Praise for C. Hope Clark

"Plot twists with grit, and a little fried okra on the side. Truly an exceptional mystery writer."

—Cindy Ervin Huff, BookBub Reviews on
THE CRAVEN COUNTY MYSTERIES

"*Badge of Edisto* further establishes Clark's well-earned reputation as a master of the mystery genre."

—Jonathan Haupt, coeditor,
Our Prince of Scribes: Writers Remember Pat Conroy

"Another excellent job of describing the mood and feel of the Lowcountry island of Edisto. It's a place like no other. The ending is explosive and wild. More great Lowcountry crime fiction from Clark."

—C. Brad Cox, Amazon Vine Voice Reviewer on
BADGE OF EDISTO

"Mystery and intrigue . . . love and romance . . . secrets . . . likable characters who come alive on the pages."

—B. Burke, Amazon Vine Voice Reviewer on
BADGE OF EDISTO

"Innovative plotting, real-life situations, and authentic characters make this novel stand out."

—Clay Stafford, publisher *Killer Nashville Magazine* on
EDISTO JINX

Rock Valley Public Library
1531 Main Street
Rock Valley, IA 51247

D1551600

The Novels of
C. Hope Clark

The Carolina Slade Mysteries

Lowcountry Bribe * Tidewater Murder

Palmetto Poison * Newberry Sin

Salkehatchie Secret

The Edisto Island Mysteries

Murder on Edisto * Edisto Jinx

Echoes of Edisto * Edisto Stranger

Dying on Edisto * Edisto Tidings

Reunion on Edisto * Edisto Heat

Badge of Edisto

The Craven County Mysteries

Murdered in Craven * Burned in Craven

Craven County Line

Craven County Line

Book Three of
The Craven County Mysteries

by

C. Hope Clark

Bell Bridge Books

This is a work of fiction. Names, characters, places, and incidents are either the products of the author's imagination or are used fictitiously. Any resemblance to actual persons (living or dead), events or locations is entirely coincidental.

Bell Bridge Books
PO BOX 300921
Memphis, TN 38130
Print ISBN: 978-1-61026-223-1

Bell Bridge Books is an Imprint of BelleBooks, Inc.

Copyright © 2023 by C. Hope Clark

Published in the United States of America.

All rights reserved. No part of this book may be reproduced in any form or by any electronic or mechanical means, including information storage and retrieval systems, without permission in writing from the publisher, except by a reviewer, who may quote brief passages in a review.

We at BelleBooks enjoy hearing from readers.
Visit our websites
BelleBooks.com
BellBridgeBooks.com
ImaJinnBooks.com

10 9 8 7 6 5 4 3 2 1

Cover design: Debra Dixon
Interior design: Hank Smith
Photo/Art credits:
Landscape (manipulated) © C. Hope Clark
Road (manipulated) © Maryia Bahutskaya | Dreamstime.com
Sky (manipulated) © Dary423 | Dreamstime.com

:Llcd:01:

Dedication

This book is dedicated to my sister-in-law, Angela, who has been to hell and back yet never fails to ask how the other person is doing. She's read everything I've written and never fails to make me feel great about it all. Love you, Fuji.

Chapter 1

QUINN STERLING wiped a trickle of sweat off her temple and cursed herself for leaving sunglasses in the house, cursed twice for setting down her Sterling Banks ball cap someplace she couldn't recall. Then she shielded her eyes and used her height to scan over the tops of heads, praying there were no complications before shutdown tonight. Almost a thousand people wandered Sterling Banks, and as much as this festival meant to the locals and the history of Craven County, she couldn't help thinking about the cleanup and reseeding of her trampled grounds tomorrow. After filling in the ruts.

And it was damn hot despite her having twisted and fastened her unruly red curls atop her head.

She hadn't had two seconds to breathe once they'd opened the farm's gates to the Fourth of July public that morning. Time to stroll the crowd again for the umpteenth time. She must've walked ten miles already in her softest, most broken-in boots, not even caring about how worn and ragged they looked. Comfort trumped style today.

Everyone was welcome at Sterling Banks on this day, and she wished her daddy were still alive to see how she continued the summer tradition. He had handled this so much more smoothly than she did, but she did her best hosting in his stead. The older folks had the manners to speak of Graham, telling her how proud he'd be.

Hard to believe Jule, her nanny and subsequent goat herder on the farm, had had to talk her into continuing these affairs after he died.

Some lines were a dozen people deep at the assorted canopied booths, people she greeted, thanking each and every soul for coming. Odors of sugar, grease, and grilled meat filled the air, each smell better than the one before, emanating from canopies outlining three sides of the open ten-acre field, some plain white and others borrowed from assorted businesses in the nearby town of Jacksonboro. For instance, the Presley Funeral Home was well represented under one of its graveside canopies, passing out end-of-life brochures and free hand fans, alongside the Raines family who received equal billing and half the shade of the shared tent where they doled out slices of watermelon grown on their farm.

A few canopies couldn't help but flaunt Clemson or the University of South Carolina, but this time of year the rivalry was an afterthought to the hot dogs, burgers, barbecue, fried catfish, or grilled cob corn served underneath. As long as there wasn't a Georgia Bulldog tent, everyone was happy.

Three dozen canopies and fifty vendors, if you called them that. Nobody overcharged a crowd on Sterling Banks, and the affordability of the event made people come and feel appreciated. Her father taught her about civic obligation from the time she could walk.

For July and Christmas, two long-time rituals by the Sterling family, they opened a section of its three thousand acres for the county's guests, and around Christmas, opened the pecan barn. As the biggest stretch of property in the county, the oldest employer with a history dating back to 1700, Sterling Banks served as a centerpiece for Craven County, a means to brag. Quinn's great-grandfather originated this particular ritual for the farm's workers, and as the plantation prospered, as workers invited more friends and families, Quinn's father realized this was a way to promote Craven County and support its hard-working work ethic.

As the last heir of the oldest family in the oldest county in the blessed state of South Carolina, Quinn preserved that responsibility.

She loved the dirt, for sure, and couldn't dream of selling an acre of it. Not with all those graves in the family cemetery watching. Not with the feel of her parents still in the house.

Bittersweet. So bittersweet. She'd given up an FBI career to come back and run this place . . . when someone murdered her almost perfect daddy. Fathers didn't come any better, and it about killed her too when he died.

She'd known that private investigative work wouldn't fill the void of leaving that career completely, but she'd gotten the license anyway. She had to in order not to feel so shackled to the farm. Worked like a charm except she hadn't had a case since the whole school board incident six weeks ago. Because the farm took a lot of her time, she only wanted cases that piqued her interest, and those were hard to find in this small rural county.

Dragging her thoughts back to the here and now, Quinn finished her fourth circuit of many more to come and reached the front of the event again. She checked her phone out of habit more than anything else since she wore a radio on her belt to communicate on the farm. That one message from earlier this morning hung there unanswered, but nothing new. She was familiar with the caller but hadn't the time or emotional investment to take this conversation today. She'd at least have to wait until the evening, when things died down. Most people understood what day this was and how busy she'd be, making Quinn even less inclined to take the message.

Back to the task at hand. Pickups and cars parked end to end on the front of the field, with overflow vehicles lining both sides of the long Sterling Banks drive. High school kids earned community service credits directing where to park under the watchful eye of a Craven County deputy.

Like Quinn, Jonah Proveaux, her beau and farm caretaker, walked the crowd, hunting how to assist the vendors, advising incoming drivers, diverting people who dared venture back into the orchard, deterring those nosy enough to see Quinn's house up close. Last month Jonah had decided to run for school board in the fall. Since then, he'd reached uber popularity amongst teachers and parents, not to mention high school girls directing cars and making no attempt to hide flirting glances at him.

Quinn watched a young, long-legged brunette in denim cut-offs go almost weak in the knees at Jonah walking within reach of her. He never noticed. The driver she was supposed to direct, however, rolled down a window and hollered for guidance, jerking her back to attention.

Jonah continued toward Quinn, smiling at the sight of her instead. He held something in his hand. She sidestepped over a few yards to find a patch of shade under a nearby oak for the break.

He handed over the item. "Here's your hat, m'lady."

"Oh, dear Lord, bless you," she said, meaning it. "Hold it a sec."

She undid her hair, which almost exploded from confinement, then pony-tailed it up to go through the back tab. "There." She shifted the bill around until the hat fit. "Thought I was going to melt out here."

"Sugar melts, Princess."

She gave him a saccharin grin. "You saying I'm sweet?"

"No." Flashing his self-assured grin, he tapped her brim. "A lot more adjectives come to mind other than *sweet*."

As though leaning forward to avoid eager ears, she acted as if she had something to say then darted in for a quick peck on the lips. "I know those words. Shame I can't bring them more to life right now."

He pecked her back and hung in close. "Who says they have anything to do with sex?"

She hung there, a bare inch between them. "Who said I meant sex?"

"Owwwww!" came the catcall from about ten feet away. "I can feel the heat from here!" One of the Sterling Banks grove tenders.

Jonah pulled back first, a grin still in place, and hollered over at the guy. "It's July, Nolan. Of course, it's hot."

The hired hand strode off laughing, not that he hadn't seen his two employers engage in a little PDA before.

Jonah ran a crooked finger under her chin. "Meet me later."

"You'll be too tired to romp."

"Who says I'm talking about sex?" he mocked and strode off with a chuckle that turned quickly into a wave at a neighbor who he trotted over to pat on the back and welcome.

Quinn stood still, admiring this man who'd arrived on the farm as a toddler with his mother, Jule, who'd originally been hired to manage a household and became much more than a housekeeper when Quinn's mom died. Jonah had promptly assigned himself the role of her protector. Not until this year had she been able to see him as more than a brother.

Way more than a brother.

Wake up, Quinn. There's work to do.

Before spotting Jonah, she'd almost reached the red canopy, the one with Jackson Hole Diner on its flaps, and she wasn't passing it by. Lenore Jackson closed her restaurant for this shindig and had donated her cooking talents on this day each and every summer for as long as Quinn Sterling had breathed Craven County air. The scent of her fried okra would've made Quinn drool if she hadn't already eaten two paper cones full.

In her branded red apron, name embroidered across the bib, Lenore tended two vats of deep friers on stands with fans in the corner keeping her sane in the heat. She could outcook everyone here, but today she tended fried okra and fried dill pickles, letting other venues fill in the rest.

Quinn slid between tables and adjusted a fan to hit Lenore better. The cook caught her steady perspiration on a headband, red, of course, and had tied one of several iced kerchiefs around her neck. A cooler under the table held more.

"Saw you swapping spit with that boy," Lenore said. "Not sure that needs to be aired out here."

"Everybody loves it, Momma," Quinn said, cherishing this woman who'd been the other woman who'd stepped up when her own mother died. "Don't you get too hot. Where's Ty? He ought to be helping you."

"He's coming," Lenore said. "Give him time. He's got responsibilities."

Now a Craven County deputy, Lenore's son had grown up beside Quinn from the time they were both five. His dad had worked for hers until Ty's dad died from cancer when Ty was fifteen, which pushed Lenore to open her diner. But Quinn wasn't the boss's daughter, and Ty wasn't the child of a foreman. Not to each other, and whether anyone else thought it, they dare not say. From naps on the porch to swimming in their underwear, they both had Edisto River in their blood and pecan dust in their bones, their feet having evolved to climb any tree in the grove.

Jonah, Quinn, and Ty . . . with her ever in the middle. She'd kissed them both in her day, and dating Jonah had caused her a lot of personal grief in having made a choice, but she'd made it, with Ty's permission, no less. Not that the big man didn't harbor feelings for her.

She didn't like thinking about that.

Quinn grabbed a napkin and wiped moisture off her own forehead and above her upper lip. "You got something to drink? You gotta stay hydrated in this heat."

"I'm good, honey. Go tend to your people." Lenore rested a hand on her hip. "And leave that poor boy of yours alone today."

"He's not a boy, Lenore."

"You ain't telling me nothing," she said, going back to shoveling more cones of okra, inserting the cones in a specialized box with holes bored the right size. "Girl, I got work to do, and so do you. Go on."

"Yes, ma'am." Quinn turned the napkin over and wiped the back of her neck before tossing it in a bin. There'd been hotter Fourths than this one, and there'd been cooler ones, but this morning started at eighty degrees and had tapped ninety by noon.

She returned to the crowd, but in scanning the parking area, she spotted her familiar buddy. A tall, broad man her age, he strolled up still in uniform, his wide hand atop the head of an eight-year-old boy clearly destined to be tall and broad, too.

Quinn stooped in front of the child. "Cole, my man, you are sprouting right before my eyes. What've you been up to?"

"Growing!" His grin showed front rabbit teeth a bit big for his mouth. "I stretch every morning to grow faster."

She busted a laugh and pecked him on the cheek, the boy winking in return. The kid was way more the flirt than his father, who popped him lightly on the back of the head to behave.

She peered up at Ty, understanding now the responsibility that Lenore had referenced back under the canopy. This was Ty's weekend with his son. She rose back up. "I was wondering where you were."

Ty Jackson patted the top of his son's head, his hand never having left. He was a deputy. He knew what happened to kids in crowds, though Quinn doubted anyone in these parts would dare touch a hair on that particular child.

But he was tense, not wanting to let loose of Cole, his crowd-control gaze at work across the sea of people. No smile. Ty almost always smiled.

"You all right?" she asked.

"Had a little dust up with Nat," he said. "I was late picking him up." His voice usually carried a gentleness but from a deep well of a place— a voice versatile enough to make a culprit stop in his tracks or a victim feel absolutely safe. Today he sounded terse, anxious . . . wary.

Quinn didn't like discussing the mother in front of Cole, and, frankly, spoke little of her with the father. Ty and his ex hadn't been on good terms since Quinn had left the FBI and returned to Sterling Banks. Too much fiction about Quinn and Ty having grown up together, too much whispering. She loved him dearly, and if she and Jonah hadn't found their way to each other. . . . Who knew? It was damn hard to take three lifelong buds and turn them into two plus one. Her heart had belonged to both for so damn long.

She noticed tightness in his jaws, pain in his eyes. "Wanna talk?" she asked. "We can sneak away into the manor."

"Not now," he said. "But later we gotta talk."

Sounded ominous. "Sure. Right now Lenore's looking for you, though. Your momma's working her butt off today."

"Granny?" Cole asked, peering straight up at his dad.

Quinn turned and pointed to the tent three tents down. "Go to the red one and no place else."

Ty released the child, which triggered Cole to take off. Ty kept an eye on him while continuing to talk. Cole arrived to the smothering arms of his grandmother, and Ty dropped his look to Quinn. "All okay out here? Seen anything odd?"

She was still concerned about him. "No problems. Thus far, anyway." She took his arm. "You're awful disturbed about something. Was it that bad with Natalie or is this about something amiss at work? You know, something I might want to know about?"

He gave her his half grin, used to her habit of picking law

enforcement business out of him. "I don't have to update you about the sheriff's department."

"Yeah," she said, grinning back. "But you do. How else are we going to keep Uncle Larry in line? Where is he, by the way? He may not own the place, but he has a reputation to uphold. Since when does he miss the opportunity to flaunt being a Sterling?"

Her uncle had been sheriff since his thirties. The same uncle who'd lost his Sterling Banks inheritance in a divorce, which her father had salvaged by paying off the ex. Uncle Larry ran the sheriff's office about as well as he'd managed his marriage . . . and as poorly as he'd hunted his brother's killer. Quinn solved the murder and, to this day, couldn't be in the same room with her uncle without a spat.

"He's not here?" Ty asked, peering around as if Quinn might be mistaken. He understood as well as she did that the sheriff loved taking credit for a Sterling event. Forget the fact he'd lost the right and everyone knew it. He was still the top cop and was closer to being Sterling royalty that anyone else. They were a small family.

"Maybe something came up," she said, though Larry usually chose strutting at events over doing real work any day. He had deputies to delegate that to.

Ty seemed exceptionally attentive to the crowd, though he had to know eighty percent of them by name. Scouting over Quinn's head, Ty's expression darkened, then his eyes widened. She went to turn only for hands to cover her eyes.

"Guess who. One try," came the voice.

She gasped.

Then she spun, breaking free, and wrapped her long tanned and freckled arms around a man she hadn't seen since her daddy's funeral. "Uncle Archie!"

She hugged him tight. He hadn't the height of her father and Uncle Larry, but that still put him at her level. Short brushed six foot in the Sterling family.

"When did you get in?" she squealed, hugging him again.

He kissed her on the cheek. "Red eye put us into Charleston about two hours ago. Baby Q, you look adorable. Better than . . ."

"The last time you saw me. Well, anything would look better than then, Uncle Archie. But you . . . look the same. You haven't aged a year."

Yet she lied. An ample supply of gray ran through what used to be thick, wavy blond hair, and he seemed leaner. More crow's feet around what she deemed the prettiest blue eyes on the planet, but more sagging under them than she remembered.

Guess they could both lie about each other's looks.

A child around six peered from around his thigh, then stepped out as if taking the stage. She brushed her T-shirt down and tipped her chin once in a silent hello.

Humored by the girl, also blond and also tall, Quinn threw a puzzled glance at her uncle before lowering herself to a less intimidating height. "Hello there," Quinn said. "And who might you be?"

"Your cousin," she said, holding out her hand, purposely drawing upon a practiced speech. "My name is Glory Bea Sterling. Nice to meet you, Cousin Quinn."

Quinn took the offered hand with the long fingers of a Sterling and would've melted if shock hadn't taken over first. "Nice to meet you, Glory. Love the name, by the way."

"Yours is pretty, too."

Standing, Quinn attempted to maintain a soft smile for the child's sake, but it was damn hard to do and still hide the surprise. "Um, when did I become a cousin?"

"I'm six," Glory answered before Archie could. "I'll be seven in eight days."

The girl was bright.

Unapologetically, Archie spoke with the pride of a father. "She's glorious, isn't she? Thus, the name," he said, gazing down with love as Glory met his look with a see-how-good-I-did smile. "Patrick and I used a surrogate. We had our sperm mixed rather than one of us choosing to be the donor."

Running her palm across the thick yellow curls cut short in Shirley Temple style, Quinn said, "Clearly your swimmers won."

"Without a doubt," he said. "Sorry, but there never seemed a good time to tell you. She was due any time when Graham passed, and you had enough on your plate. That and we wanted to make sure everything went okay. It was a difficult birth, and she had some early issues for a few months. And after the way I left, thinking I'd never return, I just kept finding excuses to avoid letting Craven County back into my world. I'm sorry, Miss Q. I really am, but I'm here now."

Quinn should be peeved at her uncle, but staring at Glory, she knew now was not the time. She remembered how good he had been with her as a child. Their one-on-one luncheons. His listening to her when she was pissed at the world. She'd assumed he would never father a child but look at him now. It suited him.

She ran her arm through Ty's, drawing him close. "You remember Ty?" she said.

Archie reached a hand. "Of course, I do. Man, you grew into a beast, didn't you?"

If Ty's complexion wasn't so dark, his blush would've glowed as red as Quinn's mane. "Good upbringing," he replied. "Good seeing you again. How long are you sticking around?"

"Wait." Quinn realized they were missing another guest. "Speaking of Patrick, where is he?"

"They live in different places now, Aunty Quinn."

She loved how Glory called her Aunty, with a Y. A better ring than cousin. "I see," she said.

"It's okay," Glory continued. "We've been doing it for years."

Which brought a slight scowl from Quinn. "Years?"

This time Archie scratched the back of his neck. "One year is more like it, but guess we have some catching up to do."

A tad stung at the revelations, Quinn wondered what else might be amiss. His appearance was so out of the blue. "Yes," she said. "I believe we do have some catching up to do." But now wasn't the time. This was an event. A Sterling event. "I hope you're not too terribly tired, because as a Sterling, you can help me greet these people."

Archie took in a deep breath scanning the grounds. He hadn't been much of a Sterling legacy fan and had severed ties years ago for reasons Quinn had never fully understood. "Not counting the funeral, it's been over fifteen years, Quinn."

"Times are different now, Uncle. And those who have a problem with you can be escorted off the property. You hear me? Hey, I'll introduce you, if you like."

"I'd appreciate it," he said, then stilled as his attention focused past her. "Guess we can test things first with him."

Quinn turned. Uncle Larry, the Craven County Sheriff himself, made his way in uniform across the field, two deputies at his side. She didn't like how he looked. "He's got a burr up his ass, Ty," she said. "Any idea why?"

"Shit," he murmured back, making Quinn wonder why. "If I get called out to something," he said, "would you make sure—"

"Cole can stay here until you get done," she said, giving a playful twist to one of Glory's curls. "Besides, he has someone he needs to meet."

Sheriff Larry Sterling reached them. Deputy Harrison, her least favorite deputy, stood to his left. She could read her uncle like headlines in a tell-all gossip mag, and this was no social call. For a second, she wondered who had died. Craven County was small enough for her to at least know the name of whomever it might be. Car accident, drowning, overturned tractor. . . .

"Ty," the sheriff said, avoiding looking at Quinn and giving his long-lost brother the bare minimum of a glance. "I need you to come with me."

Ty stiffened, a flash of panic in his eyes. Quinn touched his back for support. "What's going on, Uncle Larry?"

"Never you mind, Niece. Ty, please, son. Just come along."

Quinn's radar went up at her uncle's cryptic behavior. Ty was the senior deputy, the closest to a detective the SO had. "Wait a minute."

"Stay out of this, Quinn," said the sheriff.

He hated Quinn's curiosity in his business. He hated more that she could solve a case quicker than anyone on his force. He did his damnedest to hide Craven County crime from her to avoid her judgement, one of the many controversies that drove a wedge between them.

"Just tell me, Sheriff," Ty said, his voice lowered. He'd tell Quinn later anyway, and they all knew it.

"It's Natalie," Larry said. "She was found dead in her apartment about forty-five minutes ago."

Quinn's head did the math. A jolt of fear coursed through her.

"The Colleton County police need to speak to you, son." He started to reach out and take Ty's arm and thought better of it. "Afraid I'm to escort you to Walterboro. A witness says you were the last person to see her alive."

A weakness shot through Quinn. She almost reached for her phone and that unheard message, but now wasn't the time, was it? Any message Natalie left in Quinn's voice mail would be moot now, wouldn't it?

Chapter 2

PEOPLE PARTED around the cluster of uniforms, ignoring the cop presence to head to the food. A band made clanks and thuds in setting up in the field's back west corner. In the meantime, assorted boom boxes made music from the tents until the band took center stage.

But the world had locked still for Quinn and Ty.

"I wasn't the last person to see her alive, Sheriff," Ty said. "Because I didn't kill her."

The sheriff listened as if he'd heard it a dozen times. "I know, son, but right now you have to come with me."

Ty emotionally held his own, and Quinn wondered how. He wasn't one to crumble, but Natalie was the mother of his son. There had to be a crack in that façade. Inside he had to feel pain at losing a woman he'd once loved enough to marry and have a child with.

Quinn rubbed his back, reminding him she was there . . . while anxiously wondering what kind of message the dead woman would leave on Quinn's phone. They hadn't spoken in years. Quinn wasn't Natalie's favorite person. For her to reach out was incredibly curious . . . incredibly odd. And she wasn't mentioning it to a soul until she listened to it herself.

Ty scanned over his shoulder, across the moving crowd to the red tent. Cole dipped out batches of okra under the watchful eye of Lenore. As if sensing the attention, she glanced up at her son and smiled. Ty waved.

"Cole," he said to Quinn, trying to hold the smile on his mother.

"I got him," Quinn said, then decided she could do a heck of sight more than babysit. "I'm calling an attorney for you, Old Man," using the nickname she'd given him because he thought through everything, took measure of facts, never reacted faster than he had to. "Don't talk to a soul without them."

She then turned and faced off with her Uncle Larry or tried to. He wouldn't look at her. He knew the laser beam of hate he'd receive. The bond amongst Quinn, Jonah, and Ty was renowned, and when you took on one you took on the trio. Even Natalie had bowed to it, citing it in her reason for leaving Ty.

"May I come with him?" Quinn asked, pushing the words hard at her uncle.

Ty answered instead. "You're needed here. Keep things normal. The attorney is enough, Q." He patted her back the way she'd done his. "I got this. Please, watch him." He nodded toward the fried okra canopy.

"Goes without saying." Still, she pushed her way in front of Uncle Larry. "You be there for him, you hear?" She didn't care how the scolding in front of people made him feel.

He didn't reply and tried hard not to pay her any mind, difficult to do with her face a foot from his.

"Be decent for a damn change, Uncle Larry."

"Q." Ty pulled on her shoulder, easing her back. "Another place, another time."

He was right. She gave them space.

The four men walked off, like cops called to an assignment. Late arrivals greeted them in passing, a couple stopping them to shake hands, thanking them for their service.

"Quinn, call the attorney," Archie said, who'd stood to the side, allowing Glory to wander off a few feet to keep her out of earshot. Right now she spoke with another girl whose parents waited in line for lemonade. "You have someone in mind?" he asked.

"I do." Sliding phone out of her pocket she located a hunting buddy of her father's who'd said to her at the funeral, *Call if you need me, Quinn. Not that the Sterling family would ever need any other attorney but the white-shoe firm you usually use. Still, call me. If you need me.* "Baron Ingram," she said, grateful she'd put his name in her contacts. Right now she didn't need high powered, she needed a criminal defense guy who knew the players in these counties. Ty's reputation could be ruined by the time county law got around to clearing him.

Archie took a moment to register the name that rang a bell. Then he made the connection and whispered, "Oh, yes."

Surprisingly, an efficient message service put her through to Ingram. Bless the man for being available and not feeling the need for small talk. "Ms. Sterling. This is a surprise. What's up?"

She explained the situation in three sentences, then took longer to explain the importance of the accused. "He's my childhood friend. Daddy adored his father, and his mother stepped in to help raise me when Mom died. He's as noble and good a soul as you'd ever meet."

"That's a powerful endorsement," Ingram replied.

"I'd sell Sterling Banks for him, Mr. Ingram."

"A *mighty* powerful endorsement," he tacked on.

"I'll pay your fee," she said.

"Which I assumed. I'm about to meet a client, Quinn, so I'm sending one of my best in my stead to plug the damage." He must've noticed the hesitation at the substitute. "I'd let her represent me, if that's your worry."

"A powerful endorsement of your own," she said, more to assuage her doubts and hide her disappointment. She wanted the zenith of criminal defense lawyers and wasn't used to settling for less, thus Jonah's nickname for her . . . *Princess.*

Quinn had no choice. Time was short, and Ingram promised she'd get the job done. "Thank you," she finally said. "Now please, get her there. He's on his way to the Walterboro Police Department as we speak. Who should I tell him is coming?"

"Tassey Talmadge," he said.

Her breath caught. "Oh."

"Told you I'd take care of you."

Quinn had heard of the woman. This wasn't the junior associate she'd envisioned. Around fifty, Talmadge held her own in a courtroom and in the media, one case being that of a prominent Charleston heir whose mother's lineage dated back to not one but two founding fathers. The heir had been accused of killing his child's nanny, only to get off by claiming he thought the nanny—with whom he'd been having an affair—was killing his child. Investigations noted the child had probably been choking on a toy, but the defense also argued that the nanny neglected the child due to the father not willing to divorce and marry her.

The pampered child was made to sit through the trial, in the lap of her famous grandmother. The heir got off with probation and rehab since he'd been high at the time.

Then there was the CPA laundering cartel money only found guilty of failure to file customs forms. He got off with a hefty fine one assumed was paid by his grateful employer.

"You've heard of her then?" Ingram said.

"Yes."

"Defense law gets . . . vicious," he added.

Her ex-FBI gut told her settling for less could cost Ty dearly if things went sideways.

Unless a detective found another killer or somehow proved Ty's innocence, he would be the presumed killer and in the investigation crosshairs. There would be DNA at the scene—his child lived there, and Ty saw his child regularly. Ty already said he and Natalie had had a bit of a spat. Sometimes an overworked county squad didn't dig beyond the obvious. Ty's choices could quickly narrow to pleading to some lesser charge of whatever larger charge they threw at him, or going to court. Juries were squirrelly, the selection process a crapshoot as to who would determine your fate. You wanted the savviest lawyer on your side, and sometimes you had to ignore the callouses on their hands from whom they'd represented before.

"Send her," Quinn said.

"Done," he replied. "I'll be close if she needs assistance."

Quinn sensed he didn't expect the need to arise.

She called Ty, who'd left with Harrison, her uncle following with the other deputy. "Tassey Talmadge," she told Ty. "Speak to nobody until she gets there."

"Jesus," he said. "She's . . . malicious."

"We leave nothing to chance, Old Man," she said.

"I don't know what to say."

"Say nothing, buddy. From this moment on, say nothing."

She hung up. The sounds, the scents, the heat of the farm's festival slowly filtered back in, and the reality of her having to act normal set wrong in her gut. A scream boiled up inside, but she shut it down. It'd have to stay bottled up. A silent gnawing worry refused to be so easily corralled, and it would compete with everything else for the rest of the day.

The average person might think Justice blind, but Quinn had been an FBI agent long enough to know sometimes you had to help show her the way for real justice to be served. Human beings could be flawed, short-sighted, nasty creatures . . . on all sides of the equation.

"You look like you need to sit," Archie said. "Let's go to the house."

"No, I can't." The whole world had shifted off its axis. She was mad at Uncle Larry, when he'd only been the messenger. He wasn't a solid ally in times of crisis, though.

"Why can't you disappear a while?" Archie asked. "Everything's running taut and in sync from what I see."

She reeled on him. "I can't, Uncle Archie!" Then she overrode herself. "Oh, Jesus, I'm sorry," she said quickly before feelings got hurt. "But we'd have to explain where I was. There has to be a Sterling on site. Uncle Larry being gone is bad enough."

"I'm here," he offered. "And I fully appreciate the weight of our name, honey."

Wanly, she smiled. "I know you do." Now she felt like two cents. "I love you, but you taking over . . . like that's not suspicious, the long-lost Sterling brother flying back from San Francisco because the two local Sterlings can't be there." She stood. "Ty will call me. The attorney will call me. Right now, though, Ty expects us to protect his mother and his son."

Jonah walked up. "Hey, people have been asking where your uncle . . . is . . . is that Archie?"

"An uncle *has* arrived," Archie said with an exaggerated swing of an arm and a bow. "And he shall host this party like it's never been hosted before. Care to meet and greet people, Glory?" He held out his hand, and his daughter gladly took it. "Let's show how good we are at working a room."

Glory scrunched her nose, happy to play. "But we're not in a room."

Archie swept the air again. "All of this is our room, sweetheart."

And with that, the two ventured into the throng, his resistance to a headlong and splashy reintroduction to Craven having vanished in light of a higher calling.

That was the Archie she remembered. She was so happy to have him home, even if for a little while.

"When did he arrive?" Jonah asked, stunned. "And who is the girl?"

"My cousin," she said, not up for a detailed explanation. "We've got bigger problems."

His brow went up. This man knew her history better than anyone, and there was no cousin in the details, but he went with the flow. "I canvassed the field, Princess. Everything is running like a top, short of an underestimated ice supply in two places. Two of the high school kids got four bags out of the garage freezer."

Ice. The last thing she cared about was ice.

"Where's Larry?" Jonah scouted the immediate area, gaze stopping at the red canopy and sight of Cole handing out cones of okra. "And I see Cole. Where's Ty?" Then he caught himself. "Must've been a call in the county. Of all days for a fender bender. That wouldn't normally keep Larry away, though."

She raised both hands and scrunched her eyes. "Stop, Jonah! Just stop."

He didn't ask for what, and he didn't ask why. Instead he took her by the elbow and escorted her to the first tent and reached in from the side to ask for something cold. The vendor popped a frosted cup in his hand, understanding the perks of the people in charge, and Jonah escorted Quinn to the tree line.

Trees nourished them. Trees were what they did all day—woke up to each morning and dreamed about each night. Trees were what they grew up climbing, loving, nurturing, and living by their means. Walking her to the far side of a hundred-year-old pecan, he backed her up to it, hidden from people, and pushed the drink in her grip. "Now, tell me what's going on."

The coarse feel of bark on her back grounded her, and she slid down to sit on a gnarled root. These trees on this side had pretty much gone feral, far away from the pruned and pampered groves. Still, this one cradled her.

She took a sip, then a deep breath. "Ty's ex-wife died."

He lowered himself to her level. "Oh, no."

"That's why Uncle Larry isn't here. That's why Ty left. We have Cole for as long as it takes."

He rested a hand on her shoulder. "Of course we do. What happened? She was two years younger than you. Car accident?"

Running a hand over her eyes, temples wet from perspiration, she let it rest over her mouth, so many what-ifs pinging in her head. She knew more *of* Natalie than anything personal, so she hadn't much to draw from. They didn't gossip about Ty's ex, and Ty didn't share much about the married time of his life.

But the murdered women statistics spoke loud and clear. The spouse or ex-spouse was the first suspected in these kinds of cases. In law enforcement's shoes she'd have suspected Ty as well. Or at least known she'd have to clear him quickly before anyone would focus on the real suspect.

"Quinn," Jonah said, gentle, yet firmly enough to bring her around. "What the hell aren't you telling me?"

"Uncle Larry collected Ty and escorted him to Walterboro. Natalie was found murdered, and they're saying the last person who saw her was Ty when he picked up Cole."

He slid himself fully to the ground, letting his touch slide to her hand. "That's insane."

"To you and me, maybe, but to law enforcement he's the most likely suspect."

Shaking his head, his brow clenched, and he gripped her hand tighter. "No. No way."

Peeking around the trunk, measuring their privacy, she pulled out her phone. "Jonah . . ." She tapped buttons to the voice mail but didn't hit play. Only held it up. "I got this earlier this morning, but I was too busy with the event to stop and listen."

He watched her, as if waiting for a hammer to fall.

"A call from Natalie," she said. "I haven't listened to it."

He cupped her hand, the one holding the phone. "Go ahead, honey," he said. "Play it."

Tentatively, she hit play.

"Quinn . . . Natalie. You're probably surprised to get this. I haven't exactly been your biggest fan."

Quinn looked over at Jonah as a few seconds of silence went by. The voice mail was longer, and she hoped it contained more. Nat's voice had sounded a tad unsteady, almost humiliated.

"Um," Nat started back. "I was asked to do something . . . no, this won't do on a voice mail. Listen. I'm headed to Charleston today. I know it's the Fourth and I'm not sure if you have plans or anything, but can I stop by and talk? You probably think I'm crazy, but I promise you'll understand. Anyway . . . call me soon as you can. If I don't hear from you, I get it."

Tears ran hard down Quinn's cheeks. She dropped the phone and dropped her face to her knees.

"Awww, honey." Jonah reached over pulled her sideways against him. "You didn't know. Even if you'd listened, there was no urgency, and she didn't say it was important. You would've called her tonight. You were in the middle of all this today."

She turned and buried her head into his shoulder. "But I can't now. What if my call would've impacted whether she died or not?"

"Princess, there's no way you could tell that. Come here." He wrapped himself as much around her as he could, lightly rocking her in his embrace, as he'd done for her so many times as a child.

Finally, she calmed. Ty would need her. Nothing against small-town cops, but a lot of them traveled the path of least resistance in solving a case. She didn't know whether to show Ty the voice mail or not. She feared more what he would think about her delay in listening to it than she hadn't answered.

"Will they detain him?" Jonah asked.

She shook her head, relieved to be able to do so. "Most likely not. Not this early. Unless someone saw him do the deed, they have to investigate, and thank goodness there's still such a thing as evidence, but

I assume someone said he was the last person who saw her. Who would that be? And more, where was Cole in the middle of all this?" She threw a wave back toward the festivities. "Ty brought Cole here, and he was fine. Children don't hide things well."

"And Ty?" Jonah wiped tears off her face with one of Jule's bandanas in his pocket. She barely heard him say, "He's my brother, too."

"He wasn't himself," she said, loosening herself from Jonah.

"What does that mean?"

"It means he had something on his mind. He told me he argued with Nat but stopped with that."

No doubt Jonah sat there worrying what that meant, as she did.

"When he returns, we need to get ahead of this. I already hired an attorney for him. Baron Ingram assigned Tassey Talmadge to us."

Mulling the familiar name around, he latched ahold of the recognition . . . and frowned.

"She's good," Quinn warned, reading his expression.

"She's . . . devious," he replied.

They had to get over that. "Welcome to the world of criminal defense law," she said. "You want the best, because when authorities question you, they think you're guilty until proven innocent."

"That's the other way around," he said.

"No," she said. "It's not." She rose and dusted herself off, wiping her face on the sleeves of her shirt. "We've got to get back to the party."

Yet he seemed not quite ready to re-enter the fray. "We're supposed to act like nothing happened? What do we tell Lenore and Cole?"

She'd already thought of that. "We tell them Ty got called away, Jonah. At least we can let her get through the afternoon happily puttering with Cole and selling okra. Let's let her have those last few bits of the day without a weight on her heart. And if the festival is over, and Ty is still occupied, Cole stays with us so he can visit with Glory."

Again with the scowl. "And who exactly is Glory?"

"Archie's daughter."

"Archie . . . has a daughter?"

"Yes, gay men can have offspring, Jonah," she said, having been recently schooled on the subject. Archie and Glory showing up would've ordinarily been a huge excitement. Monstrous.

"So, we wait," he said.

She nodded. She needed to hear what the Colleton Sheriff's Department had collected already before she formulated a plan. Investigations weren't limited to uniforms.

Jonah stood. "My brain hurts. This is a lot to take in, and on this day of all days." He looked at his watch. "Eight more hours till we close down."

Her breath came up deep from her belly, and she let it out slowly, hoping for better control. "I'm glad Archie is here."

Even if he had shown up unannounced and spilling secrets. This Fourth of July had already come with a few more fireworks than expected. However, Archie understood as well as anyone how much Ty meant to her and Sterling Banks, and for the moment a murder trumped whatever he'd come home to say. Still, she couldn't stop wondering why.

Chapter 3

"GO FIND ARCHIE," Quinn told Jonah. He left with a soft, sweet kiss and skirted into the crowd.

She sighed, redirecting herself. If she had to act normal, she might as well start with introducing her uncle to the throng. More like reintroducing him, depending on who remembered him. He'd been the most minor of the Sterling men, the least public, but the most gossiped about once upon a time. Quinn wanted to show him around to the most accepting people first, starting with Lenore.

Feet heavy, she made her way to the red canopy, the fried food no longer appealing. Lenore saw Quinn coming before Cole did.

"Ty got called out," Quinn said, as routine-sounding as she could. Lenore's son being called away was part of his day-to-day existence.

"That boy and his job," she said, spooning up pickles. "He loves it, though."

"He asked if Cole could stay on Sterling Banks until he got back. That okay with you?" Quinn asked. "You'll be exhausted after all this."

Lenore winked back. "He'll probably be back before I get done anyway." With a line of more than a dozen people strung out waiting, she hadn't ceased shoveling pods and pickles.

Quinn swore that her two friends' mothers were the hardest working women she'd ever met. They never stopped. Jonah's mom tended the limited activities taking place on the farm today and running errands as needed while keeping an eye for nosy stragglers around the residence. Ever since the break-in a few months ago, the loss of her favorite nanny goat to a hoodlum, and her brief kidnapping during the school board fiasco, Jule wasn't much keen on mulling with the masses.

"See what I'm doing, Q?"

Quinn shifted attention to the eight-year-old. Cole beamed, using the same nickname his father did.

"You're a big help to your grandmother," she said. "Good thing you came along."

"Where's Daddy?" he asked, while handing over another paper

cone to a woman charmed by him judging by her smile.

"Sheriff came. Said he had to go to work."

His little exaggerated shrug would've been cute any other day. "Him and his job. That's what Momma says. She says he loves it more than anything, even you."

Quinn lost her breath a second. She wasn't fond of airing dirty laundry in front of a child. "I've got news for you, young man. He talks more about you than anyone else in the universe. I'm way down on his list behind you, his work, your grandmama, maybe even your momma, if you ask me."

Cole laughed at her. "You don't know my momma very well."

Which pained her heart, because she knew how much that would pain Ty's.

Jonah strutted up. "Here he is. Found him huddled with high school buddies."

Archie looked happy enough, so Quinn could rest easy he'd found a friend or two. But before she could make introductions, Archie strode behind the okra and pickle table and took the strainer from Lenore's hand. "Hey there, Lenore Jackson. Bet you don't remember me."

Her frown melted and sparked into the biggest laugh. "Oh my Lord. Oh my Lord. Come here, you bad boy, and give me a hug."

The embrace had a washing-machine motion to it, back and forth, both of them squeezing as much love out of each other as they could. Finally, Lenore pulled back. "You got old."

His eyes went wide, then his laugh rippled out loud and long. "I'm not taking that bait, ma'am."

Ah, there was some of his Southern drawl, and Quinn had forgotten how joyous he could laugh, a warmth spreading in her chest at realizing how much Sterling Banks had missed Archie Sterling.

Quinn felt a hand behind her, gripping one of her belt loops. Glory had taken up residence beside Quinn—once Cole spotted her—and gone coy, unsure what to do about the attention.

"Cole," Quinn started, trying to simplify the family tree down to something an eight-year-old could grasp. "This is Glory Sterling."

At the name Sterling, he perked. "Sterling?"

Nobody'd ever seen the need to explain to the child about the branches of Quinn's family tree. He was just familiar with the people who lived on the farm, not so much how they were related. Having a new one drop on him messed with his head.

Quinn motioned to Archie. "This is my Uncle Archie. He's been living in California for a long time." She gestured to Glory. "And this is his daughter which makes her my cousin. Her name is Glory, and she's six."

"I'll be seven in eight days," she reminded them. "Let's call me seven."

Cole took a step closer. "You turn seven when you have a birthday, not before."

"When's your birthday, smart boy?" Glory asked, letting loose of Quinn.

"June," he said. "So I'm a real eight."

Half smiles coated every face under the canopy and outside it.

"Okay, then," Lenore said, chuckling, leaning over with an outstretched hand. "This is Cole, and I'm his grandmother. Nice to meet you, Glory Sterling." They shook hands, then Lenore tapped a curl, making it bounce. "That's some fancy hair."

As if on cue, Glory made more curls bob with a shake of her head. "I asked Daddy to doll me up for this auspicious occasion," she said. "I believe he did a rather nice job, don't you?"

Quinn had to turn aside to not laugh aloud, but enough others did to break any ice Glory hadn't already melted with her charm.

"If that isn't a Sterling, I don't know what is," Lenore said, standing to look at Quinn.

Someone in the line purposely cleared their throat.

"Sorry, but I gotta get back to business. We can chat later." Lenore laid a hand on Cole's head, apparently a trait Ty copied from his mother. "You staying to help me or escorting Miss Glory around the grounds?"

The boy pondered which was the right answer until Lenore gave him a nudge. "Go have fun, child. Listen to Miss Quinn, okay?"

"Yes, ma'am," he said, inching closer to his new friend, then the two inching further ahead to walk in front of the grownups. A procession evolved, and they all went with it.

They hadn't gone twenty steps when Cole asked Glory, "Where's he been anyway?" Cole tried to hide his finger pointed at Archie.

"Told you. California," Glory said.

"That's weird," he replied. "I never heard of him. I thought family lived close to each other. Momma says even if they don't sleep in the same house, they live close enough to take care of each other. How far's California?"

"Real far," she answered. "Took us all night flying to get here."

Cole wasn't happy with that. "That's too far."

"Is not."

"Sure is."

Glory's pout eased off. "Doesn't matter anyway, does it?" she said. "We're here now, and I'm learning my legacy."

"What's a legacy?" Cole asked.

"It's about your grandparents, and great-grandparents, and great-great-grandparents and what they did."

Cole thought hard about that. "I have one grandmother, one mother, and one father," he said. "No legacy. We just have each other."

His words cut Quinn deep at his thinking he still had three relatives. She was glad to be behind the kids.

"That's sad," Glory said.

Cole bowed up in defense. "No, it isn't."

"Is to me."

"Nope," he affirmed. "Family is family. Sometimes God gives us lots of family and sometimes He gives us a little bit of family. I got all the legacy I need."

Jonah's arm slipped around Quinn. "Damn, kids are smart," he whispered.

But Quinn couldn't say anything. Not with the knot in her chest. She appreciated why Archie wanted Glory to value her roots. What she didn't understand is why he'd taken so long . . . and why now.

AN HOUR LATER, with the kids hot and the adults pulled in different directions to put out festival brushfires, Archie escorted the children to the house and put them under the watch of Jonah's mother. It took him an hour to return.

Archie joined Quinn in the crowd in front of the band. He swayed and swung a little at "She Thinks My Tractor's Sexy" while pulling her several dozen yards away to be heard. They left Jonah back at the stage fiddling with something electrical off to the side.

She'd listened to Natalie's voice mail several times, and Ty hadn't left Quinn's thoughts. She'd hoped to hear from him or the attorney by now. She didn't dare imagine hearing from Uncle Larry who tended to deliver bad news. She didn't want to see him anyway. Not with Natalie's voice mail eating at her. He might see through her.

Likewise, she restrained herself from visiting Lenore anymore for fear of giving off worrisome vibes.

She and Archie stopped walking, but Archie hadn't ceased moving, allowing Quinn to enjoy the humor of her uncle's lack of rhythm, even if performed for no reason other than a distraction for her. Bless his heart.

"Guess they don't listen to Kenny Chesnee much in San Francisco," she said. "You miss it here, don't you?"

He checked himself and grinned. "Maybe."

"No maybe about it, and when this day is over, we need to talk."

His head reared back. "That sounds more like my line. Darn if you don't sound all grown up, Miss Quinn."

She smiled at his drawl slipping out again and hid her recognition of his changing the subject. "Kids okay?" she asked.

"Yeah. I had to talk with Jule for a while. She's still cute, cocky, and dry as ever. And I love that dog of yours! All legs, feet, and tongue. Glory was all over him."

"And him all over her, I imagine."

Bogie was a people lover. A black-mouthed cur turned six months old, with the most expressive eyes, he loved everyone he met. She'd named him after Humphrey Bogart and his acting history as a private investigator. It just fit.

"Bet you shocked the bejesus out of Jule." Jonah's mother didn't need much scare in her life. She'd had enough in her sixty-two years. "And I also bet she scooped up Glory like one of her baby goats," Quinn said, shifting to the positive.

Archie scrunched his nose. "You bet she did."

Her breath caught at the rush of familiar. "I forgot you did that."

"What?"

"Your cute nose thing."

"Oh. Guess I haven't done that for a while," he said, marveling at the revelation.

She held her palms out in a question. "So why'd you want to talk? Not much privacy here."

A neighboring farm owner walked by and patted Quinn on the upper arm, proving her point. "Nice job, Quinn."

"Thanks, Hank."

When she turned back to Archie, he grinned with admiration. "They love you, Niece."

That last word fell ugly on her ears.

He sobered. "What did I say?"

"Uncle Larry calls me *niece* instead of Quinn," she explained. "But you make it sound nice. All's good, Uncle Archie. Don't worry about me."

She always thought Larry either hated saying her name, used the word to keep things distant between them, or loved to put her in her place. Who the hell knew? But Archie made the word sound sweet.

Empathy filled Archie's eyes. "He's never been good with people, relatives or otherwise." Then he gave her a knowing sigh. "You've had your hands full since Graham left, haven't you, Miss Q?"

Her life was charmed compared to the average person. Lots of people lost their father. Lots of people lose their dream job. She had Sterling Banks, though, and she had Jonah and Ty. And Jule. And Lenore. Now Archie and Glory.

Damn . . . how nice was it to be able to think that? Uncle Archie hadn't been here four hours and she was already hooked on him, almost leaning on him. She could already see her heart breaking at his departure.

"Jule," he began, changing the subject, choosing his words, "has aged. She's still lovely, mind you. Nurturing as ever. But time seems to have taken a toll. What happened?"

Quinn gave a sarcastic wince. "Too long a story to tell amidst hundreds of people. A tale for another time." Also, too many people for her to be questioning him about his purpose for being there. "Let's manage today first. If you see Ty, please, come get me."

"Why wouldn't he call you?"

"To avoid taking me away from my duties," she said, worry for him rushing back in like a King high tide. She still hadn't decided to tell him about Nat's voice mail.

"When's this whole affair over with?" Archie asked, scanning the crowd.

"Supposed to be done by eight, but you have to make the band quit taking requests or it drags out to midnight." She recalled the first year she ran the Fourth on her own. "The alcohol starts showing up, and then you have your hands full."

"Pull the band's plug at seven forty-five?"

She grinned. "You learn quick." Before they could start up any other topic too detailed to cover, she motioned back toward the stage.

They connected with Jonah and delegated ground for each to cover, Archie expected to take more time in his territory due to old-time Cravenites remembering him, wanting to catch up on the years.

Quinn would still try to slip away as quickly as possible, maybe even let Jonah and the farm's hands see to clearing the parking lot without her. That or cleanup could wait until tomorrow.

Time moved on to six p.m., six hours since Larry had left with Ty.

The attorney wouldn't have gotten there until two, and four hours of interrogation was nothing, especially when it involved murder.

Maybe she could make one inquiry. Slipping her phone out of her jeans, she hit a number in her favorites, though the number fell far short of being so.

The call went to voice mail.

Oh no, sir. That wasn't happening. She called again. When the call rolled to voice mail again, she left a message short and sweet. "I will keep calling until you answer, *Uncle.*" Her benign moniker for him served the same purpose as his calling her *niece,* and Uncle Larry knew it. "I'll call over and over. You aren't in the interview, so don't pretend you're unavailable." She almost stopped there but couldn't help herself. "So help me, if you get involved in this investigation, I'll do my level best to blast you out of the water. Colleton isn't your county, and Ty being yours is a conflict of interest. Pick up the damn phone." She hung up.

She gave him long enough to listen to his message and added a minute more.

He called her back. "What is it?"

"Are you in Walterboro?" she asked.

"Yes."

"Why?"

"To support my man."

"Why does that not give me comfort?"

"Because you don't trust people. I don't have time for this, Niece. What do you need?"

Good. She could cut to the chase, too.

"What was the time of death?" she asked.

"Not sure I should—"

"What was the damn time of death?" She was the wrong person for him to con with half-truths.

"Between ten and eleven this morning, they say."

Ty had arrived at Sterling Banks right before noon. To have a timeline that tight already meant they'd spoken to enough people in the vicinity to narrow things down.

"Cause of death," she said.

"Strangulation."

That made it personal. Not good.

"Who found her?"

"Open investigation."

"Not yours," she countered.

"But privileged, nonetheless. One law enforcement officer does not undermine the case of another, even if it's not in his jurisdiction."

She'd tried.

"He didn't do this," she said. "He's not capable. Murder is not in his nature," she added, realizing the big and burly size of her friend made him more than capable. His training, however, would've told him not to strangle her. There were other ways. . . .

"He's an officer of the law, so yes, he is very much capable," Larry replied, his tone demonstrating he held the upper hand here. "As to his nature, who knows what someone will do when backed into a corner?"

"How the hell was he backed into a corner?"

Natalie lived in Walterboro to be outside of Craven County and away from Ty and his allies. She grew up there with a grandmother who'd died five years ago. Natalie's dad was a complete unknown, and her mother died from an overdose when Natalie was twelve. Quinn couldn't imagine Natalie having anything to hold over Ty.

"Talk to me, Uncle," only this time she pleaded, half changing tactics, half desperate to know. "What do you mean?"

"She was leaving," he said.

"Why?" she asked. Where would Natalie even go?

"No idea."

Apparently, one of his Colleton brothers in uniform had spoon-fed Larry a taste of the interrogation, but not all. They knew of his relation to Quinn.

Who would Natalie have told this to other than Ty? Because no way would Ty volunteer that detail and incriminate himself. Not with Tassey Talmadge in the room.

"They still interviewing him?"

"Yep."

What else could she ask while she had him?

"While I've got you," Larry began.

Quinn waited, eager to hear almost anything.

"What's Archie doing in town?" he asked.

The oldest trick ever. Trading information. He'd shared a little and expected something in return.

"Have no idea," she replied.

"Quinn." He dragged out the name as if she knew better.

"He arrived around noon, and we haven't had a chance to talk. Not in this crowd." The truth.

He sighed into the phone. "When you find out, call me."

27

"What? No. He's your brother. You call him. Invite him to your place. Show him the new Sheriff's Department HQ. Take him out to eat."

"Gotta go, Niece."

He hung up.

She hadn't the energy to understand the animosity between Larry and Archie, but without a doubt she'd root for Team Archie.

Larry hadn't given her much to go on about Ty, but she did learn the police department had a witness or witnesses. Maybe not to the actual crime . . . surely not to anything involving Ty. Someone could've seen him and Cole leave, but otherwise there was nothing seen that could be incriminating.

There was one other thing she could do, though.

Someone needed to interview Cole. Someone other than the attorney. Someone other than the cops. Even someone other than Ty. If Cole witnessed something problematic, he needed to spill it without worry of repercussions. An attorney would scare him. A strange cop would scare him more. And his father would give him the sense of having to answer the question right or something bad might happen.

No, Quinn had to be the first to tease out what the child may have seen. He may have thought he'd seen nothing, but sometimes people saw happenings they didn't register at first, or didn't decipher as important.

She'd promised to take care of Cole, and this came with the job.

Chapter 4

QUINN LEFT THE fairgrounds early, but the longer she waited, the less time she had. By seven thirty, time had slid by, and as badly as she wanted Ty back, she couldn't risk his returning before she spoke with Cole. No point in Jonah knowing either. Archie didn't ask. She wished the remnants of the crowd a good evening and exited to the manor, her men chalking her retreat up to stress and her letting them.

The kids weren't at the house, but it didn't take Quinn long to find them feeding the other kids at Jule's place a quarter mile behind the main house. Who didn't like petting baby goats?

In her overalls, one of her signature bandanas in her back pocket, blue this time, Jule had parked herself in the barn's opening on a cane chair she kept for such a rest, a large box fan pushing a breeze across the floor. Her long gray braid draped over her shoulder, she'd parked a cold thermos and a stack of paper cups by her chair.

Quinn slid a bale of fescue over to park herself, her long legs accustomed to the folding up, and Bogie came bounding up to be petted, wriggling and unable to contain himself at seeing his mistress. With a practiced command, taught to both of them by Jonah, she made the lanky six-month of a pup lie down.

Inside, Glory and Cole sat on the barn floor, on a blanket not normally there, on a bedding of hay not normally there either, with a young goat basking in the incessant stroking. The nanny stood to the side, enjoying her own special treat of pellets, corn, and straw, deciding the pampering worth these humans tending her baby.

Glory wore a yellow bandana like a hairband, containing her curls. Cole's was tied around a skinny bicep. Bright red. They'd been indoctrinated into the Jule bandana club.

"Hey, where's my scarf?" Quinn asked, which made Jule smile. "How are they doing?"

Normally stoic and mostly business, Jule Proveaux wore happy on her face. "Fed them around five. Found toothbrushes for them. We've been out here ever since, having fun," she said. "The children," she added.

"Not the goats, though they don't look too put out by the attention."

Quinn chuckled. The goats *were* Jule's children most of the time. She'd been originally hired as nanny to Quinn, with Jonah tagging along, and she had a pragmatic yet nurturing way about her. Very practical. Very understanding. You listened to her, and you learned.

"Think you could distract Glory and take her someplace? I need to speak to Cole," Quinn said.

"What's going on?"

"Cole's momma was found dead this morning," she whispered low.

The worrisome wrinkles flashed then disappeared, with a glance toward the boy to remain protective and discreet. "He doesn't know?"

"No, ma'am."

"Don't you think it's his daddy's place to tell him?"

Quinn nodded. "Yes, ma'am. I want to ask Cole about his morning, before his daddy picked him up, to tease out what he may have seen. I will indeed let Ty tell him about his momma, but he doesn't need to be the one asking questions about what Cole might have seen."

"Hmmm." Jule stood, a little slow but nothing troubling. Sixty-two wasn't old, but a half-dozen decades had a way of taking up residence in your bones, she was prone to say. "You be careful with him."

"Preaching to the choir," Quinn said. "He's as precious as his daddy, and I would hurt myself first." She thought about saying something else, to get it off her chest. Jule's maternal instinct ran deep, and she always said the right thing. "Jule?"

"Hmm?"

But Quinn couldn't tell her about the voice mail recording. The need-to-know in her said not to. The guilt in her said yes. What good would it do, though?

"Thanks for taking care of these two."

"No thanks needed," Jule said. "You think first of him, mind you."

"Yes, ma'am."

"Glory?" the older woman called.

Glory peered up, her fingers still embedded in goat hair. "Yes."

"Yes, ma'am," Jule corrected.

"Yes, ma'am."

"Let's you and me go inside and fix us something sweet to snack on."

Cole's scowl flashed his concern of missing out.

Jule pointed to the baby in his lap. "Young man, you are in charge of her. Don't let her get lost. Can I trust you?"

"Yes . . . ma'am."

"Good," she said, holding out her hand for Glory to take it. The two strolled to the neighboring house, Jule asking questions and Glory more than happy to chatter replies.

Quinn moved over to Cole, settling on the blanket still warm from Glory's backside. "Having fun?"

"Oh yeah," he said. The baby nudged his hand, hunting for more treats, and Cole giggled, hiding pellets in a different hand than before. "Daddy back?" he asked, not looking up.

"Not yet," she said. "How's your mother doing?"

That caught his attention. "Fine, I guess. Why?"

Quinn didn't ever ask about Natalie. They existed on two entirely different planets in his father's solar system. Jealous of Quinn's childhood with Ty, Natalie had hated Quinn since the first time they'd met, having recognized the soft spot Ty had for Q. "Your dad was late showing up today," Quinn said, "so I wondered if things were okay at home."

She worried that Nat had sounded okay on the voice mail but was not okay when she met Ty. Another reason to keep the voice mail to herself for now.

Cole's grimace at the silly question assured her that she hadn't crossed a line, and that nothing was wrong as far as he could tell.

"Mommy always fusses at him when he shows up. She hates it when he's late, and this morning he was."

"How late?" Quinn asked.

"Twenty whole minutes," he said. "He's supposed to be there by ten when he gets me. She gives him five minutes, but she gets pissed after ten. This morning she was leaving to go someplace. She runs errands and does girl things when I'm gone, she says. Like I do boy things with Daddy."

She arched a brow. "She lets you say *pissed?*"

"Sometimes."

"Does your dad let you say *pissed?*"

He wilted a little. "No."

"Okay then." She'd diluted the subject well enough with that focus on his manners. Back to questioning. "Did they argue?"

"Oh, yeah."

"Where were you?"

"In the kitchen," he said.

"Where were they?"

"In the hallway at the front door. Daddy made her shut the door so nobody would hear. But when Mommy lost her temper, Daddy made her stop." He leaned over. "She was piss . . . um, real mad, then. She told him to leave. He took me outside to his police car, turned on the air conditioning, and left me playing a game on his phone while he went back up to get my stuff."

Quinn might understand removing the child from a grown-up argument, but damn. This was not good. Not good at all. "How long before he got back?"

Cole shrugged. "I was playing."

Kids, adults as well, plunged down rabbit holes once they fell into a video game. "Do you remember what they were arguing about?"

Cole leaned over, doubling himself in order to press his cheek against the kid's neck. "You mean besides him being late?"

"Yes," she said, noting his shift in temperament, seeking comfort in the animal.

"Moving," he said, mumbling the word. "Mommy might want to move. Not sure where. Maybe Charleston? Said there are more jobs for her there. Daddy was not happy, let me tell you. Mommy was kinda mean about it when Daddy said that was too far away."

"Do you want to go?" she asked. Not a pertinent question of interrogation, but she wanted to know. Ty would've asked.

Cole shook his head.

"Was he mad when he returned to the car?"

"No, ma'am. Maybe sad, but he tries to hide that from me."

Sure he would. "Was he breathing hard? Tired? Upset in any way?" she asked.

Cole shook his head back and forth five or six times. "Daddy doesn't get upset, Miss Q. He's too strong to get upset. We just came here. He didn't tell me Glory would be here, though."

"Glory was a secret for all of us," Quinn replied, her hand touching his as they spoiled the goat. "By the way, how do you like her?"

He sat up straight, grinning with a power to charm. "I like her a lot. She's not like my school friends. She's Cracker Jack."

Quinn laughed aloud. "Where'd you get a term like that?"

"Miss Jule," he said. "She said all the Sterlings and Jacksons are Cracker Jack."

"True," she said, moving up to stroke his mass of black curls. "At least we try to be."

Cole appeared to look behind her, and she turned, expecting Jule and a plate of shortbread pecan cookies, her go-to cookie jar recipe.

With an endless supply of pecans, Jule didn't bake a cookie, cake, or casserole without nuts in it.

"What're y'all up to?" Ty slowed as he took in the scene, not wanting to scare the animals. "Ah, got a new one, huh?" The nanny stiffened, and he softened his approach further. He'd grown up around goats, like Quinn. Nobody disturbed Jule's herd without consequences.

Quinn studied him for the stress, but like Cole said, Ty was a pro at hiding feelings. He was the stabilizing factor at every crime scene, at every fender bender, at every domestic disturbance. His emotions weren't readily shared, Ty ever letting others reveal theirs first. Even with Quinn, he reserved sentiments for particular times and places, but she'd seen as much or more of his feelings than his own mother. They'd grown up that close.

"Her name's Zinnia," Cole said, stroking. "And she likes me."

"I see that," his father said, before shifting attention to Quinn. "Come with me to the house? Attorney came back with me since it was on the way."

She stood to go find Jule, but Jule exited the house with Glory holding a tin of cookies. Jule carried a new thermos, probably of milk.

"We need to go to the house a moment—" Quinn began, but Jule finished the thought.

"And I can keep the kids until you come for them. Or they can spend the night here, if you like."

"You're a wonder," Ty said.

"Yes, I am. Now, y'all do whatever y'all need doing. I got this."

And of course, she did, because Ty and Quinn had grown up in this barn, amongst goats, savoring afternoon cookies and learning at the knee of Jule like this new generation at her feet.

They walked a hundred yards before Ty asked, "Does Jule know?"

"Only that Natalie died. Nothing else. And nobody has told Cole."

He seemed a little relieved at that.

"How'd it go?" she asked.

He shook his head slowly, marveling at the day. "I'm damn glad you hired that attorney, Q. You didn't have to, and you didn't have to go top shelf with this one."

Quinn hugged his arm in a loving *you're welcome*.

His shifted into the meat of the matter, pain in the telling. "They never told me I did it, but they damn sure think I did. I've never been on that side of the table before, and stupidly caught myself wanting to explain things. All of me itched to give them a timeline and the details about what Nat and I discussed, but Ms. Talmadge shut me down."

"Which shut them down. That's her job, Ty. People get in the way of themselves in those situations. That's when the interrogator tries to get the upper hand . . . in the opportune moment of weakness when someone is first accused."

"But I didn't do it!"

"They don't know that."

"They are supposed to seek justice. I'm a brother in blue, dammit."

"You are the suspect, the bird in the hand, so to speak. They go at you as if you did it, until somebody proves them wrong."

She almost said they were only doing their job, but that wouldn't help. Ordinarily, he should recognize that. "You know they learn which buttons to push," she said. "They hear motive you don't even think exists. You've been on the other side of the table. You know. Now take a breath and let's analyze this." In her training, the FBI Academy had trainees interrogate each other, and the learning curve was eye-opening. "Tell me what they think," she said. "I mean, the details."

"They're holding back some," he replied.

"Of course they are. Your attorney held back some of your cards, too. It's a game."

"Not when you're the target," he grumbled, as they approached the house.

She stopped him a few yards shy of the back patio leading to the double glass doors to the vaulted den. "You left her alone in there?"

"Yeah. Wanted you alone before we went in. She told me not to talk to you, but what the hell does she know?" He gnawed down hard on those last few words since it was just the two of them.

Quinn pulled him to the side of the house so their voices wouldn't travel. Lawyers were nosy by nature. Tassey Talmadge would've recognized that Ty sought Quinn as an ally, yearning to spill to someone other than a cold, calculating attorney. As a deputy, he accepted the callousness of the profession, but for even a few moments, right now, he needed a friend.

"It doesn't look good," he said.

She rubbed his arm. "Honestly, did you argue with Natalie? Cole said something about it."

"Yeah, and she has a high-pitched voice. No doubt someone heard her with the door open part of the time."

"What did you argue about?" she asked, wanting corroboration for Cole's story.

He sighed, then in a bout of frustration spilled. "She was planning to move to a bigger city, from the way she talked. I suspect a man's involved, but no mention of a name. I can't see her up and taking off like that on her own, especially to a big place, Q. She gets lost in Savannah and fusses about Charleston's one-way streets, and has never tried getting around Atlanta." He shook his head. "Someone manipulated her."

She mashed her lips in a tight, understanding way. "You didn't know where?"

"No, she wouldn't tell me. That's so wrong, Q."

Could Nat's voice mail have been about moving? God knows why, but was Natalie wanting to talk about that with Quinn? Now might be a good time to tell him about the call. "Maybe she—"

"What about Cole?" he said, loud and unruly, arms animated out to each side. "How would he see me? Where would he go to school? He's growing up, and the influences there . . ."

Dusk dropped quickly around the trees, and the gnats were out, Quinn waved a couple away from her ear, letting Ty say his peace.

"If someone heard us arguing . . ." He lowered his tone, seeing how emotional he'd become.

"Yes, and . . ."

". . . then I appear guilty as hell."

Totally correct. "What'd you say that might sound guilty?"

He moved his jaw around, remembering. "That she was crazy to leave. I didn't want them to go. I wasn't letting her run off with my son." He held up on the last one. "And there must be a man pulling her strings."

Quinn sighed at all the cliches . . . cliches that fueled the embers of a guilty fire in the eyes of a detective. "Okay."

He leaned a straight arm out, palm against the old Charleston brick wall, his posture wilted.

"I'm sorry," she whispered, easing up close. "Nobody's given it a thought that you might have some feelings about her being dead, have they?"

He grunted, validating that she spoke the obvious. "What the hell do I tell Cole?" he said into the wall. "And what do I say after he hears they think I did it?"

"You don't worry about the latter," she said. "Not yet. Not until it happens."

She wasn't a parent. She really hadn't had to break the news to anyone about death before. She'd experienced it. Words failed her in what to tell Cole, and she swatted another gnat, feeling totally inept.

She'd wait to tell him about the voice mail.

"I can tell you this, Ty. Be honest with your lawyer. No secrets. No excuses. No half-truths or second-guessing what might or might not sound good. That's her job to sift through everything and decide what serves your best interest. You hear me?"

Still leaning, he turned his head toward her. "Is there a single cell in your body that thinks I might have done this?"

"Oh, God, no, sweety. None at all." The fact he had to ask that drew a lump in her throat. "Never."

"But you've killed people I never imagined you killing," he said, his gaze darting to the living room behind those sliding doors where two thugs broke into her home and tried to take her out. Where Tassey Talmadge waited.

"Yes, I have," she said, and she had her share of nightmares about both deaths despite the fact they were deemed righteous. Both had tried to kill her. One man had killed her father. She'd be lying if she said she was ashamed of either, and she dodged those thoughts most days. Killing anyone left a dark spot on your soul.

"They aren't letting me plan a funeral yet," he said, his voice choking. "I need to take care of her for Cole. She has nobody else since her grandmother died."

"You're jumping ahead of yourself," she said. "Her body is evidence, and they'll sit on things for a while. First talk to counsel. She's been waiting long enough, okay?"

He dragged himself away and, at the sliding door, held it open for her to enter first. The attorney sat relaxed in Quinn's favorite chair, a leather recliner, a mug of milk in her hand after having helped herself to the kitchen. *Archie must be out with Jonah*, she figured.

She remained seated when the two entered but held up the glass. "What exactly is this stuff? I didn't want anything alcoholic, and I hate soft drinks."

"Goat's milk," Quinn said. "We raise goats."

"Interesting," the woman said, sipping then licking the thickness off her upper lip.

"It takes some getting used to."

"Indeed." Tassey set the glass on the side table and rose, smoothing out her pencil skirt before holding out her hand. "Tassey Talmadge," she said. "You must be Quinn Sterling, Ty's sponsor."

"Ty's best friend in the whole damn world," Quinn corrected. "And we need to make this thing go away."

"Ms. Sterling." Tassey lifted her chin in a thought, then dropped it back down. "Because you pay me doesn't mean you control me." She gently waved a hand toward Ty. "He is my client. Please understand that."

Quinn tried not to take issue with the attitude. "I was FBI," she said. "I get it."

"I'm sure you do, but this will get personal before it gets better, and lines will blur. I'm here to keep us on track, clear-headed, and as unemotional as possible. There might be some things you don't need to be involved in."

"What you tell me I tell her," Ty said. "No compromising that."

The woman wafted a hand to the sofa, as if she owned the manor. "Sit," she said. "Let's talk."

Quinn wanted to sit next to Ty anyway. Let the counselor have the *Princess's* chair for now.

"He looks good for it," Tassey said. "And they have a witness who heard the fight."

"Who?" Quinn asked.

"They aren't saying, but it has to be a resident or guest in the complex. Maybe a delivery person who happened to walk by the door long enough to take in the conversation. People are curious creatures." She turned to Ty. "Where was your son during all this?"

"I put him in my patrol car once she started scolding me for being late," he said. "He heard nothing."

"Let me decide that," she replied. "I'll need to interview him."

Ty unfurled himself, moving to the edge of the cushion. "No way. He doesn't even know his mother has passed."

Tassey's expression remained in check, as if nothing could cut through her Kevlar. "Then let's get that out of the way. Where is he?"

Ty jumped up. "No damn way are you involved in *that* conversation."

"Mr. Jackson—"

"No!"

The lawyer took in a shallow breath and tried to display a sad, empathetic smile of understanding, but Ty wasn't having it.

"Smack that look off your face, Counselor," he said. "God . . . you people." He strode to the sliding door, facing the grove.

Tassey turned to Quinn. "We have to hear what the child saw and heard, while it's fresh, before anyone else asks him in a way that reflects badly or alters his thoughts."

Quinn had risen when Ty did. "You have a lot of ground to cover to stay ahead of this. I see that."

Arms draped on each tufted chair arm, Tassey waited.

"This child needs his father."

Tassey attempted a kind, understanding tight smile. "No doubt." Tight seemed to be her middle name. Total control.

Quinn continued, fighting for Ty. "This night will change this child's life, and every word, expression, and movement of every person involved will sear into his brain for the rest of his life. I've been there."

"I get it, Ms. Sterling."

"But do you?"

Tassey released a soft sigh. "I'm trying to save his father. However the child remembers me doesn't matter."

Cold. Quinn couldn't argue with the logic, though, but tonight could change how Cole remembered his father, too.

The woman might've been right about this getting personal. If she didn't mind being thought ill of, then let her be the person for Cole to hate. Quinn could see that. But Jesus, Cole had to experience this lady's aloofness atop the loss of his mother? And any day he'd hear things and have burning doubts about his father.

Thank God Quinn had been preemptive talking to Cole to get the unadulterated story of the child.

Cole's future was about to get confusing for him, and she'd be his biggest advocate. And he had a place to land here at Sterling Banks . . . in case his daddy didn't.

Chapter 5

QUINN SAT ON the back porch in a rocker, in the dark, listening to Cole cry off in the distance of the pecan grove, her own tears barely held at bay. Someone came through the sliding doors, and in turning to see who, she blinked, sending moisture down her cheeks.

Archie slid another rocker over close, the wooden runners scraping before he lifted them up. "I love the smell of these trees." He sat. "Told Jonah I'd be out here with you. He's got his hands full with the final shutdown. Jule has Glory for the night."

"Yeah." She sniffled. "Feel bad leaving the shutdown to him." She swallowed the tears. "That attorney is a cold-assed woman."

Archie listened but waited for her to embrace the reality.

"But she needs to be," she said, resigned. "Someone has to keep their head and ask the hard questions."

Tassey had told Ty to bring Cole back to the house, then seated across from the child, the father told the son his mother had died. *How* and *why* fell out of Cole's mouth, as expected. Tassey had stood off to the side, waiting for her cue, then told the child she was an attorney helping his daddy find the answers. Cole reared back from her, not trusting her at all, with the stranger's presence emphasizing how scary this all was. Then he lost himself, fighting to place blame.

"You're the police, Daddy," he said through heavy sobbing. "Why didn't you save her? Why aren't you finding the bad guy?" Then with a gut-wrenching scream, he yelled, "I want you to kill him, Daddy. Promise you'll kill him!"

Ty tried to scoop the child up and take him away, but Tassey sat beside Cole and began with her questions, a firm hand out for Ty to stay where he was. But Cole had seen no one. Heard no one. And the conversation he had heard involved two parents mad at each other—a rehash of what he'd already told Quinn.

Quinn would try a softer hand with Cole later, after he had time to digest things, but she was more eager to get to Colleton County and knock on doors. Someone had to have seen something. If a witness enjoyed nosy listening, they tried watching, too. That possibility flashing red in her mind said the witness might be the perpetrator, too.

Colleton's Sheriff's Office wouldn't reveal that person yet. They would've corded off Natalie's apartment, too.

Quinn stopped the rocker. Cole's sobs had turned to whimpers, and she could barely hear them anymore. From the direction of the sounds, it seemed Ty had taken his son toward Windsor, Quinn's childhood tree house over on the river.

She moved a hand to her uncle's knee. "So sorry this is your home-coming, Uncle Archie."

"Couldn't be helped, little girl." He patted her hand and returned to rocking.

"How long are you staying?" She exhaled long. "Please say a while. A really long while."

"As long as you need me," he said. "I sold my architecture firm."

She stopped rocking. "You retired? What are you . . . fifty-five?"

He gave her a melancholy grin. "Only days away, as Glory is so prone to say. I wanted time with her, and the firm sold for more than expected. My investments are solid, so it made sense. But now's not the time for that discussion. I'll be around long enough to answer your questions, help however you need me to, and allow you to get to know Glory. I'm not who you have to worry about at the moment."

She pointed at him, bringing it around in his face, bouncing her finger off the end of his nose, the way he used to do to her. "I'm holding you to every word, Uncle." She caught herself. "I gotta stop calling you that. You're a far cry from being Uncle Larry."

"Uncle is fine, little girl. Or Uncle Archie if for some strange reason you're confronted with the both of us. I answer to anything and know you know the difference."

Thank goodness he was here. He was an ally. He knew how to behave like a loving uncle should. Her family had increased from three to four, but it felt like so much more. Ty appeared, Cole draped against him, head snug in the crease of his father's neck. The child had ex-hausted himself enough to sleep. Ty looked exhausted in his own right, but his embrace of his son spoke volumes.

"Back in a minute." He headed toward Jule's to tuck his son in with Glory. Quinn couldn't help but remember how she and Ty used to sleep the same at this young age. Sometimes with Jonah overseeing. Some-times with Jonah crawling in with them.

Didn't take him long to return. "Wish you could stay here," she said with a hug as Ty turned to leave.

"Need to tend to Momma," he said, his face weary around his eyes. "Praying she hasn't heard already."

"She would've called you . . . or me," she replied. "Watch out for press."

"Here, too," he said and left the porch, making his way to the drive around the corner.

Tassey had left some time ago. Quinn followed Ty to his vehicle, noting someone must've collected his patrol car from the event this afternoon. He still wore his uniform short of the weapon in his holster, probably at Uncle Larry's instruction. At least he hadn't taken the badge. She might've had to say something about that.

Everyone wanted so desperately to show their allegiance to him, but his mother would want to tend to her son in his time of need. That conversation, maybe with tears, would take them into the night, and Cole didn't need to be in the middle of that.

Quinn saw Ty off and returned inside. Jonah and Archie slumped in the living room's deep-colored leather furniture. The ceiling, high and timbered in pecan wood, plus the familiar dark paneling offered their own welcoming condolences to Quinn as she entered.

Fatigue after the annual Fourth of July event was normal, but this year the event had turned on a dime, erasing any sense of normal. Thank goodness the attendees had no clue.

Quinn plopped on the sofa next to Jonah. He reached an arm around her, and she sank into him.

"Ty?" he asked.

"Worn out but headed to Lenore's. He'll stay there tonight."

"Cole?" Archie asked.

"Curled up in bed with Glory, I'm guessing in your room, with your momma looking over them."

Even Archie remembered Quinn and Ty in their youth, his soft grin a tell-tale of the memory.

"So what's the deal?" Jonah finally said after the silence wore on too long.

"To outsiders he looks guilty," she said. "Someone says he was seen at Natalie's within the time frame she died. We don't know who. Uncle . . ." She caught herself at using the same word for both uncles. "Uncle Larry won't say much, assuming he knows anything. Not his jurisdiction, and Ty works for him. Who knows?"

Jonah rubbed Quinn's back, her long torso drooped over her knees.

"So what now?" he asked. "We just wait for detectives to do their jobs?"

She peered over her shoulder at him, a brow cocked up as if he ought to know better.

He released a hard sigh. "No, you're right. My bad."

But Archie couldn't decipher the unspoken between the two. "What?"

"I'm going to Colleton County in the morning," she said. "If it weren't so late, I'd go now. Time is everything, and you talk to witnesses before they start thinking too hard or talking too much to each other. Before the press gets ahold of the story and spins it."

"What witnesses?" the uncle asked.

"People at Natalie's apartment," she said. "I want to nail down who saw what."

Archie peered at Jonah for clarity.

Jonah cocked his head at Quinn, his look remaining on the uncle. "Quinn doesn't wait for others to do the investigating. She doesn't trust Larry, of course, but she isn't all that trusting of uniforms either."

"They go after the first person with the least shadow of a doubt on them," she said. "Lazy investigating."

"Wow, aren't you the discriminating one," Archie said. "I'd have thought you on their side."

"I'm tainted by Craven County," she said. "You would be, too, Uncle Archie, if you'd been around."

Disappointment set across Archie's face.

Jonah tapped her shoulder blade. "Now, now, Princess."

Quinn dropped head in her hands. "I'm sorry, Uncle. I'm tired. I'm worried." She stopped short of saying she was scared. "I don't know many in the Colleton SO, but I can't see leaving Ty's future in the hands of people who haven't earned my trust. That sound better?"

"We're all tired," Archie said, standing. "That red-eye flight was eons ago. We can talk about this in the morning."

Abashed at the oversight, Quinn rose as well and took two long steps into her uncle's hold. "I'm so sorry. Of course you're tired."

He kissed her temple and squeezed her into himself. "No apology necessary, Miss Q. I'll find my way to a bedroom. I believe I remember the way. Get some sleep and we can talk game plan tomorrow."

She kissed him back on the cheek. "Where's your luggage?"

"In his old room," Jonah said.

She loved everyone remembering things as they used to be. Archie had lived in the house until he had gone off to college, then came home thinking he would assist with the grove and pecan business that generations of Sterlings had managed as their pre-ordained legacy. He left at twenty-seven, when Quinn was Glory's age. While he'd come home often in his earlier years flying solo, by the time Quinn entered middle school, he'd sold his inheritance to Graham, Quinn's father, and vowed never to return.

She was never made privy to the motivation, and many Craven County people had frowned upon such spoiled behavior. What else did you call turning your back on a third of a plantation with a three-hundred-year birthright?

She saw him to the foot of the stairs and watched until he disappeared into the upstairs hallway. Bogie sat at the base looking up, waiting. Then he peered at Quinn, ready to hit the sack as well.

"We're going up in a sec," she said to the droopy pup.

Why had Archie left to begin with? And what prompted his return after twenty-eight years? She'd love to hear about the in-between as well. She'd always loved this uncle, but in all honesty, didn't have much awareness of who he really was. It was amazing how birthday cards and Christmas cards and the occasional phone call lulled you into thinking you were connected. All it took was one surprise seven-year-old cousin to remind you that you didn't know jack.

Her great-grandmother's clock chimed on the mantel. Ten thirty.

"Staying here tonight?" she asked Jonah.

He dragged himself upright from the sofa. "Since my bed's taken, I was thinking about it."

"Would appreciate the company, but on one condition."

He posed hands on hips, wilted but leery. "What?"

"You don't get upset when I leave in the morning for Colleton," she said. "I need boots on the ground before the people who lived around Natalie get too caught up in each other's stories."

Jonah pulled his shoulders back, cracking his spine. "Not surprised. Want me to come?"

Did she? She normally took Ty on such treks. He kept her reined in and offered detective ideas of his own. Jonah would only be company—not help, and he had so much to do here. She shook her head. "No. We have guests. There's cleanup left to do."

He peered down his nose at her a bit.

"I know, I know," she said, reading his body language as if it were her own. *"You're spoiled, Princess. You're getting out of work, Princess."*

Jonah put away the chastisement and lightly laughed at the mind-reading. He grabbed her hand to lead her up the stairs, but at the landing halfway up, he stopped and turned to face her, the humor gone from his expression. "This is Ty we're talking about. I don't care what you do as long as you don't get in trouble for it. Just stay out of trouble."

"Jonah," she started.

He covered her lips with a finger. "At least before you get in too deep, come get me. Drag me in with you. You won't have Ty to keep you in check. There's nothing we won't do for our guy, and that means me as well as you, Quinn. I don't want both of you in jail. Don't do that to me. Don't do that to Jule." He tapped her lips once again. "Keep. Me. In. The. Loop."

She got it. She would tell him the same thing if their roles were reversed, but he wasn't accustomed to the world of crime, accusations, and law enforcement in a world that was a far cry from black and white and often anything but fair. She understood where to cut corners and where to overstep. He didn't.

Jonah kept Sterling Banks running, the home fires burning, so to speak. He had plans for a pecan store on his small acreage that butted against hers. He was the favored son for one of the school board trustee seats.

In other words, Jonah was an extremely good guy, and she didn't like him tainted with anything she might do. Not that she planned to do anything inappropriate, but sometimes such decisions were impromptu. Sometimes the bad guys waved a knife at you, or chased you through a pecan grove with a gun, or as he had learned not that long ago, rammed your truck with theirs.

Jonah was the good she could come home to, the sanity that made sense when the rest of her universe unraveled. She wasn't sure if her decision was for her sake or his, but she didn't want him hurt.

"You're thinking way too hard," he said, taking her hand to go upstairs.

"Not sure what I'll be doing in Walterboro," she said. "So no promises, okay?"

Abruptly, he stopped halfway up the second set of risers, dropped her hand, and peered down at her from two steps up. "Are we a couple or not, Quinn? Some days yes, but there are moments, like now, when you wall me out, when I wonder where you stand. You know that?"

Taken aback, she wasn't sure how to respond.

"I'm not stupid," he continued. "The hairs on my neck go up each and every time you leave the farm on a case, even when I know what you're up to, so imagine how I feel when I'm in the dark. That's not fair.

It's almost deceitful, and it's damn sure disrespectful."

His lecture hung like an ultimatum between them. She tried to take his hand back, and he rested it on the banister instead.

"Don't say that, Jonah. I respect you more than anyone I know."

"Then quit underestimating me. Quit using me as your landing place, your chance to escape from the bad in your life. If you cannot share your bad with me, then what good am I?"

He wasn't letting up, meaning she'd cut meat, hurting him with those two words . . . *no promises*. She wasn't sure what to say to undo that.

Quinn giving Jonah culpable deniability made the most sense to her. Protection. But he'd been her protector since she could walk and preferred to remain actively so.

"I promise to keep you informed," she said.

He held a gaze on her, as if measuring her truth. "I'm holding you to that," he finally said, and reached for her hand.

They didn't speak of the subject again. Ten minutes later, they were under the covers in her bedroom, him pulling her to him, her head on his shoulder as his breathing quickly became deep and even. He was drained.

However, her brain churned. She tried to calculate the odds of Ty going to jail, remained anxious about a murderer running loose and how they'd behave now that the anthill had been kicked.

And she worried if, intentional or otherwise, she was capable of keeping her promise to Jonah. She'd told him about Natalie's voice mail, though. That had to count for something. But he wouldn't settle for that.

Chapter 6

IF BOGIE HADN'T shifted to lie in the warm part of the bed, Quinn wouldn't have realized Jonah was gone. Seeing six thirty on the clock was reason enough to snuggle back against the dog and drift back to sleep. By seven thirty, she woke enough for her brain to engage and process that Bogie was now gone, probably in the grove with Jonah. The dog had been his gift to her, but the pup shared his allegiance, such as in the mornings when Jonah slept over. Those times, Bogie understood he would be fed earlier and could romp in the trees longer when he chose Jonah.

Quinn loved that he was loved so much. Between Jule and the farm staff, the dog had more attention than any ten dogs.

With Jonah gone and Bogie not needing tending, she reached for the phone to make her first call of the day, and it wasn't to Ty.

She got Tassey's voice mail. "Call me ASAP, please, counselor. I have a suggestion."

Knowing how efficient this attorney was, Quinn leaped into the shower, but still, the phone rang as she stooped over wet and clean, toweling her tangled red mane. She ran back into the bedroom, threw the towel on the bed, and sat bare naked taking the call, understanding that a game of phone tag only meant more numbers on an attorney's tab.

"Ms. Sterling?" Tassey Talmadge sounded crisp and very much at full throttle.

Quinn shifted the towel's wrinkle out from under her backside. "Yes. I want you to hire me as your investigator."

"I have an investigator."

"Who charges you way more than I would."

"You get what you pay for," she said.

"I certainly hope so, because I'm paying you plenty. However, take a dollar from that ten-thousand-dollar retainer I sent you last night and call it even. I'll shoot you my standard contract unless you want to send me one of yours."

The attorney gave the slightest of hesitation, and Quinn took advantage. "A dollar. I don't need the money. I'm vested in this. I'll dig deeper. I know most of the PIs in Charleston, and I stand toe to toe with any of them. Baron Ingram will vouch for me. I'm FBI trained." She took a breath. "Plus, this is my only case."

Quinn expected a sigh, a harrumph, something, but the woman remained silent, again, as Quinn had noted last night, the control in her strong.

"Do you fully understand the seriousness of this situation if you let emotions interfere, Ms. Sterling? Do you realize how you could jeopardize Ty's future if you fuck this up?"

Funny how this woman even made the curse word sound professional.

"I do," Quinn replied. "But this is my neck of the woods. You know that a Charleston PI will face more obstacles than I would."

"People wouldn't see you as impartial."

"The cops, maybe, but not the average person, and especially not those living in Colleton County. I can be quite convincing, and a woman can be less intimidating." She began thinking about what to wear to tone down her first impression.

"You'd have to keep me informed," said the lawyer.

"Of course."

"Before Ty," she added.

That might be more difficult, but at least she hadn't told Quinn *not* to talk to Ty. "Agreed."

"You start today," Tassey said.

"I'd have done that anyway, whether you hired me or not."

"That's what I figured. Best you work with me than independent."

Exactly. "Good, then please contact Colleton SO and let them know I work for you, because I'm headed out to the apartment complex as soon as I'm dressed. It's the day after the Fourth and most people aren't working. I want to catch as many as I can."

Tassey exhaled this time. Not loud but enough. "I hope you're as good as you claim."

"This is for Ty. I'll be most excellent, Counselor. I fully understand the gravity of the situation."

"Which is why I hired you."

If the situation weren't so dire, Quinn would've pushed back at the idea having come from the attorney. She didn't.

Tassey reiterated, "Keep me informed," then hung up without a goodbye.

Excellent. Now she could phone Ty. He answered sounding sluggish.

"Hey, Old Man," she said. "How're you doing?"

"Fine," he said, though he sounded nothing of the kind. "How's Cole? I'm about to head that way."

"Good. He spent the night with Jule and Glory, so all's good, by the way. He's sad, but he has a lot of support here, Ty. Family. He can take Glory around the farm, and no doubt Archie and Jule will be right behind them. Jonah will check in. Trust me, he's well taken care of and he'll have something to do to occupy his mind. Now, really, how are you? And how is Lenore?"

He grunted. "She's cooking for me, worried and demanding we should stay with her. She'd love to have Cole stay here, but that means he'd be at the restaurant, and I'm torn over that. He's a handful, and she works hard enough as it is. He needs more attention than she has time to give him there, though I'd never tell her that."

"Like I said, Cole's well taken care of. My turn to repay the favor. God knows how much she tended to me after I lost my mother, then my father." She paused as an idea struck her, then said, "Both of you can stay here. It's not like we don't have the bedrooms. Think about it. Anyway, on another note, Tassey hired me as her investigator."

"What?" The sigh came hard in her ear. "Someone murdered Nat, Q. A murderer is still thinking they got away with it."

"I know all of that, Ty."

"I couldn't stand to lose you, too, Q. That would be the end of me."

"And I can't stand to lose you," she said. "That's why I asked Tassey to hire me."

"Let me come with you," he said.

"Ty, you know better."

"Then who's going with you. Jonah?"

This time she scoffed. "Trust me, he and I have already been down that path, but no, at least not today. I need him here on the farm."

"You cannot do this alone."

"You forget who you're talking to."

He moaned. "Don't give me more to fret over, Q. Be smart, please. Watch your back. I can't help but wonder if . . . never mind."

"If you're targeted?" she finished for him. "Who better able to sniff that out than me?"

"Just . . . be careful."

"I have to be, Old Man. For you."

They hung up, him saying he'd get there soon but first he'd spend a couple hours assisting Lenore at the Jackson Hole diner. He said she was rattled, and she'd aged before his eyes. She needed assistance getting the diner open without coming undone.

Poor guy was accused of murder, yet he worried about taking care of his mother, his son, and now Quinn. Initially her gut told her to keep him apprised even before his attorney, but now she wasn't so sure. The big guy had a lot on those broad shoulders. She'd keep the voice mail to herself for now.

Quinn was motivated now. She threw on dark slacks, the color and cut accenting her five-feet-ten height, then added a white oxford shirt to look proper yet casual. Claret leather flats. Hair down, she pulled the front back into a barrette, thus the feminine touch. Simple gold studs and a thin cross necklace. One more addition needed, but it was downstairs.

At the end of the hall she heard activity below. Her phone read nine, way too late for Jonah to be readying for the day and too early for his break. By the time she reached the landing, she heard the kids, and a split second later she smelled pancakes.

"Aunty Quinn!"

Damned if her heart didn't skip at the joy of hearing her name from that child. "Good morning, Glory."

Dressed in a lavender shorts set, the sleeveless top a floral daisy print that hung wide with a ruffle at the hips, her little cousin all but beamed at the hope for a new day. "Can you take us to the tree house after breakfast?" she begged. "Please, please?"

Quinn welcomed the hug around her waist, sucking it in. This child had people skills in spades. "Afraid I have a job this morning. If Jule or your dad can't, I'll take you there this afternoon."

"Awww."

Quinn heard someone in the kitchen. "Where's—?"

"Shhh," Glory said, waving up at her too-tall aunt to lean down.

Quinn squatted to the child's level. "What?" she whispered, as if they shared a secret.

"His mother died," she said, hushed. "He's awful sad, Aunty Quinn. Awfully. He cried sometimes last night. I hugged him, though, and took care of him."

Stroking the child's hair with curls too tempting not to, Quinn asked, "Can I trust you to take care of him again today until his daddy gets here? He's probably going to want to show you some things. There are a lot of good places to see on Sterling Banks, and he might feel a little better if you did things like climb trees, walk along the river, visit the tree house, and of course, tend to the baby goats. Jule might even let you sample her pecan pralines and sugar nuts in the barn."

Her little eyes widened with each option. "I can definitely do all that."

"Good. Where is he now?"

Glory pointed to the sliding doors. "Out there. Jule took him to the rocking chairs. I think he's sad again."

"Oh, poor little guy."

"Yeah," Glory said.

No point interrupting them, either, since he obviously felt comfortable with Jule. So Quinn changed the subject. "Your daddy making y'all breakfast?"

"Yes, he is. He's good at avocado toast, but you didn't have avocados, so he's making pancakes."

Typical California, but avocados would go bad before being eaten in this kitchen. Quinn stood and held out a hand, which Glory instinctively took. "Right now I need to pick out a scarf. Want to help?"

Quinn escorted Glory into the master bedroom at the end of the house, down the hall from the kitchen. She opened the door, and they entered a room she'd preserved since her father had died, who'd preserved it since Quinn's mother had died. For thirty years, this room had remained intact with the belongings of Graham Manigault and Margaret Kennedy O'Quinn Sterling. For years, Quinn had envisioned this moment to be one with her own child.

"This room belonged to my parents," Quinn said, and when Glory screwed up her eyes, Quinn explained. "Your uncle and aunt." Then when Glory seemed still stymied, Quinn redefined. "Your daddy's brother." She started to say she and Glory were cousins in reality, but no point screwing with the child's head. Besides, Aunty Quinn sounded so perfect.

Glory let loose of her hand and wandered into the great chasm of a room. Quinn left her studying frames photos on the dresser and went into the walk-in closet for what she had originally come for.

"It doesn't smell old," came from the other side of the wall.

"That's because I keep it clean and put an air freshener in here." Then the voice in the doorway caught her a little off guard. "What're you doing in the closet, Aunty Quinn?"

"Finding a scarf to match my outfit," she said, stroking the rows of material, from mohair to simple indigo cotton. From gauzy to silk. "My mother loved scarves. Which do you think I ought to wear today?"

Glory peered up at the colorful array, most too high up for her to touch, so Quinn pulled over a small three-step ladder once used to reach the shelves of the fourteen-feet-high room. Glory climbed up and went straight to a thin, floral chiffon. "That one," she said, slipping it loose from its loop.

Whether it matched or not, Quinn would've worn it, but the soft, pastel celadon green held an oriental touch with a claret accent in the flowers and their branches, matching her shoes. "Excellent choice," she said, helping the girl down. They'd be back and explore this room properly later. Girl to girl. Generation to generation.

As they exited, Quinn shut off the lights and closed the door, with Glory skittering out to check on Cole.

She held herself in the hallway a moment before following her cousin. Gracious, never before had she desired a child of her own so much. That connection between her parents and offspring suddenly carried more weight. Family trees were one thing, but emotional connection between generations held more meaning when watching a child make the attempt to understand where she came from.

Her eyes moistened. She missed her parents. She wished them here to explain things to Glory instead of her. She wished they could hold her on their laps, and be the ones escorting her around the grounds. She wished Archie and Graham could be brothers again.

"It's on the table," shouted Archie, and Quinn swiped at her eyes and strode in. She only had time for a quick bite, regretting the need for rush, but Ty sat worried at Lenore's, mired down in a wait-and-see world as to whether he had a future inside or outside a jail cell.

Fate had given her such lovely guests at the most inopportune time. Thank God that Jule and Jonah could tend to Archie and the kids, because Quinn's total focus had to be on saving Ty. These people would rally for all they were worth for Ty, too, which would likewise keep her strong.

Then, so she wasn't breaking her promise to Jonah, she texted him. *Headed to Walterboro. I'll be careful. Will text when I'm on the way back.*

She wolfed down the pancake and half a glass of milk. Archie found a thermos and sent her packing with coffee laced with goat's milk, along with a kiss on the cheek and a warning to stay safe.

Reluctantly leaving such a wonderful new feel to the manor, she still left, pushed by the urgency that warned her: if she didn't solve this, Ty was going down for murder. She had this sick, sick feeling things weren't what they seemed.

Chapter 7

QUINN POINTED HER personal white pickup, plain without the brown Sterling Banks logo, toward US Highway 17, heading south. She picked up Wood Road to shortcut through to Green Pond Highway and headed north toward Walterboro, another twenty miles to go.

Colleton and Craven Counties could be one in terms of landscape, farming, and variety of housing and small businesses, each having claimed Jacksonboro as its county seat at some point in history. Today, Colleton had the larger county seat of Walterboro sporting a whopping six thousand people, almost as much as Craven County's entire population. Neither county had much to write home about to the average tourist, but natives to the area understood the history. The Revolutionary War, the Civil War, and Native American pasts left huge footprints. Plantations were still tucked down long roads, a handful open to the public with marshes, Spanish moss dripping off live oak trees, and enough woods and fields to feel feral and unmodern.

Roots ran deep in this mixture of loamy, sandy Lowcountry soil, some acres wet and others not, with many lineages tracing back like the Sterlings to three centuries ago. In Craven, Ty and Lenore's heritage reached back to slave days, to a property in the possession of the Jacksons who established Jacksonboro. The family tree sported more dark than light faces today, but residents recognized a Jackson with respect, regardless of what color the first Jackson was.

The Jacksons stuck together, for instance, Ty's nuptials. Quinn came home from college when Natalie Wright married Ty Jackson, her beaming as if she'd married royalty, which she unofficially had in this region. The Jacksons threw a wedding with three hundred people in attendance. When a Jackson celebrated an event, family came out of the woodwork.

Quinn had tried to hug Ty after the I-do's only for Natalie to insert her white-laced, manicured self between them, demanding their relationship cease in thought, word, and deed, and demanding it loud enough for folks to whisper.

The incident embarrassed Ty to no end, and embarrassed Quinn for him since he had to live through the gossip. She could go back to college.

Natalie's jealousy had no basis. Quinn and Ty had kissed but once, in tenth grade. They'd grown up as best friends. Quinn had been afraid of becoming more than that to either of her guys—Ty or Jonah. Maybe she carried a smidge of glum at the time as she had slipped down to girl number three in Ty's life, behind his mother and new wife, but she'd been genuinely happy for him. Natalie, however, couldn't differentiate between the platonic and the romantic, and since Quinn was considered a whale of a catch for eligible men from Myrtle Beach to Savannah, to Natalie she was competition. Having Sterling family money and the privilege that followed only made it worse. Not that Quinn recognized any of those social issues back then. Her goal had been to finish school, become FBI, and leave Craven, like her Uncle Archie. Her young self saw Sterling Banks as an anchor, a burden she hadn't asked for. She never saw the flip side of that coin and how her life had given her advantages so many didn't have.

Thinking back, she'd been such a child then.

The weight of Natalie's death hit her harder today, especially after listening to the voice mail again, listening harder for clues. She should've tried more to bridge the gap Nat was ever keen on keeping deep and wide between them. That gap made Quinn wonder if the imaginary relationship Nat saw between her husband and his childhood girlfriend had festered into a wound that wouldn't heal. Ashamed, Quinn saw how she'd felt rather proud of having the upper hand back then, while having done nothing proactive to earn it.

She wasn't wearing that pride very well today, and wished she'd grown up sooner.

When she returned after her father died, Ty and Natalie separated within four months. Ty mourned not seeing his baby son every day. Quinn mourned her father. Jonah nursed his injured mother back to health, as she'd almost died herself walking up on Graham Sterling's murder.

In the aftermath, the JQT Club as they'd called themselves since children, became a mess and not strong enough to be particularly attentive to each other. Each hurt too much to be of much good. Ty and Natalie's marriage had been affected as well.

When Nat divorced Ty, she'd left the small house they'd built in Jacksonboro and gravitated back to The Front Porch of the Low-country, as the town of Walterboro was nicknamed. Even though she'd been raised in the town, she had no more relatives. Quinn guessed the relocation was as close to returning home as Nat could get, while still being far enough from Craven County to give her peace. At least she kept Cole within reach of his father.

Quinn's truck passed several farms, some fencing an immense number of acres. Lowcountry dirt leaped in value daily, and she wondered how much of that fencing would rot, too expensive to replace, especially with taxes becoming obscene. She wondered how many might be forced to sell. Developers pursued undeveloped acreage like bucks in rut, blinded to doing anything but getting what they wanted and willing to shed blood in the process. They ignored what ground meant to history, to the community, to the environmental, pristine soundness of the region.

Quinn blew by a mile marker. Damn, she needed to stop driving ninety miles per hour or she'd get pulled over. Without Ty or Jonah there to talk with, she could get immersed in the wrong thoughts.

She refocused on the task before her—visiting the crime scene. As required, or at a minimum as a courtesy, the attorney for the accused had to notify the police when needing to see a crime scene. Trouble was the police didn't have an obligation to share the crime-scene results with anyone until that someone was accused, i.e., charged. Charging meant they were pretty damn sure they had their culprit, because that's when the defense attorney gained a certain degree of authority, too.

Regardless of Ty not being charged yet, Tassey had asked permission for Quinn to enter the apartment. The sheriff's office, unwilling to give her and her high-powered reputation a solid no, countered with the requirement that one of their deputies be present. Tassey told Quinn to play nice and be grateful for the privilege. Quinn expected a seasoned deputy, maybe even a detective, but she could wish for a novice and hope the SO preferred their experienced people doing more than baby-sitting a gumshoe.

Either way, Quinn wanted nobody interfering with her efforts to interview neighbors and study the scene. To those uniforms, she was the enemy coming to town to see how much she could muddy up their case. She hoped she was overthinking this.

State Highway 64 took her through town and out to the other side where I-95 catapulted Northerners to Florida, along with a lot of drug traffickers. Its other name, at least in South Carolina, was The Corridor of Shame for even worse reasons. A strip where the counties alongside it represented poor, rural areas where public school held a history of inequitable school funding and poor student achievement. Craven

County fell in that line of counties, one of the many reasons Jonah wanted to be on the school board. Like every state, the rural counties didn't have the political clout, and in this state Charleston, Columbia, Myrtle Beach, Rock Hill, and Greenville received the lion's share of public monies, ironically where the higher incomes lived.

Maybe schools had something to do with Natalie wanting to move to Charleston, or wherever. Quinn didn't have a child, so she wasn't sure what she'd do in Nat's shoes, but she was beginning to understand Nat may have had justified reasons and reservations.

Quinn had already passed the small, two-attorney law practice where Natalie clerked, primarily handling real estate closures and family court cases. Quinn had been asked to handle a couple of the latter types, but she'd declined due to Natalie working there, without giving the real reason. Best to keep peace in the family.

Past the interstate overpass, two meager motels, and a handful of eateries, the area quickly turned rural barely a mile out. She took a right onto Jones Swamp Road, coming to an apartment complex of six buildings. Natalie had taken the most affordable address closest to her workplace, Cole's school in town, and a small shopping mall that supplied most of their needs. Efficient and frugal.

Quinn didn't have to hunt for the letter F, painted black on a two-by-two white sign which would have identified Natalie's faded-yellow, vinyl-sided building. A sheriff's patrol car sat in the parking lot right outside the entrance.

She parked beside the vehicle and exited with only her phone and keys. She'd take her notes on her phone, and record if possible.

Quinn reached the deputy's door before he had a chance to unlock it. She backed away for him to rise to his feet with a husky grunt. He was fifty, she guessed, with the girth representative of someone who'd paid his dues, and from the name plate over his pocket, he came with heritage as well. Though of the blue-collar nature, the name Raysor meant something in Colleton. He had to be related to a tenth of its people.

Someone like him could be an all-too-convenient sabotage to her efforts. He knew the turf, the people, and how it all fit together. He'd talked to the other deputies, maybe even the detectives . . . maybe the people she was about to interview. He'd report back what she knew, and he might. . . . Crap. The more information the better, right? She needed to toss the paranoia and get the damn job done.

At least eighty pounds senior to her weight, he rose to his full height, which equaled hers. She was accustomed to being the tall woman in the room, but this deputy gave her a no-holding-back looking over, deducing what he was up against.

She went first. "Quinn Sterling, investigator for attorney Tassey Talmadge who represents Tyson Jackson." She reached out for a shake, holding it there, letting him know it was his turn to meet her halfway.

He gripped her hand, with strength. "Deputy Don Raysor."

"Thanks for meeting me," she said. "Care to show me which apartment?" She fully knew which one, but there were games to play, and then there were games to master. Right now it was an issue of earning trust, or at a minimum, make him feel the superior so he let down his guard.

He nodded at building F behind her. "That one. Top floor, apartment one." He squinted up at the landing. "If you get confused, try looking for the crime-scene tape. It's a dead giveaway." With that, he gave a clipped laugh.

He was pushing buttons. Quinn might not have been close to Natalie, but Nat had been Ty's significant other. However, Deputy Raysor had no need to know any of that.

"Here, I'll show you." He led the way. The steel stairs were sturdy enough but creaked at his heavy footfalls. At the top, he turned left and took them toward the front. Yellow tape zig-zagged across the doorway of apartment one. Quinn didn't see that man fitting through the gaps.

He snatched them down. With a key from his pants pocket, he opened the door. At least he motioned for the lady to go first, but he stopped her at the threshold. "She was found here, in the entryway. The door hit her feet when the landlord tried to enter."

"Who found her?" she asked, taking in the setting of markers, tape, and fingerprint powder. She'd been taught at the academy to study a crime scene from the inside out, beginning at the body, and surprisingly, Raysor had wisely stopped her from traipsing atop the scene before getting her first overall view. "Can you talk me through this?" she asked. She'd determine here if his knowledge came from firsthand experience with the crime scene or secondhand chatter after being briefed on how to meet the nuisance of a private eye.

"Landlord was called by a neighbor," he said.

"Which neighbor?"

He searched his brain, eyes darting a quick second. Nope, he hadn't been on the site before and was operating on what he'd been told. "Someone on this floor," he said. "Best talk to the landlord so you aren't getting it secondhand."

You mean like all the information you've given me thus far?

"Sounds good," she said, reaching over to pull the door closed. "Let's go see him, or her, or whomever, first before we enter the crime scene."

This time she led down the stairs, across the parking lot to the first building where she'd already seen the *Office* sign on a bottom unit. Usually the landlord was offered free or discounted rent to live on the premises, and on a weekday, during business hours, they ought to be in.

The name plate on the door to A1 said *Manager*. A squirrelly-looking man about fifty, gaunt but far from healthy—judging from the sagging belly, neck, and arms, skin a pale yellow from smoke and drink—answered the knock. Like Raysor, he gave Quinn an up-and-down assessment, more up than down since he couldn't have been more than five foot five. "We're filled up," he said, choosing to speak to Raysor instead of her.

Quinn moved into his line of sight, surprised the man was willing to lose so much air-conditioning to the July heat. Nobody living in these inexpensive rentals made a lot of money, and from what she could see inside, the man decorated in early Salvation Army. "Sorry, sir, but we're not here for a rental. We're investigating the Natalie Jackson death in apartment F1."

"I was told you'd show up," he said.

She turned to peer at Raysor who gave no reaction one way or another. She chose not to ask if the manager referenced her or the sheriff or the authorities as a whole, and she held off asking his meaning, preferring that the odd little man feel obliged to deal with them because of the uniform if that's what made him click.

"Hello, Mr. . . ."

"Pratt," he said. "Gunner Pratt."

"Nice to meet you, Mr. Pratt. Would you answer some questions for us?" she said.

"Already answered a bunch of questions."

The expected reply. "Well, sometimes the mind remembers new things a day or two after. And having someone fresh ask them often shakes the tree a bit more. May we come in? Or would you like to talk to us in Ms. Jackson's apartment?" Then she thought again. "Maybe you have a meeting room or community center in one of the buildings?"

"What do we look like, Hilton Head?" He held his door open wider. "Come on in. Don't have refreshments, though, unless you want water. Don't get paid until the first of the month."

From the color of his skin and what used to be the whites of his eyes, he had more than water in his pantry but wasn't willing to share.

"We're putting you out enough as it is," she said. "Thanks for talking to us."

They entered the room holding a warm light scent of mildew. Pratt was frugal with the AC from the eighty-degree feel to the place. They took the sofa, the cushions worn thin, Raysor on one end and her on the other, with Pratt in a recliner christened with a layer of beige body oil where elbows and heads had left their mark around small slits in the leather.

Quinn pulled out her phone and opened a page to take notes.

"You're not recording me, are you?" Pratt asked.

"No, sir. I'd have to ask your permission to do that anyway," she replied, when in fact she didn't have to as long as she was one of the parties of the conversation. Cops didn't have that latitude. "I type fast, jotting reminders of what you tell me." She grinned as if in apology. "I can't remember everything. I hope you don't mind."

He waved her off as an okay.

She showed him the screen and how she'd already typed the date, place, and time to make him feel better. "Now, who found Ms. Jackson?"

"The neighbor across from her. Frannie Bean."

"Unusual name," she said. "Bean is her last name?"

"Nope. It's her preferred name."

"And her real name is . . .?"

"Frances Bean Salvador."

That drew a grunt of humor from Raysor.

"Yeah, right?" Pratt said, open to conversation from another male. "Weird lady, and she's the chief instigator around here. She'd be the one most voted to find a body, too. She leaves notes on car windows about dog poop and kid's toys. She even got into it once about Ms. Jackson's son's bike being left at the bottom of the stairs. She took the damn thing and made Ms. Jackson come knocking on her door for it. Bike went upstairs after that, chained to the stairs. She tries to get all kinds of petitions signed."

"Great," Quinn said, happy the man felt talkative with Raysor present. The deputy had a purpose. "We'll talk to her."

"They already did yesterday," Pratt said.

Quinn nodded, and Raysor turned his head to stare out the window, probably agreeing that all this was repetitive. Both of them could get over themselves.

"About Natalie," she continued. "Had she given notice about leaving?"

"She mentioned the possibility of moving but hadn't given notice. Takes a month's notice in order to get a security deposit back. I told her that, but she never gave it."

Maybe Natalie was only fishing about moving.

"Did she ask for a referral?" Quinn asked.

"No."

"How long has she lived here?"

"Seven years. Had to look it up for those guys from yesterday. Wanna see the lease?"

She shook her head. The timeline matched the Jackson divorce closely enough. "I'll take your word for it. Any staff on duty yesterday that would've been around when she was killed?"

He shook his head. "Only me. But I don't check on when people have cable or the like come to their residences. Electrical, water, and sewer usually route through me, and she had none of them scheduled. With it being the Fourth, I doubt anyone was here unless it was an emergency."

Raysor sat straighter, staring at something in particular out the window. "Like that guy?"

The other two followed his gaze to a plumbing van, a man in uniform shirt and navy slacks reaching into the back for whatever he needed.

"I got him," Raysor said, rising with an effort from deep in the sofa. "Y'all continue doing your thing." He left.

Quinn continued with the landlord. "What about cams or CCTV?"

Pratt relaxed without Raysor, less on stage. "They're on the parking lot and my door only. Seems people don't like cams on their doors. Some of them have those RING doorbells installed, though. We allow those."

"Did Ms. Jackson?"

"Nah. She fussed about her ex wanting her to get one. Being a cop, I can see where he'd want her to, but she wasn't having it. He did coax her to live upstairs. Said less breaking and entering happens on upper floors, though I can't vouch for that here."

Sounded like Ty, and yes, he was correct on that statistic.

"I'd still like to see the cam footage," she said. "Say between nine and eleven a.m.?"

"Already gave a copy to the sheriff's office."

"Again, we're sort of checking behind them. Doesn't hurt to check twice."

Pratt rose slow and reluctantly from his seat. "What's your email?"

She gave him her nondescript Gmail address. As he pulled up footage and did his thing, she confirmed Nat's employment and her routine of coming and going. "Did she have a boyfriend?"

"Neighbors say yeah, but nobody can name him. I can't. Never seen him, either, but if I were her, I wouldn't want that big beast of an ex of hers to know. He looks like he'd break someone in two. If you ask me, he did it," Pratt said.

"Which he? And why do you think that?" Quinn asked, not loving the manager's supposition and wanting him to absolutely confirm the who and particularly the why.

"The deputy," he said. "Her ex-husband. Mr. Jackson, though I'm not sure of his first name."

"All these years and you don't know his name?"

"Ain't ever seen him up close. Gets his kid and goes. Brings his kid and goes. And Ms. Jackson wasn't one to ever talk about herself, you know?"

Nat had still used the wiles learned from being in a cop family.

"Why do you suspect him?" she asked, fingers hovering over her phone, wishing she'd put the phone on record after all.

"He has the skills. His visits always made her start yelling."

"You heard her yelling all the way over here?" she asked.

"Nah, but the neighbors told me."

Only twenty-four hours later, these people had already shared enough of their stories to muddy each other's versions. It's why you interviewed people quickly, before they had a chance to pollute each other's version.

"He was mean," Pratt added. "He didn't want her to move. You know how cops—" Then he stopped himself, realizing that plain clothes or not, the woman before him probably rooted for the other team.

Quinn rose, trying not to show a distaste for his opinions. "We'll go talk to the neighbors now. Thanks for your time, Mr. Pratt. You've been helpful."

"I hope so," he said, making no effort to walk her to the door. "We don't like cops here. They bully. You may think otherwise being who you are and what you do, but people like me in the world are beginning to recognize the bad in these people." He added, "Hope I haven't insulted you."

"Not in the least," she said, hand on the door, knowing good and well if someone broke into Pratt's apartment, the first person he'd want on the scene was a big, beast of a cop like Ty Jackson. She bet this scrawny two-bit piece of a man had a record, too.

She left before she said something wrong. Time to go see what the neighbors thought about Natalie, Ty, and whomever Natalie had been seeing. Ty mentioned some unidentified new man had convinced Natalie to move, and hopefully a neighbor could confirm that identity.

Another name, another suspect, another someone could cast reasonable doubt into this case before it overwhelmingly cornered Ty and tainted the entire jury pool of Colleton County.

Chapter 8

QUINN LEFT THE manager's apartment, headed toward building F. If Raysor wasn't shadowing her any better than this, it was on him. Out in the parking lot, however, Raysor and the plumber laughed and exchanged conversation alongside the van, a huge graphic faucet along the whole side. The two seemed to know each other, the man about the same age as Raysor. She expected the deputy to break away and catch up, realizing they were changing gears and returning to the crime scene, but instead of following her, the deputy gave her a glance and remained where he was, chatting away with his buddy.

Fine. She didn't need a babysitter anyway. Time to interview the neighbors, and she'd opted to leave the nosy neighbor who found Natalie until last. Quinn climbed the stairs once again, stopped and knocked on the apartment to Natalie's right, the one with F2 on its door.

A woman in her mid-twenties answered. Cropped brunette hair complimented her heart-shaped facial structure, and she'd been enjoying a relaxing day judging by her jean shorts and sleeveless tee. She looked innocent enough.

Quinn smiled down at the five-foot-two person. "Hey, I'm investigating Natalie Jackson's death. Would you be available for a few questions?"

The lady peered behind her, as if seeking backup. "Um, we weren't even here yesterday when all that happened. Not sure we can help."

A man appeared of similar age and hair color and pulled the door back wider. He wore dark-red hospital scrubs, seemed freshly showered, and his wedding band matched hers. "We're sorry about Natalie, but honestly, my wife is right. We can't tell you a thing."

"Actually, we're broadening the investigation," Quinn said. "We'd like to ask you about Natalie's life and routine. It might help us."

"We?" he asked.

Kudos for him to finally ask for identification. "I'm Quinn Sterling, a private investigator, here with a Colleton deputy who's in the parking lot interviewing someone else."

The husband held up a finger, left from sight, then shortly returned. "I see him outside."

Quinn smiled, as if she were happy he was happy, then she wiped away a trickle of sweat on her temple to remind them this was July with the sun at its prime.

The couple kept peering at each other for what to say, not wanting to say or do the wrong thing, not wanting to insult the law while remaining uninvolved. Quinn deduced they hadn't been married long with neither being the alpha, and neither wanting to make a decision without the other's approval.

"I promise not to be very long. I still have to interview your neighbors. Sound good?" she added, nudging them to take the path of least resistance and say yes.

"Can't hurt anything," the wife said.

"Sure, come on in," the husband concurred.

Quinn hoped the interview wasn't this much of a group-think ordeal.

Laid out the same as Pratt's, the apartment instead smelled of citrus, and while the curtains might be from Walmart and the furniture from CostPlus, the couple had been selective enough to turn a low-rent unit into a cozy home. A framed cross stitch indicated Troy and Tee were less than a year married. Textbooks on the table said nursing student, with the red scrubs telling Quinn the husband studied at University of South Carolina, the Salkehatchie campus.

"What year are you in nursing school?" she asked.

"Third," he said. "I'm on scholarship, but that doesn't pay the bills. I'm finishing while she works, then she'll go to school while I work."

Tee beamed at her husband's explanation.

They were cute as buttons. Too cute to be murderers. Besides, a nurse surely would come up with a better method than manual strangulation, but then, nurses weren't trained in killing.

"Sounds like you created a well-thought-out plan," Quinn said. "Congratulations."

He beamed. Wow, had she ever been that sweet and naïve?

Now that she'd gotten them to let her in and even smile for her while releasing personal information, it was time to get to work. She sat where they told her to, accepted the glass of iced tea, and began. "How long did you know your next-door neighbor before she died?"

"Nine months," Tee said. "As long as we've been married. This is our first home. Natalie introduced herself to us the first day we moved in when she and Cole brought us homemade brownies, still warm." The mention of Cole brought about a realization. Tee gasped a little. "Where is Cole? Oh my goodness, how is he doing?"

"He's with family," Quinn said. "He's sad, as you might imagine."

"Oh course. We babysat him a few times. He's adorable. Quite full of himself but never any trouble."

"So you knew Natalie well?"

Troy intervened. "Well enough to be friendly, but not all that close, really. The babysitting wasn't often, but she had no family. We knew that much." He looked over at Tee, mentally telling her he was going to say more. She tightly smiled and shrugged. "Did her husband kill her?" he asked.

"Still an active investigation," Quinn said. "Nobody's been charged."

"It's in this morning's news," he said, which Quinn hadn't seen, though she wasn't surprised. "Online," he said. "*The Post and Standard* is only published weekly so we read the daily online version."

She'd checked *The Craven Chronicle's* online blog that morning, likewise published weekly with a daily abbreviated online version. They mentioned the murder in about two inches of news that listed Ty only as the ex-husband and a local. The physical paper wasn't due out for a couple more days, enough delay to throw a juicier story together. The home county editor would be clamoring all over people for a lede and a few juicy quotes, and Quinn would warn Ty again to be on the lookout. Jonah, too, so he could watch the farm's entrance. The whole county understood the inter relationships of Sterling Banks's people.

"Did they mention a suspect?" she asked, typing in a note to herself to look up *The Post and Standard's* blog and social media.

"They said Natalie's ex-husband was a *person of interest*," he was careful to say correctly.

"Did they mention her boyfriend?" she asked.

The couple exchanged glances. "Boyfriend?" Tee said for them both.

Quinn tried to seem stunned. "Yes, the boyfriend." She set her phone down, as if this subject needed her whole focus since they were in the dark. "There was talk of her moving to be with him. You sure she didn't mention him?"

The couple seemed genuinely stunned. "Not at all," Tee said.

"Not that we were best friends or anything," Troy amended.

"Did you ever see her with someone?" Quinn asked.

Troy chose to take the lead now. "Just the ex. A really big man. The silent type." He did a one-shoulder shrug move. "We've heard her get loud some weekends when he picks up or drops off Cole."

"Ex-couples can do that," she said, returning focus to her phone, to make Troy less worried about what he might say and make it seem they were harmless in whatever they did. "Ever hear what they said?"

"Only common stuff exes say to each other."

As if newlyweds would know.

"Yeah," Tee said. "Like he was late for pick up. Or she could use more money for Cole. Make sure he doesn't eat sugar or make sure he does his homework."

Quinn had a thought. "You say Cole spent the night with you?"

"Not often," Tee replied. "My hours are business hours, Monday through Friday, so sometimes on the weekends. Three times, maybe? When she went out of town overnight, Cole usually went with his father."

"Where did she go?" Quinn asked, eager for the least glimmer of hope at any evidence of Natalie having a beau.

Troy held up his palms. "She never opened that door. We knew because she told us she wouldn't be there and to watch her place. You know, like neighbors do."

Tee laughed. "She knew we couldn't afford to go anywhere, so we were always here!" Then she turned serious. "I sensed she didn't want anyone to know where she was. She apologized once for not telling us. Said she didn't need her ex to hear. We never asked again."

Not good. "Have you met Tyson Jackson?"

"Only know him by sight, ma'am," Troy said. "We didn't dare introduce ourselves. Didn't want to be involved in someone else's marital problems."

"I hear you," she said, uneasy at everyone thus far seeing Ty as a threat. "You weren't here yesterday, you said. Mind my asking where you were?"

Tee seemed surprised. "It was the Fourth of July, Ms. Sterling. We were with relatives at the lake, and stayed long enough to see fireworks. We were shocked at the yellow tape on the door when we got home. We were trying to get the manager when one of the neighbors came knocking . . . about scared us to death—"

"She told us what happened."

Again, this cross-cross of conversations between potential witnesses motivated an investigator to reach witnesses, neighbors, and relatives as soon as possible. "Her being Frannie Bean?"

"Yes. Have you met her?" Tee asked. "She's a professional busybody, if you ask me."

Troy sniggered. "Only this time her nosiness took her to a body the rest of us might not have discovered for days."

"Thank heaven she did," Tee almost whispered. "Would've hated to have smelled her to find that out."

Seemed Frannie Bean had infiltrated everyone's space and spread the news, and if she were anything like meddlesome observers who relished being the discoverer of important issues, her story grew with each telling. "What about the other neighbor? The one in F3?"

Tee almost whispered. "The vampire."

Her husband's scolding came quickly. "Tee, come on. He just keeps to himself."

But Tee was beginning to enjoy the audience. "He keeps odd hours, and we think he must work from home. He's not old enough to be retired and not disabled that we can tell. No visitors. Never. And he doesn't like you to speak to him."

"We tried once," Troy added.

"And he got angry looking, and I swear he growled," his wife tacked on.

"Not a growl," Troy said, as if his wife were a child, "but he glared for sure, turned, and disappeared into his apartment."

"At least he leaves you alone," Quinn said.

They nodded in unison.

Quinn had pretty much confirmed these two had little to contribute. The Colleton SO would tie down the timeline where these two were on the Fourth. The neighbors could corroborate.

Quinn gave them a card, as she had the manager. "If anything comes to mind, please call me. Any time day or night. We want to catch this person. For Cole's sake if nothing else."

Troy took the card, read it, and handed it to his wife. "Thought the husband did it. Isn't that what *person of interest* means? The person most likely to have done it?"

Oh, hell no, she wasn't leaving on that note. "Person of interest means only that, someone who is close enough to be worthy of questioning. They have more information or are closer to the victim than the average person, but until he's charged, they don't have enough to think he did it."

"So y'all are fact-finding," Troy said.

"Yes," Quinn replied.

"Everyone here says he did it," Tee said. "I hope he doesn't come by here. And it scared me a little that he might get custody of that poor boy. Cole loved his mother."

This neutrality stance she fought to maintain was difficult. Thank goodness Raysor wasn't here. Where exactly was he?

Quinn handed back her half, now lukewarm, glass of tea. "Thanks for your help."

"Don't feel like we said much," Tee said.

You said enough.

"You were more than helpful," Quinn said. She headed for the door, super eager to exit this Barbie-doll residence where Ken and Barbie drank whatever Kool-Aid someone handed them.

Outside she peered over the landing, the rails blistering on the palms of her hands. It was two in the afternoon, and the July temperature was still on the rise. If it wasn't ninety-five, she wasn't a redhead.

The plumber had disappeared, with Raysor nowhere in sight. She bent over to see below, to check out the patrol car. Still there.

"Checking on me?" came the deep voice from behind her.

She jerked, hoping it hadn't shown to him, giving herself a second to turn around. "Yeah, guess I am. Where have you been?"

"The plumber is Trevor Meyers, a second cousin on my father's side. When someone has a water problem out here, he's the most local. He was here yesterday."

Interesting. "Why didn't the manager mention this plumber?"

The deputy threw a half sneer at her. "Because he wasn't at Natalie Jackson's. He was on the grounds, only at another apartment. He saw our Jackson fella arrive, then come back down and put his son in his patrol car, and then go back up to F1. Saw him leave, too. About half past nine."

"Who else went into her apartment during that time?" she asked.

Raysor grimaced. "He didn't say he saw anyone else."

"Did you ask him?"

"No."

"What the hell did y'all talk about so long, then?"

His humor disappeared. "Like I said, we're cousins. You stroke people to get them to talk. You might take a lesson in that. The manager wasn't too fond of you, in case you didn't notice him turning to me. Part of why I left." He leaned in. "As a courtesy to you, Legs."

She stiffened. "Legs?"

"You got 'em. Own 'em," he replied.

Was this man for real?

"I own them, all right . . . Dough Boy." And she almost pointed a finger into his belly as the off-screen person did to the biscuit character in the commercials.

He rubbed his belly as if she had.

She should've talked to the plumber. Maybe Raysor could've gotten more out of the manager.

Standing on that upstairs landing, they stared a few seconds at each other in a mental game of chicken.

She finally spoke up first. "Someone else entered that apartment. Had to."

A bushy brow raised over the deputy's left eye. "Why's that?"

How was she supposed to answer that? "Because I work for Tassey Talmadge, who works for Tyson Jackson, which means I look for other options. Everybody, to include you, thinks Tyson Jackson did it, without anyone trying too terribly hard to seek an alternative as far as I can see. The manager and these people in F2 think Mr. Jackson did it, when neither one laid eyes on him yesterday."

"My cousin did."

She leaned in, still tempted to prod that gut. "Did he see Tyson Jackson kill her?"

Raysor delayed answering, so she answered for him. "No. Did he have eyes on that apartment long enough to say nobody else went in there?" This time she didn't give him the chance to speak. "No. Did he see which neighbor found the body?"

"Didn't ask him that."

"Again, another no."

However, the plumber was damaging. He saw Ty go in and out of the apartment close to the estimated time of death. She needed more. She needed someone to have seen someone else.

"Who's this Ty fella to you?" Raysor asked.

"Just doing my job," she said.

His squinted eyes sent a gaze down his nose at her, loaded with doubt.

Great. Now she suspected even more that this chunky, middle-aged uniform was little more than a snoop, sent to oversee her and report back to the sheriff's office. She ought to leave and come back later without telling anyone, but she wasn't sure how much that would sabotage Ty's case.

"Well, Dough Boy," she said. "We have several more apartments to visit. You in or do you need a fast-food fix? Wouldn't want you fainting in someone's living room. Would make me look bad."

A sneer climbed up his cheek. With his hands still on his gut, he patted his shirt. "Ate a big breakfast, so I'm good, Legs. Let's find us a witness."

Raysor wasn't flinching. The sheriff's office had already spoken to people, and maybe this was little more than Raysor ensuring she didn't muck up whatever they already had.

For the umpteenth time, she had to dash aside the skinniest of worry that the only evidence to be found was against Ty.

Chapter 9

"WHERE NEXT, Columbo?" Raysor asked, still happy with himself for catching Quinn by surprise on the apartment landing.

"Apartment F3," Quinn said, chin motioning toward the unit across and down one from Natalie's. "What happened to *Legs?*"

"Thought it might be too non-PC," he said.

She laughed once, and none too kindly. "A little late for that, Dough Boy."

He laughed back, equally sarcastic. "You judging my size?"

"You judging my legs? Or me as a woman?"

Sniffing, Quinn recognized cigarette smoke, Raysor scrunching his nose about the same time. Turning, they realized they were putting on a show for an older woman standing outside the apartment F4 doorway, listening so hard she might've written their words down on the palm of her hand if she'd had a pen.

"Hey, keep going," the neighbor said, in anything but a Walterboro drawl. Nowhere near Southern either, but Quinn wasn't gifted enough in dialect to tag which state. "This is entertaining."

Very puffy in size, F4's arms were twice the size of her neck, her black, thin-strapped tank giving a clear view of their pudgy circumference. The tank tucked into the waistband of a red floral gathered skirt which did anything but trim her appearance. Thick-soled sandals matched the color of the tank. A wide headband kept curly gray hair away from her face, most of it piled in an unkempt knot atop her head. The red lipstick was so loud Quinn swore she must've just swiped it on. Quinn had seen a lot of vividly decorated people in her day but none quite as tacky.

She'd bet a month's sale of Sterling Banks's pecans this was the nosey neighbor referenced by Troy and Tee and the complex manager, the lady who'd discovered Natalie's body. No way on God's green earth was this woman the recluse.

While Raysor stared, Quinn slid out one of her cards. "We were about to knock on your neighbor's door. Then yours, but you just won our attention."

"What the hell for?" the woman asked, moving a cigarette from her right hand to her left to take the card. Her words were without rancor, though. Just her way of asking.

"We're inquiring about what people may have seen yesterday when Natalie Jackson died."

Quinn tried to act as if this woman wasn't a shock to one's system. The deep, gravel voice, the daring to show crepe-wrinkled skin . . . deep-gray eye shadow and eye liner that curled up into ample crow's feet on the sides. And all of the poorly done makeup amplified by saucer-sized glasses dating back to the eighties. The way she used the corner of the card to dislodge a piece of tobacco from between her teeth would leave an imprint on Quinn's brain for years.

"I may have been here at that time," the woman added, spitting the piece on the porch.

"Where are my manners?" Quinn said, trying to take control of the conversation as well as get a name. "I'm Quinn Sterling."

The woman held up the card. "So it says here." She leaned against the doorframe, taking time to enjoy the moment.

Raysor tired of the contest. "Ma'am, could we have your name, please?"

The resident of apartment F4 stepped toward him, then forward again until her belly, accented by the gathers in the skirt, almost brushed his. Raysor fought not to look down.

"Name's Frannie Bean. Surely you need my phone number too, big man."

Raysor cleared his throat, but in that second of time, Frannie Bean reached up and felt the man's chest, massaging his pocket. She went toward his pocket.

He backed up. "We already have it at the sheriff's office."

She stepped forward again. "They have my name, too, yet you asked. But I want *you* to have my phone number. Where's your cop notebook? All you police have them."

Instinctively, he put a hand over his pocket. "Ma'am, may we come in and talk?"

"Sure, honey." She reached for him as if to drag him in.

He moved enough to escape and waved toward the opening. "You first."

His action lit her up like a Christmas tree. "I love you Southern boys and your genteel ways." Frannie Bean's attempted sashay assumed more of a waddle.

They entered a time warp, a sixties-retro affair of turquoise, rust, and gold. A silver lamp hung on the end of a sweeping curve of an arm, curled over the sofa. A brash rug with overlapping circles pulled the colors together. At least it wasn't shag, because Quinn wasn't sure she wanted to touch—even through shoe soles—something so prone to collecting crud over that many years. From the cloying scent, it had already absorbed decades of cigarette smoke, then LSD orgies came to mind. Between Pratt's place and this, she already craved a shower.

Frannie Bean didn't ask what her guests wanted, just went to the refrigerator and brought back canned Cokes, setting them on a glass coffee table still showing signs of the last dozen or so canned Cokes. An orange ceramic ash tray held a week's worth of butts, assuming she smoked only one pack a day.

Chivalry be damned, Raysor sat in a gold vinyl-covered chair before Frannie Bean had a chance to corner him on the sofa. Quinn took the opposite end of the sofa, however, putting Frannie Bean between them, partly to assist in the interrogation, and partly to mess with him.

"What do you do for a living?" Quinn asked.

"Retired school teacher," Frannie Bean said. "I stay active, though," and she pointed toward the window facing the parking lot.

A cardboard sign sat propped behind the sheers, and even from her vantage Quinn could tell the front was bright red, saying something about a school board. "You help the local school district? I'm sure they appreciate it."

"The hell they do," Frannie Bean said, and cackled a laugh. "You people are so far behind the times down here. That board needs to go. I'm considering running next time, you know, to bring some variety into this place." She pointed her cigarette at Quinn. "You live in Colleton County? Would love your vote."

"Sorry, I don't," she said, and left it there, glad for Jonah he didn't have to politic in this district.

Frannie Bean turned to Raysor on her right. "Your sleeve says you live here. You vote?"

"Yeah. I'll watch for your signs. Now, may we ask you about yesterday?"

"Sure!" came out loud and aiming to please, or maybe more about enjoying the attention of guests. "I'll tell you like I told the others. I heard Natalie arguing with her ex, and I mean she was screaming like a banshee. I could hear her over my television. Then he escorted the child to his car, a cop car, and returned, and the screaming commenced again."

"You say she screamed," Quinn said. "What about him?"

"Low mumble more than anything. Couldn't make out his words. She did most the talking saying things like he didn't control her, and she couldn't live her life for his convenience . . . yada, yada, yada. Typical divorcee stuff. Been there, done that. Seems so crucial at the time, and you look back and realize it was idiotic." She swatted Raysor on the knee, and he flinched. "Amazing how stupid we are when we are young cads and sluts, eh my man?"

Raysor seemed stuck between insulted and shocked.

"My colleagues," Quinn started again, "claim you were quite helpful with details. Said you had an eye for them."

Frannie Bean's smile crawled up into her eyes. She was eating this up.

Quinn could milk this, her, all of it. "We're following up for additional thoughts you may have had. For instance, did the ex-husband have a key?"

"No, he had to knock. The first time and the second." She scoffed. "Like she didn't know he was coming back." Her expression almost exploded with sarcasm, as if she had to perform. Her ample body rocked once on the sofa so she could lean forward more, closer to Raysor. "That's when she really cut loose."

"You heard?" Quinn asked. "Did you happen to see anything? I mean, you're right across from her door."

"I was rearranging those pictures." She pointed to the wall, the one fronting the porch. Photos of assorted people represented Frannie Bean's past, the dress and coloring an assortment of decades. "I went to the peephole, honey," she said, "I mean, once I heard her carrying on the second time, mind you. Stayed there to see what would happen. He left, the door slammed behind him, and all was good." She leaned over like telling a story around a campfire. "Only it wasn't, was it?"

The woman ought to do a podcast.

"When he left, you thought all was good, huh? So he didn't leave angry?"

Animated, Frannie Bean shook her head. "Cool as a damn cucumber, coming and going." Then she ceased moving, squinted her eyes and whispered, "But that's how the evil ones are. Stealth and methodical. He also had to put on an appearance for the child since he'd right then killed his mother."

Son of a bitch. Quinn tried not to drop her head. Speculation everywhere, with assumption about Ty morphing into supposed fact. "You said the wife slammed the door."

Raysor raised his brow then righted himself back to neutral.

"Is that when you went over to check on her?" Quinn asked, scared to hear the response. "After she slammed the door?"

"Oh, no," Frannie Bean said, rapidly mashing out the cigarette butt she'd sucked down to barely an inch, matching the rest of them in the ashtray. The woman wasted little of her nicotine. "That's when I went to the laundromat."

Quinn stiffened a little. "Immediately after he left?"

"No, I waited about five minutes, in case the show started up again, but since things were quiet, I went on."

Quinn saw a glimmer of hope in this timeline. "How long were you at the laundromat?"

Nodding at Raysor first, as if assuring him she was telling him the same as she told the others of his kind, Frannie Bean continued. "I did a wash load, waited for it to finish, then crossed it into the dryer and came back. Maybe thirty minutes. At the last minute I'd thrown one of those box cakes in the oven and needed to take it out. One wash load is about equal to a box cake. Done it a dozen times." This time she bent toward Raysor and winked. "I'm a multi-tasking genius, sweet cheeks."

"So, let me see if I follow you," Quinn said. "Through the peephole you watched Mr. Jackson leave Natalie's apartment."

Frannie Bean snapped a nod. "Right."

"Natalie slammed the door."

"Yep."

"Then you thought about a cake, mixed it up, and put it in the oven."

"That's correct."

"Then you carried your laundry across the complex to the laundromat, washed a load, then returned in time to take out your cake, give or take approximately thirty minutes."

"Thirty-*five* minutes to be exact," came the reply. "Bet the box is still in the trash, telling me to cook it that long. The timer was going off when I walked in. Took the cake out, shut off the oven, then thought, *Natalie might need a piece of this cake.*"

"Nice neighbor," Quinn said.

"I try to be." Frannie Bean enjoyed the stroke and looked over to see if Raysor admired her for it, too.

Quinn continued. "So you took the cake straight out of the oven, carrying it over in the hot pan——"

Head shaking time. "No, no. Apparently, you don't bake, Ms. Sterling."

Quinn tried to appear sheepish. "My bad. Educate me."

"I gave it a few minutes to cool then put it on a plate I don't care much about in case I never got it back. I keep several of those in the pantry. Get them from the Salvation Army Store."

Flashing surprise, Quinn peered at Raysor, as if this woman had won the Nobel Prize for physics for such genius. "So . . . you put the now-cooled cake on a plate and went across the porch to her place. Take it from there."

Frannie Bean pretended as if she had the cake plate in both hands. "I tapped the door with my foot since my hands were full, and I called her name. It was open a couple inches, so she would've heard me." Her hands dropped back to her lap. "When she didn't respond, I nudged the door again. It swung in a couple of feet then stopped, like there was a heavy box or chair or something substantial behind it. I pushed with my shoulder. It opened a couple more inches but stopped there."

Quinn typed notes, fighting to hold a gaze on the storyteller, to keep her engaged. "And you found . . . what?"

"I found the poor girl on her back, eyes wide open, mouth open, arms all which away, legs crumpled, maybe from where I'd pushed the door, but that couldn't be helped. Deader than dead, and trust me, at my age I've seen dead a half-dozen ways."

Frannie Bean gave her the time authorities arrived, and when they left. When others came and went like the manager, the press, and the onlookers from other buildings that had no business being there. Quinn finished typing and looked back up at the waiting woman. "Did you see anyone else up here, outside your door, outside Natalie's door, in the parking lot, anywhere . . . anyone not a resident?"

"Nobody but the ex," she said. "Pretty sure he did it. The cops are, too."

Quinn tried not to look at Raysor as if he were such a conspirator, too. "What makes you think that?"

"Heard two of the deputies talking on the landing," she said. "I kept the door cracked."

"And rearranged more pictures?" Quinn asked, to which Frannie Bean smiled a satirical smile. Quinn returned one of her own. "Gotta admit you're good. The deputies say anything else?"

"Nah. One of them heard me, saw me, anyway, they shut my door."

Quinn didn't blame them. "Well, you've been a help. Thanks. You have my card if you think of anything else."

"I do," Frannie Bean said, then slid closer to the deputy to her right. "Mind if I have your card? You know, in case I can't get this pretty detective over here? Nothing against her, but you seem more capable of protecting me from evil than her. Every lady needs a hero in her contact list."

Raysor, bless him, pulled out a card. This woman was too mouthy to turn down, and the last thing he needed was a complaint that would only engage the two of them more.

While they exchanged awkward words, Quinn reread her notes. She needed the investigative file ASAP. Ty was guilty in too many eyes, the likely culprit by the simple fact he was the only one seen. Natalie had fussed enough to draw attention. People loved putting two and two together, whether or not the sum added to four.

Quinn liked witnesses like Frannie Bean, though, and she might come back later for clarity. Tassey would be pleased. Assuming Frannie Bean didn't switch her story, there was indeed hope.

Per Frannie Bean—the one who heard the most, saw the most, and discovered the body, the best witness they had thus far—Ty had left with Natalie slamming the door shut. Natalie . . . not Ty. And what was initially referenced as a half-hour span between that slam and Frannie Bean finding Natalie was more like an hour plus counting preheating an oven, mixing a cake, walking across the parking lot to the laundromat, doing a load, then coming home to take the cake out of the oven, even letting it cool enough to transfer onto a plate.

Frannie Bean only then ventured to Natalie's to find the door ajar.

No telling how many sets of prints were on that doorknob, but Quinn would like to know. She couldn't wait to tell Tassey that there was a window for someone else to have killed Ty's wife, and ample room for reasonable doubt.

Raysor pined to leave, but Quinn appreciated his being present and professional enough to vouch for this interview and what he heard from Frannie Bean, in case there was anything contrary in the sheriff's office files.

"Let's go," Quinn said. "Thanks for the Coke, Frannie Bean."

The F4 tenant saddled up to Raysor. "Thanks for introducing me to this gentleman. I'm hoping he'll find a reason to come back by."

Quinn made her way around the coffee table, toward the door.

"Oh, there's a good chance of that."

Raysor glared back.

Frannie Bean's face took on a kid-on-Christmas-morning wide-eyed appearance. "That would be damn lovely." She read the deputy's card in her hand. No telling where Quinn's had gone. "Donald Raysor."

"Don," Quinn said. "He likes to be called Don."

And yes, Don would be back as many times as it took. In the name of justice, the man was gonna do what it took if Quinn had to deliver him herself.

Chapter 10

"SURPRISED SHE didn't ask us to lunch," Raysor grumbled once the door to F4 shut behind them.

"She's at the peephole, Dough Boy," Quinn said under her breath.

He hushed, darting his eyes then correcting himself. "Now what?"

Quinn moved out of sight of the peephole, and Raysor followed. "We still have F3," she said, striding to the door about twenty feet down. She knocked, glancing back up the porch, halfway expecting Frannie Bean bold enough to poke her head out of F4 and offer advice. Come to think of it, they should've asked her about F3.

Sure enough, her door clicked open. "He won't answer," Frannie Bean said.

"What kind of car does he have?" Raysor asked, heading to the railing to peer down into the parking lot.

"He's had a moped, an old Toyota, and a squatty Ford thing. Weird fellow. He parks in different places to not be seen." She lowered her voice. "Some say he hides to throw off aliens."

Raysor look stymied on that one.

"What's his name?" Quinn asked.

"John Jefferson. Hasn't lived there long."

This complex was diversely weird. The murderer could live here and nobody be the wiser, because everyone came from a different planet.

Quinn knocked again. No answer.

"He ain't going to answer, I'm telling you," Frannie Bean said. "Assuming he's there."

"Thank you, ma'am," Quinn said, hoping the woman would retreat, but she didn't. "Let's go," she told Raysor and headed down the stairs.

"Hell," he said, once out of earshot. "That crazy woman could've done it."

"Yes, she could have," Quinn said, though Frannie revealed no motive. "But we have some doubt now when it comes to Ty doing it. We keep digging."

"We." He huffed. "Like I'm your flunky."

"Or partner."

"Ain't that either. Sheriff pays my salary, meager as it is. I'm dancing on a line hanging with you. And that's the second time you've slipped up and called this man Ty," he said. "I take it you know him?"

"Grew up with him. He's a deputy for my uncle, Craven County Sheriff Larry Sterling. Ty is honest as the day is long, and he didn't kill Natalie. His attorney hired me to assist in his defense. And you probably knew all of that already."

Raysor stopped at the bottom of the stairs. The plumbing truck was gone, and he particularly noticed that she noticed. "Don't go blaming the plumber."

"Don't go blaming the cop," she replied, and took note of the bottom floor of building F. Apartment F5 sat immediately below Natalie's place. Unless someone had strangled her and eased her to the floor, or strangled her on the floor, there was a chance someone had heard a thud if they were home. She headed there.

Raysor got to her about the time she reached up to knock, only to change her mind and ring the doorbell—one with a cam that had the potential of seeing anyone going up or down the stairs. When nobody came when she pushed the button, she resorted back to three hard knocks.

An elderly gentleman answered the door, blinking, his thinning hair askew from an apparent nap. "Can I help you?"

"Sir, we're here to ask questions about the Natalie Jackson incident upstairs yesterday."

"Here we go again," he said, turned and retreated into his apartment, the door left open.

Quinn and Raysor entered. The old man already sat in his recliner, and from the natural fit, it was his routine respite. He ran fingers through his hair, as though only now realizing he looked half asleep.

Quinn made introductions. "And you are . . .?"

"Baxter Randleman," he said.

"You live here alone?" Quinn asked.

"Yes, ma'am. And I saw nothing yesterday. I heard nothing. I need to wear hearing aids, but I can't stand them. Leave them on the dresser half the time. Told 'em yesterday like I tell you now, I can't help you."

He stopped talking, planted a stare on Quinn, and seemed to slowly gnaw on something he found in his teeth. She didn't want to know what.

"Does your doorbell work?" she asked, eager to see the footage.

"No, ma'am."

So much for that hope. "Ever thought about fixing it? Might've helped catch a murderer yesterday." That little dashed bit of hope had pissed her off more than if there hadn't been a doorbell at all.

"It's his choice on whether he puts batteries in his doorbell, Quinn," Raysor said.

She knew that and curbed her frustration. She ran through the other questions . . . did he know Natalie, did she have a boyfriend, did he see Ty that day. He gave negative knowledge of all.

Bummer.

"Who's taking care of Cole?" he asked.

Suddenly he knew something. "You're familiar with Cole?"

"Sure," Baxter replied. "Plays outside my window. Shows off for me on his bike." Then his face clouded over. "Caught him crying once, poor boy. Said he was mad at his mother. She had a new boyfriend, and the kid was none too pleased."

And now he knows of the boyfriend after just denying same. Quinn's pulse spiked a little at the potential. "Did the boyfriend have a name?"

Baxter shook his head. "He never said and I never asked. Said the man called the boy *Chipmunk* because of his chubby cheeks. The kid hated it. Said his mom told him to get over it. Said her nickname was *Chiquita.*"

She saw a spark in Raysor's eye. Bet the sheriff's office didn't have that in their notes.

Yes, Cole had chubby cheeks, and as cute as they were to family and friends, he hated the attention about them. It was all Quinn could do not to poke or kiss them. She'd never utter *Chipmunk* as an endearment. That might indicate the new boyfriend was a jerk, but *Chiquita?* Odds were that said boyfriend wasn't black like Nat, but Hispanic. Here was more to talk to Cole about.

Apartment F2 had babysat Cole. Apartment F4 had scolded him for his bicycle. Now F5 had watched Cole perform bike tricks and listened to the child's woes. These tenants may not have seen a boyfriend, but they confirmed there was one. Cole could even identify him.

Baxter confirmed he heard and saw nothing the day of the murder, and Quinn believed him, so she and Raysor left. Apartment F6 was another couple who had been out of town for the Fourth, who knew of Cole but little of Natalie and hadn't lived in their apartment six months.

The lone twenty-something woman in Apartment F7 lived the farthest distance from Nat's place and heard nothing until after the police arrived. She answered the cops' questions and retreated inside. Kept to herself, she said. Didn't even know Nat's name. She'd graduated tech school two months prior and had started a job at a local car dealership that kept her busy. When she wasn't out with friends from work, she visited her mother on the other side of town, still addicted to her mother's leftovers and washing machine. That included on the Fourth of July when Nat died. F6 and F7 knew of there being a recluse that nobody liked overhead, and they knew of Frannie Bean from whom they kept their distance because of her nosy ways.

Apartment F8 sat beneath F4, aka Frannie Bean's place, and the woman who answered said she'd lived there for quite some time. Almost since the apartments were built.

"May we come in?" Quinn asked. A tenant around this long could be every bit as good as a manager, if not better.

"Why don't you have a uniform?" the woman answered instead, only a couple inches over five feet, old enough to have retired early, still young enough to be active and astute. She'd answered the door in short leggings and a tank, barefoot, a tad of perspiration glistening at her salt-and-pepper hairline, a damp towel around her neck.

Quinn handed over a card, but what she expected to be a formality only backfired.

"You're nobody," the woman said, flipping the card once, then twice, as if it were as good as blank, glancing at Raysor then wincing as if he weren't much better for accompanying Quinn.

"I'm—"

"A private investigator. A snoop for hire. I don't have to talk to you, either." Miss F8 again stole a look at Raysor, for him to confirm. He acted as if he hadn't heard a thing.

The July day beat down, even under the stairwell of the bottom floor, and Quinn wiped the side of her face, for the umpteenth time trying not to wipe the moisture on her clothes, pretty sure her armpits showed perspiration if she moved wrong. "Ma'am, may we ask you about Natalie Jackson?" Then she added, "Please? I work for the attorney representing her son and his father."

"So what's with the deputy?" the woman asked.

"Nobody has been charged with the crime, so when I asked to talk to people and examine the crime scene, the sheriff's office regulations required I be accompanied. He's a pretty decent guy, and from the pink in his cheeks, he's as hot doing this as I am." She hoped she'd bridged this conversation somehow. "Were you doing yoga? You look fit."

"Yes," she said. "I teach it on Zoom. I'd been teaching Natalie, too. Nice girl."

Bingo. Finally, someone who knew Nat more than in passing, someone Nat had been willing to spend time with. Quinn hadn't realized how little she was familiar with Ty's ex until now.

F8's nose went up an inch. "And you're the Sterling woman she spoke of."

They weren't making headway, and the longer they stood on the threshold, the more irritated this woman seemed to get. "May we please have your name?" Quinn asked. "You seem to know more than everyone else in this apartment complex put together. Surely the sheriff's office interviewed you."

"I answered their questions. Volunteered nothing. Like I said, I saw nothing, but what did you expect on a holiday? Good day for killing someone, I'd say."

Raysor's wiry brows went up. "Odd choice of words."

"Grow up, deputy," the woman said. "And my name's Becca Blevins. I've lived here longer than anyone else in the complex and make it a point to know who lives where. Need to keep up with the comings and goings of people or you don't recognize who shouldn't be here."

"You just became my favorite tenant," Quinn said.

"You don't know me well enough to say that," Becca replied.

"You're bright. You're aware of your surroundings, and you befriended Natalie. Trust me, the way my day's gone, you are golden, Ms. Blevins."

To that Becca almost brightened, then she quickly dropped the look. "Her ex is a cop. I can't afford to get involved."

No, no, no. Don't back away now.

"You're worried about her ex coming after you?"

"No," Becca replied, curt. "I'm worried about cops as a whole." She nodded toward Raysor and backed into her home, on the way to shutting the door.

"Becca," Quinn said, a little too loud. "I can meet with you without him, if you like. He's babysitting me. If you don't want him in your place, he doesn't have to come in."

"Wait a minute," Raysor said.

Turning to him, Quinn put a hand on her hip and tried to stand taller than she already was. "You are to oversee me in terms of the crime scene, Deputy. You don't have the authority to stop me from talking to a resident in their home. You also don't have a warrant forcing her to let you in."

Raysor's complexion, already rosy in the heat, reddened. "Not in your best interest to buck me . . . Ms. Sterling."

"Nor is it in hers to allow you inside."

Becca quit retreating, taking in the repartee.

"So wait for me in the car," Quinn said. "I still need to see Natalie's apartment afterwards."

"I'm not your errand boy."

"I'll tell them you left early without taking care of my requests."

By now his chest heaved but not so much she worried that the chunky uniform was at risk of heat stroke or the like. The hint of a wink when he pivoted to leave told her he was playing along.

Both ladies watched him enter his vehicle.

"He bully you like that all the time?" Becca asked.

"Most of them try," she said, meaning it, but stopping short of telling Becca that Quinn had been one of them not terribly long ago. A camaraderie was needed. "Is there any way I can come in and pick your brain about Natalie? I represent her family."

"Sure," Becca said, stepping back to allow her guest in.

As Quinn guessed, yoga had been in play when they knocked, a DVD paused on the screen, the mat sprawled in the small living room with a minimal sofa, a chair and an end table pushed back, probably left there most of the time if Becca was serious about her downward dogs.

Quinn stepped around the mat. "Sorry to interrupt your exercising."

"Only had five minutes left. Want some water with lemon?"

"Sure." Quinn assumed her place in the chair.

Becca took her place on the sofa's end, setting two glasses between them. All this proper etiquette, with drinks softening conversation, was about to tax Quinn's bladder.

"How did they treat you yesterday?" Quinn asked, taking a sip, hoping to finally get a barometric reading of how in depth the sheriff's office had been.

"They asked if I saw anyone, if I heard anything, and how well I knew Natalie and her ex."

Quinn waited, not wanting to appear anywhere near as pushy as Becca seemed to feel she'd been treated.

"I was friends with Natalie," Becca said. "Darn good friends. But the sheriff's investigators weren't interested in our sharing iced tea while Cole played video games or two ladies watching movies on weekends until the early hours of the morning."

There was a poutiness, a defensiveness, an insulted sense of disregard in her description of the friendship, which told Quinn that Raysor's people hadn't adequately handled this tenant. Becca was strong-willed. She'd told them what they minimally needed to know since they'd seen her interview as nothing more than ticking off a box.

Quinn sensed more to Becca Blevins than first expected.

"And I knew Ty," Becca threw in.

Which was what Quinn had hoped for. "Please, tell me your impression of both of them, particularly about each other."

She didn't ask if Ty killed Natalie. Becca had lost a friend. If she suspected who did the deed, she'd say so.

"Natalie loved Ty, but they'd grown apart, as cliché as that sounded." Becca sat back on the sofa and crossed her knee-length soft blue leggings, more at ease. "I remember when she moved here, all hot and bothered, closed off from the world with a toddler to manage." Becca shook her head and rested the water glass on her knee. "If anyone needed a girlfriend, it was her."

"Glad you befriended her," Quinn said.

Becca gave her a sideways glance. "Why would an investigator say something like that?"

"Glad you did the right thing, is all."

A sneer climbed up one side of Becca's mouth. "I recognize your name, Ms. Sterling. Natalie spoke often of you."

Quinn had to resist hard explaining herself. How she'd been friends with Ty her whole life. How Ty had married Natalie while Quinn was at Quantico. How something else had to be wrong with their marriage for Natalie to walk away.

There was no way to kill the rumor that the princess of Sterling Banks had stolen Nat's husband, so Quinn remained mute, not giving it much life.

The hostess rocked her leg ever so slightly. "She felt she had no chance against you."

Quinn sat there and took it. The woman could call Quinn a sorry slut and a hustling hussy, for all she cared.

Lie. She did care. She cared a lot. Natalie dying while hating Quinn didn't set so well on a conscience, which was maybe what bothered her most. Not having done a thing.

Especially since Natalie had reached out the day she died.

Becca's gaze turned coy. "By the way, I've talked to Ty a few times as well."

Hallelujah. Becca was the first tenant who dared to say they'd spoken with the *suspected killer*. "What's your take on whether he murdered Nat or not?" Quinn asked, feeling a different depth to this woman than the other neighbors.

"He was a noble man, in my opinion," Becca said, giving a sly grin. "I'd have dated him myself."

But she hadn't answered the question. Quinn waited expectedly, attempting to keep this talk amiable, respectable, and on Becca's terms.

"I didn't see him go in," she said, "but I saw him go up the stairs yesterday. Twice. I heard Natalie yelling, but not him, but then, she could be loud. That's how they were. She had more fire. He took it. I told her to let the man off the hook. She couldn't hold Quinn Sterling against him forever."

That remark stabbed deep.

"What about Natalie's boyfriend?" Quinn asked without the first sense of nuance. "Where's he from? How close were they?"

Becca's chin went up a bit, and she hesitated, gauging. "What boyfriend?"

"The one Natalie told Ty about. The one Cole spoke of. The one who called him *Chipmunk* and called her *Chiquita*."

The boyfriend couldn't be denied now, and Becca nodded, losing the attitude. "She was seen with a man."

"Have you met him?"

"No."

"Was Natalie planning to go off with him?"

Becca gave a hint of a wince, as if she ought to rethink trusting Quinn and this line of questioning. "What gave you that idea?"

Quinn was accustomed to holding facts close, leaking them only as needed, but Becca wasn't talking without someone teasing it out of her. She preferred holding the upper hand, or that was Quinn's interpretation. This dance would take hours if Quinn didn't bold-faced get to the point.

Putting down the drink, Quinn leaned elbows on her knees, phone in both hands to keep her phone note-taking app at the ready. "She told Ty she might move to Charleston or some other city. She'd been seeing someone, but Ty hadn't made his acquaintance. Cole met him a few times."

Becca didn't say anything, looking wary.

"All the tenants heard Nat's yelling," Quinn said. "Ty put Cole in the car to remove him from fallout. When he returned, she resumed the yelling, supposedly about a potential move."

Easing back into the sofa, Becca seemed to ponder what she'd heard but said nothing.

What part of the story wasn't correct? She'd spoken to Ty and Cole and received enough supportive discussion from three neighbors that there was a beau.

Becca, however, had held Nat's confidence. Girl talk. Quinn would bet a hundred acres that the tenant of apartment F8 understood way more than she'd told the Colleton County Sheriff's Office, which was more than she was willing to tell Quinn, for reasons that had the potential to exonerate or crucify Tyson Jackson.

Chapter 11

QUINN ACHED TO see the version of Becca's interview with the sheriff's office, but that wouldn't be available until after they charged Ty, which she was desperately trying to avoid happening. That left Quinn on her own dealing with Becca Blevins who apparently held her cards close. She may have told the deputies very little. Quinn's guess was that she had revealed barely enough to show she knew Natalie but not enough to nail Ty to the wall. Otherwise, they might've held him.

Her phone vibrated, a message scrolling across the top of the screen of her note-taking app. An 843 area code, the Lowcountry, but she didn't recognize the number. She let it go to voice mail, and as she watched, the caller proceeded to leave a message. She had no time for telemarketers or even vendors or clients of the Sterling pecan business. Not now.

"Becca," she continued. "Who was the boyfriend?"

"You mean a name?"

"Of course I mean a name." Though irritated at Becca's false ignorance, Quinn couldn't afford to be impatient, but with Ty's future in the balance, her patience ran thin. She would've thought her best interview tactics would come out instead.

"Only know his first name. Gabriel."

"How close were they?"

"Not as close as they used to be."

Used to be? "Meaning . . ."

Becca sucked the bottom out of her ice water and set the glass on the end table. "Meaning the shine had worn off. Nat broke it off but was embarrassed to tell Ty. She'd been taken advantage of, and even though she and Ty were divorced, Ty might've wanted to deal with him."

Becca had definitely read Ty correctly. "What did Gabriel do? Was he abusive?" If Ty caught a whiff of Gabriel being shady in any capacity, he would have delved into it, and done it clandestinely. He might not have even told Quinn. Ty wasn't one to broadcast his motives, but to people who didn't know him, this couldn't have been motive to go after

Nat or Gabriel, the end result being Nat's death.

Motive. All she could find was motive that damaged Ty.

"Nothing physically abusive that I could tell." Becca dipped her head saying, "Believe me, I asked. She denied it, saying she wouldn't allow that behavior in Cole's world. I don't know the details, but he lied to her."

Spurned lover. Motive for the boyfriend.

Surely the sheriff's office hunted for Gabriel.

"What did he lie about?" Quinn said.

"She said he wasn't who he said he was, and he asked her to do things she was not willing to do anymore. Said it went against her conscience."

Sex moves? Or maybe something illegal? "And she didn't tell you—"

"Again, I asked if this was about abuse, and she denied it. I never saw bruises, cuts, or limps, so I can't suspect otherwise, and I really didn't want to know if it was anything else, for reasons like this right here. If I don't know, I don't get dragged into it."

A lie could be anything. His identity. His marital status. His financial status. An unwillingness to continue doing whatever. *God, this could be anything.*

But Nat was still considering a move. Even after breaking off her relationship with Gabriel, maybe she'd fallen in love with the idea of finding another job, in another town, at a place where Ty wasn't as big a part of her life. She might've felt stuck being in Walterboro, in a two-bit apartment complex, with little future ahead. She might've been running from Gabriel. Hell, even the voice mail said she was headed to Charleston.

"Ty was surprised Natalie considered moving anywhere," Quinn said.

"She liked Charleston better than anywhere else, because we talked about places we'd like to live. I know for a fact she met Gabriel twice at a motel in Savannah in their early days. Frankly, I never liked the sounds of the man, but she had to learn for herself."

"Why Savannah?"

Becca scrunched her mouth. "It's only an hour's drive from here? It's in another state? He hid from a wife? When I asked too much, Nat clammed up, so I served as more of a sounding board."

"Do you think he killed her?" Quinn asked. "The boyfriend, I mean."

"Nope." Becca shook her head. "I'm not forecasting. I never met

Gabriel, and honestly, I'm glad I never did."

"You think he could be dangerous?"

Hands waving in front of her, Becca tried to back up the conversation. "Stop. Nat said she cut things off with him. Period. One minute she's smitten, and the next she's vowing to not to take his calls. Said he wasn't what he professed to be, she felt like a fool, and she shut that door forever."

"That's it?"

"That's it."

Hard to believe a friend like this only knew a fraction of the story. "Okay, you say you've met Ty a few times. Mind my asking if that was lately?"

Becca's lips flattened. "Two days ago."

"Where?" Quinn asked.

"Here."

"The apartment complex?"

"No, here. In my apartment."

Quinn's fingers stopped. This was too much to type and capture it all. "Please, do you mind if I record this?"

"I'd rather you not," came the reply.

Damn it. Quinn set the phone on the table and focused on what was about to be said, intent on mentally recording the phrasing best she could. "Continue."

"Ty asked to come by. He showed up around three, before Natalie and Cole got home. Asked if he could ask my opinion since I was Nat's friend." Becca gave a lighthearted one-shoulder shrug. "I said I'd answer what I could but wouldn't violate a confidence."

Ty was protective of those he loved. It was his nature, and he'd been honed by his training. Protective of his mother, his son . . . Quinn. Nat would make the list as well. "What were his questions?"

"Was Natalie still seeing this new man. He didn't know his name, and I didn't volunteer it. I told him no."

Quinn admired her for being so pragmatic. "His reaction?"

"Very relieved. Then he asked if the man took it well."

Sounded like Ty. Sounded like any cop, to be honest.

"I told him to ask Natalie. I didn't know."

"Sounds like he had his suspicions," Quinn said.

"The child," Becca said. "Cole gave him reason to be concerned. When he asked if Cole had been treated improperly, physically, mentally, verbally, I again said I didn't know, just that Natalie decided the man wasn't right for her or Cole."

Maybe there was more to why he confronted Natalie the next day, and from the number of tenants who'd heard Nat yelling at Ty, she didn't like the interrogation.

"How did Ty leave? Relieved? Frustrated? What?" Quinn asked.

Becca squinted. "I really can't say. He's rather stoic."

Quinn understood. Ty could hide his feelings. "Anything else?"

Becca shook her head, and took a strong glance at the clock on the cable box.

"Another question or two, and I promise I'll wrap this up," Quinn said. "Did you tell anyone with the sheriff's office about this conversation with Ty?"

"Nope."

"Did they . . . ask ?" Meaning, had she lied or held back?

"Not in so many words," Becca replied. "That's all I want to say about that."

"Did you tell them about Gabriel?"

"Only that there was an old boyfriend no longer in the picture."

Who could blame her? Someone killed Natalie, so why fess up to anything she had no firsthand knowledge of in case it rebounded against her. But she seemed to be the best friend Nat had. Becca knew more, no doubt.

"The residents," Quinn said, shifting topics before Becca got too distrustful. They were close to that line. "How well do you know your neighbors?"

To which Becca laughed, then faded to a chuckle. She counted on her fingers.

"F1 is . . . was . . . Natalie. Tee and Troy live in F2. Nice, sweet, harmless. Knew Natalie, liked Cole, but they don't have the common sense to fill a thimble. F3 is some kind of nerdy recluse. I've seen him, but he doesn't like to be seen, if that makes sense. Don't care to know him, either. He's rude. F4 . . ." A smirk appeared on her face. "That is a strange woman. Frannie Bean doesn't like me. Nosiest damn person in this complex. She creates gossip where there's none, stirs trouble when she's bored, and if you think you'll get a straight honest answer from her, think again."

Becca hadn't taken a breath, and stopped to take one before launching again. "I can't see Natalie telling a one of them about Gabriel. Most have surely seen Ty at one time or another, but I'm fairly confident they don't chat with him. He's visually intimidating in that uniform."

Quinn let the woman keep on, not daring to interrupt the lightning speed she'd taken up talking. She heard about who spoke to Natalie, who knew Cole, covering everyone. Becca confirmed what Baxter had said. Apartment F6 was a couple who had been out of town for the Fourth. Apartment F7 was the twenty-something girl repeatedly off at her mother's place. She hadn't been seen over the holiday.

The diverse array of neighbors both intrigued and frustrated Quinn. Between what Becca knew, what Pratt said, and what Quinn gleaned from Frannie Bean, she knew how long everyone in building F had lived there.

Tee and Troy less than a year. Frannie Bean almost since the place was built, like Becca. The recluse, John Jefferson, was about a year, and Baxter five. The young couple on the ground floor less than a year, and the young lady hanging onto her mother a few months.

Quinn asked the next question quickly, aiming for a straightforward reply before Becca lost her momentum. "Any of them have a reason to kill Natalie?"

Becca busted out laughing. "For what?"

But Quinn was serious. "For vengeance, jealousy, sex, money . . . secrets."

Becca sobered.

"Yes," Quinn said. "Do a mental tour of this building. Who could be that angry? Who could be bought? Who had motive?"

The woman thought, her frown not liking what she found. "I don't even want to think about that."

"Because somebody comes to mind?"

"Because I don't want to think I live around someone like that."

Which wasn't an answer. "Well, somebody committed murder yards from your front door. Maybe you *should* think about it. Aren't you the one who said be aware of your residents so you know who doesn't belong?"

Becca stood. "All I got to say, Ms. Sterling." She was done.

Quinn made a conscious act of looking at her business card on the table. "You've been a lot of help, Becca. If you think of something, call. Day or night. This is important not only for Natalie, but also for Ty and Cole."

Becca retrieved the card. She walked Quinn to the door and silently shut it behind her.

The heat hit Quinn like a wall, the humidity sauna level and thick. Raysor sat in his cruiser, the motor running for the air conditioner, his eyes closed and mouth open. She thought about leaving without waking him, but he'd been accommodating. Besides, she still needed to see Natalie's place.

Quinn rapped on the glass, and when he didn't budge, she knocked and shouted, "Hey, Dough Boy!"

He fought to open his eyes, the snort not audible but clearly taking place as he reoriented himself. He rolled the window halfway down. "Legs, thought you gave up on me."

"Open up," she said, and moved around the car without waiting for his answer. Inside, she angled the vent off her, the blower strong enough to clear leaves off a lawn.

"Get anything other than recipes and yoga moves?" he asked through a voice gravelly from sleep.

"As a matter of fact, I did, and now I have a question or two for you."

From Becca's door to the patrol car, Quinn grew some hope and lots of urgency. There was another suspect. And there was still John Jefferson in Apartment F3 to account for. A recluse without solid hours, who could've had his eye on everyone else. Whom nobody liked.

The rest of the tenants weren't exonerated until their whereabouts were confirmed, though. The hand size of the bruising around Nat's neck would clear some of them like Tee or the young girl in F7. But that didn't eliminate Troy or any boyfriend of the young girl.

But there'd been no mention of a suspect other than Ty. If Tassey was aware, she would have shared the chance of other suspects with her hired investigator.

"Who else are they considering in this murder?" she asked Raysor.

"I'm not an investigator," he said.

Pivoting in her seat, she addressed the big man head on. "Don't bullshit me. There's a window of opportunity here from the time Ty left. There's a dumped, disgruntled boyfriend. And there are a handful of potential suspects living in the damn building. Why are they leaning on Ty?"

Raysor didn't flinch. "Legs, I've been around the block a few times. They may be leaning on several people other than Ty, but they don't have to tell you or me. Did you learn who the boyfriend is?"

"First name only. Nat's phone should show something. I need access—"

"God, I wish they'd given babysitting you to someone else. I ought to be on Edisto Beach."

She tried not to be disgusted with him as the image of the sheriff's office. "What do you mean Edisto Beach?"

"I'm on loan to the police department there. Been doing it through six police chiefs and a lot of years. They caught me this morning before I left and assigned you to me. Tickled me damn pink in case you couldn't tell."

Maybe Raysor didn't know much after all with Edisto being his main beat. He hadn't done anything today to make her distrust him, and since he wasn't active in this investigation, he might be open to questions. "Are they targeting Ty?"

"Even if I knew, why should I answer that?" he replied.

"Because you aren't involved and have nothing to lose. I won't tell anyone."

"That's a big ask, Ms. Sterling."

"Why, because I'm on the other side? Thought this was about justice and the truth."

His jowls floated around as he moved his jaws, entertaining her angle.

"Tyson Jackson is law enforcement, Raysor. He's never disgraced his oath. Put yourself in his shoes."

"A badge doesn't buy him an out, either. He has the responsibility of honoring a higher standard."

"I get that," she said. "But if you and your people were worth a damn, you'd be working hard to prove he did it, which suits me fine, because that would mean you'd prove him innocent. You ought to be digging up all the evidence you can see, find, think of. It's your responsibility to get this right, and you fall down on the job if you stop short of a thousand-percent effort to find who killed this woman."

She could tell she'd hit a nerve when he faced forward, staring out and up at Apartment F1.

"Help me here," she continued. "What do your people think?" Then she tacked on, "What does your gut tell you?"

"That he's the easy candidate," he said, but quickly tacked on, "However, that's not knowing what my people have done. I'm not an investigator. I'm a beat cop at the beach and like what I do. Point me in the right direction, wind me up, and I write tickets and break up spats."

"Ever been shot at?"

"Yes."

"Ever taken a bullet?"

He wasn't sure where this was going. "Yes."

"Then you're more than a wind-up doll, Raysor."

How could he argue at a compliment? "Can you find out if your people learned Gabriel's whole name? Where he was from? I'd hug your neck for a driver's license picture."

He grunted. "You'd have to do a lot more than hug me to make me snoop against my own."

She ought to feel insulted but wasn't. "You're the most non-PC cop I've ever yet, yet for some reason it doesn't bother me." She blew out a quick breath. "You're an odd duck, Dough Boy, and not as limited as you'd like people to think."

He laughed. "Good. That's how I like it. Think of me as the stupid fathead who never could make sergeant, eats donuts when not napping in his cruiser, and steps on his dick when it comes to wokeness and pronouns. Underestimate me. Take me for granted." His scowl eased into a wicked grin. "Because that makes people ignore me until I'm all over their ass with cuffs and throwing them in the back of my cruiser. I possess a damn sight more horsepower when you look under the hood, Legs."

Well, well, well. "Okay, I'm willing to take a chance that there's more to you than a pretty waistline, and that you really can find out what we need."

He released a gruff humorous grumble. "We? Pray tell."

"Find out if they're looking at anyone other than Ty."

One of his bushy brows raised.

"And get his, or their, name, beginning with someone named Gabriel who might be from Savannah. That last part is iffy. Natalie caught him lying to her and cut things off, so no telling what he told her is the truth."

"Name might be iffy as well, Legs."

Yeah, she knew that. "Guess we see how amazing you really are then. What did they find on the phone about him? On the laptop?"

He didn't appear quite so pleased with himself now. "I'm not a techie kind of guy."

"Not asking you to put hands on. Only talk to your buddies."

His pudgy self-assured countenance held a pose. "Who says I ought to bring you anything?"

"The horsepower under my hood thinks your horsepower doesn't want a fellow law enforcement officer run over by a short-cut investigation. Have you heard who Tyson Jackson's attorney is? Who I'm working for?"

"No."

"Tassey Talmadge," she said.

"Jesus Christ and all the angels," he said.

"Amen and amen. She's going to get intel one way or another, and we all know how she loves stepping on the people in her way to put a win on the board."

"I'll see what I can do, but no promises."

She grinned. "I knew there were redeeming qualities about you. Now, show me the apartment. Then I gotta pee something fierce."

Chapter 12

RAYSOR OPENED Natalie's door. An air of death remained, and a supernatural sense of the unreal. To Quinn, the trace of Ty's ex on the carpet, the seen and the unseen, didn't seem to be hers. Training told her not to touch anything, but the déjà vu made her hand grip the door-frame.

Years ago, Quinn had arrived home to step into the manor's foyer where her father died. Though his body slept in the morgue, she felt something when she stood where he had transitioned, where she could still see the faint tint of his blood in the grout. For days she felt his presence, as if he'd hung around as long as the powers-that-be allowed. It wasn't his time. He had too much to do. He had too many people to love and grandchildren he'd hoped to meet.

Natalie had been half his age, with an eight-year-old left behind. If her soul wasn't stuck, nobody's was.

"Talk to me, Nat," Quinn whispered. She dragged her gaze from the floor up and out . . . around. She delayed crossing the threshold, aching for a sense of discovery to come back and find her.

"You can go in," Raysor said.

But she gave herself another few moments, inserting herself into the body, the eyes, the mind of the killer . . . then the body, eyes, and mind of the victim. "Give me a sec," she whispered.

Natalie had let the culprit into her apartment. He didn't hesitate long to do what he came to do. He was big enough to do it clean and quick. Quinn wondered if her neck was broken, but the report wouldn't be available until after the autopsy. No real fight. None of the neighbors heard another male voice. They only heard Natalie, and even then, associated her arguing with Ty's coming and going.

But the timing wasn't quite right. Natalie had slammed the door shut behind Ty, meaning she reopened it for someone else. Even if Gabriel or some random killer of opportunity did the deed, the murder had occurred after Ty left with Cole.

But couldn't Ty have come back as well?

There was a small window of time in which Ty could have *returned* to the apartment. However, even if he went back before arriving at Sterling Banks, Cole would've known.

Yet again, Cole was key to the facts, or the facts as an eight-year-old could perceive them. God, she cringed to think Cole might be considered to testify. There was law that said children didn't have to testify, but when it came to minors, the court would appoint a guardian, and no telling how traumatizing that would get for Cole. Even if he did give a statement, a prosecutor could say Cole had lied to protect his remaining parent, worried what would happen to him if he lost both his mother and father.

Quinn needed to find this damn boyfriend.

Too many had seen Ty come and go. The fact he was barely heard or not heard at all, only went to prove he was stealthy. Imagine how silent he could be with intent.

Quinn finally entered the apartment.

A robot sort of toy, maybe six inches tall, sat as though carefully placed on the credenza by an adult, straight and on its feet. Quinn found that odd for it to be there and not in Cole's room, lying on the living room floor, or tossed someplace once its owner lost interest. Not like this, so neatly parallel to the furniture's edge, its jointed legs locked straight. The investigators hadn't taken it, either, thus labeling it unimportant. Quinn took a picture. More proof Natalie had gone down quickly.

The kitchen had been cleaned up, as if expecting company. Every pillow and knickknack in the living room held its proper spot. More pics. She passed Cole's bedroom first, way straighter than a child's room should be. Natalie's room, however, had endured the gloved hands of deputies, investigators, and forensics, judging from the askew drawers, bed linens, and toiletries in the bath.

Quinn would've tossed the entire place.

A small suitcase sat open in the middle of the bed. Nothing in it. Nat's voice mail had stated she was headed to Charleston. Maybe she was about to pack? Or had she started to and changed her mind?

No phone, no computer, both taken as evidence as expected. "We need to know who she communicated with, Raysor."

"Best I can do is chat people up, like I said."

A bona-fide offer from someone who ought to be on the other side. She couldn't ask for much more than that.

The odds were Nat knew the killer. The act was pretty damn quick, not even knocking the robot or the artificial flower arrangement off the credenza. Unless someone had put things back to right, and what killer would take the time for that? What investigating cop would bother? They were trained to hunt and toss, not put things back in order.

A text came through from the vibration in her pocket, but she had her head in the apartment and its imprint on her mind, its recorded pictures going home with her on her phone. The caller could wait.

She made another circuit around the apartment, noting its cleanliness, neatness, and nothing out of place short of the suitcase on the bed and the robot on the table. Well, the notations on the entry-way floor where Natalie fell.

The killer had been allowed access.

Reluctantly and disappointed, she turned to leave. Raysor locked up, making a half-baked effort at returning the crime-scene tape to its rightful place.

"What else you need?" he asked, trying for the third time to anchor the end of a tape, then letting it flutter down in defeat. "It's not worth my time to drive to Edisto now."

"Let's go sit in your car," she said, heading down the stairs, pretending not to notice Fannie Bean's attempt to strategically hold the handle to slip her door closed unnoticed.

Inside the vehicle, Quinn shuffled the day's details. She itched to get back, needing a one-on-one with Ty, another with Cole, then of course a check-in with Tassey. That didn't count time with Archie and Glory, and she'd totally shirked her duties cleaning up Sterling Banks after yesterday's celebration, having left it all to Jonah.

But she had this new asset in the seat beside her, and right now he was worth the extra time required to groom him. "Chat things up and give me a call," she said, handing him her card.

He reared back a bit, holding off taking the card.

"Sorry," she said, palming it. "That sounded like an order, didn't it?"

"Pretty damn elitist, if you ask me."

He was right, and she'd been known to fall into that habit. "Let me start over," she said, and did a redo. "You," and she waggled the card at him, "are the biggest asset I have at the moment. Add to that you are not investigating the case and you haven't been tainted."

Raysor squinted as if Quinn still weren't explaining herself properly.

"Sorry . . . again." She sucked in a breath to begin anew, but he interrupted.

"You know as well as I do that emotional partners are responsible for the grand majority of deaths," he said. "Seventy-five percent, sixty percent, the number doesn't matter, but it's the spouse, boyfriend, girlfriend, lover, paramour, whatever the hell you want to call them these days, that likely kills the other. Being an ex puts Ty in tighter crosshairs, and it scares you to pieces."

Okay, he was right, but Quinn wasn't letting him hammer that first point, as if statistics had Ty half guilty already. "Raysor, you can't deny that poor investigators allow bias to guide their investigations. A lot of people have gone to the gallows, so to speak, on circumstantial evidence."

"But the wife was taking his kid away," Raysor said.

"Confirmed from Becca Blevins," she said.

Raysor looked puzzled. "Who?"

"F8," she said. "The lady who didn't like cops."

He nodded, waiting for more.

"She was friends with Natalie. She said Natalie broke things off with the boyfriend." But Quinn stopped short of telling Raysor about Ty driving to Walterboro to meet with Becca to talk about said boyfriend.

"So why was there a suitcase on the bed?" he asked.

"And why was it empty?"

"She hadn't started packing," he said. "The apartment was damn tidy, if you ask me. As if she expected company."

"Some people clean before they go out of town, too."

If only she had Nat's phone. "I'm not asking, Raysor. I'm pleading with you to see what you can learn." Urgency rose into her throat. "Ty's a friend since childhood. He wanted to be law enforcement his whole life. We solved mysteries together in my daddy's pecan orchard and joined the Craven County Sheriff's Office together when we graduated high school. I know this man like my own brother," she said. "He's—"

"I get it," he said. "I'll see what I can do. Don't go calling me though. I'll call you."

So Raysor indeed had a heart. This man was more than she came here expecting, a total lottery win. Chances were zero to none she'd get this level of assistance from any of the other deputies. "Thank you," she said, laying a hand on his broad, hairy forearm resting on the console between them. "I'll owe you, Raysor."

"Yeah, yeah," he said, pulling his forearm back.

"No," she said. "A Sterling promise carries a ton of weight and comes with a long memory. It's solid, trust me."

He peered up from under those middle-aged brows. "I know who you are, Quinn Sterling. I understand your wealth, your reach, and your influence. I'm not in need of any of that. What I do is purely about doing the right thing, and I'll decide where I draw the line. Obligations and favors get you in trouble, and what I do results in neither, you understand?" He took a sniffy breath. "That sort of shit gets you in trouble. I ain't yours."

"Fair enough," she said, intending with all her heart and soul to keep her promise with this man . . . somehow.

She made him shake her hand before she left the cruiser, and she watched him drive out of the parking lot. Time for her to return home and revisit Ty and Cole.

First her texts and messages.

One from a bulk pecan buyer in Charleston, a confectioner who'd been trying to get her to dinner for two years. He needed to schedule his fall order and had discovered an incredible new restaurant that had recently opened its doors on King Street.

Another text from Jule, saying that sometime in all of the family chaos, she needed to sit down to nail the fall line of pecan gift baskets, her forte. No rush, but don't drag around either. Come August, people would be tired of summer, and by Labor Day, people would be rushing into thoughts of autumn, meaning the website decisions and price list for Sterling Banks products bordered on late.

A long text, Jule's habit. She hated phones, loved texts but typed them as if she penned a letter. She'd not long quit signing her name to them.

Jule's message gave Quinn a soft moment she much appreciated. But then Quinn read the more recent text, and she had to read it again to understand the message from Jonah.

Hope Ty caught up with you. Love you. STAY SAFE. Check in, please.

She reactively glanced at the time on her phone. After three. She dialed Jonah.

"On your way home?" he asked. "Everything okay?"

He didn't kid her about shirking the cleanup after yesterday's celebration or tease her about her private investigator urges. If the case hadn't been about clearing Ty, this might have been a lighter, different discussion.

But the three were a unit. This wasn't Quinn choosing PI work over Sterling Banks. This was choosing family over business.

"Quinn?"

"Sorry. Just left the apartment."

"Sorry you had to see that, honey."

She'd talk later about there not being much to see. It was more feeling than anything else. "Thought I was on my way home until your text. What do you mean Ty was catching up with me?"

"You haven't seen him?"

Ty didn't lie to the two of them. "No, I haven't. Replay what happened," she said, a fear rising in her chest.

"Oh, man," Jonah said. "Quinn, he came by right after you left this morning, asking where you were."

"What did you tell him?"

She could envision his shrug. "That you went to Walterboro to Natalie's apartment, to talk to people."

Okay. Simple enough, but as many times as she'd investigated alongside Ty, he might've been stung at being left behind. But he couldn't accompany her. He knew better.

Jonah continued. "He ate breakfast with us then tended to Cole for a couple hours before Glory and Jule took over. He spoke to his attorney some, or at least that's what Archie said. I was in the grove when I wasn't on the field with the cleanup. Then two hours ago, he called me and said his attorney wanted him to do some things, but he didn't say what. We offered to take care of Cole, then he was off, saying he'd catch up with you and he'd update you on what his attorney told him."

Quinn scanned the apartment complex, halfway expecting to see Ty's Jeep waiting for her. "Well, he didn't find me. How was he acting?"

"He's worried and it shows, but he's managing." Jonah would read Ty as well as Quinn. Ty was a deep pool of water, and he had his ways, but the two of them knew them.

"Yeah," she said, worried Ty had no intention of meeting up with her. "I need to find him, so guess I'm not on my way home. That a problem?"

"No. Find him, Quinn. He doesn't need to be alone stewing in his thoughts." He hesitated. "He worries me now. You learn anything? Please tell me it's something good."

She sighed into the phone. "I learned a lot, but I haven't decided how much of it is good yet."

"Well, like I told you earlier, check in, okay? There's a murderer out there who recognizes that people might be hunting for him. And if he isn't a total stranger, he understands you're involved. Don't need a target on that luscious back of yours, Princess."

"Or any of us," she said. "If they've heard of me, if they learned anything from Natalie, they're aware that more than Quinn Sterling lives at Sterling Banks. Poke one; poke all. God knows we've experienced that enough times."

Jonah did a grumbling thing in his throat, likely remembering his mother being injured, scared, and kidnapped, a nanny goat slaughtered for effect. "I secured this place after our last situation, and I'll alert the workers, but we can't protect three thousand acres."

"Don't care about the acres, Jonah. Just the buildings and the people in them."

"I know," he said, his voice back to the regular Jonah who served as a mainstay for Quinn's world and all those on the farm. "I'll speak to Jule and Archie," he said. "You be careful, and don't take long. I don't want you out at night." He hesitated. "Love you."

"Love you back," she said, and hung up.

She held off on the next two voice mails from numbers she didn't recognize. Her mission had been defined by Jonah. She cranked her truck's engine.

Ty . . . what the hell are you up to? And where are you doing it?

Chapter 13

QUINN LEFT THE apartment parking lot, not bothering to tell the manager. He didn't seem to be one to care anyway. He'd already proven he hadn't given a damn about Natalie.

Retracing her route back to Walterboro, Quinn waited at a red light near the interstate. The familiar Jeep passed her before she registered who it belonged to. The connection clicked as the driver made his way to I-95 South.

Ty.

And he would've noticed her.

Anxiously waiting for the green, she u-turned to head the other way. She'd lost sight of him, but the interstate was straight and easy, and if he wasn't driving like an idiot, she'd catch up to him within two to three miles.

But three miles came and went. Apparently, he drove in a hurry, because by the time she passed the Cracker Barrel at exit 53 she still hadn't caught up. Hell, he could've gotten off at that exit, and she'd be at the state line before she realized it. She spoke into her Bluetooth to dial Ty.

He didn't answer.

Oh, no, he wasn't dodging her call. She redialed him again and again, and when he still didn't answer, she pulled over and texted.

I'm on your butt. Answer or I'm following you into Georgia.

She hated sitting there, anxious about his potentially gaining distance.

Finally his call came through. She didn't wait for him to speak. "Where the hell are you?" she said. The why could wait until they met.

"Ahead of you," he said. "Don't follow me."

She had her suspicions *where* he was headed along with somewhat of a *why*, but no way on earth was she letting him do this alone. He shouldn't be doing it, period.

"Turn around, Ty. I mean it. You're going to screw things up for you, not to mention Cole."

He didn't respond.

"I don't care where you are, get yourself to the Hendersonville Rest Area," she said. "I'll meet you there."

The call disconnected.

"Oh you didn't . . ." she said, looking at the phone in her hand.

Quinn pulled back onto the interstate. He might've pulled into an exit, but common sense told her Ty was goal-oriented and wasn't up to killing time over coffee at Cracker Barrel. Not with Cole mourning his mother. And the fact she was the investigator on his case and he still took off with some clandestine purpose without her knowing, told her he wasn't thinking straight.

I-95 was known for fast traffic connecting Miami to the Canadian border, a melting pot of license tags wearing out the asphalt with speeds fifteen to twenty over the limit. Quinn slid into the draft of a trucker doing eighty and made time, inching up to eighty-five when he did. She couldn't see up the highway, but she could make up distance, maybe passing Ty en route.

By Yemassee, she began to wonder if he'd stopped for gas, as much to miss her as to top off his tank. Not much further was Ridgeland, then twenty-something miles onward, Savannah. She bet Ty headed to the city where his dead ex-wife and her lover once rendezvoused on weekends when he had custody of Cole.

She called him again, and was forced to leave a voice mail. "Pull over now, Ty. And do not cross the state line. You know it doesn't look good, you being in Savannah."

She hugged the truck, until she finally decided this wasn't working. She sped up, slipping around the trucker, and took off at ninety, willing to risk a state trooper's ticket.

I-95 was known for its fast pace, but she managed to keep up with the fastest, staring as far up the road as she could for the tail end of that dark-green Jeep.

Almost to Ridgeville, she spotted it, too afraid to text or call at that speed, so she gunned the gas to reach him. He must've seen her in his rearview mirror, because he slowed to a sane person's speed to let her catch up. She glared at him from the fast lane, but he didn't glare back, instead aiming two fingers ahead as if telling her to follow. She eased in behind him.

They got off at the Ridgeville exit, and he led her to the McDonald's. Ty parked his Jeep facing the highway, got out and went in, not waiting for her. Dressed in jeans and a polo, he almost didn't look like a cop.

She parked two slots over and sat there a second, letting him do his pouty thing of going in without her.

By the time she entered, he was sitting down with two coffees, having selected a booth in the back corner. Scents of assorted items fried in peanut oil should've tempted her to place an order since she hadn't eaten since Archie's pancake hours ago, but she wasn't up to eating. She wasn't sure she could stomach more than the cup Ty had waiting for her.

The place wasn't full, but there were still enough people to force her not to slap the ever-loving hell out of him. Instead, she leaned over the table and mumbled, "You know better than this." She sat back down, uncomfortable with her back to the door, but Ty had instinctively snared the side which put his to the wall.

He set the extra coffee before her, but she set it to the side. "I'm so mad with you right now, Old Man."

"I don't have to tell you everything," he said.

"If you aren't telling me everything, then you're not telling your attorney everything, and that's suicide in a case like this, Ty."

He was a smart cop and the closest thing to a detective Craven County had, but murders weren't common enough to train him thoroughly. The two cases they were both familiar with had involved her father's murder at Sterling Banks and a private investigator in the Jacksonian Motel. The sheriff's office, including its illustrious leader Larry Sterling, had fallen way short in solving either one. Quinn had solved them both.

All Ty understood about running a murder investigation was what he had learned from shadowing Quinn. Not only was he not thinking straight, he hadn't enough training to know what thinking straight meant.

He'd put a lot of cream in her coffee, the way she liked. They knew each other that well. He recognized she'd be mad. She felt how scared and angry he was, feeling incredibly impotent at being sidelined because he was the prime suspect and there was little he could do about it. So he must've decided to do something, regardless of how misguided.

"I didn't want you to talk to Becca before I did," he said. "But you left without me."

"Of course I did, Ty." It hurt her heart to see him this way, hear him this broken, and she couldn't help but lose the anger.

"I hung around the apartments, waiting, debating on whether to join you, until I saw that deputy," he said.

"Deputy Don Raysor," she filled in. "He turned into a decent guy once we quit getting in each other's way."

His eyes tried to squint, but he seemed too spent to get mad. "He's on their side."

"Officially, but not really." How was she to explain this? "He's trying to glean information from his people and get it back to me. What might be on the computer, what unexpected numbers were on her phone, things like that."

He still hadn't sipped his coffee, the cup sitting protected between his hands.

"I did speak to Becca, by the way. She said you went to her two days before Natalie died, asking about Gabriel. Do you know his last name, by the way? Becca didn't."

"The name's an alias."

Quinn had assumed the name was made that up. "And how would you know?"

"I used to go to Walterboro on Sundays, watching for when they returned from Savannah. He isn't from Georgia." Finally, he drank from the cup. "The car was a leased 2020 Lexus with South Carolina plates, tag number STG 346. Leased to someone named David Wescott of Charleston."

She shook off the shock of his findings to pepper him with questions . . . and the obvious warning that scared her to her core.

The perk of being an LEO was access to all sorts of toys. "Did you get his driver's license?"

"Yes."

"Match his face?"

"Yes."

"And yet you were driving to Savannah."

"To try and confirm how many nights and when. It's a Comfort Inn in Port Wentworth." He took to his coffee again, then set it down. "I followed them there a couple of times."

Her heart in her throat, Quinn was definitely stunned now. "Jesus, Ty. What does it matter where they used to go? She broke things off with him, and you know it."

"I wanted to talk to the motel manager for his impression."

"That's a phone call."

"I wanted to see his eyes when he talked."

"And he would've seen yours and been scared to death. You're not on duty nor authorized to investigate."

"You would've done the same thing, and you know it."

A young mom managing two young boys peered over at Ty's rise in tone, then turned back to her children, hurrying them to finish.

Quinn rubbed a hand across her brow, not surprised at the furrows. "Like none of that looks wrong."

He leaned in to avoid disturbing the mother again. "I've been to his address in Charleston. At least the one on his driver's license. A decent apartment." He sighed, stared down at the table, and mumbled, "I had to see what Nat and Cole were involved in, you know?"

He'd practically been stalking the man, which reflected badly on him atop what the neighbors thought of him. While she understood that need, if any of these details came to light, she wasn't sure Colleton County SO would bother looking any further than Ty as the murderer. Oh, they'd run down this David, but who's to say he wouldn't turn the tables and say he and Natalie were concerned about Ty and his obsessive tailing of him, her, both.

Quinn wondered how many other unspoken things Becca may have told the sheriff's office and not revealed to Quinn, and was she for or against Ty? Had Natalie told Becca she thought Ty was fixated on her and her new beau?

Suddenly, Becca seemed a time bomb.

"How well do you know this Becca?" Quinn asked.

"Probably as much as you do. She didn't distrust me," he said. "She let me in her apartment, offered me a drink, and we chatted for close to an hour. She said Nat was over this Gabriel. He'd lied to her, but—"

"But Nat wouldn't tell Becca what he lied about."

"Yes. Which makes me all the more suspicious," he said.

Quinn listened to him list the whys. He might as well have been reading her mind.

"Scorned lover," he said first. "Or she got coaxed into something illegal she wanted out of. Twisted sex maybe."

He was hitting all the bases, for sure.

"How was Nat supposed to trust that?" Quinn said. "She was smart enough to get out."

"Exactly," he said, so grateful his friend finally agreed with him on something. But then he wilted, which looked so odd on such a big man. "That's not the worst of it, Q." He peered around the room, as if spies waited to hear what else he had to say. "I saw Natalie yesterday. The day she died. Right?"

Quinn tried not to frown at what sounded like a big BUT. "Right. You picked up Cole. Neighbors saw you and heard Natalie yelling at you. I corroborated that. You got Cole, Natalie got angry, you put Cole in the cruiser, then returned to finish your conversation. She slammed the door behind you. You left."

"All correct. But on the way home, maybe five miles toward home, Cole remembered a toy he'd meant to bring. I called Nat and told her we'd turn around and come get it."

Quinn tensed. *Please, please tell me you didn't go back.*

He let out a quiet, breathy laugh. "I can read you so well, Q. Yes, I went back. But when I got there, the door was cracked open. I pushed it further. It hit something. When I peered in—" But his voice cracked, and he couldn't look at her anymore.

She reached over to cover his hands still holding his cup. "Ty, what did you do?"

"I backed away," he said, moisture in his eyes. "I knew what it looked like, but I had Cole with me."

"You—" But she contained herself. How the hell did he walk away? Who did that?

But she let him sit there, understanding he was searching for words, hoping for her understanding. Her thumb stroking the back of his hand, her heart beat like a marching band on homecoming night. "I'm here," she said.

"I didn't just *leave* her there," he corrected, clearing the tears from his throat. "I saw her face, the scared terror in her eyes . . . wide open and staring at the wall, Q." He tried to swallow and couldn't, and she removed her hands off his and nudged the coffee cup. She waited until he took a swig of it.

He continued. "Her mouth was open, like she tried to cry out and couldn't." His voice shook. "It was all I could do not to go in and scoop her up, you know?"

"I know," she whispered back, returning a hand to his forearm.

"But . . . but she was gone. I could tell. You know, right? You've seen more than I have, but you just . . . I reached inside and took her ankle pulse. Or tried to."

Silence fell hard over them. Real hard.

She didn't ask why Ty didn't call the authorities. He'd recognized he would be the likely suspect as the ex who'd just argued with his wife. Quinn couldn't help but see race here. If she'd found Nat and done what he did in the name of preserving a crime scene, she might've been suspected but no doubt would've gotten off. Ty . . . not so easily. As a trained officer of the law, now he recognized he should have stayed at the scene and called it in, but at that moment something in him flipped, telling him for the sake of self-preservation not to.

Son of a bitch. Son of a stinkin' bitch.

He was so scared . . . and he had a right to be.

"We tell Tassey," she said.

He jerked his head up.

"Don't even think about telling me no," she quickly added. "She has to know all the facts to prepare a proper defense, you hear me?"

Son of a bitch. Son of a stinkin' bitch.

Guess now she would check out the details of David Wescott. Sooner or later, he'd be talking to the sheriff's office, with his attorney in tow, getting ahead of things. And once his attorney heard about Ty, his visit to the apartment within an hour or so of when she died, he'd play the nervous victim. No doubt Nat had confided in him about her ex, maybe exaggerated about his being an intimidating cop, or opined about their arguments about Cole. That could be inflated into Ty having erratic behavior, especially with the attitude the neighbors already had. Hell, it's what she would guess, particularly if he was still feeling scorned.

Someone had killed Natalie in the fifteen or so short minutes it took for Ty to leave, turn around, and return. That someone had been watching Ty, waiting for him to leave. The timing could not be that tight and be coincidental.

In a way, Quinn saw what Ty had thought in that moment. He had envisioned what would ensue if he stuck around and called in a murder. Telling a couple of deputies that he had left and someone swept in and killed his ex-wife after Ty and Nat had argued loud enough for Fannie Bean and Becca to hear, all but said *cuff me.*

God, they needed to talk to Tassey, but not here. Not while driving, either. Ty needed to be seated, with Quinn beside him, and focused, listening hard to his counselor. This might even merit Tassey coming out to Sterling Banks.

Sure it did. It damn sure did.

"Let's go," she said, sliding out of the booth.

Ty followed. "Sterling Banks?"

"Sterling Banks," she said, hitting the attorney's number. "Hopefully, Tassey will be waiting for us by the time we get there."

Chapter 14

TASSEY AGREED TO meet them at Sterling Banks but wouldn't arrive until after they did. She was good, but she couldn't always drop everything when beckoned, she said, but would be prompt. Quinn deduced after some quick calculations that meant within an hour after Quinn and Ty got home.

Ty drove ahead of her, keeping to the speed limit as she ordered him to do. He didn't need attention by authorities, not even that of a traffic ticket. Nobody needed to hear he'd tried to go to Savannah and dig dirt on his competitor for the murder rap.

They'd backtracked and exited the interstate, the hot summer sun finally at their backs. In spite of the air conditioning, the Lowcountry swelter infiltrated the glass, and no matter that Quinn grew up in this wet heat, hot was hot. A person could tell themselves it was a far cry from the hotter August days, but that didn't stop the sweat.

They headed through Walterboro and back toward Craven County when she received a call from the person who'd left a voice mail while she visited Becca.

Since she had nothing better to do than drive, she took it, letting Bluetooth take over. "Hello. Quinn Sterling."

"Thank God," said the male voice on the other end. "Did you get my voice mail?"

Scammer? He sounded a bit dramatic, though. "Um, care to identify yourself?" she said.

"Oh, sorry, sorry. Of course. Quinn, this is Patrick French, your Uncle Archie's friend."

He let that set in.

Because she needed to let that to set in. The bounce in his voice, the way he clipped the ends of his sentences, the man's persona rushed back to memory.

She hadn't seen Patrick for well over a decade. He hadn't come to her father's funeral, which she'd found odd at the time, but per Archie's explanation yesterday, Patrick had remained behind, tending to newborn

Glory after a difficult birth.

But the two men were divorced now. Quinn wasn't sure for how long since she hadn't had much chance to corner her uncle and learn what his life had been about. "It's been a long time," she said.

"Yes, regretfully. I liked you from the first time I met you. You and Archie share a lot of Sterling traits."

She took that as a compliment. "What can I do for you, Patrick?" She damn sure hoped it had nothing to do with his and Archie's personal drama. She didn't have the emotional energy for that, and she preferred hearing anything personal from Archie anyway.

"Two things. Two very important things," he said. "I wish we could meet in person, but I'm leery of doing so."

She assumed because of Archie. A bad sign. "I'm not keeping secrets from Archie."

"Wouldn't ask you to," he said, sighing a rather mournful breath. "First, has Archie talked to you about why he came to visit?"

Please, no marital drama. "No, but we've had a bit of a family crisis the last two days, so we haven't had the chance. Listen, I don't want to get in the middle of whatever happened between you two." Pondering how he even knew Archie was in South Carolina, she quickly attributed it to Archie making Patrick aware of where Glory might be. No telling what that custody arrangement looked like.

"Quinn, we're past that. I still love him, but we . . . fell apart. But that's a conversation you need to hear from him, not me. No, this is about Archie himself."

That last part shot electricity through her. "Why, what's wrong with Archie?"

"So he hasn't told you," he stated.

Come on. . . . "Like I said, we've been rather occupied."

"Oh my," and he sighed again. "Corner him. Make him talk to you. He's got to quit weathering this alone."

She'd almost let Ty get out of sight and had to speed up. "Weather what?"

"You talk to him. It's not my place to break the news."

Her pulse stepped up, dread taking up residence in her throat. "I will. Tonight." So many options played out in her head. Cancer. Financial ruin. Legal issues. Something to do with Glory's adoption, maybe. Surely DNA could put that last dilemma to rest, but family-court law could be a crapshoot.

"You said two things," she reminded him, as much to change the subject off of Archie as to get to the point.

"The next one is much more delicate." He spoke as if to hide the call from anyone nearby. "I live in Charleston, in case you didn't know."

Yet another surprise. "No, I didn't," she said, envisioning future dustups between the exes. She adored Archie under her roof, but she hadn't counted on the divorced significant other living right up the road. Made her wonder who had followed whom to the East Coast. "Thought you took over the architecture firm from Archie. He said he was retired."

"He sold me his shares, and a few months ago I sold the entire firm and went solo thanks to an offer here in South Carolina. He knows."

Not even one of the questions pinging in her head. She had no room for another crisis. "I'm on the road, Patrick, and I have to meet someone as soon as my feet hit the drive on Sterling Banks. Say what you need to say."

"Sorry again." But he didn't immediately carry on the conversation. "Patrick?"

"I hear you're familiar with Ronald Renault."

Her blood froze, a vision returning of a man named Chevy dead in her living room. Another man shot dead at her childhood tree house Windsor, the henchman's blood spoiling innocent memories on those steps. Blood that she'd welcomed as an alternative to her own.

The vendetta between the Renaults and Sterlings had been front-page news not so terribly long ago after Quinn killed Renault's blind daughter after being bitten by her seeing-eye dog and shot in the arm. The wound still ached at night.

A car passed her. Hell, she'd slowed again. She couldn't even see Ty now. "Yes, the name means something to me. He's rather famous in this part of the world, in case you haven't heard." The passing car braked to turn onto a side road. She almost tapped the bumper getting around the vehicle and doubled down to make up distance.

She didn't like this conversation, and she was keenly conscious of the fact she had no business driving while dealing with Patrick's riddles and focused on Ty's situation, which continued to push to the front of her mind. But Patrick's encrypted way of speaking had her hooked.

There was nothing encrypted about the name Renault, though. No way could she hang up now. "Why are you asking?"

"I don't want to think this, but I'm beginning to wonder if I've been duped," he said. "I was asked to come work for the Renault real estate empire, in both development and renovations."

She almost exclaimed, *What?*, but bit her tongue.

"The timing amazingly suited my needs," he said, "but now I'm thinking too much so. I already had a buyer for my firm, and I was toying with retiring like Archie, even wondering where to move to since San Francisco has gone downhill so much, but then this opportunity came out of the blue. I mean, the firm was respectably known, which is why Archie and I could afford to retire to begin with, so Renault finding out about Sterling & French was no surprise."

No, there were no coincidences with Renault. Quinn couldn't afford to believe in coincidences when it came to that man. He didn't make the slightest move in his universe without the next ten moves strategically choreographed from his wardrobe to his real estate deals. He never sat still. He never stopped planning. He never accepted second place.

"How long ago was this?" she asked.

"I've been in Charleston six months."

Meaning Patrick had seen the Charleston headlines when she killed Catherine Renault. "Then you recognize the animosity between the families."

"I do. At least now. Didn't know before."

Ronald Renault was a rabid, self-absorbed, driven man unaccustomed to being told no. He'd been after Sterling Banks since Graham's death, and in bits and pieces Quinn learned he'd been so for considerable years prior.

She was convinced the Renault / Sterling feud wouldn't end until one of them was dead. The multi-millionaire, if not billionaire, had had her father killed. In a strange turn of fate, Quinn had killed the only Renault heir, a daughter, in self-defense. She was convinced this year's mishaps and all-too-convenient run-ins with the criminal element were related to the man who was damn good at distancing himself from anyone paid to pull a trigger.

Quinn had barely gotten off the hook for the daughter's death. If not for the Sterling name, if not for the dog bite and bullet she'd collected in the fight . . . if Catherine hadn't died but rather remained alive long enough to skew the story, Quinn would be in jail.

She hated discussing those weeks. "Why are you calling me, Patrick?"

"Mr. Renault scouts nonstop for land, asking my opinion on development potential, to include properties not for sale. I understand that someone at his level thinks on a higher scale, hunting for a prospect before it's even close to being one, and I enjoy the freedom the job provides of envisioning development. Such latitude to conceive fresh designs without the weight of cost is freeing and inspirational."

"Patrick, please," she interrupted, realizing she wasn't five miles from the Sterling Banks brick and wrought-iron entrance. "I'm really pressed for time."

"The point is one of those mythical plans included Sterling Banks."

She would love for a few pieces to fall into place, like a Tetris puzzle, and tell her something she didn't know, but she was aware of Renault's obsessive desire for the farm. She'd worked hard to write off her incessant uneasiness about Renault's fixation as paranoia and hadn't succeeded. Even as affected as Jonah had been by Renault's deceitful, cunning machinations—one of which involved his mother's injuries, he had counseled Quinn that staying guarded was one thing. Preoccupation was another.

He hadn't been the one chased through the pecan orchard by a hired killer. He hadn't been the one forced to kill two people that night.

And in this phone call, she wasn't the one being paranoid or prejudging. Someone else saw an issue, too. Patrick's gut feeling about being a very intentional cog in Renault's scheme machine had merit, and she now understood what he meant about not seeing Quinn in person. He was a fool to work for the man.

Patrick's trepidation about meeting wasn't about Archie. Disloyalty to Renault came with a price, and Patrick was wisely wary. Quinn had witnessed how cutthroat that price could be, and it was far worse than Patrick could imagine.

"I understand the limb you're on." She was afraid to go into much else. The less Patrick knew the safer he was, but she couldn't help but relish the realization she had a connection inside Renault's realm. "Watch yourself, Patrick. You're smart to be cautious."

"Not feeling so smart, Quinn."

"Let's say you're smarter now. Let's remain in touch."

"Yes, I agree."

"Thanks for calling. Truly, thanks so much."

"Please, talk to Archie," he repeated.

"I will."

He hung up.

Renault would use Patrick in any attempt to take Sterling Banks. Quinn wouldn't trust Patrick visiting the farm, but in light of Archie and Glory, how could she tell him no if Archie wanted it? Patrick—Sterling connection to the enemy camp or not—would ever be a Renault scout in her head now.

God, first Ty's situation . . . then something amiss with Archie.

Ahead, Ty pulled through the farm entrance. The old sense of coming home to those pecan trees and their history usually eased her nerves. She took her time driving in, fighting to feel the dirt beneath her tires, but she couldn't settle. Instead, the closer she got to the manor, the more nervous she felt, as if they were on the brink of a bad, bad turn of events.

She pulled behind Ty's Jeep. He stood on the steps leading from the garage into the house. Quinn waited a second to catch her breath. Ty's crisis was more than enough, but seeing Archie would throw some unrevealed issue to the forefront of her mind. As insane as it sounded, she'd have to push Patrick's damn truckload of Renault crap to the back, a rather difficult effort with something so . . . visceral.

She laid her forehead on the steering wheel. *Okay, think. Sort who you talk to and what about.*

Jonah would ask about Ty and had a personal need to know about Renault, and he deserved to be informed. They'd fallen out too many times about her harboring secrets that could potentially impact them all. To do so again was not prudent with the man who practically ran the place, whom everyone expected to propose at any time.

But to tell Jonah about Renault was to tell him about Patrick, which was to tell him about Archie, about whom she had no idea as to what was wrong. The conversation exhausted her thinking about it, and she hadn't the strength to deal with that talk before coping with Ty's mistakes.

Archie. As she suspected, he'd had a purpose returning to Sterling Banks.

Regardless of what she promised Patrick, Quinn wasn't questioning him until after Tassey left. No telling how long her visit would be with the buckets of new information that could shift strategy. She would not be pleased at Ty having pulled his stunt today and having kept other facts from her.

Ty remained waiting at the steps. "I'll go on in," he said aloud, sadness in his posture, misery in his eyes. Quinn let him go, not wanting it to appear that she'd dragged him home.

Yes, she had to hold off on Archie for now.

When she entered the kitchen, Ty stepped through to the living room. He turned back around to the adults making dinner. "Where's Cole?"

"The goat barn," Jule said. "Too young to leave them alone in the tree house that close to the river. We've babied them for the better part of the day so felt it time to leave them to themselves a bit. That girl's good for him, by the way." Then in afterthought she added, "Bogie's with them. Dog hasn't left their side all day. Jonah told the workers to check in on them when they're in the area. Once they go home, Jonah will bring them to the house."

Quinn was glad. Bogie deserved the spoiling, and the kids merited the pup's affection. "How's Cole?" she asked.

"Cries in waves," Archie said. "He'll be doing that for a while, I imagine. Any headway on what happened to his mother?"

Quinn toyed with how much to say. Better less than more. "Nothing definite either way," she said. "No real witnesses. Still have a few issues to ferret out." There, that was general enough.

Quinn peered over at the meal prep. Pulled pork sat in a foil tin off to the side, most likely from Lenore's restaurant since the air wasn't saturated with the aroma of a pork shoulder having roasted for hours on a slow heat. Baked beans cooked in the oven, however, and Jule's hands deftly prepared a cold corn summer salad.

"Give Jonah a bit," his mother replied, focus on the bowl. "Beans'll be ready in thirty minutes. We'll get the kids and start without him if he isn't here."

The lock on the sliding doors clicked then the huge glass frames glided apart in a hush. Ty moved through to the outside. "Gonna check on Cole and call Momma," he called back, not waiting for anyone's reply before he left.

Jonah probably hadn't told the others about Ty's detour of the day. Jonah not only kept secrets but knew which ones merited safekeeping.

"Ty's attorney will be here in an hour," Quinn said to the two in the kitchen, snaring a slice of bell pepper. "Don't be surprised if we see more of her."

"Nothing surprises me around here, girl." Jule finished chopping the last of the pepper, shook moisture off her hands, and wiped them on a towel habitually tucked in her waistband like her bandannas.

Quinn went to the sliding doors, watching Ty disappear up the gravel road to Jule's place and the goat barn. She texted Jonah.

Just got home with Ty.

He gave her a thumbs-up, then a note saying, *Need me to come in?*

No, attorney is on her way, though. Jule has dinner almost ready.

He answered with a kissing emoji. No denying he was way better at romantic gestures than she was.

Quinn moseyed back to Archie while Jule continued with the meal.

From the looks of things, dinner only waited on the beans. Jule began throwing quilted placemats on the kitchen table. This might be dinner in stages with the way people were coming and going.

As Jule messed with the table settings, Quinn bent to prop elbows on the counter next to Archie's stool. "Hey."

He halfway turned to her, waiting.

She leaned closer. "Patrick called me today."

The news drew him up short but only for a second or two. "How much did he say?"

"Only that I need to talk to you. Said it was your story to tell."

"Hmmm." He pivoted his head away. "Can I help you with anything, Jule?"

"Nope," the older woman replied, pretending not to see their heads buried in discussion.

Quinn let her forehead come over and touch his ear. "Don't you think it only fair that if you drop in on me that you say why? You came here in need, I can see that."

He didn't answer.

"Got my hands full with Ty tonight," she said. "If Tassey leaves early, maybe we can talk then. Otherwise, tomorrow. Can it wait?"

"It's damn sure not going anywhere," came his reply, a stoic impression taking over his jaw. She didn't remember ever seeing him so solemn. Not the Archie she remembered in her teens.

He'd always been the happiest, most jovial of the three Sterling men. Graham. her father, carried the stereotypical leader-of-the-pack trait of a first born, and his diligent determination to protect the family legacy put the three-hundred-year-old farm in his hands. While Larry was the second, he missed the boat when it came to the middle-child graces of diplomacy, generosity, and need to please. He fell far short of them all, losing his inheritance to a nasty divorce, the acreage salvaged by Graham. Wearing the sheriff's badge served as its replacement, with nobody daring to run against Larry in almost thirty years.

Archie, the baby boy, inherited the charm. Pleasant and willing to take risks, he'd put the family behind him and headed to the West Coast, deeding his acreage to Graham for a minimal price that was used to start his architectural firm.

Fact was, Archie and Larry hated each other, and nobody understood why. As in couldn't-stand-to-be-in-the-same-room-level of hate. With Archie gone, their feud became a moot issue. Now that he was back, Quinn wasn't sure how the two would behave.

With all the other nastiness simmering under this roof, Quinn had no desire to visit that problem. It had lain dormant for more than twenty years and could remain so a while longer.

Uncle Larry might not own the manor, but he'd grown up in it and lived locally, so Quinn hadn't ever had the heart to take his key. Hopefully Archie's presence would deter Uncle Larry from one of his impromptu drop-ins.

She hated when he did that.

A knock sounded at the front door. Quinn's thoughts immediately went to Uncle Larry until she realized Tassey must've made good time driving south from Charleston.

Quinn answered. The attorney carried a tight jaw and a stare that could laser steel. "Let's get to it," she said, not waiting to be asked in.

Quinn showed her down the hall to the living room. "We were about to grab a bite to eat. You are welcome—"

"I've eaten. I need you and Ty now. Where can we meet in private?"

Quinn peered around, as if she hadn't lived there her whole life. She had never entertained use of the formal study, shut off since her father died. Quinn had gradually picked at the paperwork until it now resided in the corner of the massive living room on a roll-top desk twice the size of the average, with a wall safe holding the most important papers. The study still held ghosts, in her opinion. "The dining room okay?"

"The laundry room is fine if we have room for three." She looked around, judging. Her eyes came back to Quinn as to which direction she should go.

Quinn pointed to a set of double doors. "Through there."

"Get Ty's ass in here," Tassey said, marching to where directed, slinging a briefcase off her shoulder with an unexpected strength.

"He's with Cole. They'd haven't seen much of each other today, but I'll—"

"Don't care if he's taking a crap. Go get him," the counselor said, not caring who heard but loud enough for Jule and Archie to come forward from the kitchen. They stood stiffly at the kitchen's entrance, watching and listening but not about to say a word.

Quinn texted Ty before breaking into a trot out the door toward the goat barn, but not before she heard the attorney's briefcase hit the polished pecan-wood table with a thud that couldn't help but leave a mark.

Chapter 15

QUINN REACHED the goat barn before Ty answered the text, but when she arrived, she understood why he hadn't bothered.

The evening sun sent a sharp angled band of light through an open window into where he was, the light giving a postcard look to the yellows, browns, and beiges. The big barn fan droned from the other side of the facility, keeping the heat bearable.

Ty stooped next to Cole and his new friend, listening to their day's escapades, making the appropriate noises about how exciting a day they'd had. Amidst three juvenile goats, one standing and two on the barn's hay-strewn floor, the children's hands were embedded in white or gray fur, sitting so close that Cole's leg touched Glory's. Archie's daughter reached over and hugged the boy once in the telling of their tales. She had her daddy's warmth and empathy, for sure.

Quinn hadn't the heart to interrupt. Ty had left Cole's side on probably the most emotionally vulnerable day of the boy's life in order to investigate. Cole had weighed on him the whole day, no doubt, in his mission to clear his name so Cole kept at least one parent.

But the attorney's time was limited, and she didn't come cheap for the time she allowed them to have. "Tassey's in the dining room, Ty," she said. "You kids ready to come back to the house?"

"Who's Tassey?" Cole asked, his young complexion tired, eyes a bit swollen from the roller-coaster day of tears.

"The lawyer you met last night," Ty said before Quinn had a chance. "She does important stuff. Come on." Ty stood, a bit of a creak in his unfolding.

Cole clenched a fuller handhold of goat fur, enough to make the animal flex a muscle, a shiver running across its ribs. "I want to stay here."

"I'll stay with him," Glory offered.

Ty looked at Quinn. "Can you . . ."

But she shook her head. "Tassey wants me there, too, and, after today, I need to be."

Doubtful, Ty seemed uneasy at leaving.

"We'll stay right here," Glory said. "Uncle Jonah said he'd come get us."

"We'll stay right here," Cole repeated.

The father sighed and caved. "Don't leave the barn till someone gets you."

Both kids said, "We won't."

Quinn hooked her arm through Ty's and escorted him out, wishing this could be a long, slow stroll, but they hadn't that luxury. "Come on," she said, pushing her long legs into a fast walk back to the house.

Inside, Tassey sat at the head of the table for twelve, having done no more than pull out a legal pad. A cup of coffee on a sweetgrass coaster sat at the top of the pad, off to the side. She motioned for Ty to sit to her right, Quinn to her left.

"Investigators think you did it," Tassey said. "Even more than they did yesterday, and I need to hear why from you."

Tassey spoke to Ty, but he sat back, giving the floor to Quinn. "They'd already interviewed the building by the time I got there," she began. "Three neighbors admitted to being home when Ty arrived to pick up Cole. Two of them heard Natalie yelling. Nobody heard Ty, but he was seen coming and going, the first arrival and the second after he tucked Cole away in his vehicle."

Tassey held a hard stare on her while Ty studied his lap. He wasn't himself. Maybe he understood he'd screwed up the other day meeting with Becca. Maybe he regretted going out today. Maybe there was even more she wasn't aware of. Quinn left her concerned glance on him to further educate Tassey. She had to hear it all.

"Those people think he did it, too," she said.

"No shit," Tassey replied.

"Nobody else was seen going into the apartment after Ty left, but someone had to have, Tassey. Ty did not kill Natalie."

"Convince me," Tassey said, to which Ty looked up, a confused, earnest stare at Quinn to do as his counselor asked.

"The neighbor in apartment F4, right across from Natalie, has a one-hour gap in her story after Ty left. She tried to say he must've done it, but she couldn't tell her own story straight. Natalie slammed the door when Ty left, but the neighbor found it ajar later when she found the body. But during that hour, she was doing laundry and baking a cake. There are gaps."

Again, Tassey studied her client, like a teacher asking a student why they'd cheated on a final exam. "What about when Ty went back?"

Quinn's nerves pinged. "I told you. After he took Cole to the car—
"

"Not then. Later," the attorney said, making tick marks on the pad with her pen.

She knew.

Quinn did the only thing she could. "Ty, that has to come from you."

The man sat straighter, and related the call to Natalie about Cole wanting his robot. How he returned to the apartment. How he found her dead on the floor. How it caught his breath.

Quinn held her own breath.

Then, remorsefully, he described how he'd eased away and hadn't called the police.

Tassey didn't react. Not the first extra blink of an eye. "And what about the two days before?" she said.

"I didn't meet with Natalie that week except for when I picked up Cole."

"Not Natalie," Tassey said. "Becca Blevins. When you asked her about Natalie's boyfriend."

Shit. Becca wasn't as altruistic as she seemed to be. She had spoken to the cops about meeting Ty that two days before, and the questions he'd asked her, probably, not to mention the fact he slipped over there without Nat's knowing, all of it painting him as a jealous ex-lover.

"Apparently, she hid things from me," Quinn said. She wasn't about to say Ty had as well. "Apparently, she can't be trusted."

"No," Tassey said. "She just didn't trust *you*. She told enough to Colleton County, though."

The attorney took this moment of stunned introspection to sip her coffee and give everyone a mental break. Two sips, to be exact. She had no time for long breaks. "And they've spoken to a Mr. David Wescott, after he voluntarily came forward with his attorney this afternoon."

"Gabriel," Quinn said. "Shit."

She'd worried about that, even mentioned to Ty how smart it would be for the man to show himself first. Quinn wondered how, being an ex in Nat's life, he'd found out so quickly. There was the empty suitcase on the bed, though. And the apartment had been so clean and neat. Had she been planning a reunion? A trip to Charleston? Becca might not be aware if Nat didn't want her friend knowing Nat had changed her mind about her old beau.

Tassey set down her cup, giving Ty her full attention. "I believe you've been told by both Quinn and myself that honesty was your best defense, because without it I cannot perform at full potential. You're a cop. I hate representing the police. They second- and third-guess what people think and say, predict what attorneys will do, surmise what juries will decide. They think they have magic powers of foresight, and as a result, they are their own worst enemy. While disappointed, I am not surprised at you, Mr. Jackson."

"Tassey, Ty isn't—"

"Shut up, Quinn." The attorney never let her focus off her client. "Now, Mr. Jackson, let's start over. Tell me every word of every conversation you've had with Natalie, her neighbors, your mother, and anyone else who could be called as a witness about your behavior, your feelings, and your anger about what your ex-wife was doing to your family. She was taking away your son without your permission, with a man you didn't approve of. Let's start there. From your gut this time. Go ahead."

Ty looked to Quinn, and all she could do was softly nod to proceed.

He spilled to them both. Listening to him, watching him flay his soul, tore Quinn up. Every muscle tensed on it in the telling. She bit her tongue countless times waiting for Ty to finish. She was a troubleshooter. Always had been. Yet sitting here listening to a truth that did nothing but depict him as the guilty party ripped her to pieces.

Where were the holes to this story? Where were the soft spots? While Tassey made Ty repeat himself, each time a deeper cut than the last, Quinn scoured the so-called facts she'd learned today, angry at how the details only served to better cement the prosecution's case.

With cold expectation, she envisioned Tassey talking about a plea downstream, accepting a lesser guilty charge rather than stand before a jury and judge and roll the dice. While juries were a game of chance a hundred percent of the time, no science whatsoever, even a negotiated guilty plea meant at least two decades in jail, minimum. The extenuating circumstances for the death penalty weren't there.

Heavens, it crushed her thinking of Ty in a jail suit.

Quinn began scheming. She needed to corner Becca again. She had to learn more about the recluse, whom Frannie Bean had identified as John Jefferson. Recluses kept to themselves, but they also were insanely observant about their surroundings in order to shelter their privacy. He could have witnessed more than the others. Though an odd bird, he had as much credibility as Frannie Bean. "I'll do background on these apartment people, to include the manager," Quinn blurted. "I'll go back and talk to them again."

"Quinn," Ty said, reaching a hand over to hers.

Caught up in her thoughts, Quinn had spoken over them. "Sorry," she said.

Her vocal expression of desperation had only served to make her friend more aware of their odds.

Cries broke the silence. Wailing, high-pitched children's cries tangled into long hound-dog barks from Bogie.

Ty's chair flew back to the floor. Quinn tossed hers aside and scrambled around the end of the table.

A dark anger coated his face as Jonah pushed aside the sliding glass doors on the back porch. He rushed in, Glory in his arms, Cole stumbling alongside, clinging. Bogie bounded in, throwing his two cents into the excitement.

Ty took Cole before Jonah could fully cross the threshold.

Archie flew from the kitchen and grasped Glory.

"Take them someplace else," Jonah said. "I'm calling the sheriff. I've already radioed a few men to cover the place from Jule's house on out."

"What the hell—?" Ty started.

Jonah gripped his friend's shoulder. "Take care of Cole first. Calm him down. We'll talk in a minute. I don't think they were touched, but Cole fell over himself running to me."

Archie didn't wait to be told, whisking his daughter away from whatever ugliness this was. Ty, however, stood torn between wanting to handle matters and needing to tend to his son.

"Take him to one of the bedrooms," Quinn said, pointing to the stairs.

Jule grabbed Bogie's collar, removing him from the fray.

"Take him to one of the kids and he'll hush," Quinn told Jule, then over her shoulder to Jonah, "Don't call 911."

"I know," he replied, the private number already dialed, phone to his ear. "Larry? It's Jonah. Someone slipped onto the farm and scared Ty's and Archie's children in the goat barn. The kids say they aren't harmed, but they're mighty shaken up. I have my people combing the groves." He took a breath, listening. "We'll get what we can from the kids, but all I got is male, about my age because they first thought he was me, and dark hair. A baggy windbreaker. Yeah, in this heat."

Quinn took in the vague description, eagerly waiting for Jonah to get off the call and get down to finding this creep. She had already snared the handgun she kept atop a kitchen cabinet, telling herself that with kids in the house, it would be locked up in her safe upon her return.

"Hell no I won't," Jonah said into the phone. "Just get here." He hung up, Quinn knowing without asking that her uncle had told Jonah to wait for him and his people.

"Out through the garage," she said, snaring keys off a hook. "I have another handgun locked in the truck console."

Jule took care of Bogie upstairs, leaving Tassey alone, electric energy still in the air despite the silence. Observing everything from the dining room entrance, Tassey spoke up. "Why not take the dog?"

"He's not trained," was all Quinn felt the need to say.

Tassey stepped closer. "And shouldn't you wait for the sheriff's office?"

Jonah scoffed and went toward the garage. Quinn barely hesitated to reply. "My home has been violated, our family threatened. This is not Charleston, Counselor." She shouted up the stairs. "Jule?"

Jule shouted back. "Yeah?"

"Make sure every door is locked," Quinn hollered.

"I'll help her," Tassey said, calmly, as if promising to do the dishes before they returned home.

Quinn bolted after Jonah. He had snared the extra firearm. Quinn caught up with him and they jogged toward the goat barn.

"Where was Bogie in all this?" she asked. She hadn't trained him to be anything but a farm dog. He'd never met a person he didn't like, and suddenly she wasn't comfortable with that.

"Found him standing in the doorway, facing the woods, hair up on his back. I'd like to think he chased the guy off, but he's still pup and, frankly, we haven't trained him to do anything but come, heel, and fetch." He huffed between phrases.

Whoever it was could've easily killed the dog.

The farm was three thousand acres, but the land between the county road access and the building complex area of two houses, a goat barn, and the pecan-distribution building, represented closer to fifty. Jonah had fifteen men who hadn't left for home yet, and he had already scattered them strategically across various sections to cover acreage they knew like their own backyards.

"What am I looking for?" Quinn asked. "And which way?"

"Around the barn and Jule's house," he said. "I told the sheriff all I got from the kids. You heard."

She trotted alongside him. "Did he threaten them?"

"Not exactly."

"Then what the hell did he say *exactly*?"

"He told them that Ty killed Natalie."

Jesus Christ!

Jonah was as furious as she was. "You cover north and east around the buildings," he directed, concern furrowed in his forehead. "I'll cover the rest. He could be hiding so watch yourself, Quinn."

She followed instructions. Her training excelled over his tenfold, but good advice was good advice. And he was looking to regain some semblance of control over the situation. He had found the kids, probably kicking himself he had missed the culprit by mere minutes. She should be worried more about him, but while she owned the place, Jonah was the foreman of it all, and he had to feel like the guardian right now.

This year had been menacing and dangerous to all on Sterling Banks, and if Jonah had learned anything these last few months, it was security. He'd rigged outdoor cameras on all the buildings and could handle the weapon in his hand. She held no doubt he would do what was needed for safety on the plantation in his charge, not for the responsibility of the place but for the love of its people.

Larry arrived in fifteen minutes with four deputies and the promise of two more coming. They canvassed the land and every nook and crevice of the buildings and landscaping around it. They found nothing between the houses and the exit to the highway, tire tracks impossible to discern with the comings and goings of farm trucks and now the patrol cars, the light having dimmed.

Quinn had ventured through the grove, following an uncommon path that led to another vehicle exit not readily known by other than Sterling people. Tree by tree she walked guardedly, weapon at her side, recalling how she, Ty, and Jonah were expert at hiding, then leaping out at one another as children.

Her phone vibrated.

"Anything?" Ty asked, that low voice more bass than usual, tapping the impatient, defensive father in him.

"Nothing," she said. "I believe he's gone. I'll be in in a few minutes."

She made her way to the exit, unable to find tracks in the orangey summer dusk. Whoever this was had been stealthy entering and inconspicuous leaving, the only witnesses being two small children too scared to recall much of a description.

Quinn returned to the house, leaving the uniforms and farm workers to continue the search in the off chance the idiot stuck around. She felt better closer to home. She found Uncle Larry in the living room with Tassey, so typical of him to assist with a search from a recliner, but right now she needed to talk to Ty.

"Come, update us," Larry said, to which Quinn replied, "Didn't find anyone," and scurried to the kitchen.

Yeah, rude, but she wanted Cole's description of this guy before the poor kid got befuddled from attention.

"Anything?" Jule asked, seated at the kitchen table, patiently being the backup anyone needed.

"No," Quinn said. "Listen, I'm going upstairs to see Cole. Try to keep everyone else down here if you can. Especially Uncle Larry."

Jule went straight to the coffee pot, hit a button, then opened the pantry. "Got it."

Before Tassey or Larry could grab her as she passed through again, Quinn ran upstairs. Archie and Glory were sequestered in the last bedroom on the right, across from Quinn's. She heard a whine and yip of a bark from that direction, telling her where Jule had put Bogie. Quinn found Ty and Cole in the second bedroom on the left.

As she eased the door open, a force gripped her forearm and pulled her to the room, into the corner nearest the closet. Cole, in a fetal position on the queen guest bed faced away from them, totally still. Ty positioned himself between his son and Quinn, backing her against the wall. "We've got to find these people," he said, teeth clenched.

People, as if the intruder was part of a bigger script being run. Quinn agreed.

Resting her hand softly on her friend, she peered around him to the bed. "Is he awake?" she whispered.

"Yes," he said, relaxing his jaw as pain filled his eyes. "He won't talk to me. I have no idea what happened out there, Q, because he won't talk to me."

Hand still on his arm, she massaged the spot. "Let me try," she said. "Better me than the cops, okay?"

Inhaling deep, Ty stared at her and gave in. "Okay."

"You . . ." and she pointed to the doorway.

He understood, walked over to glance one more time at his son, the little body clenched tight. With heavy weight in his steps, he left, pulling the door to within an inch of closure.

Easing down on the bed, Quinn touched the boy's shoulder. "Cole, can you turn over and talk to me?"

He sniffled, remained in a ball, and murmured into the quilt. "I'm scared, Miss Q."

"Oh, honey." She eased down to embrace his little body in hug. "I know you are. But you are the best witness we have. You're smart. You're older than Glory. I need you to sit up and talk to me, okay?"

"Don't talk to me about Daddy," he said, mashing into the pillow.

"Okay, then let's talk about the man you saw," she said. "I have police in the grove right now, hunting for him, but they aren't sure who to hunt for. Can you describe him?"

He spoke toward the wall. "If you find any stranger, it's gotta be him."

As she always bragged, the kid was smart. "In case he gets away, how would you describe him for other police?"

Cole rolled over, still on his back. "Tall like Mr. Jonah, but not as big as . . . Daddy."

Quinn nodded. "Good, what was he wearing?"

"Dark-blue jacket. A cap. Jeans. Black running shoes."

"Excellent," she said, validating him. "Hair?"

"Brown."

"Age?" This would be tough. Children didn't judge ages well.

"Like you and Mr. Jonah and . . . that's it."

He didn't want to mention his father.

But he was going to have to.

"Now," and Quinn rubbed on the child some more. "Sit up for me."

Cole did with wriggles and scoots until he was upright and cross-legged. He still wasn't looking her in the eye, though. His downcast expression about broke her heart.

"Where was the man standing?"

"Right outside the big opening to the barn. Bogie wouldn't let him come close."

Good for Bogie. He was more of a guard dog than she thought. She counted her blessings the trespasser hadn't shot him.

"Did he know your name?" she asked.

"Yes," he said. "He talked to both of us."

Of course he did. They were seated side by side. "But he only said your name, right?"

"No." He wrapped arms around her, and she squeezed him back. "He said Glory's, too."

Ice water coursed through her veins. How the hell did he know about her?

128

Chapter 16

THE CHILL IN QUINN'S bones clung tighter than the child in her arms.

A trespasser had ventured onto Sterling Banks property and found his way to the goat barn without being noticed. How had he known to go there? How many times had he been on the place before tonight? How did he learn about the children?

Not that Glory took precedence to Cole, but Natalie's death sort of put Ty and Cole in the public's eye. At least in Craven and Colleton Counties, maybe a mention in Beaufort and Charleston media.

But Quinn hadn't even known about Glory until yesterday. How had anyone else?

Patrick's words came back to her. *I'm beginning to wonder if I've been duped.*

Suddenly, they applied to her, too.

Cole squeezed her tighter, so she cast aside the worries to attend to the boy. She eased him back to see him. *He would recognize the boyfriend.* "Cole, had you ever seen this man before?"

Was this David Wescott, aka Gabriel?

He shook his head.

"Good." She gave him another hug.

No. Not good. The thought of another hired henchman on the grounds escalated her concern. No, her anger. Made her want to hire henchmen of her own.

She fought tensing up, to keep him from doing the same. "What did the man say to you?"

Tears still welled in Cole's already swollen eyes. He had to relive the moment to speak the words. A quiver began in that small body, resonating into Quinn's, and he tucked himself into her shirt.

"You're safe now, sweetie," she said, stroking his head. "You can tell me."

Regardless of how hard she hugged him, the shivers continued, but he answered bravely, nonetheless. "He said Daddy was a dangerous man. He said Daddy killed Mommy, and he was going to jail for the rest of his life." He busted out in sobs.

Dear Lord Almighty.

She hadn't the heart to ask him more. She rocked and rocked, praying he'd find some peace in the motion.

Poor baby, he'd lost a parent and been told the other one was dangerous. His family had been destroyed. He didn't know where to turn, whom to trust, and he couldn't see what his future would be.

"I don't want to hate Daddy," he said, bawling.

Tears wet her cheeks. Cole's absolute confidence in a father who caught bad guys by day and read bedtime stories by night, had been stained.

Quinn rested her chin on his head, still rocking. She glanced over at the door where Ty had to have heard, and she softly cried some more.

Ty lived his life to protect his family and do right, and now his own child had doubts about him. This had to have torn him in two.

But Quinn would do right by him, by them both. She could gather information from Cole, research this Gabriel dude, and work with Tassey in any way possible. In no scenario could she envision someone as noble as Ty behind bars. No way.

Ty eased into the room.

Head turned away, Cole didn't see him at first, but he heard the rustle and looked around. Seeing his father next to the bed, he gripped Quinn, burying his face again.

Quinn could see Ty break into pieces. Fighting hot, silent tears, he slid out of the room, this time pulling the door all the way shut.

God, she had to fix this.

Cole made sure his father wasn't there and sat back, wiping his face. "I'm never going to see the goats again!"

"Oh, don't blame the goats," Quinn said, trying to smile through her own sadness as if she hadn't cried as well. "They've become used to you and Glory. They don't get nearly as much loving as you give them. If you like, we can pick one out for yourself. Keep him here, but he'd be yours."

He brightened, then clouded over again. "But I don't even want to leave the house."

Personally, she didn't want him to, either. He could identify both his mother's boyfriend and this visitor, with either potentially a murderer. Glory could identify the visitor. Poor Archie. How the hell did people endure parenting when the world threatened to hurt their children like this?

"Hey," she said, giving him a little shake of a hug. "How about I bring Bogie in here?"

"And Glory?" he asked, moisture drying on those infamous chubby cheeks.

She comically puckered lips as if he'd asked the obvious. "Of course. Give me a second to find them."

He'd brightened, but a wariness remained, and he wrapped arms around his own knees when Quinn stood, not eager to move from his safe place in the quilt.

Quinn slipped down the hall to Archie's room. He sat in the corner in a rocker, Glory in his lap, her palm over her own cheek, alongside her mouth as if trying hard to avoid sucking that thumb.

Archie rocked in a slow, barely moving rhythm, singing low to his daughter, her body spooned into his. Not a Brahms lullaby but something so much more perfect.

Hugging the doorframe, Quinn could barely make out the words, but she knew them. In a gentle tenor voice, Archie sang "Dream a Little Dream of Me," a Mamas and Papas melody. A song familiar to his age and easy to listen to for her. A tune to soothe them both. He noticed Quinn waiting, giving her a bare smile, and she waited until he finished the verse to enter.

Bogie raised his head from his place on the bed, tail thumping. His legs had grown lanky of late as he grew into his big feet, and Quinn ran a hand over his head and down his back. The thump double-timed on the bedspread.

Glory followed her daddy's attention, and smiled at her cousin's presence, then held out arms. Quinn went right in and scooped her up. Face in those blond curls, Quinn took in the scent, relishing the wrapped cocoon of arms and legs around her.

All her senses took on keen new levels of desire, along with the need to shelter. God, she never thought she could want one of these of her own.

"How are you, little girl?" Quinn asked, sitting on the bed. Bogie shifted over to touch his owner and nose the creature in her lap.

Glory snickered at the cold nose and pet him on the head. He nudged for more, and she obliged him. "I like it here, Aunty Q."

Oh, thank heavens. Quinn was sure tonight had turned the child against Sterling Banks. She might be made of sterner stuff than Cole, despite the difference in ages.

"Tell me about the goat barn," Quinn said, fingers entwined behind

Glory's back, holding her in a seated position on her lap.

Glory pouted. "He didn't introduce himself, if that's what you mean."

Sterner stuff for sure. This child cracked Quinn up, but she'd seen Glory almost sucking her thumb, too, seeking the safeguard of her father. Six almost seven was almost toddler-esque in Quinn's opinion, and any stranger with ill will could easily take advantage.

"Well, that's part of it," Quinn replied. "Definitely bad manners there, but tell me what he said."

"That Cole's daddy killed his mommy and would go to jail." Ever so little, she inched closer to her aunt. "Said his daddy was a dangerous man."

Quinn hugged her again and let her loose. "He was the bad man, Glory. Not Cole's daddy." Quinn went with bad instead of dangerous, a word she wished Glory hadn't learned yet. "Cole's daddy is Mr. Ty, by the way. Let's call him that. He's been a friend of mine since I was your age, and he's one of the sweetest grown-ups I've ever known. Does that make you feel better?"

But Glory peered back at Archie, seeking what to say. She was still leery of Ty. Archie only smiled assuring, not validating or debunking her feelings.

Giving her a small pat on the back, Quinn said, "I'd like to talk to your daddy a while, if you don't mind, sweetheart. I haven't been able to since y'all arrived, and I've missed him. Can you tend to Cole for me? You and Bogie?"

Quinn started to say he was alone and needed someone with him, but that would slide into the question of why his father wasn't in there with him and water the seed of doubt already planted by this damn stranger.

"He asked for you specifically," she said instead.

The child's sense of duty shot forward. "I can do that. Where is he?" Glory slid out of Quinn's lap before Quinn could say more, reaching for her cousin's hand. "Take me *and* Bogie." She slapped her tiny thigh twice. "Come on, Bogie. Come on, boy."

The dog hopped down with a clunk, his back up to the child's waist. Quinn left Archie in the rocker and escorted her duo down the hall. Cole lit up when they walked in, and Glory hopped onto the bed in tandem with the dog. She gave Cole a hug and pushed at Bogie to move to a different spot so she could be closer to her buddy.

Quinn's insides warmed, her heart flipping once. If only her mother and father could see this. "Y'all okay if I leave now?"

"Yes, ma'am," Cole said, with the manners his parents taught him.

"Door open or shut?" she asked, hand on the knob.

"Shut," Glory said. "We don't want people to eavesdrop."

Smiling, Quinn did as ordered and returned to Archie.

He remained in the rocker. She returned to her seat on the bed, their knees only a couple feet apart. "She's incredibly strong, Uncle Archie. You've done a remarkable job with her."

"Patrick taught her a lot, too. She misses him more than she admits."

"So," Quinn said, not wanting to launch straight into Patrick. Not yet. "How do you think she really is?"

"She's fine," he said. "Not so sure about me. I wanted to find my old Henry .22 and hunt that guy down myself. Haven't felt that urge since I left the South."

Quinn liked this old side of Archie showing itself. "I'm sure I can find it. Be happy to clean it for you if you're serious about putting it back into use."

"No, no." He returned to a small back and forth. "I'm sure nothing will warrant that."

He didn't know the details of events of this year or he'd think differently. "I don't want you to regret coming home," she said.

"I do and I don't, but the *don't* outweighs the other, Miss Q. You especially. Glory already adores you and this place." He laughed. "And Bogie."

"Yeah, I think he's already traded owners."

He raised a brow. "Is that—"

She laughed back. "Not a problem at all. The more loving anyone gets the better." She had gotten used to having that warm body, albeit a dog, in the bed each night. Just the idea of another heartbeat in the house made a difference, and Jonah had given her the pup because of that void. With several heartbeats hanging around these days, Bogie could play musical beds now. The manor wasn't so tomb-like anymore.

Her phone dinged.

Jonah texted. *Everything all right up there?*

She needed to get back to the people in her living room, but she wasn't done here. *Getting there. Can you go through the farm's cams please while I speak to Archie? Explain later.*

Thumbs-up.

The intruder had surely made his presence known on one cam or another, from the manor's corners to the goat barn, from Jule's place to the pecan-production barn. The way Jonah had rigged up the system after a prior intrusion, thinking ahead, he'd measured angles in hope that a face could be captured on at least one camera.

She set her phone on the bed, face up, in case.

"What's going on, Quinn?" Archie asked, when she showed she was his for now. "Glory's strong, but she's rattled. She might be leery of Ty for a bit, and you can't blame her. We raised her not to fear everyone she meets but still taught her to believe in herself when her instincts kick in about people." He wasn't upset, wasn't on edge, but a thread of uneasiness still ran through his words. "She can't be expected to tell the good guys from the bad at six years old."

"Almost seven, remember," Quinn said, trying to keep the chat from turning too dark too soon. "Someone's trying to frame Ty. That's what's happening."

He wasn't accusatory, but he deserved the right to ask, "Are you sure?"

"Swear the farm on it," she said.

His nod said he believed her. "Making sure this was the same Ty I knew. Who did he piss off in Craven County to warrant this, though? He's a cop. I get that, but this isn't someone mad about their DUI, is it?"

"Probably has nothing to do with Ty's job or Craven County," she said. "Might be nothing more than Natalie dismissing a boyfriend who didn't take no for an answer."

Paranoia hummed in the background of her mind, thanks to the danger she and her Sterling Banks family had experienced this year, but she didn't need to share this early. Besides, she wasn't sure she wanted to describe it all, some of it going all the way back to Graham's murder. Without sounding obsessive, how was she supposed to tell Archie that she couldn't rule out this being connected to her? Someone getting to Nat because she was connected to Ty because he was connected to Quinn. All because they were affiliated with Sterling land.

Paranoia hummed louder.

She had zero proof, and admittedly, she questioned herself for thinking along those lines. What if this wasn't about her? But could she afford to dismiss the possibility?

"Got nowhere else to be," Archie said. "Talk to me."

"Well, nothing I'd love more than to cover things top to bottom." A lie she needed to tell in the moment. "But I've got Ty, Uncle Larry, Jonah, and a high-priced attorney downstairs. I came in here to check on Glory first, but secondly to have a brief chat about you."

He smirked. "Listen to you, all in charge and pushing a mission."

"I've had a lot happen in my world. Might've grown up a little."

"You were always tough, but you've hardened a bit, Niece"

"Guess so." She let a moment pass to think about that, then changed the tangent of the conversation. "Patrick's worried about you."

"He's lost the right," Archie said, plain and simple without rancor.

"He sounded sincere," she said.

Archie shifted his attention off her to the spot on the bed where Bogie had been.

"He said to ask you to elaborate about yourself," she continued. "You asked me questions about my world, how about what's happened in yours? Let's start with why you two broke up."

Archie thought, and Quinn sensed him trying to find the best, briefest way to tell it. "He stepped out on me."

She wasn't here to judge, but. . . . "Why would he do that? Not that I've been an active part of your life, but I thought y'all were solid."

"We were," he said. "But when I needed him, he wasn't there, and he found another bed like he was the one who needed the help. It opened my eyes, and changes had to be made."

"What sort of *need* are we talking about here?" she asked, scared of what the answer might be. "Something medical?"

"Maybe."

She cocked her head. "That's a yes-or-no question."

"Okay, yes," he said, sighing.

That sigh launched a somersault in her chest. He had no choice but to finish that thought.

"I have Parkinson's," he said. "Diagnosed eighteen months ago."

"Oh, no," she whispered, then regretted her reaction. She'd heard of the disease but never knew anyone with it. She understood it robbed you of muscle ability and eventually turned into a sort of dementia, but did that mean months? Years? Did everybody face a clock? "How long . . ."

"How long do I have?" he asked. "It's what most people ask."

He said it with a smile, thank goodness. It made her smile, too, though she didn't feel like smiling.

"Nobody has that answer," he said. "It affects everyone differently. The average person is diagnosed at age sixty. They pegged me at fifty-three, though, truth be told, symptoms go back a couple years before that. Thought it was age, or something minor . . . or something that would go away."

She reached over, hand on his knee. "I don't even know what questions to ask, Uncle."

He covered her hand with his. "That's shock. I was the same. Then an hour later a tsunami of questions poured out of me. They've discovered a lot about the disease, but there's no pill to cure it."

She'd come in the room with plenty of questions, just not about this, and suddenly the other questions didn't exist anymore. All she could think about was how bad he was, how would it affect his future, and how long a future did that mean.

For both him and Glory.

"How did you . . . know?" she asked, looking at him through a different lens. She hadn't noticed any signs, but she hadn't exactly been hanging around since he arrived yesterday.

"Hand tremors. They came and went, and sometimes I wouldn't even notice them. Patrick made me see a doctor." He didn't seem to like bringing up Patrick. "Staying healthy and seriously exercising combats the symptoms. When you tax the muscles, they behave better. I have an exercise regimen."

She caught herself studying his hands, his legs, watching for the textbook tremors.

He caught her, his smile holding the rare quality of eternal reassurance. "Good days and bad days, Quinn. The way things are going around here, a bad one will pop up soon."

Oh, God. "So, being here isn't good for you?"

"Honey, I can't be anywhere without something interrupting the calm. Stress is, for lack of a better word, a stressor."

Quinn settled hands in her lap. People like her, on the outside looking in, probably looked for physical, mental, and lifetime limits. People like her uncle, afflicted, had to think how to live in the here and now, how to find quality of life, trying not to count down to an end.

He went back to rocking. "I retired but soon learned that being isolated worsens the symptoms. Memory issues can seem bigger if I dwell on them too long, and they get worse with some of the meds. Depression can happen. It was when they said get my affairs in order for downstream, however long that is, that I realized my home wasn't San Francisco." He let out a long breath. "I have no support system there. Friends, yes, but nobody willing to take this on. Family and potential caregivers? Again, nobody ready to catch me."

Quinn couldn't crawl in his lap like Glory, so she patted the bed for him to sit beside her. He did. Sweeping both arms around him, she laid her head on his shoulder, wishing to hell she could fix this.

He still called Sterling Banks his home. Their family was small, but it was all he had. Quinn had two uncles left in the bloodline. Two uncles and a cousin. The two of the three she loved most wanted to live with her. Or so she hoped.

"While I'm . . . sad about your diagnosis, Uncle Archie, I'm thrilled you brought your burden here. I hope it's here. I mean, under this roof." She wanted to say how quiet it got being alone in the big house, with the exception of the overnighters by Jonah. Hearing voices from someone other than some podcast on Alexa would be wonderful.

"I'm glad. Turns out Patrick worried more about my diagnosis than I did," Archie continued, "and that's saying a lot, Quinn. He got angry, he mourned, he obsessed on the internet. He started making plans for the both of us without consulting me, as if the day the doctor told me I had Parkinson's meant I no longer had the mental faculty to think for myself. We argued incessantly. About three months into things, he stormed out. Didn't come home for four days. Texted me that I'd see him when I saw him."

He took another breath, a shaky one, making her wonder if it was emotion or Parkinson's.

The word *asshole* came to Quinn's mind about Patrick. What a selfish prick. "Was that when he slept with someone else?" she asked, hoping she made this easier.

"Yes. They shared pills, drank, and he dragged home looking like hell saying he couldn't do this long-term caregiving thing. He couldn't handle watching me *deteriorate*. Managing an architectural firm, taking care of a child, and taking care of an invalid surpassed his abilities, he said."

"He was willing to give up Glory over this *deterioration*," she said with a pause and air quotes with her fingers.

The side of his mouth swept up. "Yeah. I felt like a fool."

"You? Why you?"

"I thought he had more substance than that, Quinn. I thought I had better taste in men."

Her phone dinged.

Jonah texted. *Come down, please. We found him.*

Chapter 17

"GO ON, THEY need you," Archie said, standing from the bed. "Enough of my story."

Quinn welcomed the pardon, but this conversation was far from over. "How long are you staying?"

"A week?" he said. "I'm open."

She took his hand and rose. "Good. I love you, Uncle, but Ty's situation is pretty dire."

"Go, go." He let loose of her, brushed the air, shooing. "I'll check on Glory and meet you downstairs. I'm on Team Ty, too."

She left him and scurried off. She came down the stairs noting nobody on the sofas, until she reached the bottom and found everyone hovered around her makeshift office in the far corner. Chairs had been pulled over, and while Jonah sifted through footage, Larry, Tassey, and Ty watched. Larry would point, then Ty. Jonah couldn't be enjoying the back-seat drivers to his efforts to piece together the start-to-finish movements of the trespasser, but that horde of onlookers had a lot of experience to draw from. Multiple sets of eyes couldn't hurt.

"Quinn's here," Ty said.

Jonah peered up. "Come on over. We see the guy, and it is a guy, but he recognized we had cams. We thought Bogie kept him out of the barn, but I believe he stood outside the doorway on purpose. Shadows and angles and the damn hat kept us from getting a clean view. Then we got this between here and the barn." He clicked and clicked, stopping. "He didn't expect the one on the tree." He adeptly isolated a piece of footage.

Quinn leaned over, a hand on Ty's shoulder. "Not a bad image."

Jonah scrolled more. "Then we studied the one I set low, here." There was the guy approaching, looking up, but the angle allowed them to see the man from a totally different view.

Quinn leaned further in. "Nice job, Jonah!"

In the violator's effort to hunt for cams he expected at the height and locales where cams usually were, he missed the one hidden in the shrubs, anchored on a lone fence post installed for a situation like this.

Jonah locked in on four stills, saving to a flash drive before sending them to Quinn's printer. He printed one of each for every person present, which by then included Archie.

The man paused in mid-step in the image Quinn studied. Dark hair, age late thirties to early forties, medium height and build, jeans, sneakers, and a windbreaker with an emblem on the left front breast. She had no clue who this was. "Any of y'all recognize him?" she asked.

Three no's from the sheriff, Ty, and Jonah, meaning he probably wasn't from Craven County. Tassey added her own negative, as if it mattered.

"He looks familiar," Archie said.

The whole crew turned attention on the man who barely knew a soul in the county anymore. Especially someone nobody else recognized.

Archie shrugged. "Can't place him, but he rings a bell. Maybe he's got a doppelganger in San Francisco, but I've seen him or someone close like him not too long ago."

With no conclusion to that, they moved on.

"Zoom in on the emblem," Quinn said.

Resolution somewhat blurry, Jonah printed it off, but upon closer examination and a united effort, they identified it. All but Archie had seen the ads on billboards and television. Absolute Landscaping. *When you want the Absolute best.*

"Add that to the other photos," Uncle Larry said. "And send them to the Colleton and Charleston police and sheriff departments. And the towns of Walterboro, Beaufort, and Ridgeland."

"Cottageville, Middleton . . ." Jonah added, emphasizing the smaller towns.

"Wouldn't hurt to send them to Beaufort, Jasper, Berkeley, and Dorchester counties, too," Ty said.

Tassey raised a hand. "Pump the brakes, y'all. Don't you think the Colleton Sheriff's Office should be contacted first before you spray these everywhere? Maybe they should even be the ones sending these out? And whose contact information do you put on there?"

Larry stood, his stature taking up room. "This crime happened in Craven County, on Sterling land, ma'am. We put my office's contact information on there. Nothing connects this man to Ty's case."

Tassey scrutinized him, blatantly so, unaccustomed to being second-guessed. "The man mentioned Ty and the murder."

"Which still doesn't give them jurisdiction," he countered.

Quinn wasn't sure she agreed with him. "Will you be sharing every-thing with Ty, Tassey, and me, Uncle?"

"Open investigation, Niece. Can't share."

She snatched the papers out of Larry's hand. "The hell if that's so. The murder investigation isn't yours, and this current crime happened on my property." Then a revelation flew into her head. "I'll send these to my FBI buddy in Charleston. With their facial recognition tools, maybe we'll luck up."

Jonah peered around, and she reined herself in. In the space of just a couple seconds, she'd slighted Larry for no longer being a key owner in Sterling Banks, and she'd rubbed her FBI contacts in his face. *Ouch.* The cat in her had leaped out when he threw that small-county weight around.

But this was not the time to count coup or be petty. She stopped short of refusing him the images, because the more help they had the better for Ty . . . and Sterling Banks security.

Larry's harrumph meant he'd probably cooperate. Quinn usually relied upon Ty to dance the dance between her as a PI and her uncle as the sheriff. Ty got her what she needed, and Uncle usually looked the other way, but Ty was benched at the moment.

Nothing stopped Quinn from placing strategic calls to her favorites in these police and sheriff's departments, and wouldn't hurt for Ty to make some of those calls to his fellow brothers and sisters in blue, too.

She'd contact Absolute Landscaping at first light. Nobody benched her. Telling them that someone caught on camera wore their wind-breaker while trespassing and had threatened children in the process might get her a name. No point mentioning Ty or the Natalie case.

Archie had silently stood back, and when everyone rose and dis-persed, he'd moved further, excluding himself from conversations. Quinn caught the split second of a razor-blade stare between her two uncles, then the breaking away and pretense of nothing having happened.

Add that to her list of future conversations.

Larry didn't hang for long, grumbling about having to jump on this trespasser situation and file his reports and spread the word to the other law-enforcement entities. Jule had long returned to her place, and Jonah left to check on her. Archie went upstairs to the kiddos. It was getting late.

Ty and Quinn saw Tassey to her vehicle, her saying the normal things about remaining quiet, not doing anything stupid . . . and nothing being over until it's over. Quinn assured them she wasn't waiting on

Larry. Quinn wasn't sure Ty heard a word.

Tassey's speculative gaze settled on Quinn. "Who hates *you* so much to murder Natalie and set up Ty to take the fall?"

Quinn tried to sound appalled. "Who says it's about me?"

"Don't bullshit a bullshitter, Miss Sterling. Despite his recent bad judgment, there's not a damn thing in Ty's history to merit this setup. There's gobs of reason in yours. Study the odds, Miss Ex-FBI-know-it-all."

"Not disputing those odds," Quinn said. "But nothing points to anyone in particular, and I don't know the guy on the footage."

Tassey accepted that. "I agree with your uncle now. We have two cases here, regardless how much we think they might be connected. We do not spill what we learn, you hear me? Let Colleton do their thing, and we'll do ours. Larry and the others don't need to hear my thoughts. Let them focus on their tasks. We'll focus on ours."

Quinn got that. "We can afford to pursue the what-ifs while they chase the concrete evidence."

"Exactly." Tassey reached for her door handle, her touch automatically releasing the lock. Quinn appreciated she'd locked her doors in the first place. She liked this woman more and more, so she put some cards on the table.

"You're aware of Ronald Renault, I take it."

"Why do you think I said what I said?"

Fine, Quinn got that, but she worried that someone as high-powered as Renault could still sabotage Ty's legal representation. Tassey didn't hold back on her, so why not ask the hard question. "Does Renault intimidate you, Tassey? I mean, he's a pretty powerful guy."

Ty looked at Tassey, waiting for the answer.

"No," came the reply. "You can't be an attorney at my level and get intimidated, by Renault or anyone else. Know your enemy. The name Renault only means I reassign my lesser cases to junior lawyers in the firm to open my calendar." But there was something unspoken about her.

"You aren't about to get rid of me, are you?" Quinn said. "Because of Renault?"

Tassey didn't answer, that stoicism of hers at play.

"You fire me as your investigator, and I'll keep working at it, regardless," Quinn warned.

"No, I'm not firing you." Tassey dragged out the words. "But between Renault's taste for vengeance and that red hair of yours, keep your head down. If he's involved, he'll expect you, and he can pay for enough feelers to see you coming."

The attorney changed gears. "Let me know what you find out about the landscape company. You and your motley crew need to dissect Natalie's life, too. Mainly post-Tyson Jackson. Her education, employment, finances, social media. Tear it apart, Quinn. The sheriff's office doesn't have the motivation you do. If I need to hire a second investigator, tell me soon."

"Not needed," Quinn said. Not yet, anyway. Not with Ty and Larry and Larry's deputies at her disposal. Tassey would hire a Charleston PI if she hired anyone, and Quinn had suspicions that Renault had already tainted a lot of them. Money spoke in that world, too.

"Get to work, people." Tassey eased into her Lexus, backed out, and left.

The further Tassey drove, the more a new reality set in. What started out as wrong place and wrong time for Ty, had turned into a setup going so far as to ruin Cole as a witness.

Watching the taillights leave the property, Quinn could feel Ty through the arm she held onto. He was down. He was worried about his son. He struggled seeing his way out of this.

Quinn scoured her brain for what to do now, meaning tonight. "What time is it?" she said, turning the big man back toward the house. "We haven't eaten."

"I'm fucked, Q. Purely, unadulterated fucked."

The f-bomb wasn't in Ty's vocabulary—more frequently in hers. The uphill climb to clear him stared them both down. A very tall, avalanche-ridden, greased rope, uphill climb. "Let's go back inside," she said, unsure what else to do, though standing around feeling sorry wasn't doing anyone a damn bit of good.

She took him in and sat him at the kitchen table before pulling out leftovers from the refrigerator. In two minutes, they each had a plate of food, but Ty acted as if it weren't there.

"My own son could crucify me on the stand," Ty said, taking the fork handed to him only to rest it on the plate. "I can't let them interrogate him, Q. Little man's so mixed up right now. He would grow up torn about putting me in jail while hating me because he thinks I killed his mother." Elbows on the table, he lowered his head in his hands, staring at the plate's edge.

She gently pried his hands away, then lifting her own fork, she pointed to his food. "Eat. We're not at that stage yet." She went back to her meal, and on second thought repointed her fork at him. "You're staying here tonight." She wasn't letting him be alone, not in this state of mind. His sanity begged for the Sterling Banks support system.

Support system. She'd spoken of that with Archie. How sad to move cross country for a support system, particularly after learning that after having lived so long someplace else you had none.

Which in turn made her think of Glory. Her father ill, her other father gone, and a stranger threatening her. That was a lot to toss at a seven-year-old. Quinn cringed that some faceless man had recognized who she was on Sterling Banks, which was supposed to be a safe haven.

People knew Cole and people knew Glory, but nobody was familiar with both . . . except people who had met them on the Fourth. There was no way to sift through all of them.

Her mind shot immediately to Patrick, but she quickly discounted him. He didn't know Ty, much less Cole. Archie hadn't known Cole before yesterday.

Wescott merited research, but he'd have little to no clue of Archie and none of Glory.

Broken loops.

"Not sure I'll be able to sleep, regardless where," Ty said. His food sat untouched. Sitting at the table picking at cold baked beans wasn't solving a thing.

"I doubt I'll be sleeping much either," she said.

But he didn't act as if he'd heard. "Can't stay with Cole. Not in his present state of mind. Not even sure I ought to be in the house. Maybe I'll go to Momma's—"

"No," Quinn said. "She has a restaurant to run, and you'd feel obliged to help her like you always do, but you cannot be seen in public right now." She palmed his chin to make him look at her. "Stay here. If you're worried about Lenore, she's welcome, too."

"Momma'll be better where she is," he said, twisting his head out of her touch. "I can't stay in this house, not with Cole here. Think Jule will put me up at her place? That lets me still be close."

"Of course she will." Best solution for all of them. Her fingers had typed the text before she finished the sentence.

Jonah's reply was instant. *Send him whenever he's ready.*

Might be late, she texted back.

Give him your key, he answered. *Love you.*

Quinn pushed back from the table, taking both plates. "Come on. You're staying on the farm not only tonight, but as long as it takes. Cole may not want you right now, but you crave Cole. We must vouch for your every move until this deal is over. You hear me?"

She dumped dishes in the sink and returned to the living room to her business corner. She found scribbles on notes left behind from the others, but none of them told her anything she didn't already know. "Pull up a chair. We got work to do."

Tassey was right. Time to delve into Natalie's history. Might take no time and might take hours, but she had Ty at her side to feed her information and expedite that effort.

The obvious next step was to tear into the name David Wescott of Charleston. Ty had already started down that path so he could be of help there, too.

Then she'd send him to bed and delve into all the other people in apartment building F. She couldn't believe these people weren't more aware of Nat and Wescott and their comings and goings. She'd explore their lives thoroughly, too.

Then tomorrow she'd rise early. Charleston was an hour away, and landscapers started work before dawn with summer being a busy season. She didn't care to chase the owner of Absolute Landscape from job to job all over the county.

Ty would hopefully sleep in.

She typed Natalie's name and social security number into one of her databases. Ty keenly watched as the screen populated. "May I?" he asked, taking the mouse. She let him. He needed to feel useful, and he would recognize the correct information, the erroneous information, and the fresh information they needed to take note of. As a trained deputy with a modicum of investigatory experience under his belt, he had some skills.

Then a thought struck her. Tonight Ty and Jonah would be at Jule's. Cole and Glory would be upstairs, probably in the same bedroom tonight. Quinn would be up before anyone and gone.

Was Archie up to being the responsible adult for both Cole and Glory in that small window after Quinn left and before others arrived? Or was Quinn horrible for thinking him disabled? Patrick, in similar manner, had treated Archie as incapable of making decisions.

Maybe she ought to discreetly text Jule and ask her to come over when Quinn left in the morning.

Crap, that made her feel like a heel about Archie. No. If he couldn't take care of the kids, he'd say so. After all, he'd traveled cross country with Glory.

So this is what it's like juggling family.

"Quinn," Ty said, flipping screen to screen. "Not seeing anything that jumps at me."

"Glad you're sifting through it rather than me. I'd be ten times longer."

"You're feeding me work to keep me occupied," he said, his attention still parked on the screen.

"Guilty as charged," she said. "But I'm not lying that your knowledge beats mine about Natalie."

"Hmmm." The mouse's small clicks sounded loud with the room devoid of people.

He continued for an hour through several databases Quinn subscribed to, her logging him in and satisfied to watch beside him as he scrutinized his ex-wife's history. "Wish we had her phone and computer," he said.

"Might have somebody working on that," she said, wondering how long before she could justify calling Raysor, wondering whether or not to honor her promise not to call him before he called her. However, he'd had but a few hours to work on this. She had to give him a couple days. Two days felt like an eternity, though.

"We could check her credit report," he said, his voice almost signaling a question.

She reached over and pulled up a free credit report site. "You're right. She's deceased. Did she have a will?"

"Yeah. She worked for an attorney's firm. They convinced her how important it was after having Cole. They did it for free."

Quinn keyed in Natalie's email and social and handed over the mouse to Ty for the identifying questions. "Who's executor of her estate?"

"I am," he said. "Unless she made changes I'm not aware of, but obviously I get Cole, and she didn't have much else to bequeath nor others to bequeath to."

"That's what I thought." She nudged him. "As executor, it's actually your responsibility to prevent identity theft which happens a lot from crooks reading the obits. Go on and let's see what's there."

He hovered the mouse, as if on the brink of entering forbidden territory. "Wait. If I'm found guilty of killing her, I probably can't inherit like the will says which nixes me being executor, too. Doing this might not look good."

"You have not been found guilty, Old Man. You haven't even been charged. It's the responsible thing to do."

Yet he hesitated.

"I took care of Daddy's will and estate, Ty. I know this stuff. Do it."

With Ty's knowledge of Nat, they opened the account and in a half-dozen steps entered the site.

"Emails will show up in her account about having done this," he warned. "Someone in Colleton SO might see."

"Jesus, Ty." She took the mouse from him and clicked through. "Look. Do you see anything new or unexpected?"

He squinted.

She noticed. "You needing reading glasses now? Want me to make the font larger?"

"That's not it. There. The apartment address is correct, but what's that other one?"

Quinn clicked and copied the address then opened another screen, doing a lookup for it. "It's a UPS Store in Charleston." Puzzled she leered sideways at him. "What's that about?"

"Damned if I know. David Wescott is from Charleston, though," he said.

"Finally, something to sink our teeth into." She wrapped her arms around his muscular one and squeezed. "Keep going."

He scrolled and quickly stopped. "She banked with Enterprise Bank in Walterboro, and has since high school. She has two credit cards with small balances. Her car is paid for."

"Pretty thrifty then," Quinn said, trying for positive. "And she was on time with her rent."

Ty stopped. "Wait, she has an online bank account. One of those without-brick-and-mortar branches. I've heard of this one."

"Heck, I have one of those, Ty. Their interest rates are friggin' awesome compared to the traditional banks."

"She never had that before." He swiveled his chair toward Quinn. "She had no need for that, nor a Charleston address."

"And now we have something," she said again.

He gave a wan smile at having a crack in the case. A tiny one but one, nonetheless.

But he would see Nat as the victim. The credit bureau had the wrong person. Maybe someone with the same name had the bank account, and it wasn't hers. There were a lot of Jacksons.

Yes, she was the victim in terms of being the murdered party, but Quinn wondered what if she'd gotten caught up in something that would label her more a perpetrator? What if she'd pursued something she shouldn't have and paid a price rubbing elbows with the wrong sorts?

The woman had a secret address and a secret bank account. She wasn't selling homemade products on Etsy nor writing romance novels on the side. Natalie was a legal secretary. Those people weren't dummies, but they weren't rich either.

Ty saw his son's mother as decent, focused, and hardworking— never crossing a line. Quinn, however, had to study the clean and the dirty angles.

If Nat needed a post office box, what was wrong with Walterboro? And even if she did earn money on the side, why not have a second account at the bank that knew her?

If Natalie hadn't been such a close part of Ty's life once upon a time, and if she were somebody unrelated and an arm's-length case, he'd take a stronger stance in considering the clandestine, possibly undesirable, side of Nat.

But she was and he wasn't, and Quinn had to keep reminding herself that he wasn't a hundred percent himself.

She could tell Ty that Natalie might have a dark side, but he wouldn't listen. To think that meant he'd shirked responsibility for his son or hadn't been shrewd enough to notice.

Quinn might need to investigate further in solo mode. They'd shared their lives as if they were each other's shadows, but to preserve that friendship *and* save Ty's neck, she'd have to investigate first and share with him later. Assuming he had a need to know.

Sometimes secrets were necessary. Sometimes secrets were in the best interest of love.

Chapter 18

QUINN'S GRANDMOTHER'S crystal mantel clock rang midnight. "Time you went to bed, Ty. I won't be far behind you. Let me get the key to Jule's place—"

"Her social media," Ty said, ignoring the advice. "She wasn't heavy on it, but she was on Facebook and Instagram."

Quinn had hoped to do this alone, this delving into tangents that Ty might not like nor care to think about. "Start with Facebook," she said. "How tight did she have her security on it?"

He lightly chuckled. "It was wide open. She lived life like she had . . ."

"Nothing to hide?" Quinn finished his sentence, not giving him time to feel sheepish, and flipped into Natalie's page. She'd used her real name Natalie Jackson, and her real home in Walterboro, South Carolina.

Last post was two days before she died. The same day Ty had met with Becca, Nat had come home from work and visited the neighbor as well. The post was a selfie of the two of them in Becca's living room with a comment about how rare true-blue friends were.

"That woman told Nat about my coming by," Ty said.

"Yup," Quinn replied. "Meaning Becca told you what Nat wanted you to hear and no more."

Ty watched the screen. "Also meaning we don't know if she broke up with Gabriel, aka David Wescott, or not. We don't know if the story about Gabriel lying to Nat was even true."

Good. Hopefully he was becoming more open minded. "Right."

"She might've really been meaning to leave with him, not even knowing his real name," he concluded.

Seriously?

Quinn snapped fingers inches from his nose. "Ty, come on, man. For God's sake, she knew his name. She may have opened that account in Charleston because she was very much aware he lived there. Maybe she was moving there. Maybe the online account hid her mad money, or Christmas money, or vacation money."

"She couldn't afford vacations," he said, expression darkening.

"But what if she could? A side hustle maybe? Overtime? It wasn't like she didn't have babysitters at the apartment."

He glowered. "I'd know if she had that kind of money."

"We don't even know what *that kind of money* is. Consider the possibility that you weren't clued into her reality, Old Man." Quinn went back to the posts. No point accusing him of being short-sighted. No point in fueling a fight. He had to come to terms on his own with Nat's life not being an open book to him, and Quinn pushing him to do so wasn't the way. But she'd planted the seed. Hopefully he'd grow into the truth.

Nat posted three to four times a week, nothing much. She preserved routine moments such as activities with friends and Cole mostly, and the occasional motivational quote. Selfies hugging Cole were common, accompanied by posts of how proud she was of him. She beamed in a shot of her receiving a letter of appreciation from the firm where she worked. More pics of Becca, which seemed to happen when Cole wasn't around, jiving with what Becca had said.

After more scrolling, up rolled a picture of an outdoor gathering, and Quinn detected the buildings as the apartment complex. From the short sleeves on people, the weather was warm, the date May 25, Memorial Day.

"I assume you had Cole that weekend?" she asked.

"Yep," he replied, scouring the picture. "Make it bigger."

There had to be twenty people in the photo, gathered in the wooded area where two outdoor grills cooked away with two men, including the apartment manager, tending with aprons on. Nat posed in the foreground with Becca and others.

"That's David Wescott," Ty said, pointing to the man about four feet behind and over from Natalie. He slid the driver's license photo of the man from his back pocket. "Look."

Sure enough it was him. He wasn't in any sort of romantic pose with Nat, but he looked admiringly at her as she flirted with the camera. None of the neighbors said they'd laid eyes on him yet there sat several of them, picnicking away with him in their midst.

Ty leaned elbows on the desk, a finger rubbing his temple in slow motion, silently taking in the event.

"What do you see?" Quinn asked, wanting to know where his head was.

"Someone I'm not sure I knew," he mumbled.

She patted him softly on the back. "And this is why we do not investigate cases close to us."

"So what do you see that I don't?" he countered.

He was hurting. She wished she could stop the pain.

"I see Natalie attending a cookout like everyone else. Wescott is there, probably as her date. He seems to like her. She's having fun. Honestly, I don't read her any differently than I did before." Her rub turned into a light scratching of his shoulder blade, something he used to like as a teen. "You're angry, Ty. Angry that you were on the outside looking in. Angry that she didn't confide in you. Angry that you may have done something to no longer warrant her trust. If you'd been aware of everything, you might have saved her somehow. That about cover it?"

"More or less."

"More rather than less, I take it. Anyway, look at this one." She found another picture from that same day and expanded it. About a dozen people this time, under the trees. People held glasses, some at picnic tables with remnants of chips and burgers on red paper plates, with lots of laughter, most likely generated from the contents of the plastic cups.

"There's that couple I met," she said, pointing at Troy and Tee, the wife drunk judging by the loopy drape over her husband. "And Frannie Bean." The nosy neighbor posed mid-scowl with a repulsed expression at Tee's antics. Natalie watched smiling from a table, Becca beside her. No sign of Wescott. Maybe the picture taker.

"Quinn," Ty said, warning in his tone. "Bigger."

"Wescott isn't on there, Ty." She expanded the pic enough not to lose resolution, studying hard for what Ty thought he saw. A shockwave coursed through her as an image smacked her between the eyes. Not six feet from Frannie Bean was a man against a tree, soberly watching Tee's antics.

"Son of a bitch, that's him," she said. "That's the guy from the goat barn, Ty!"

"Print it," he said. "Several copies. First thing in the morning, I'm heading—"

"Nope," she said, hitting keys, the printer clicking as it caught the job then spit out copies. "That's my job. You think anyone's gonna talk to you at those apartments? You think this guy is not going to see you coming?" She grabbed pages off the printer. "You don't see how you can easily make this worse?"

He spun on her. "You own Sterling Banks. He trespassed on your place. Are you telling me he won't see you coming either? He might not even live there. Could be a guest like Wescott."

She took a huge inhale, exaggerated for him to take note of. "Doesn't matter who he is or how he got there, you are a person of interest in a murder, Ty. I've already broken the ice with people at the apartments. I'd be expected. You won't, and they'll be scared silly to see you much less talk to you. Let me do this, okay? Let's not give them a reason to hang anything else on your head."

While he sulked, his silence showing he agreed, Quinn flipped into her email and shot the two social media photos, the cam photos, and a scan of the driver's license pic to her FBI friend in Charleston. Agent Knox had known her when she worked for the Bureau, and had been known to do her a favor or two. Up until he learned of Jonah's recent claim to Quinn, he'd done the favors for dinner dates. Some he got and some he didn't. He kept offering to endorse her if she reapplied to her old job, but she couldn't run Sterling Banks and be an agent at the same time.

A day didn't go by that she wasn't bittersweet about that.

Ty watched her and recognized the agent's name. He'd actually met the man during a visit he and Quinn had made, asking for one of those favors. "We going to talk to him?"

We.

"No. He'll call and tell me if he can help," she said. "I'll inform you when he does."

But she wasn't informing him of much else, frankly.

Who could blame Ty for wanting to stay involved. It's what they did, the two of them partnering cases. What she knew he validated, or vice versa. It was eerie how their logic balanced.

Unaccustomed to sitting on the sidelines, Ty would leap at the chance to pursue someone, something, anything, but he couldn't, or rather he shouldn't. He didn't have the compartmentalization tools he'd need to investigate without drawing upon the past, mixing in the Natalie he'd loved, the Natalie he thought he knew, with the secret Natalie coming out with all these new warts and foibles. And they'd only been investigating an hour. What more would they find the deeper they dug?

Or rather, the deeper *Quinn* dug. He'd make an even bigger mess if more Natalie secrets spilled out. He wouldn't handle well her having a covert life.

All he'd do was get frustrated and prove he possessed the emotional trigger to kill her.

She let him do more searching in Instagram which basically

duplicated Facebook. Any time a reel came up showing Nat moving, laughing, talking, he got stuck a bit, replaying it at least twice. Seeking intel, he said. Quinn did nothing to shake him loose.

He'd be better off in bed, leaving Quinn to her solo sleuthing. This emotional struggle exhausted him more than he already was. By one a.m., he looked ragged.

"That's it for the night," she said, powering down the desktop. "We aren't thinking clearly."

He didn't argue. Instead he stood, then held her chair. She smiled up at him in thanks and stood. Then as she turned, he stopped her and drew her to him. Instinctively, she hugged him back, feeling his hurt. He laid his head on her shoulder and glued himself there. Her heart swelled and ached at him needing this so badly.

He exceeded six feet, his bulk broad, but she was a tall woman, only three inches shorter than he. With a squeeze she told him she was there for him, as long as he needed. It took about twenty seconds before she felt the quiver then the warmth against her collarbone.

Ty made no sound as he cried, but he did. She cuddled him closer. Nobody was here to see him weep, and she cooed to him, "I'll be here for you, Ty. I'll do whatever it takes to make this right."

Finally he pulled back. Before Quinn could give him her best reassuring smile, he covered her mouth with his, hard.

Mashing against her, he took that kiss as far as he could, as if he had to taste her while he had the chance.

A tsunami of emotions crashed over her, drowning her in the unexpected, confusing her about the right and the wrong, the psychological need versus . . . whatever else this was. Her rationality told her to let him have this. He was broken. He was adrift. He had divorced Natalie and no longer loved her, yet felt responsible.

So many rushing thoughts . . . but then she realized she'd let him have that kiss for a while, then another. And one more.

Finally he came up for a breath, and in pulling back seemed to justify the action. He snared her in close again. "I need you, Q," he whispered, forehead against hers. "More than any other time in our lives, I need you."

Their swims in the river, their secret huddles in the tree house as kids. The pretend mysteries they solved in the grove, and the real ones they pursued as deputies, then later when she returned as a PI. They'd kissed once in high school. They'd danced at more social affairs than she could name, his claiming the slow ones more often than Jonah with the joke being Ty was the much better dancer.

Jesus . . . Jonah.

Weeks ago, Ty had given his blessing to her being with Jonah, even pushing her toward him, saying Jonah had it bad for her and Ty wanted her to be happy. She sensed his reservation at the time, but then judged him as noble.

"Ty," she started, then couldn't decide what to say.

"I know." He wrapped those large bulky arms around her, claiming his feelings and daring to look at her. "I have no right to push my desires on you. I told you . . ." Again, his head rested against her as the eye contact appeared too painful. "But I want you."

Pulse doing triple time, she scrambled for what to say, at the same time worried why she was so disturbed, so cautious, so moved . . . so drawn. So afraid to tell him no. More afraid to tell him yes.

If she pushed him back, she best have something profound to say, something highly definitive as to where this was meant to go, but the words jumbled like bingo balls, nothing coming together in any order.

She gently eased him arm's length, and he released his hold, waiting.

"You're under stress, Ty. We're tired. Go to bed," she softly said.

He waited for more, needing more of an interpretation of what they were doing.

Think of Jonah sat on the end of her tongue, when steps sounded on the stairs.

Quinn darted back and around. Ty remained in place, hands withdrawn to his front jeans pockets.

"Couldn't sleep," Archie said, his movements feigning innocence, his gaze at his feet telling Quinn otherwise.

"Tea in the fridge and the coffee maker at the ready," she said. "Oh, and goat's milk for either. The only way we drink coffee around here."

Archie didn't ask what they were doing up so late. Quinn wished he would. "We were in my databases checking for intel on Natalie and the guy she supposedly dated."

"Too late for me to be thinking that hard," he said. "I just can't sleep. Must be the strange setting."

"I hope it's not too strange for you, Uncle."

He'd reached the bottom and headed toward the kitchen. "Just different," he said. "And things have been crazy," he added over his shoulder. "You two go on with whatever it was you were doing. Don't mind me. Be out of your hair in two minutes." He disappeared in the kitchen.

Quinn scrubbed palms over her eyes and down over her mouth. "Ty—"

A grip on her arm spun her back into his grasp, and again she found his lips on hers. A more affectionate embrace this time. Sweet, gentle, shooting current down her, into her, spiraling around her . . . confusing her.

But not confused enough not to kiss him back. He was as familiar as a brother, but they'd parted being brother and sister years ago. They hadn't crossed any romantic lines, before or after the divorce with Natalie, so why now?

"Losing Nat made me see how giving you away was a mistake. I can't lose you, too."

Damn you, Old Man. "Ty . . ."

"Don't talk," he said.

But they had to talk. This was wrong.

They say danger is an aphrodisiac. So why wasn't she sold on that right now?

They separated, he as much as she this time, his taking in a couple deep breaths. Quinn took one of her own then turned and listened for Archie. The downstairs sounded like a church on Monday. Holding up a finger for Ty to stay where he was, she eased to the kitchen, stutter-stepping at the realization the lights were out.

Archie'd already gone upstairs. There was no climbing those steps without taking in a full view of them.

Instinct told her to whirl on Ty and blister him for initiating all this. Damn him. Damn Natalie, too. But she couldn't. The friend in her said let him be but keep him out of the investigation. Keeping him out of jail drove all of them right now. To chastise him for a slip would send him to bed thinking he had nothing left in this world.

From behind her, big hands brushed up and down her arms, and his voice came in low and easy from over her shoulder. "Sorry, Quinn. Where's the key to Jule's?"

"I'll get it." Not wanting to see him, she slipped out from under his touch to the kitchen, lifted the chain off its hook, and returned to drop the key into Ty's hand without missing a step on the way to her desk in the corner.

He left through the sliding glass door, into the grove, toward the other house.

She returned to one of her subscription identity services, but she couldn't make out much more than headers and titles, the print blurred.

Betrayed by her feelings, Quinn snatched a tissue out of a box on an end table, then on second thought, grabbed the box. Blowing her nose like a snorting buck in the woods, she cleared away the tears and refused to cry. Still took her three tries to put in Frannie Bean Salvador's name and Walterboro, South Carolina, but finally she did. Before the night was over, she'd acquaint herself with these apartment people inside and out.

She snatched another tissue and blew her nose again. "Last sniffle," she said, hitting the keyboard as if the keys had misbehaved.

An hour later, she'd emptied the box, nose sore and eyes raw and blinking hard, but she'd soldiered through half the names in building F. She'd learned who had parking tickets, who'd been arrested, who'd been divorced, and who had lied to her earlier today.

She wasn't sure she had it in her to do the rest. Her body could slink to the floor right where she was and go comatose; she was that tired. But she wasn't sure her brain or her conscience would let her off the hook that easily and give her the couple hours of dreamless sleep she craved.

Trouble was, she would dream. For sure she'd dream, and either Jonah or Ty would be in it.

Going back to the apartments in the morning didn't mean rising as early as she'd planned when she thought she was going to Absolute Landscape, but she hadn't the courage to stick around the manor long. There was something about sitting across the breakfast table from Archie, from Ty, especially Jonah and even Jule that made her want to rise with the sun and miss the awkwardness she couldn't explain.

She laid her head on her forearms on the desk, fighting the foreboding.

Someone gently shook her shoulders. "Quinn, wake up. You didn't sleep here, did you?"

Throat parched and eyes puffy, she fought to roust herself, the stiffness in her upper back not making it any easier.

"Quinn?"

She straightened, neck creaky, wiping her face, hoping nobody noticed all the tissues in the trash can.

Jonah chuckled in empathy. "Pardon me, Princess, but you look like crap. What the heck did you do last night?"

Chapter 19

"WHAT TIME IS IT?" Quinn said, slowly coming to. Taken aback by the gruffness in her voice, she sniffled hard once and cleared her throat.

Jonah bent at the waist and pushed hair from her face. "Seven. Damn, honey, how late did you work?"

Stiffly, she moved a bone at a time, testing the cricks from being so long in one position . . . hiding her guilt about Ty behind the motions. "Last time I looked at the clock it was after three. You said six?"

"Seven," he repeated.

Leaping up, she had enough of her bearings now to grab papers off the printer. "Gotta run. Was supposed to be gone by now!" She slipped him a kiss on the cheek, scurried past, and took the stairs two at a time to avoid his seeing the heat in her cheeks. He stood in the same place Ty had kissed her. And kissed her some more.

Took her twenty minutes to shower and dress, falling back on her best go-to khaki slacks and a cream short-sleeved blouse. Her long, wet hair would take an eternity to dry, so she braided it quickly in one long rope that reached between her shoulder blades. Her mother's pink-and-brown paisley cotton scarf lay in a puddle in a corner chair, along with scarves, hair bobs and socks from the past week. She tied it loosely under the collar of her shirt. Donning the closest boots to her grasp, she was off.

Jonah was outside, about to get into his pickup when she entered the garage. "Hey, you're like on fire. What'd you find out to help our man?" he said, speaking from twenty feet away.

"Gotta to talk to some people," she said. "I'll be in Walterboro." She halted before getting in. "Do *not* let him leave this farm this time this time. You hear?"

"How many people am I officially babysitting?"

But she acted as if she hadn't heard, got in and took off, offering a quick wave on her way up the drive.

Her pulse ran faster than she cared to admit. She could admit, however, that she'd dodged her almost-fiancé and would have to confront him later. She could keep quiet. Question was whether Archie could. The bigger question was Ty. He was almost too honest to be a cop, and Quinn wasn't sure he could hide last night from Jonah.

The three of them had been besties all their lives. She couldn't decide if he'd tell Jonah to clear his conscience or to truly try and win her. Or if he'd keep a secret and run around looking sheepish.

She drove five miles before she realized it, wondering if she should've stayed behind and dealt with the situation. Dealing meaning talk with Ty and assure him last night was an anomaly. She wasn't up to breaking Jonah's heart. She was damn sure not up for her two best friends facing off over her, or, worse, making her choose between the two.

She'd convinced herself months ago that Jonah had beat out Ty by at least a length. Nobody questioned her feelings for both men, many women calling her lucky, some thinking she'd already slept with both. Discussing future with Jonah, dancing around banter of marriage with him during pillow talk, felt safe. She loved him, and he was crazy nuts about her.

But she had love for Ty as well, and if something happened to Jonah, she'd be all over Ty. Question was, was that wrong?

God, she thought she was over this conflict when Ty gave his blessing. She never imagined his taking it back.

She drove by a state road sign several miles out doing ten under the speed limit, people heading to work lined up a dozen cars behind her. She slowed at the next drive, a dirt road of an old wood-siding home place, and stopped.

Five minutes after eight. Not only was it a little early to be knocking on doors, but she had another stop she ought to make beforehand. God, she wasn't thinking.

Once the traffic passed her, she backed into the highway and returned the other direction, almost from whence she came, only into town. Her next stop was Jacksonboro, not Walterboro. Sheriff Larry Sterling warranted a visit. She'd waste little time doing so, bring him up to date on the pictures, and see what assistance he could offer. In and out. She prayed he was at work on time for a change.

Ten minutes later, she pulled into the parking lot of the law enforcement complex, an attractive blond-brick, one-story affair paid for by federal grant funds since Craven was notoriously underserved and under the poverty line on so many levels. Craven was too small to offer commercial industry enough tax breaks to make it worthwhile to locate to the small county. Even Colleton was wealthier, and, of course,

Charleston reigned as queen bee of the Lowcountry.

Carla perked up as Quinn walked through the door. A throwback to the eighties, the main receptionist and gatekeeper had a weak spot for Quinn, a known fact that the sheriff had come to live with since Carla's inherent knowledge of the county and its last thirty years of mischief and mayhem was priceless. Word had it she'd dated the sheriff once upon a time, but nobody dared confirm. Would've bothered him way more than her.

"Ooooh, look at you," Carla said, tapping a pen on her desk in triple time. She dropped it and got up. "Turn around and let me see how you did your hair."

Carla held an incessant fascination of Quinn's thick, curly red mane, a stark contrast to her own thin light brown, though the fluff and puff of what she did to it went far in catching attention. Her earrings rarely hung less than three inches, and she'd perfected and nailed mall bangs since before Quinn was alive.

"You were born looking good, girl," Carla said, returning her ample backside to its seat.

Though eager to get back on the road, Quinn played the game. It's how she maintained a jovial, inside relationship with the staff, plus she liked Carla. Quinn had them all feeling sorry for her because she was related to the sheriff. "Carla, if I ever need uplifting, I know where to come. I'm digging the key necklace. Is that vintage or new?"

Carla's giggle had an alto tone to it. "Vintage, baby. Wore it in high school."

"You're amazing," Quinn replied. "My uncle in or is it too early?"

"Just got in." Carla leaned forward, bust on her forearms, pencil back waving in her fingers. "Not in the best mood, in case that matters."

Quinn shrugged. "Since when is he in a good one? Mind if I scoot to his office?"

Carla shrugged back. "No appointments. He can't fuss at me for that. Can't promise he won't at you though."

Letting herself through the swinging door, Quinn chuckled at her. "Well, he can, not that it would do him any good. Thanks, girl."

Various deputies and admin staff gave her hellos, easing close enough to tell her to tell Ty they're thinking of him. Each offered to be there for him, he only had to call.

Everyone was familiar with the sheriff's niece and her carte-blanche access, often in the name of a recent case, most often ending in a huff and puff and a clash with the big man. They were also aware of how close she was to Tyson Jackson.

The deputy she liked least tipped his head as if he doffed a hat. The one who helped Larry bring Ty in. "Hey, Quinn."

He didn't ask about Ty. Nobody ever said he was smart.

"Harrison," she said in passing. *Ass wipe,* she thought.

The only deputy she'd bedded, having regretfully learned the next morning he was getting married that day. Though it had happened years ago, he never failed to flirt.

The long hall smelled of strong cheap coffee. Her boot heels clicked against the linoleum, and when she rounded the corner, down the hall she spotted the sheriff's door wide open. She knocked, nonetheless. "You got a second?"

Larry Sterling looked up from reading his morning emails, cup still steaming in his left hand. He waved her in with the other. He wasn't as grumpy as Carla had warned. Holding up his cup, he motioned with it toward the hall. "I'm sure there's some left."

"I'm fine," she said, taking one of two seats across from his desk.

"Everyone doing all right out there?" He then took a long sip. Putting the cup down, he asked, "The kids okay?"

"Everyone was still in bed when I left, except Jonah, of course. Left Archie with the kids."

He clicked his cheek, not her favorite of his many habits.

"They don't come any better than Jonah," he said. "I'll be glad when he puts a ring on your hand. Sterling Banks would be—"

"We need to talk about what happened yesterday," she said, not comfortable discussing Jonah right now. She laid out the two Facebook photos on his desk blotter. He already had the cam pics.

He leaned over, the desk pushing in his tie. He wasn't an overweight man, but there wasn't anything fit about him either. His Sterling height kept him from looking fat.

Lifting a photo as if to see it better, he then reached into his pocket to retrieve readers, putting them on to try again. From his top drawer, he pulled out the cam picture, laying it by the two Quinn brought. "Where'd you get these?" he asked, darkening and quite serious.

"Stayed up half the night researching Natalie Jackson," she said. "Found it on her Facebook page."

"I hate social media," he said under his breath, and returned to examining the pics.

Ordinarily, as was their custom, in response she'd toss out something about her being a PI in the current century and him being a dinosaur, but it was too early. She wasn't in the mood with Ty on the line. "Pretty sure that's our trespasser," she said.

Larry didn't disagree. "Name?" he asked, peering over his glasses.

"Not yet," she said. "Sent it to the FBI in the hope their face-recognition program can help. Whether they can get to my request today, if at all, is anyone's guess. Right now I'm headed to Walterboro to talk to the people I do know in those pictures. They might identify him quicker than the FBI."

He lifted the pics again. "Why would a guy like this take the risk of trespassing on Sterling Banks?"

She wasn't sure what *a guy like this* meant. "I hope I can find that out. Can you see what you can find on Wescott?" She laid the driver's license copy on the desk.

With that photo she was in essence asking him to delve into the Colleton County case. "They're connected. Have to be," she said. "However, I don't trust that sheriff's office to look much further than Ty on the Natalie murder."

He grimaced at her. "They're more professional than that, Quinn."

"Maybe, maybe not," she said. "I can't afford to sit back and rely on them to cover all bases. I'll learn soon enough what to think when I go back to Natalie's apartment and talk to her neighbors again. I also might check in with someone at Colleton County and see if they've delved very far into Wescott. He's the ex-boyfriend who Natalie dumped."

Sitting back and removing his readers, Larry studied her. "You can't afford to piss them off."

"I'm not striding in and making demands, Uncle. Besides, I have a source." She hoped Raysor was her source.

Larry nudged the photos. "You ought to be sharing these with them, to be honest. At least with your source. You'll be in their good graces if you do."

"I'm not so sure," she said.

"You don't think they check social media, too? Hell, I'd even have someone check it."

"Yet here I am showing the pics to you." Her skin prickled at the scent of opposition. One never could count Larry Sterling on one's side.

"Then no need for the talk," she said, jaw a little tight. "Ought to be interesting to see what they do with what they find."

He sighed and cleared morning phlegm, swallowing some more coffee to assist. "They aren't aware of the trespasser or the fact he was at the same event as Wescott. Tell them."

Yes, sharing was common sense if you assumed cops did everything right and they assumed everyone innocent until proven guilty. Didn't take long at Quantico to learn otherwise. Didn't take long as a PI to hammer it home. Sometimes the easiest to charge went down for the crime.

In other words, this conversation amounted to nothing more than to do their investigation for them, then trust them to take the results and use them properly. No, sir. No way. Ty was more important than that. There was a reason you hired an attorney when the cops looked sideways at you.

She'd stiffened and realized he'd irritated her. Took longer than normal this time, but he'd done it.

Last night he'd claimed the trespasser a Craven County case. Today he sends Quinn to Colleton with it. He'd slept on the matter, realizing the case made for effort he didn't want to waste. Like water seeking level, he was avoiding work as he was known to do.

Or in his brain, was his suggestion in Ty's best interest?

Ty was becoming more than a person of interest . . . he was a friggin' target. "You're suggesting the defense show its poker hand to the opposing player, Uncle."

"This isn't cards." His grumble showed he was willing to take her on.

"This is Ty, remember."

"This is a murder investigation, whoever's involved."

"Don't start," she replied. "Don't make me talk about your track record with murder investigations." She stopped short of saying he had not a damn clue how to handle one. She'd solved several for him, and he'd yet to accept the fact.

A deep crease showed in the rise of his brow. "You came to me for assistance, Niece. Yet you still bring attitude."

"Habit. Sorry." Lots of truth there. "But I'm sitting here only because Ty isn't on duty to help me instead."

His eyes narrowed. The unspoken had been said. Ty accessed official property to aid a private PI. "I could fire him for what you said."

"Don't feign ignorance with me. He's always fed me information, and he wouldn't do it if you weren't aware." Fire him? Ty was the best uniform in the county, hands down. "You wouldn't dare."

Narrow-eyed, he weighed what to say. "Don't back me in a corner, Niece."

He casually leaned back in his chair. "I'll give you a second to rein yourself in, while I get me another cup of coffee." He left the room, leaving the door open.

It was all she could do not to walk out that door, trying not to let her boot heels make any noise on the way out.

Chapter 20

DAMN IT. QUINN regretted her temper, but it was too natural for her
to go up against this man. One on one, both of them reacted too quickly
to perceived or real slights. Sometimes Uncle Larry screwed up. Sometimes she did. Since her father's death, the Sterling family consisted of
only two people, and they couldn't get along for more than ten minutes.
The whole county was well aware that tempers flared hot in the Sterling
clan. The whole county avoided crossing either one, to be truthful.

But it was no longer just the two of them. Now the Sterling family
contained two more, Archie and Glory. What Quinn wouldn't give to
have them here permanently. Archie clashed with Larry, too, only was
more passive aggressive about it. She didn't understand why.

Larry walked back in, closing the door.

"Tell me about Archie," she said before he had a chance to sit.

"I'd rather talk about Ty," he replied, the emphasis conveying the
subject was closed. "I'm tired of these pissing matches, Quinn. I got work
to do."

Always his go-to tactic, dismissing her made her feel juvenile. The
trouble was she acted more juvenile when he did it.

Her mother's Irish ire crept in, heat climbing up her neck and into
her face, flushing her infamous freckles a rusty pink in its takeover.
Without a mirror, Quinn was still aware that her hair accented the
feeling. Her father used to say he loved and hated seeing her this way
when all those Margaret Kennedy O'Quinn Sterling genes flashed into
Quinn.

"I think we're all tired of secrets, Uncle. You couldn't take care of
your older brother's murder because of secrets. You chased off your
younger brother from his inheritance, because of secrets. But you know
what? I have no secrets."

"You care for that Ty boy like he was your husband. I see that
much, Niece. Not that you don't have feelings for Jonah, but you got
two men on leashes, and you think nobody sees that you haven't gotten
married because of it. Everybody has secrets. Including you." He didn't

smile; he didn't frown. He only sat there all sure of himself. "Show me yours, and I'll show you mine, little girl. Otherwise, get the hell out of my office."

Her teeth clenched. "I don't want to go home and find Archie gone because of you."

"Well, it won't be because of me," he replied. "I've kept my distance." He reared back as if the conversation were closed.

"So you won't chase him off again?"

His breath came out pushed and annoyed. "It's up to him whether he stays or not."

"In only two days, Archie saw Ty arrested for murder and suffered his daughter threatened by a stranger, Uncle Larry. Deputies swarmed the farm, and Glory's new friend Cole cries half the time from losing his mother. Archie downright ignores you, and you in return. The aloof grudge between you is almost palpable. What the hell?"

Larry said nothing.

"I have no time, patience, or desire for a sibling feud to explode amidst everyone's attempts to save Ty's life," she said, to bring things around. "He's our focus. Only him, you hear me?"

"It's a long story," he said, attempting to shut things down. "Let it go."

"Long ago, you mean. It's ancient. He left when I was a child. That's a heck of a family feud, Uncle." She told herself to settle down. "Any chance y'all can forget about it?"

He stacked the photos with the cam pics from the night before, neatening the sides. He set the papers to his right, atop some files. "I'll look at this stuff and see what I can find."

So. . . no.

Family was exhausting. She needed to get back on Ty's case.

She stood to leave. "Don't call Colleton SO," she warned.

"Can't promise that, but if I do, I'll talk to you first."

That was about as good as a compromise got between them.

In thirty minutes they'd gone from case work to family warfare, and they'd gotten enough under each other's skins to leave marks. She stood and gave him a hard look of disappointment. "I'm headed to Natalie's apartment complex again."

He'd promised to call her, but she didn't trust that. She wasn't a uniform, and he didn't have to. As a result, she stopped short of telling him she'd inform him of her findings. A lot depended upon what she found.

She left the sheriff's complex, fewer people being social on her way out, also the norm, since her private meetings with her uncle rarely ended well. Carla smiled and gave her an all-knowing wink.

The meeting had been necessary. Her uncle wasn't the best at being sheriff, but he had access to intel and tools she didn't. He gave her some semblance of latitude because of blood, maybe her experience. Not the best collaboration, but it was what it was. Good thing she had a twenty- or thirty-minute drive to the apartments to cool off and make plans. She threw the truck into gear and headed toward Walterboro.

Ten minutes later, her pulse back down, she turned attention to that ahead. She wasn't sure who at the apartments would be up and dressed this time of day, on a weekday. Almost nine. Some of the people in building F worked jobs, some were retired, some attended school. With this being two days after a holiday, the odds were in her favor many would be home, but she hadn't prepared the first question to ask.

From the photos on Facebook, she knew some had lied to her. The question was how to approach them for another round. The next was in what order, because she wouldn't put it past one or two to coincidentally disappear once they saw her knock on the first or second door. Then there was the recluse whom she'd missed altogether.

On the other side of town, she approached the interstate but at the last minute turned into a Waffle House. Rummaging through the console, she found one of many small notebooks she tucked in hers and the farm's vehicles, found a pen that wrote well enough, and went inside.

The full-fledged eggs, bacon, hashbrowns, and toast breakfast served to stall for time and calm her nerves while the coffee perked her up. She'd left home without the first bite of sustenance. By the time she'd downed her coffee, she'd filled a page for each resident of building F, and the manager.

Better prepared, yes. Excited about learning more, without a doubt. Anxious about one or more of them turning on her or, worse, Ty? Definitely. She had questions, but strategy hadn't quite gelled. Ty's life was on the line.

By the time she reached the apartments, she opted to park on the other side of building A, out of sight of building F. She'd interview the manager first, then depending on his answers, take it from there.

But first a second to collect herself. She had more to accomplish than apartment interviews.

She'd emailed Knox the pics and texted him this morning to be on the lookout for that email.

Raysor said not to call him, but she wasn't sure if this new information trumped that. After this second round of apartment interviews, she might phone him. He wasn't aware of what happened on the farm last night.

Nobody had spoken with Natalie's employer, and that rankled. Such a simple task for Colleton, but to hers and Tassey's knowledge they hadn't bothered—holiday weekend and they already had a bird in the hand. Fine. Tassey could do that, hopefully. She could call one of those attorneys at home and sound perfectly entitled to do so. Quinn needed to update her about the Facebook pictures anyway. As much as Quinn had scolded Ty about not being wide open with his attorney, she best practice what she preached as the hired investigator. An attorney was only as good as the information in her grasp. Quinn was paying Tassey too much to piss her off.

Quinn dialed, getting voice mail. "Call me, Tassey. Someone needs to talk to Natalie's employer, and not next week. Thought you'd get them at home better than I would. Ask if Natalie spoke of Gabriel or David Wescott, if she changed her will recently thanks to this new love in her life, or if she'd spoken about giving notice. Has she missed work more than usual. If you want to break the ice and introduce me, then have me query them, fine, but I don't want to tick them off." There, got it all in one breath, one recording. *Wait.* "I'm at the apartment complex. There's been a break on the trespasser and on David Wescott. No, I haven't told the cops. I want to run it by you first."

The beep sounded, ending the message. Good enough. Mentioning there was a break with the pics would intrigue the counselor to call back as soon as she could.

From her truck's front seat, she gave a quick scan of the grounds, recognizing the wooded area where the picnic barbecue had taken place in May. Nobody strolled around, the place appearing lazy and very holiday-sluggish.

Her phone rang. Tassey.

"So you are in," Quinn said.

"I don't jump to take phone calls, Ms. Sterling. I was in the middle of making coffee."

The woman had to run her own show. "Well, can you call Natalie's bosses?" Quinn asked. "Makes better sense—"

"I had to chuckle at that long list of orders. Listened to it twice for the humor of it." She chuckled for Quinn. "Funny . . . you thinking you're in charge."

Having just settled herself down from Uncle Larry, she seized her own reins before she gave a repeat performance of temper.

But the attorney had mental powers. "Simmer down, Quinn. Not trying to get under your skin. I already made a note to call them, but sooner might be better than later. Thanks for the pointer."

Okay, that was better teamwork. Quinn quit gripping her phone so hard. She gave Tassey an abbreviated version of the pics and an update on how Larry suggested all the facts be turned over to Colleton County. "I'm about to interview the apartment manager, then depending on how that goes, the residents of Nat's building. Got a problem with that? Means these people will see the photos before Colleton does."

"I never have a problem with common sense, nor with what works best for my client. Let me know what you learn, especially about the guy from last night. There's a gaping hole in this case, and I'd rather we find it before they do."

"Ten-four, boss."

Tassey clipped a laugh. "That was cute." She hung up.

She was glad Tassey was on their side.

Quinn gathered her little notepad and pen. After last time, she'd decided notes on paper would be better than the note app in her phone and when possible, a recording in lieu of the notes. She slid the notepad in her hip pocket, wiping her temple at the tickle. In the little time Quinn had parked and spoken to Tassey, the truck had absorbed enough July heat to draw beads of moisture along her hairline down to the nape of her neck.

She slipped out of the truck and went to Gunner Pratt's apartment, knocking beside the *Manager* sign. She heard him at the peephole, but he said nothing.

"Mr. Pratt? It's Quinn Sterling again. From yesterday. I came up with a few more questions. May we speak?"

"They told me I didn't have to talk with you."

"Who?" she asked.

"The police."

Legally Pratt *didn't* have to talk to her, but when had that conversation taken place? Had they contacted him to throw up a hurdle? Or had he called them asking questions, maybe informing them about her?

"I'm simply trying to find out who killed Natalie Jackson, Mr. Pratt. Nothing more."

"Not sure I want to get involved."

She stood there, letting words settle like dust. He hadn't moved away from the door.

"I have pictures of you, sir," she finally said.

She heard rustling on the backside of the door. "What kind of pictures?" he asked, wary.

She smiled friendly at the peephole. "Guess you'd have to let me in to see." She held up the photos, but at such an angle he wouldn't make out anything.

After a short delay, the door clicked and opened. "I ain't got nothing to drink for you," he said, as before.

"I ain't here to drink anyway," she said, owning his slang. She made her way inside.

The old sofa worked this time same as before. The place smelled less musty. She hoped that didn't mean she was getting used to the scent of grunge.

"You look spiffier," he said.

Quinn hesitated at the unexpected compliment. "Why, thank you very much," she said, not wanting to say much more, counting her blessings he might've warmed to her. Score one for her, maybe.

"Whatcha want?" he said, sitting across from her in the old recliner. "Like I said, they said I don't have to talk to you."

"You don't have to talk to them either."

He laugh was edged with phlegm. "Who tells cops no?"

So they had contacted him, not the other way around. "You saw them after me yesterday, huh?"

A light shrug. "They didn't like you being here. This is supposed to be about right and wrong and finding the bad guy, but it's never that simple, is it?"

Quinn wasn't sure how to answer that one. "Everyone wants what's right. But people have their own version of what that is."

"That don't make sense." He no longer sat forward, now wallowed back into the permanent indentations of the chair, the angle an odd one with one leg bent, the other stretched. "They're doing the same thing you are, I guess."

"They show you pictures?"

"No."

"Guess I'm ahead of them then."

He sniggered. "Either that or they didn't think me important enough."

"Everyone's important until they're not, Mr. Pratt. You mind if I record us talking? Beats you sitting there watching me write your words down. Answer only what you want." She hesitated. "Or not. I respect whatever."

Downplaying made the request less important . . . less need to worry.

"Whatever, sure," he said, giving her a rubbery arm wave.

She hit *record*, set the phone on the table beside her so it wasn't so obvious yet aimed at him. Then she quickly laid the two pictures on the coffee table to snare his attention, her hand catching a chipped notch exposing particle board beneath.

He came out of his slump to see better, then, as her uncle had, fished reading glasses from a pocket. She smiled to herself at what Larry would think about her comparing the two.

"I've circled the ones I knew," she said, pushing the one with Wescott toward him, the one with a lot of people in it. Wescott, of course, was left open, falling into the list of those she didn't know, with her wanting to see what Pratt had to say.

Surprisingly, he went around naming residents without reservation. He didn't point at Wescott. So she did. "What about this guy?"

"Don't remember him much. I spoke to him, I think. He wasn't interested. Wasn't interesting either, so I didn't give him another thought. Why, is he somebody I ought to know?"

She studied him, testing her bullshit meter. She believed him. "That's Natalie Jackson's boyfriend," she said. "You don't keep up with the guests at your events? Anyone could walk in off the street and you'd feed him and let him drink your beer?"

"Now, now," and he laughed. "Once I knew he came with some-one, I let him be. Yes, he was with Natalie and Becca and that crew, so I gave him a pass. Can't say I saw him as her fella, though. I mean, her ex is black. This guy's anything but." He snapped a finger. "But like that, he was out of my head. Had my hands full grilling."

In that strange discriminating style of his, he hadn't made the connection. Quinn believed the moron.

"What about this other picture?" She exchanged their positions. A bit of dust moved around with them.

This guy, the one who'd entered Sterling Banks and scared children, was the main thrust of this talk, and her pulse inched up a bit. He stood at a picnic, scrutinizing people. Not with anyone but close enough to look as if he'd been invited, yet a tad uncomfortable with the crowd.

Pratt busted out a guffaw. "Son of a bitch, somebody got the hermit in a photograph?" He continued a rough cackle, enjoying the joke Quinn wasn't grasping hold of. "This picture the same day as that one?" he said, shoulders silently laughing in an up-and-down bounce.

"Yes. What do you mean the hermit?" she asked, anxious to put a name with a face.

He hit the paper with a finger. "That's John Jefferson."

Then it clicked. "The recluse?" she asked. "The guy who lives in the same building that Natalie did?"

"Yeah," he said, grinning at being the one in the know. "You ought to go buy a lottery ticket, lady. Nobody catches that guy in the daylight. Hell, I haven't seen him since he signed his lease."

Chapter 21

GUNNER PRATT'S chuckles went on longer than Quinn enjoyed, and he fell back in his recliner with a twinkling gaze. He thoroughly enjoyed having one up on the investigator. He knew nothing about the Sterling Banks trespasser, but he'd identified someone Quinn hadn't. "That's our recluse, all right. Don't rightly remember Jefferson being at the cookout," he said. "That was Memorial Day, if I'm correct, right?"

"Right," she said, happy for him to fill in blanks without being asked. "How do you not remember him being there?"

He shrugged. "Just don't. Man don't socialize. I was cooking that day for the entire complex. Maybe he grabbed his burger and went home."

Quinn took another hard look at the pic. The people caught in the photo had been there a while, judging from the dirty paper plates and wadded napkins. Jefferson leaned against a tree with no one close, watching. Not there for the food. No point asking Pratt who might've taken the picture. He wasn't even aware the man had been there.

She heard what Pratt said earlier, but she asked for confirmation for the recording, "When was the last time you saw him?" In case his story changed.

"When he signed and paid his first month's rent," he replied. "Cash. And each month an envelope with cash comes through my mail slot. Each time, on time, six times. Long as I get paid and the neighbors aren't harassed, I don't care if a tenant's breathing or not."

An inappropriate remark, but Quinn got the gist. He'd identified the Sterling Banks intruder, almost too damn good to be true. Question was whether to get the police involved.

Thinking about police gave her another thought. "You ever check on apartments, or the people in them?"

"Whatcha mean? Unless I get complaints, I steer clear of these people."

Bet he's well beloved out here. "I mean bug treatments, repairs, pet issues . . ."

"Don't allow no pets."

"Okay, but say you worried about someone who hadn't been seen in a while. They don't answer their phone. You're worried the water or the stove has been left on. The neighbor feared for them as they could be sick on the floor, unable to get up, like the commercial."

He listened, giving little bobs of his head at each instance. "Sure, if I need to. Isn't that what the police call a health-and-welfare check? They've done them a couple of times."

Pratt had been cooperative. He'd been downright friendly this time, which she attributed somehow to how she looked. And she gathered the police hadn't been too gracious with him yesterday afternoon, so how could she make this their loss and her gain?

"Right. Think you might have a need to check now?" she asked.

The suggestion didn't take hold at first, but the light soon came on. "You mean, since we haven't seen him since . . . this." He flicked the edge of the photo.

She gave him an atta-boy grin. "Exactly."

"Sure," he said, rising. "I assume you mean now?"

"Exactly again."

He grinned at being part of something. "Let's do this." He took a step and spun back toward her. "Hey, I have a letter going out about updating vehicle information for our records. Been having too many nonresidents parking in spots assigned to our people. I can hand deliver one. How's that sound? Ain't quite as lame as a health-and-welfare check."

Quinn smiled. "A thorough manager. I like that."

Pratt leered back. "Damn straight."

With the master key in his pocket, she assumed, since he retrieved no keys, they left the apartment and lit out across the parking lot, in broad daylight, out in the open for anyone to see. She might've thought this through better. She hadn't wanted to expose herself to everyone in case some ducked and hid or notified others, but too late now. Not so sure Pratt would feel comfortable skulking behind buildings to reach building F anyway. Sneaking up on someone contradicted the excuse of a welfare check.

She'd widen the search on Pratt's video footage from the parking lot cams. Last night she'd given her copy of what she'd already gotten from Pratt to Jonah, No sign of Wescott. She'd have loved to have gone back further, see how he came and went in the past, how often. At least back prior to the Memorial Day picnic. She was also interested in how Jefferson came and went as well, and what exactly he drove.

Skin prickled a little on her neck. Her firearm was in her truck's glove box, on purpose, to not scare interviewees, but she felt naked without it. When she caught a glimpse of a Colleton County SO unit parked in the shade of a pine, near the picnic area, she was glad she wasn't wearing it. She was authorized, but they'd be less guarded around her unarmed.

Nobody got out of the cruiser, and she sure didn't detour over to shoot the bull with them. Guarding the crime scene maybe, though guarding was a loose term for sitting in your vehicle's AC. Sure as hell better not be following her. She slid on sunglasses, acting as if she hadn't seen them.

Damn, it was hot. The summer heat already radiated off the asphalt beneath their feet.

"That the deputy who came back to see you yesterday?" she asked.

Pratt was shrewd enough not to stare at the car. "Can't tell through the glass. Didn't see him arrive. Sure didn't run anything by me." He spit on the ground, and it almost sizzled. "Damn pigs."

Nobody else wandered about. They had no idea if any of the other neighbors saw them coming. If they struck gold finding Jefferson, she might have to postpone the other chats anyway. That deputy better not get out and hunt her down and ruin what she was trying to do in finding Jefferson.

At the building, they took the stairs, Pratt doing his thing not caring who saw, Quinn scouting for blinds cracking or heads peering out doors.

The crime-scene tape on Natalie's door hung limp in the humidity. Pratt didn't even notice it being violated and continued past apartment F1 to F3, over and down from Natalie's place.

Without hesitation, Pratt strode up and banged his fist as if he were on "Law and Order," serving a warrant. "Manager. Need to inspect the apartment."

God, like that wouldn't bring out the looky-loos. Guess she should've been more descriptive about how to do this.

Nobody answered. Quinn imagined Frannie Bean at her F4 peep-hole, wondering whether to venture out and take a proper accounting of matters.

Pratt raised another fist, and Quinn stopped him. "No point making this a spectacle. Remember who lives over there." She tipped her head toward F4.

"Yep, you're right," he said low and held up the key.

She gave him an approving nod to go on in.

Arctic air hit them from a thermostat set well below the norm, even for July.

"Son of a bitch is gonna have a hell of a power bill if he keeps the AC like this," Pratt said. "Surprised he don't have icicles on the furniture."

Indeed. Yet the odor was still incredibly stale, almost sour.

The residence came across as more of a business address than a bachelor pad, with two desks along one wall of the living room, and a sectional sofa filling most of the rest. Three large monitors, two on one desk and one on the other. Wadded and strewn, lightweight blankets appeared left after a nap. Tee shirts and light jackets hung wilted and askew, three items deep over the backs of two desk chairs. Nothing on the walls but a television, turned off. The only sound was air through the AC vents. The ice maker kicked in, making Pratt look that way.

"What does he do for a living?" Quinn dared step toward one of the desks while scouting for cams, a habit of hers.

"Day trader," Pratt said. "Don't ask me the particulars, but he buys and sells stocks, bonds . . . stuff on the internet. Guess that gives him permission to be a recluse."

"Yet he isn't here," she said, moving papers with a pen, not making sense of them.

"Jefferson? You here?" Pratt led toward a short, two-person bar, the divider between the living area and kitchen. He rounded the end.

"Holy shit!" He leaped a foot off the floor, screaming two octaves higher.

Quinn dashed over. "Pratt?—*oomp*." The manager slammed into her, bounced off, then, scrambling, he rammed her again like a linebacker and disappeared out the door.

She went down backward, shoulders and head into one end of the sectional. When she opened her eyes, she understood.

Lifted to her elbows she looked down past her own boots, noting six feet away the bottoms of someone's Adidas.

Clambering up, she took in the person, a man . . . and quickly deemed him dead. Small bits of gray matter glued to the white-refrigerator front, with dried trails having taken bigger pieces to the floor. More clots decorated the white-and-gray vinyl.

Unless he had a houseguest, this was John Jefferson.

"Ms. Sterling?" Pratt called from outside, voice still weak and wobbly.

"Stay out there," Quinn shouted. "Don't even touch the door."

She took pictures. His gray T-shirt wasn't as soaked as it could've been but messy enough. Blood on the kitchen counter, hand smears through it, told her he might've tried to remain erect, but judging from the massive blood pool beneath the body, he'd not stood long. The killer had bashed him over and over again, standing, slumping, kneeling, maybe even after his victim went down.

Skull was busted open, eye sockets caved in, nose smashed flat and to the side. Clotted blood made the hair stiff and wiry, the face a palette of red from apple to merlot, cherry to garnet. Couldn't even see the death pallor. The blood had turned to glue on the floor. No point checking for a pulse.

Not a murder weapon in sight.

She started to yell at Pratt to call 911, but changed her mind. There was a perfectly good deputy in a car outside. After a couple more snapshots, she eased herself out of the apartment. On her way, she noted the location of the thermostat in the living room. No blood on it from what she could see, but she would hope for a good fingerprint since the killer had likely adjusted the thermostat to frigid in order to buy time and delay anyone noting the impending smell. It had to have happened sometime after he'd left Sterling Banks, and forensics figured time of death pretty well these days. The killer had been scared.

"Watch the place," she told Pratt. "Don't let anyone near, much less inside. I'm grabbing the deputy in the parking lot."

"Shit, he isn't going to think I had anything to do with this, is he?" Pratt asked, disgusted. "I'm so damn sick of cops."

She hustled toward the stairs.

"Wait," Pratt said, trying not to be loud. "He is dead, isn't he?"

"Oh yeah," she said. "Quite dead."

"Damn, two murders in a week. I'll never be able to fill my vacancies now."

She started to tell him to hope he didn't lose the renters he had left. Quinn took the stairs down two at a time. Becca waited outside her apartment, talking to old man Baxter Randleman. Both hushed and waited for Quinn to reach the bottom and tell them something, but she strode past.

"Excuse me, Ms. Sterling." Becca spoke up for the two. "Whose apartment is it this time?"

"Jefferson's," Quinn replied, not stopping. "Don't go up there. It's a crime scene." She turned back in afterthought. "If you aren't going anywhere soon, I'd really like to speak to you."

Becca blanched. In a quick stumble, Randleman put distance

between him and her, and before Quinn got ten feet, she heard his door click in his retreat.

The driver's side window rolled down as Quinn approached the patrol car. She almost slowed up, stunned to see Raysor. "What the hell are you doing here?" she asked.

"I was about to ask you the same thing, gumshoe. Someone from my department has been keeping an eye on this place from the git-go, and since I *wasted so much time* here yesterday, they said, I was told it was my turn." His brow furrowed. "What's wrong?"

"Body in apartment F3," she said. "John Jefferson. Male, white . . . well, barely from all the blood, approximately thirty-five years old. Blunt force trauma to the head, multiple times. Not sure when but probably after midnight."

Raysor radioed it in, asked for detectives, stating he had a suspected homicide. Then he got out. "Need your help securing the scene, if you don't mind."

"Sure," she said.

By the time they reached the top of the stairs, everyone stood outside their place, watching, listening, some chatting across the gaps to each other, each afraid to stray far from their protective threshold. Pratt talked to Frannie Bean, halfway between Jefferson's and her place. "Is it really him?" Frannie Bean asked Quinn, trying to sound like an innocent old woman to see what she could learn. Quinn motioned for her to get her gossip from her landlord.

Raysor donned gloves. "Either of you touch anything?"

"I did, more than Pratt," she said. "He freaked seeing the body, and in his stampede to escape, he plowed into me, knocking me down. So, I've touched the floor, the sofa, and the doorknob when I shut it behind me on the way out. Moved papers on a desk with a pen. Pratt touched the doorknob going in, but I don't recall him touching anything else. His feet barely touched the ground leaving."

"Are you in charge, Deputy Raysor?" asked Frannie Bean, playing coy.

Raysor ignored her after a snatch of a look.

Lookers now stared up the stairs, two belonging to a couple she hadn't seen before. Then she heard voices from the parking lot. "Dead or murdered?" "They know who did it?" "Weren't they supposed to be watching this place after what happened yesterday?" People from neighboring buildings were gathering for the show.

Raysor went in long enough to see there was a body, and that it was definitely dead, then returned to stand guard, easing the door closed. He started a list of names present. "What were you doing here?" he asked under his breath.

"Got a lead on this guy," she said. "Somebody got to him before I could, although I dare say with a much different purpose."

"Just keep people away," he said, watching the stairwell filling with folks.

Quinn went to them. "People. You must be fearful of all this, wondering how two crimes happened in a week right under your nose. Anyone see anything?"

People craned their necks left, then right, studying the person next to them, across from them, down the stairs from them, wondering which of them would say anything. Which might be a criminal. She expected no hand to raise, getting only mumbles and head shaking.

"You sure?" She made hard eye contact with each this time. Didn't take long for a few to back down. "If you don't want to speak up in the open, here." She pulled out her business cards. She didn't have enough for everyone, but she began doling them out as if standard protocol. More people left.

Nobody gave her concern. Then it hit her. *Ty.* She had to call Ty.

As she dialed, a shot of last night's guilt coursed her veins, but what was most important was pinpointing where he was when Jefferson died. He'd had no alibi for Natalie and had been blamed. If he was holed up at Sterling Banks, he was good.

His phone went to voice mail, and her adrenaline kicked in, dosed with fear. So she dialed Jonah. He always answered her calls, and these days he'd be even more inclined to jump at her caller ID.

"Quinn? You okay?"

"I'm fine, Jonah. Where's Ty?"

"Last I saw him, he was at my place. Heard him in the kitchen, I think."

"Can you check, please? I mean put your eyes on him. How far are you from your house?"

"Um, okay. Not far. I'm in the truck. Me and a couple guys were cutting up a limb. Had a big one fall in the third quadrant for some reason. Has me worried about that particular tree."

He told a worker where he'd be, then she heard noises of a truck moving on a dirt road. "Give me a minute to get there," he said.

Somebody tried coming up the apartment stairs, and she met them, motioning to turn around. "Crime scene," she said. "No one allowed."

The guy began his retreat, grumbling, "What the hell gives you the right, then?"

"Quinn? What's going on?" Jonah had heard *crime scene*.

"Later," she said. Another body had dropped, and Ty had to be found. Her mind did the math. He'd been with her until after one this morning. Right now it was elevenish. The body was at least six hours old, maybe more. "Spot Ty for me, please. Listen, was he in his bed when you got up this morning?"

Jonah was the earliest riser on the farm, and Ty had slept in his guest room.

"I didn't check," he said. "Should I have?"

"When did you last see him?"

"Um, right before I woke you up."

Quinn needed to narrow this window tighter still. She'd seen Ty at one a.m., and Jonah had seen him at seven. Not on the phone, but later, when Quinn got home, she'd ask Jule, then Archie, even the kids.

She caught herself rubbing knuckles on her chest, anxious, telling herself she did this to cover his butt.

But what if Ty did go out? What if he'd gone out for the reasons she might if she were in his shoes.

"I'm at the house," Jonah said, and she heard the truck door slam. "Jule?" she heard him call, using his mother's first name like everyone else, having done so since he could talk.

Quinn caught her voice but not her words. Jonah came back. "He left a while ago. Not sure when."

"Can you ask around? See if anyone saw him between one and seven?"

"Quinn, what's going on?"

Nothing good.

"Jonah, call him, please. He's not answering me, and I'm stuck over here in Walterboro. I found our trespasser."

"That's great, Princess. I'm proud of you! Ty ought to be happy. I'll find Archie. Did you get your guy arrested or is he getting out on bail? I need to put everyone on notice in case he—"

"Jonah, stop!"

He did. He waited. Then he said, "What's wrong?"

"He's not in custody, Jonah. His name is John Jefferson. He's a neighbor of Natalie's, and I found him dead in his apartment about thirty minutes ago. Died between the time he came to Sterling Banks and early this morning. So . . . where's Ty?"

Chapter 22

QUINN WATCHED two patrol cars and a plain wrapper pull into the apartment complex parking lot. She still had Jonah on the phone, and so far, he couldn't find Ty on Sterling Banks. Worse, Ty wasn't accounted for between one and seven that morning.

"Hunt for him, Jonah," she said. "Gotta go. Detectives are here."

"I'll go to the manor and ask Archie and the kids. Surely Ty checked on Cole this morning."

"Check our cams, too, Jonah."

Detectives made their way up the stairs, asking people to move out of the way and go home.

"Call me with what you find out," she said, rushing to get off. "If I can't take the call, leave me a voice mail."

Two men in plain clothes arrived with four uniforms, three men and a woman. With this much hoopla, the press would be here any time. She remained outside the apartment, helping Raysor keep people away.

Detectives pulled Pratt aside quickly, then short seconds later, Raysor pointed to Quinn. They separated her from Pratt, far enough for them not to hear and duplicate each other's stories.

The fit, younger detective had an up-and-tight haircut. He queried Pratt. The taller, fifty-ish detective queried Quinn, his Colleton SO polo too tight for his belly, a belt curling along the top of his pants. He wore an Elvis-sort of do, the poof making it look thicker. "So you're Quinn Sterling, the private investigator and ex-FBI," he said, his tone leading with a you-should-know-better sound to it.

She tacked on, "And niece of the Craven County sheriff, and an ex-deputy, if that's what we're doing here."

The man introduced himself. "Detective Anthony Parker."

She smiled, waiting for him to give her another run for her money. That's what cops did with her. They tested her because she was ex-FBI, niece of a sheriff, a woman, young, and wealthy. She wore a lot of targets when it came to these people.

"What were you two doing here?" he asked, glancing over at his partner with Pratt, then at Raysor taking names, numbers, and addresses of the neighbors.

"Did she do it?" someone asked Raysor, and both Quinn and the detective pretended they didn't hear.

"We were delivering a notice and doing a health-and-welfare check. When I told the manager I was on his premises and needed to speak to Jefferson, he admitted he hadn't seen him in months. No one has, really. He agreed we could go together to see if everything was okay." She almost said they were killing two birds with one stone.

"Once we saw the body," she continued, "we left the scene and pulled the door closed. I don't recall touching anything other than my head hitting the sofa and body the floor when Mr. Pratt knocked me down to distance himself from the body. I didn't touch it since it was clear Jefferson was gone from this world. No sign of a murder weapon, not that we hunted for it, but I have a decent enough eye when entering a scene."

"Anybody wandering around the apartment building?" he asked.

"No, and I was looking. Looking for him, a neighbor, a stranger, anybody."

He gathered why, too. She represented Ty, the only person of interest regarding Natalie. Parker might not like Quinn hanging around a crime scene, but he would understand why. She would've interviewed anyone about Ty or Natalie or Wescott. What Parker didn't know was she also needed intel about Jefferson's whereabouts and comings and goings now that she'd learned who he was. No way was she telling the detective about the trespass incident on Sterling Banks. Plenty of time for that later.

Parker seemed to be attempting to read her. If she had time, she'd mess with the man, but she didn't . . . he didn't . . . and on went the dance. He was doing his job, and Quinn admitted he really wasn't so bad, but one didn't let your guard down with a seasoned detective, local or federal or anything in between, because they all had tricks. She was still a representative from the other side of the other murder which was way too convenient to this one.

"You've been here two days in a row, Ms. Sterling," Parker said.

"As have your people," she replied. "Murder tends to prompt an eagerness to solve the puzzle, doesn't it? You know, before the bad guy gets away."

"Speaking of the bad guy," he said, and she didn't like where this might segue. "Where's your guy, Ty Jackson?"

He knew better than to make that inference, but she wasn't picking that fight. "He's at Sterling Banks. Been making him stay there to have witnesses around, as well as offer him and his son protection from harassers or the press."

"Convenient."

"A smart move," she corrected.

A call came in. She glanced at it, not surprised it was from Jonah, and as she'd warned him, she wasn't able to take it. A moment later, she got the ding about a voice mail. Soon after, a text dinged in. She glanced at it. *Call me ASAP.*

"You need to take that?" Parker asked, being polite while sounding perturbed he wasn't her priority.

"Not sure." She didn't like that text, but she wanted to be done with the detective before getting pulled away and having to come back and finish. She pushed the phone in her pants pocket. "It can wait until you're done. What else can I do for you?"

He liked that. He proceeded, his questions not hard nor long nor out of line, and she appreciated all three. She answered briefly, offered no more than was asked, and smiled when he said he was done . . . for now. "We have your contact information," he said.

She pulled out her last business card. "I'm sure, but here's my info, just in case." She held up her phone, motioning that she needed to get back to her messages.

There wasn't a spot on the upper-floor landing far enough away from a cop or observers, and any moment, the press. So, needing to find a more secluded spot, she made one more stop to speak to Raysor before making her call.

He was caught up with Frannie Bean who wasn't letting him go, despite the deputy's keeping them outside and sweating.

"Frannie Bean," Quinn said, not asking if she could interrupt. "Something's come up, and I need to borrow the deputy here." She turned to Raysor. "Get all you needed from her?"

"And more," he said.

Frannie Bean smiled as if she'd been complimented.

Quinn drew him aside best she could in case the onsite detectives had keen hearing and noted she asked questions which had nothing to do with the *current* murder case. Watching the detectives continue doing their thing, she related to some of their behaviors, winced at others.

"Find anything?" she asked.

"Lots of calls between her and Wescott," Raysor said low. "For about five months. Here and there to start with, then almost daily the last two months. There was definitely something between them."

Predictable. "Any other odd activity? Any trends other than Wescott?"

He shook his head. "She checked him out on her computer, though. Paid for one of those people-searching sites."

Quinn nodded, wondering how Nat had known to search under the name Wescott. She thought Natalie called him Gabriel. Had she stumbled across his alias, or worse, did Wescott find out she was doing her own sleuthing and killed her for learning too much?

She remade her point. "Ty didn't kill her or Jefferson. Natalie's murderer is likely hanging around, watching, and I'm seeing Jefferson as a loose end." Her best deduction for now.

Raysor's cartoon scowl would've been funny any other day. "Wrong place at the wrong time, huh? Saw too much?"

"Not sure," she said, thinking about how Jefferson was watching everyone at the picnic, which would include Wescott. Jefferson also could've been nothing more than a straggler who dared attend the Memorial Day cookout out of a need to belong. "Did you learn anything else?"

"Not yet, but—"

Detective Parker came up behind Quinn. "Anything additional you need to tell me, Ms. Sterling? Deputy Raysor?"

"No, sir," Raysor said. "Ms. Sterling was just—"

Quinn jumped in. "Saving him from a groupie. Apparently, the lady in the next apartment seems rather smitten with the uniform."

Cocking a brow, his lips inched up one side. "With Raysor?"

Smiling, pretending a leer, she ogled the deputy. "I don't know. There's a lot to love there, don't you think?"

The guffaw made people turn, but Parker couldn't care less. "To each his own, I guess. Anyway, I need you, Raysor. Ms. Quinn, you can go."

She hated being dismissed. She despised being dismissed. Her uncle tried that all too often, but this time she appreciated the release. She wanted to walk around the building, to the back that fronted the northwest and an undeveloped couple of acres, because Wescott, or any person plotting murder, wouldn't stroll in off the main parking lot for all the Beccas and Frannie Beans to see. Per Pratt, there were no cams out back either.

Quinn would request the apartment's front-cam footage for the last fifteen hours or so, but she couldn't at the moment. The detectives would get to it first. However, expecting the culprit to park down the road or behind a building or dumpster, she wouldn't hold her breath for much revelation from the footage. Not if there was intent.

She gave a mild wave to Pratt, indicating their joint work was done, and she wasn't halfway down the stairs when Frannie Bean caught up with her. "He's dead, right?"

"Yes," Quinn said, halting on the ground floor, not wanting to be followed.

"They know who did it?" She was almost breathless in her zeal to be one of the first in the know. As bad as paparazzi, two of which hustled toward the stairs, stopping to speak to people collected at the bottom, going for interviews of neighbors and friends.

Quinn moved toward the back before she was identified, leading Frannie Bean with her, the last person they needed to flash up on the evening news. "No, Frannie Bean. They still haven't identified who killed Natalie either."

"Oh," she poohed, skeptically wincing. "We all know who did that. It's a matter of time before they connect the dots." Her expression morphed into one Quinn would just as soon smack. "And my money is on him doing in Mr. Jefferson, too. Bet Mr. Jefferson saw Mr. Jackson when he killed Natalie, or at least put him there when they believe it happened. Two murderers hitting one apartment building?" She shook her head, those short gray curls prancing. "Not seeing two killers, and I bet the cops don't either. Jackson did all of it, I'm telling you. You're backing the wrong horse, girlie."

Incensed, Quinn bit her tongue, amazed the woman had the truck load of audacity to make accusations in front of the investigator on Ty's team. With serious restraint, Quinn forced herself to appear unaffected, hoping to keep Frannie Bean distracted from the camera.

However, Quinn was surprised when the eccentric woman headed toward the back of the building, away from the people gathering around the reporters. She pulled cigarettes and matches out of her skirt pocket for a smoke. In a twist of circumstances, Quinn wound up following her to where Quinn meant to go in the first place.

As with cheap apartments, little emphasis was placed on the rear with no parking or public exposure. Just a gradual slope of grass that slid into weeds that slid into brush and woods. Though Frannie Bean had only now lit up her cig, the place held a stench of the wealth of tobacco use that had gone before her. A tall container with sand in the top stood to the side, chockfull with butts, with half as many more scattered around the rock-filled bed that used to hold some sort of bushes, the dead stumps a mystery.

"Beautiful, ain't it?" the woman said, taking in that first long drag as if it were water after two days in the desert. "Used to think I'd put flowers back here."

Irrigation emitters stuck up out of the arid dry flower bed. Clearly they hadn't been used in ages. A few weeds crept between rocks, barely alive because even they needed water, too. "Any chance you saw Mr. Jefferson's comings and goings the last two days?" Quinn asked, checking her phone like anyone killing time. She relaxed against the vinyl siding and flipped on the recorder before slipping it in her breast pocket instead of the tight one on her backside.

Frannie Bean blew smoke away from Quinn out of the corner of her mouth. "Why ask me?"

"Because you are the famous busybody around here," she replied.

The same smoke-blowing corner of her mouth grinned up. "I could take offense at that."

"You could, but you're pretty calloused from what I hear. From what I've seen."

"True that," said the woman, removing her stare on Quinn to the woods, raising the cig again. "Been around longer than anyone else."

Like Becca, Frannie Bean was proud of that fact. Maybe she didn't have much else to be proud of.

Quinn spoke as if she had nothing better to do. "Mr. Jackson apparently didn't do Jefferson this time. I was hoping your skills might shed light on someone else, but if you don't know, you don't know."

The smoker raised her brow but not in surprise. She waited to be asked for assistance.

Quinn continued. "Did you see or hear anyone else during the night or early this morning? I doubt anyone did, honestly."

Frannie Bean flicked her cigarette ash into the grass. "Thought I heard arguing in the middle of the night, but this is a multi-family housing affair, you know. You hear stuff like that all the time. Unfortunately, I was too sleepy to get out of bed and peek outside." She winked. "That suit you?"

"You didn't go check on him?"

"Nope."

"Good. Might've gotten killed yourself."

"Sort of my logic."

Quinn had her talking. "You weren't the least bit curious once you got up?"

"Nope. Would've been a bit rude asking someone hours later what they were up to in the wee hours of the morning. Could've been rough sex for all I know."

"Hmm," Quinn said, staring off into the trees. Nobody had busted into Jefferson's place, and the killer had locked the door behind them, because Pratt had had to use his master key to get in. The door would've likely been locked when the culprit arrived, too. Recluses maintained security. Therefore, he'd known the person, and the way he'd been overcome, and considering the height and power of the blows, it was a man as big or bigger. Didn't take long, Quinn guessed.

Frannie Bean turned rocks with her sandaled foot. "Anything else?"

"Ever seen anyone go into Jefferson's apartment before?"

"Never. There's a reason they call him a recluse."

"Did you see him at the picnic on Memorial Day, this past May?"

She snapped her head around. "He was there?"

"Yep. Found a picture of him on someone's Facebook page."

She looked worried. "Was I standing near him?"

"Close enough they got both of you in the same picture. Maybe thirty feet apart."

"Jesus," she whispered, her cigarette hand down by her side, as if forgotten.

Quinn perked at the change in demeanor. "Frannie Bean. Does he scare you?"

Jerking herself back, seeking normal, denying the emotional shift, the F4 resident puffed up. "Nope. He was this unpredictable recluse nobody trusted," she said. "The fact he lived next door to me didn't set well, though. I told Pratt I felt uncomfortable, but he said nothing he could do about it."

"About what?" Quinn asked. "What did Jefferson do?"

The woman acted as if she hadn't heard.

"Tell me," Quinn continued. "What did he ever do to make you uneasy? Seems he scared you, and I bet you can tie it down to a specific incident."

"I want to see that picture you talked about," Frannie Bean said instead.

Quinn pulled it out of her pocket. In the photo, Frannie Bean stood off to the side, scowling at Tee. There was Jefferson in the background, against an oak, watching them all.

The woman shivered. "Jesus."

Curious, Quinn folded up the paper and tucked it away, watching Frannie Bean try to hide her feelings again. "Talk to me, my friend."

"He's creepy," she said. "One time he caught me peeking outside. I mean, he'd been there maybe three months, and nobody'd seen the man. I was entitled to see what he looked like, I think. One has to feel safe around their neighbors."

Funny the way Frannie Bean thought. "What did he do?"

She sucked on the end of the cigarette, close enough to almost burn her fingers, as if she needed that last jolt of support. She blew out long and slow, enough for Quinn to marvel at her lung capacity.

Frannie Bean finished and coughed once. "He marched toward me so I went to shut the door, but he rushed to block it with his foot. I backed up, thinking he was coming in to rape me or something."

Yep, that might be scary. "What did he say?"

She swallowed hard, remembering. "He closed the door behind him, which about made me pee my pants. I backed further, but he remained put."

Having been in the apartment, Quinn pictured the scene.

"He talked spooky soft but deep. Sent chills down my spine." She worked to recall, to get it right. "He said, 'Best you don't pay me no attention, lady. If you see me, look away. If we meet, walk away. I am not someone you want to know.' Then he left."

Okay, creepy fit well. "You poor thing. When was this?"

"The first of May." She pointed at Quinn's butt, where the picture was. "What if he was watching me at the cookout, to see if I'd watch him, or even try to talk to him? Damn, if I'd seen him, I'd have gone home."

"I believe he was watching everyone," Quinn said, to settle the woman. "And who says he hadn't told everyone something like that?" In truth, to some, hearing that this man threatened so readily meant he might've been casing apartments and the people in them, not wanting anyone to note anything he did. To Quinn it meant the opposite.

He could've been weird and taken issue with anyone watching him, like with Frannie Bean. What if Natalie had caught him at an inopportune moment, registered something wrong, something he couldn't afford for someone to see, and he'd acted on it and killed her?

Frannie Bean leaned down and mashed the butt in the ground. "That's odd," she said.

"What's odd?" Quinn asked, trying to see if this was still about her memory of Jefferson.

The woman rose still staring down. "Not aware of anyone but smokers spending time out here. Mostly me, honestly, but I used to put out my cigarette on a particular rock. We smokers have our habits." She showed Quinn a loose fist. "About that size. But it's gone. It was here last night before I went to bed. I take a smoke once in the morning and once in the evening."

Quinn stooped to observe better. The rock's imprint remained, an imprint that had been there for some time from the indentation and the way rain had moved soil around it. The way the other rocks were discolored from being against it.

"You remember a rock?" Quinn asked.

"Yeah, been there for years. Had a dent in it where water collected after a rain. Like a mini bird bath." She gave a sigh noisy from years of nicotine. "Stupid, but I liked that rock."

Quinn patted her on the shoulder. "Well, hope you find it. And I'm happy you don't have to worry about Jefferson anymore."

Frannie Bean spun to her. "Don't tell anyone about what he did, Ms. Sterling. I don't want people seeing me as a fearful old woman."

"Then don't tell it like a fearful old woman. Own it." Quinn pointed toward the second-floor landing. "March up those stairs and tell that detective that you had doubts about the man, and that he was a weirdo. And that you told him to leave your apartment on no uncertain terms after he violated it. Don't feel like a victim, Frannie Bean. Be proactive and strong."

The woman hesitated, soaking in the words. "Damn right."

"Better you tell them than me, too."

Frannie Bean gave a sharp nod and took off to find her a detective.

And Quinn followed her, to speak to one of her opposite number. The investigative team might think it stupid, but she'd be remiss not to tell them that there was a chance the murder weapon had formerly been an ashtray and might now be tossed into that two acres of woods.

She got another text and checked it on the way up the stairs. *CALL ME!*

Abruptly she stopped, straightened, and hit Jonah's contact. "I was outside talking to a witness," she said. "Did you find Ty?"

"Got interrupted, Quinn. We need you home. Now. It's Archie."

"Be right there. Hold on."

She scurried to the stairs and hollered up at the wide backside still taking the steps. "Don't forget to tell them about the missing rock, Frannie Bean. It might've been the weapon."

The woman turned on the steps, eyes wide, and a grin blossomed on her face. She'd take full credit for being so deductive, but that was fine.

Quinn raced toward her pickup. People pointed at Quinn, and a reporter shouted, "Can I speak to you, Miss Sterling?"

But she pretended not to hear, trotting faster. She hoped the Colleton team was shrewd enough to listen to Frannie Bean. She'd check in with Raysor later and see.

"Talk to me, Jonah," she said back to the phone. "What happened?"

"Stroke, heart attack, I have no idea. Jule found him. He couldn't use his arm or his leg, and he made her leave while he locked himself in his bedroom. I didn't ask if he needed 911; I just called them. He's asking for you."

She mashed the gas harder. "On my way, Jonah."

She could carve a thirty-minute trip down to twenty, but that twenty would seem like two hours. To fill them, she tried to call Ty again and was forced to leave a message.

"Call me. Where are you? We have another body, and damned if you aren't going to be the most likely suspect if you don't make your whereabouts known. You're about to get on my last nerve, Ty."

Then she called Tassey. Damn she hated doing that. It was like ratting on her best friend, but her best friend no longer seemed to have a grip on common sense. Slowly, she was having some serious doubt as to what he may have really done.

Ninety-nine percent of her said he was innocent, of both murders, but a small piece remained that whispered, *but what if he did something?*

Chapter 23

EVEN AS RURAL as the area was, the EMTs reached Sterling Banks before Quinn. She rolled up and parked, leaped out, and ran inside. Nobody was downstairs. Not a soul.

She took the steps two at a time to the second floor where she found the activity. Jonah stood in the doorway to Archie's bedroom staring in. Seeing him made her break into a trot. "Jonah? How is he?"

He backed up as if saying, *See for yourself.*

"Where are the kids?" she asked quickly.

"Jule has them. And Bogie."

Thank God for that woman.

Quinn went in. One standing, one stooped before Quinn's uncle, the medics were putting away a blood-pressure cuff and other medical paraphernalia with no sense of urgency. Archie sat in the same rocker he'd rocked Glory in the day before.

"Uncle?" she said, making her way in, sitting on the bed again as she had last night.

"Wish Jonah hadn't called 911," he said. "Wish you'd been here to explain."

If wishes were horses, beggars would ride. Something her father used to tell her as a child in one of his many teaching moments about being privileged. Everyone had wishes. Graham made sure she understood she had more of her wishes granted than most.

"Is he okay?" she asked the nearest medic.

"He's fine for someone in his situation," came the reply, adeptly skipping the word *Parkinson's*. "Needs to touch base with his doctor about some changes. We've talked to him about it." The medic stood, all packed up. "If you don't mind, we'll head on out since he doesn't want to be taken in."

Archie shook his head. "No need."

The medic smiled. "Then fine, Mr. Sterling. You take care."

"I'll see you out," Jonah said from the doorway.

The two men followed him, and Quinn waited until she heard them most of the way down the stairs. "Walk me through this," she said, turning to Archie. "If I'm to understand, you've got to educate me. Is this normal or not normal? Whatever *this* is. I'm not sure what happened."

"I'm tired, Q," he said, looking every bit as he stated.

"I know you are . . . or I can imagine you are, but I'm not letting you off this easy. Give me the abridged version, and I'll let you rest."

"I know, I know," he mumbled. "You're entitled."

She sat upright, waiting. He looked pale, and he favored his right arm.

"After last night . . . after all that happened with the kids . . . I stayed up later than usual. Like all of you, my stress level was up there. You saw me when I came down for something to drink. What time was that . . . one?"

"Thereabouts," she said, trying hard not to blush at being caught in Ty's arms.

"I hadn't slept a wink. So I read, checked on Glory, listened to songs in the dark hoping I'd drift off. I say all that to lead into this," he said, speaking as if he hadn't slept in days. "I woke this morning with the issue with my arm. It wasn't working properly, and when I tried to stand out of bed, the leg gave out on me. I'd underestimated the exhaustion of the trip, the thing with the man sneaking onto the grounds, and Glory being scared to death. My brain wouldn't shut down so my body wouldn't shut down, and I haven't exactly been precise with my meds on this trip. For someone with Parkinson's, that can create an episode, especially in the morning. Morning akinesia, they call it. Either that or my meds need adjustment. It's a dopamine thing, without going into the science." He made little eye connection during the explanation, as if ashamed.

Quinn reached over and took his hand, purposely taking the one with the bad arm. "If you rest and take your meds, you'll be better today, right?"

"Probably," he said. "It's not like I've done this before, Quinn. It's a learn-as-you-go thing."

She gripped his hand a little tighter. "What can I do for you to make it better?"

"Nothing," he said, staring at her hand over his.

She got it. He wasn't wanting to add tasks to her life. He'd dropped in on her, and unless she was ridiculously stupid, he was having second thoughts about coming to Sterling Banks. "Tell me what *you* can do to make it easier then," she said.

"Talk to my doctor. Lighten my load. Plan ahead for when my off episodes may happen, since they do have somewhat of a clock affiliated with them. Take my meds, for one. Set things out in advance like clothes and make them simple to put on, like fewer buttons. Prepare meals ahead when times are good, and when the harder times come, have someone to help." His breath released softly, and he hadn't looked at her yet.

He was breaking her heart. "Uncle Archie."

When he peered up, he had tears in his eyes. "I was wrong to bring this to Sterling Banks. Y'all have so much on your plate already."

"Oh, no," she said, blinking back tears of her own. "This is exactly where you should be." She wanted to hug him but feared breaking him somehow. "You are a Sterling. You are a wonderfully good person, and your needs are our needs. Please, please stay here. I mean permanently."

But the stress. She wasn't doing a good job of fixing that. The timing of Archie's arrival with Ty in this mess totally sucked.

"I'm so sorry." She gripped harder, then worried that hurt him. "We caused all this, didn't we?"

His good hand pushed her grip off his less able one, and he flexed his fingers, testing. "You didn't cause any of this, Niece. I separated from Patrick to avoid stress. I sold the company to avoid stress."

"You came here for some peace, and we ruined it."

Leaning forward, forearms on his knees, he resumed his role as the elder Sterling in the room. "Stress is everywhere," he said. "It's how you adapt, the attitude you take, that dictates how you handle it. With or without Parkinson's, I haven't been doing a very good job at adapting."

He needed family. He'd lost his partner and had won custody of Glory. But was Patrick entitled to know if Archie started declining?

"What about Patrick? Should we call and let him know?" she said

"Quinn . . ." Cutting him her scolding look, he trailed off. He was about to say he wasn't up to it, but Patrick had to be very much a part of the stress that haunted Archie. To help her uncle, she had to make sense of his partner. Divorce was one of the biggest stressors there was, and the aftermath could maintain that stress level for years. She was stressed at the very real fact that Patrick worked for Ronald Renault. That continued to boggle her mind.

"What's with Patrick?" she repeated. "I'm your family. You are moving to the farm if I have to tie you down to keep you from leaving. We aren't doing secrets here anymore, Uncle."

His expression slid into one more stoic, maybe parental, then in an instant she realized the corner she'd backed herself into.

"Then what about Ty?" he asked, and she understood he wasn't talking about the murders.

"It's . . . complicated," she said, cringing at the cliché.

"All relationships are," he said.

She struggled to give this explanation the respect it deserved. "Jonah and I are serious. We talk marriage, though we haven't exactly nailed it down."

He let himself relax his back against the rocker, listening.

"The three of us are tight, Uncle. Tighter than any three people on this planet."

"I remember," he said.

"Jonah has stepped up his game, and I feel like we will eventually do this thing." Ugh, that sounded more like a business deal than a lifetime commitment. She scrambled to give it more polish. "Ty even gave his blessing not more than a month ago."

"Must've hurt," he said.

"You have no idea," she whispered, recalling the dance they'd shared in his mother's empty diner one evening, when cleaning off tables turned into Ty assuring Quinn that Jonah was the best choice for her . . . the stronger partner. *He's got it awful bad for you*, he'd said, which was true. It had pained her to hear him say it, but they couldn't stay a threesome forever.

Ty had found Natalie, which would've been fine except for Natalie's leaving Ty when Quinn returned home. After Ty's kisses last night . . . God, how had she let him do that . . . she realized that Natalie might've been wiser than them all.

"It's hard to break us up," she finally said. "I love Jonah most, but that doesn't mean I love Ty much less. Loving him at all hurts when I commit fulltime to Jonah, Uncle. How can I make it not hurt?"

"Start with not kissing him back," he said, then his attention got redirected to the doorway. A brief pained expression appeared and went, and Quinn wondered if this was what you called an episode.

"When did this thing with Ty happen?"

Quinn spun around at the new voice to find Jonah in the doorway. Archie looked away, with no place to disappear to and no strength to do it with.

"Not here," she said, heart slamming in her chest. "Archie needs to rest."

Leave was all she could do. She'd get the lowdown on Patrick and how to handle Parkinson's later. Dealing with last night's kiss—kisses—

had shot to the forefront of her things to handle at the worst possible time ever.

After kissing Archie on the forehead, she turned to leave but then had a thought. "You need help getting to the bed?"

"No," he said, a sad smile at the offer. "I'm good."

Yes, he was good. He was an excellent human being and had been her favorite uncle by a mile. She'd hated Larry since her teens for ostracizing him. That was another story yet to be told, but that one had to wait as well. For avowing no secrets allowed in the Sterling household, it damn sure seemed to be full of them.

Shutting the bedroom door behind her, she followed Jonah down the hall, watching his walk, watching his stiffness, wondering how hurt he was. She'd take anger all day long over hurt. She had no clue how to explain this.

He went in the kitchen. A call came in on the radio on his belt, and he quickly handled the small issue with a farmhand in one of the back groves before coming back to where Quinn stood, waiting for her sentence.

"First, Ty," she said.

"Haven't found him," he answered firmly. "Is it dire we find him right now? At this moment?"

"Maybe not dire, but before the authorities need to talk to him." She much preferred talk about the case.

"So, the trespasser is dead?" Not much emotion there.

"He is," she said.

"Archie know?"

"No. I, um, thought you were telling him. I didn't get the chance."

Jonah's forehead creased. "Don't you think you should've told him that before discussing Ty? To take some of the load off his shoulders?"

"You told me you would."

"Well, I got busy looking for Ty," he said.

Archie's mention of Ty had thrown her off balance. Their chat had suddenly become about her . . . about Ty. In hindsight, she saw Archie had wielded a mighty deft hand at taking the spotlight off himself.

"Go tell him now," Jonah said. "You didn't see how he was earlier. Were you aware of his condition?"

"Just enough to put a name to it. Parkinson's. He came here pondering whether he could move in permanently. I told him by all means he could. Then Ty happened, then the trespasser . . . I'm not sure how Patrick is involved, but any kind of divorce is no fun, and stress messes with his health. Now he's having second thoughts about living here. Which is better? Having a trespasser loose or knowing someone murdered him? You and I know Ty wasn't involved in any of this, but how can Archie trust that with a child at risk?"

Jonah gave her a cool stare at that last one. "Go tell Archie."

"First, did you pull up the cams to see when Ty left?"

"Not yet. I'll do it while you go upstairs. Go on, before he dozes off. Give him some decent sleep."

Monotone. A hundred-percent business with disappointment mixed in . . . and a small thread of animosity. Jonah hated confrontation and served as the best mediator of the three of them. He always hunted for a way out of a situation, while Ty and Quinn often mired down in the clues and obstacles, which frequently made him the leader, regardless of how alpha the other two behaved.

Quinn had wished more than a few times that these two men could be welded into one.

She walked to the stairs, taking them two at a time. Over her shoulder, she saw Jonah sit at the desk to pull up the cam footage, glancing up once at her before going attentive to the screen.

At Archie's door, she rapped a knuckle softly, then when she got no response, harder. Unsure if he heard and worried he wasn't answering, she eased the door open.

He lay on the quilt in the same clothes she'd left him in, one arm over his eyes. In case he was asleep, she slid like silk to his bedside, watching closely for the rise and fall of his chest.

He released a deep inhale, like a person taking in a catch-up breath in his sleep. She hadn't realized she held hers until then. "Uncle Archie?" she said, above a whisper.

No response. He was out of it. He did, however, lower the arm from his face, his head lolling to the side. That's when she saw the tears. Fresher tears. The poor man had cried himself to sleep.

She left him and returned downstairs. "Jonah?" she called about the time she hit the landing. "I didn't have the heart to wake him. He . . ."

But Jonah wasn't at the computer.

She trotted the final steps, roundhouse-walking around the bottom banister toward the kitchen, the only other place that made sense for him to be. Either that or he'd gotten called out to the farm, but he'd have sent her a text if that were the case. Besides, it hadn't been ten minutes. He should still be going through the cams.

"Jonah?" she called, only finding an empty kitchen. She ran to the back sliding door, to see if he'd stepped outside. Nothing. The garage, maybe? He left something in his truck? She scurried to the door into the garage, off the mudroom. Maybe one of the hired hands had driven up with a problem. Hell, what did she know these days? While Jonah was her foreman, she found herself more than a few times letting him just manage the place.

A convenient farm manager. A convenient boyfriend. These were the ideas running through his head. But he wasn't one to pout. He was the level in the group.

And she'd hurt him.

Outside, Jonah's truck was gone.

Quinn started to phone Jule, changed her mind, and jogged up the quarter mile of dirt road that connected the manor to the smaller home near the goat barn. "Jule?" she called, in case the woman was keeping the children occupied with the animals.

Bogie bounded up from around the house, bowing then hopping, seeking affection. She petted him on the head, scratched him under the chin, then went the direction from whence he came. She found Jule leaning on the corral.

"Jule? Where are the kids?"

Dressed in her usual overalls, she pulled out a yellow bandana from her back pocket and wiped her brow. "Inside playing with the goats, just now put the fan on them. Can't keep them out of there." Pragmatic and even-tempered, like her son, Jule still wore concern. "Archie okay or did they have to take him to the hospital?"

"He's resting," Quinn said. "It's a condition he's got, so we're learning. When he's awake, I'll have him explain it to you." She didn't want to sound upset to Jonah's mother, but his leaving Quinn without notice was so abnormal as to be highly worrisome, if not frightening. "Where's Jonah?" she asked.

But Jule frowned. "Last I knew, he was at the manor."

"He was, talking to me, but after I went upstairs to check on Archie, I came down to him gone. Thought he came here."

Suspicion caught the creases of Jule's eyes. She pulled out her phone and dialed a number. After a few moments, she clicked it off and returned it to her pocket. "He's not answering," she said. "You try."

Quinn did with the same results.

"Girl," Jule started, a hard stare saying there had to be an even harder reason for Jonah to ignore calls.

"I made him mad," Quinn said, before Jule could corner her. Then before she got too far on the defensive, she mentally tried to piece things together. Jonah had left, purposely not telling her. This was about more than Ty kissing her, because he'd have stayed and addressed that. What was worth going dark and shirking his job responsibilities?

"Jule, did you see Ty come in your place last night? Once we got done doing research at the manor?"

"Haven't seen him since last night at the manor, girl. Since I took the babies and brought them back here."

Quinn wasn't hearing this right. "You didn't see him this morning?"

The woman shook her head.

"He hasn't been with Cole?"

Jule broke eye contact, a sadness in her body language. "No. Cole didn't want to see him, so I called Ty and suggested he not try, at least not yet. The boy will come around. Once y'all fix all this mess about Natalie, he'll come around."

Quinn might've missed the opportunity to lift stress off Archie, but she wouldn't with Jule. "We identified the trespasser from last night," she said.

Jule's face lit up. "Praise be. Did you catch him?"

Any other time, Quinn would appreciate the trust this woman had in her to capture the bad guy. "Didn't have to," she said. "Someone killed him sometime last night."

The woman's relief quickly shifted to suspicion. "Which is why you're hunting Ty," she said.

Quinn didn't have to say a thing. Jule was not dumb.

"So what does Jonah have to do with this?" Jule asked.

"I'm trying to find them both. Seeking answers. Both are keeping things from me, Jule."

Jule froze, the bandana-holding hand on her hip. "Girl, you better get your damn act together. The three of you might as well be triplets, and if you lose control of that, I'm not sure how you'll be saving Ty."

Stating the obvious, Jule.

But Quinn didn't want to mince words. That's not what one did with Jule.

"One more thing." Jule bent forward, as if the five-foot-nothing lady had any height to spare. "Don't you get Jonah hurt in all this, you hear me, girl?"

"Yes, ma'am."

This case had taken a turn for the worse, as if that were possible. Ty hadn't been seen since he left the manor in the middle of the night, and Jonah seemed to be his accomplice. Unless Jonah was angry with Ty. She had trouble envisioning them tangling. This wasn't what the JQT club was about.

As juvenile as it sounded, the Jonah/Quinn/Ty society had been in existence since they were children, and it meant something. It meant everything. They took care of each other. They never held secrets. They'd never flown solo. Now look at them.

Ty had run off without her, Jonah had lied to her about their friend's whereabouts . . . and she had kept Jonah in the dark.

They had previously thought as one, but right now they were shattered. Quinn stood frozen in place, peering down, boots dusty from the very soil that had nurtured all three of them, bound them, and taught them into adulthood about what mattered.

So why did it just look like dirt now?

Chapter 24

UNABLE TO SIT AND wait for the guys to touch base with her, Quinn ran back to the manor and got on the computer, pulling up cam footage going back to one in the morning. Ty had left Quinn around that time, and slowly she moved forward. There he was, walking toward Jule's.

He had at least gone where he said he was going, but she didn't stop there. The cams she watched were some of the same they'd used to identify the trespasser. Unless you walked way around through the pecan trees to avoid them, you were captured on a recording.

And he knew that. Is that why he'd gone? He already knew the camera would tell Quinn the truth of something? With a sinking stomach, she watched the action unfold.

Ty wasn't thinking about cams or he didn't care about being seen, or maybe he changed his mind about where he needed to be, but he reappeared around one twenty, this time with Jonah on his heels. Jonah gripped him on the shoulder. Ty snatched loose, his body movements jerky and demonstrative of frustration. They glared at each other, bracing like arguing friends were prone to do. The video had no audio, but one didn't need to hear what they were saying to see they were at odds.

Ty shoved Jonah at one point, tired of hands on him, tired of their conflict, whatever. He spun and left toward his vehicle in the manor's drive, per Quinn's estimate. Jonah remained in place for another few minutes, watching long enough for the Jeep to leave.

She flipped to the manor's cams, and saw Ty leave the grounds. Jonah returned to Jule's, head hung at what looked like defeat.

Quinn had been so deeply embedded in her research at the computer during that time she hadn't heard a thing. Too ashamed and wrapped up about being seen kissing Ty, maybe. So guilt ridden she'd dove into demographics and reports with an intensity so deep to block out all else.

Jonah had woken her from her sleep, head on her arms at the desk. She wondered what he thought. Was he testing to see what she'd heard?

Did he wonder what she knew?

Of course he did, and she'd proven she'd missed it all.

She was a better investigator than this, and for the first time she reflected on the fact she might be too close to this case to be objective. As she'd warned Ty.

Regroup. Rethink. Get your damn act together.

The mantle clock chimed two in the afternoon. It felt like a fortnight since she'd sat up with Ty studying Natalie and Wescott's backgrounds. Neither guy answered his phone, and both had turned off the people-finder app they'd forever shared in case one of the trio needed another. She had no idea if they were upset, angry, or sad. Was Jonah mad at Ty or protecting him? Leaving her out of the loop, however, was a first. They just didn't do this.

She felt on the edge of a change, an irreversible shift in their friendship, and she prayed she was overthinking this. Their lifelong relationship was crazy valuable if not almost sacred, and if it could not weather this conflict, especially this particular conflict, they likewise ran the horrible risk of not keeping Ty off of Death Row.

Her phone rang, and she jumped to grab it. Raysor spoke up in his gravelly voice. "Hey, Legs."

He could call her *Lover* for all she cared. "Hey, how's it going?"

"I'm stuck in my patrol car watching the scene, or shall I say scenes? The detectives and forensics are still doing their thing. From what I saw, they'll be a while. Not nearly as clean as the Jackson murder."

"Okay." It wasn't like Raysor to call and chitchat. "Something you wanted to tell me? I mean, you said don't call you, let you call me."

"Heads-up. They're wanting to speak to your client but say he isn't answering his phone. They left word on the attorney's voice mail. She hasn't called back, or from what I can tell. Have either called you?"

Ty wouldn't, and Tassey hadn't. "No."

"Any idea where your client is at?"

No wonder Colleton investigators hadn't called her. They'd told Raysor to do it. "No," she said, offering nothing more.

"Thought he was staying with you, so people could account for his whereabouts."

"I came home from Walterboro and he'd gone out, Raysor. I didn't exactly freak that he wasn't under lock and key. Are you telling me to forward a message when I see him, or is this where you tell me to find his ass and tell him to contact his attorney?"

His throat clearing went on like he'd finished a cigar. "Giving you a heads-up, is all . . . Legs."

She tried to smile, reminded—despite the nickname—that he had been a stand-up guy so far. "I'll tell him he is needed for questioning. Thanks for the heads-up. We'll get his whereabouts in order. What's the time frame?"

He laughed once. "Now who's using who? Just passing the word. Take care." He hung up.

This situation was about to heat up. The media was only getting started. What was her next move? Damned if what popped to mind didn't rub her wrong. She rethought the instinct, yet came to the same conclusion. Call Sheriff Larry Sterling.

She attempted another call to each of her guys, leaving voice mails. Then she dialed Larry's private number, wishing she had the time to go to his office, but she'd lose time hunting for Jonah and Ty. She knew where she wanted to go, assuming her hunch was right. She hoped so, because it was the only hunch she had at the moment.

"Niece?" he answered.

"Uncle," she replied. "I need to update you on the trespasser, and we may or may not have a problem."

"I heard they have another body in Walterboro."

"John Jefferson. A neighbor of Natalie's who turns out to be the man who threatened the kids yesterday."

"They didn't tell me that," he replied.

"That's because they don't know it," she said. "I went to the apartment complex to talk to the neighbors again, to show them the picture of him we found on social media last night. The manager identified him. He took me to the man's apartment, and we found him with his head bashed in."

Big sigh. "Jesus, Quinn." He waited. "What else? I can hear it in your voice." He waited as if it were her turn but then beat her to it. "Where's Ty?"

"Unaccountable."

"Son of a bitch."

"Exactly. Jonah, too. Ty disappeared in the middle of the night. Jonah this morning. I'm asking that you simply tell everyone in your shop to keep a lookout for both. Tell them to check in with me ASAP. No more than that. Is that doable for you?"

"Hmmm," he grumbled. "Is Colleton hunting him?"

"They would like to speak with him, yes. No more. I take it they haven't told you that yet."

"A matter of time," he said. "But yes, of course, we'll put out a watch. His attorney know?"

"My next call," she said.

An internal urge to ask him to keep this close to his chest came and went. This was Jonah, his favorite, and Ty, his best. He wouldn't purposefully sabotage his own family and his own office, or at least she hoped.

"Any of your deputies can call me if, say, there's a sighting but no contact. I just need to know where they are."

"Quinn?"

"Uncle?"

"Did they cross the line?"

"You mean did they kill anybody?"

"Any line that jeopardizes me and my people if we don't turn them in to the Colleton SO."

"Then no," she said. "It's a long story, and it's as much personal as it is connected to the trespasser. Please trust me on this, Uncle Larry." It was a big ask considering the history between them.

"I'll be in touch by day's end," he said. "One way or the other."

"Thank you. I mean it."

"It's Jonah and Ty, Niece. I'm sure you do."

They hung up. She instantly dialed Tassey.

"I was getting ready to call you," said the attorney. "Ty isn't answering his phone, and the sheriff's office left me a voice mail I didn't want to return until I spoke to you and Ty. Update me. What's this about another body?"

Quinn filled her in about them ID'ing the trespasser as Jefferson, then finding Jefferson dead. "Per my farm cams, Ty left Sterling Banks in the middle of the night. Neither Jonah nor I can reach him. I've left voice mails telling him to come in, but, honestly, I didn't want to leave a message about Jefferson. He'll put two and two together, get fifteen, and lose his mind," she said.

"So, his whereabouts are unaccounted for during the window Jefferson was killed, I take it."

"For now." Quinn had to remind herself that this was Ty's attorney, and not to bend the truth too much. She needed to be kept in the loop.

But she wasn't telling her about Jonah missing. Ty, yes. Jonah, no.

"I need your gut feel on what Ty might be doing," Tassey said.

"Digging up clues of his own," Quinn replied. "We were going to the landscape company this morning, the company with the logo was on

Jefferson's windbreaker until we found him on Natalie's Facebook."

"So he knows nothing recent about Jefferson?"

"No." However, Jonah knew. Whether he'd told Ty was anyone's guess.

On second thought, no, it wasn't. Jonah *would* tell him. Anyone's guess was whether he'd punch Ty for coming on to Jonah's girl first, then tell him.

"Have you spoken to Natalie's employers?" Quinn doubted she had in this short a time, but time seemed to rush around them, dredging up damaging material against Ty as it did. Quinn felt a critical urge to do all she could as fast as she could. She ran ahead of a tidal wave. Everything being uncovered continued to count against Ty, which only meant she had to run faster, hunt harder, and turn over more rocks than the others did, until she proved him innocent.

"I spoke to one attorney," Tassey said. "Could be helpful. Could be totally foreign to what we're looking at. Maybe not pertinent at all."

"Let me decide that."

"Once again, Ms. Sterling, you forget who the attorney is here. I do the deciding."

"And you forget that I investigate anything and everything first so that there are things to sift through on your end to make the damn decisions. Don't hold anything from me or you're hamstringing what I can do for you. Understood?"

Tassey gave a low *hmmm* over the phone. "All this is upsetting you. Maybe you aren't the proper investigator—"

"Right now you are upsetting me for wasting yours and my time. Time I pay you quite handsomely for. For God's sake, give me something worth paying for and tell me what Nat's employer had to say, Tassey. I've got a lot on my plate without arguing with you. And I've kept you in the loop as promised."

"Let's get on with it then," the counselor replied not the least bit plussed. "Several months ago, he wasn't sure when, Natalie came to her employer asking if it was illegal for someone to pay her for information. Of course he asked her to explain more, because he assumed it was information on one of their clients, which would certainly be inappropriate. She assured him it was not a client. Whoever it was knew she traveled in that person's orbit. Whatever she could learn about that person could be compensated. Her employer offered to review any sort of contract, but there was none. He found that odd, but he trusted Natalie and let it drop, with a warning that it not reflect on the firm."

Son of a bitch, this *was* worth pursuing. "Did you ask about whether they'd heard about a boyfriend?"

"He said she was seeing someone, yes, but she never divulged who. During this time, she also updated her will."

Quinn inhaled at the potential of that. "Is Ty still the executor?"

"He wouldn't say, which I can understand, Ms. Sterling. Focus."

Tassey was right. "Try to get Ty to contact you, Tassey. I'll do the same. In the meantime, I'm heading out looking for him."

"Continue to keep me informed, please. No secrets."

Quinn hung up. She'd update the attorney after she found Ty, understood more, and pieced this crap together.

Double-checking her firearm still in the glove box, ensuring her phone charged, she texted Jule she was headed out after the boys. Then she texted Archie to take it easy, not to worry since the trespasser had been caught.

She wasn't sure he was ready to hear about Jefferson's brains sliding down the cabinet fronts of a cheap rental in Walterboro. She also wasn't sure he needed to hear Jefferson's murder might be connected to Natalie's. And she damn sure knew he didn't need to hear that Ty might be a suspect in both murders. If all that wouldn't send Archie packing back to California, nothing would.

Chapter 25

QUINN HEADED TO Charleston, nervous that time was limited and Colleton County would be on Ty's butt any moment. At three in the afternoon, traffic shouldn't be bad entering the Holy City, but it crawled slower than desired.

Heat waves rose here and there off the asphalt lanes. The killer had been smart to put Jefferson's air conditioning on max. This time of year wasn't kind to corpses.

Quinn could read Ty as well as anyone, and she assumed he'd reached the point of thinking if nobody else was going to solve this case, he was. While it had been barely three days since Natalie's death, those days had dragged out long enough for Ty to doubt whether any investigation could conclude in his favor. Quinn almost didn't expect Ty to come back until he had something, had someone, or gave up trying. From Boy Scout to double-homicide murderer. Had to mess with his head.

Charleston was big compared to most cities in the state, but deep urban it wasn't. It sprawled on a couple of peninsulas—the main peninsula holding real estate worth its weight in gold—and being on a peninsula, the development was rich, the traffic congested. Quinn usually scanned the scenery on this drive, watching how the rural turned semi-rural then suburban, and how much had changed each time.

Today, she barely saw the road, thinking so hard about Ty. Born and raised in Craven County, he'd been respected both as a Jackson and as a tight friend of the Sterlings. He'd earned more respect being a kind, congenial, firm but fair deputy. The public and the sheriff's office held him on an unassuming sort of pedestal. It was the only world he knew.

And Jonah. She couldn't be sure where he was, and whether he was hurt by her urgency in siding with Ty against any evidence to the contrary. Once upon a time, he'd understood that a thousand percent, just as Ty had understood a month ago when she had to focus on Jonah.

She gripped the steering wheel so hard her fingers were numbing. United . . . that's what they were, damn it. Unconditional friendship was a rare commodity these days, and she wasn't ready to say theirs was fading.

She wasn't going all the way into the Charleston this time. Her GPS had her on the outskirts of West Ashley, about six miles from where Wescott's address supposedly resided on Ashley River Road.

Turning off Highway 17, she made her way up Bee's Ferry Road until she reached Ashley River Road. Didn't take long to find the community.

Ashley Vale wasn't the meager level of Natalie's and Frannie Bean's apartments, but it was a far cry from the East Bay Street living of downtown. If this represented Wescott's standard of living, he either belonged in middle class or lived in places where he could sign shorter leases and be gone.

If he had a place here, then why Savannah? Unless he and Natalie really had had a fling. Working together could stir up such feelings. She'd been a prime example of that three or four . . . maybe five times, with Jonah being the most recent . . . and the last, she'd promised herself.

She crept through the parking lot, spotting Ty's Jeep in a strategic corner where the majority of the comings and goings could be observed. A dozen buildings. Per building signs, Wescott lived in the one in front and to the right of the Jeep's vantage. Parking about a dozen slots distant from the Jeep, she faced the road instead of the apartment buildings, to avoid the attention to those in the Jeep or anyone inside the units. She tied her red hair back and tucked it up under a cap.

She could no longer make out the Jeep from where she sat, which meant they couldn't see her. Easing out of her truck, she crept behind hers and the other vehicles until she reached the Jeep's taillights. Ty had combat parked, his visor down. He sat slumped in his seat, and, surprise of surprises, Jonah sat in the passenger seat doing the same.

She tapped on the glass, and Jonah about leaped out of his skin. Upon recognition, he unlocked the doors, and Quinn slid into the back seat. Keeping it light, her words aimed to return them to their comradery, before everything had splintered. "Boys, I'm hurt. You're partying without me."

"Wescott is a killer, Quinn," Jonah said.

Straight to the point. "Jonah tell you about Jefferson?"

"That's his name?" Ty asked.

"Apartment F3 near Natalie. Sounded like a rather creepy sort."

"Let me tell you my story, then you tell me yours," he said.

Even as the prime suspect, Ty would still describe the situation in a procedural manner. She held up a finger for him to wait a minute. "First, the kids are fine, and Archie is resting comfortably. Your mother texted, and I told her you were fine, too. Don't make a liar out of me." Then she poked him. "Go ahead. Start from when you ran off last night and bring me up to speed."

No talk of kisses. Not that she was naïve enough not to think the hurt of all parties didn't still prickle under the skin, but she had hoped the trio still could prioritize the more imminent concerns. Like Ty going away forever for murder.

Ty gave her a split second of eye contact about sidestepping the obvious before he launched into Quinn's request. "I came here first after I left the farm," he said.

First? "At two in the morning?"

"What better way to study Wescott than to come to where he lives and stake it out until he got up and went about his business," Ty said. "I arrived, narrowed down where his apartment was . . ." He pointed to the third of four apartments, counting from the left of the two-story building directly in front of them. Passing between that building and the one beside it was a common area with a pool and clubhouse.

Ty continued. "I'd identified his Lexus from before, so it was easy to find." He pointed to it parked right outside the apartment door. An SC tag.

"Do you realize that sitting here all night has made you yet another suspect, Ty?" She wanted to wring his neck for going off half-cocked with a half-assed plan in mind. "Follow the other guy and see what you find? That was your strategy? Jesus Christ, Ty, you're smarter than that. You should have been on Sterling Banks, with witnesses who could protect you and Cole and, more so, vouch for you. Damn it, Old Man, what the hell is wrong with you?"

Her voice bounced off the low ceiling. Ty was turning into his own worst enemy. How was she supposed to fight that?

"Q, take it down a notch," Ty hissed back.

How often had he corrected her temper? Hearing his stunned her into silence.

"He didn't park here all night," Jonah said, his tone lower, again the mediator. "Let him explain, Quinn." He reached down and lifted a notebook, filled with Ty's recognizable longhand. "Look at this."

She reached for what she recognized as a surveillance log, but Ty interceded. "Let me tell it first."

She repositioned herself in the middle of the back bench seat, her long legs squeezed between the two front seats. She had to shift a couple times to find a comfortable place. "I'm listening."

"Wescott came out of his apartment a little before four," Ty said.

"Four?"

"Let the man talk," Jonah corrected.

Ty dipped his chin at Jonah, a mild sign of appreciation. Surprisingly, she was the odd person out.

"I followed him," Ty began, "praying he stopped somewhere, anywhere, to get a benchmark other than me since my words aren't worth a damn right now. And he did. Filled up at a convenience store, the one right before you get to a Kentucky Fried Chicken on Highway 17."

She was aware of the spot. *Smart going, Ty.* That put Wescott on someone's security cam. Quinn sat on the edge of her seat, literally and figuratively.

"After that, I followed him all the way into Walterboro," he said.

Quinn's heart beat harder, but she told herself to hush.

"He went onto the road alongside the apartment complex, like he was turning in the side entrance. Since it was pitch, my headlights would've been obvious, so I drove on past a quarter mile or so, turned around, and gave it a minute or two. Then I drove back, headed down that road, and continued to where I saw his car on the side, him still behind the wheel."

"Facing the back of the buildings, right?" she asked.

Jonah gave her a glance of reproach, but Ty did a palm up that it was okay. "Yes," he said. "Some of those woods stood between him and the apartments, but still, he could see. The point is that he didn't want to *be* seen."

This was good.

"I turned into a drive that didn't have a car, shut off my lights, and went out on foot." He held up his phone. "I have pics from when he left his place, benchmarks along the way, and when he pulled into the road. Once I parked, I took pics of where I was in relation to his vehicle, then along the way in the edge of the woods, until I reached his Lexus."

"Friggin' awesome, Ty." She was proud of him . . . to a point.

He'd been in investigator mode and doing well at it, but he should've taken her. Not only could they have done all that he did, but done so with a witness. A tainted witness, but two people versus Wescott. But unless Ty told her something incredibly fresh and indictable, he still wasn't out of the hole.

Someone came out from between the buildings and headed toward them. All three sagged out of sight. They heard the SUV two cars over crank up, pull out, and leave before they rose back up.

"You got to the Lexus," she said, coming back to where he left off. "Whoops, incoming."

They slunk down and up three times before Ty could get back to the storytelling.

"He wasn't in the car when I got to it," he finally continued. "I hugged the tree line until I could see the back of building F. He was there, on the outside landing, back against the wall, waiting."

Quinn visualized the location, the same smoking spot where she and Frannie Bean had spoken. Where the cigarette butt rock used to be. "Video or photos?" she asked. "I mean, of that spot and what he was doing?"

"Video," he said.

Her heart jumped. "Go on."

"He went in the corridor there, you know, where it leads to the stairs."

She nodded.

"I held the video on, afraid to stop it. Lasted six and a half minutes. He ran out. I retreated into the trees, stopping the video when he got to the car so I could run back to mine. I heard him scratch the dirt leaving as I got into my car. I caught up to him in a half mile since the stupid moron stayed on the main road, the same road he'd come in on. I followed him back to West Ashley, then here. Drove past the apartments, entered via another entrance, and stopped on the other side there." He pointed to around the corner, where the parking spots weren't visible. "Saw him as he went into his apartment. After twenty minutes, I moved my vehicle here. He hasn't come out since."

"Give me your phone," she said, almost breathless. "Jonah?"

"Ma'am."

"What time did you get here, and are you in any pictures?"

"Got here about forty-five minutes before you did," he said. He looked to Ty for the second answer.

Ty shook his head. "No way was I placing Jonah here, in the middle of whatever this turns into."

Quinn pulled out her own camera and put it in video mode on herself as she recited the current time and date. She did a short recitation about where she was and why she was there, to watch Wescott. Not abnormal for a private investigator. She kept the view in tight and hoped nobody could tell which vehicle she was in. She'd save this in case her presence was needed to make this legit.

Then she went to Ty's videos and pics. Throughout his accounting, she held a robust concern. It was the pitch of night in the very wee hours of morning before the sun even thought about rising. What would be the quality of Ty's work?

The collection he took was immense, and as soon as possible, they'd preserve these on several hard drives and flash drives so some rogue element didn't get their hands on Ty's phone and conveniently make them disappear. She was that convinced that they'd soon come for Ty. The public would demand it of the sheriff, and the sheriff would demand it of his people.

She reached the long, six-and-a-half-minute video and held her breath. She hadn't been out there at night. What if Pratt's slack maintenance not only meant dead bushes in rock flower beds, but also no bulbs in the rusted coach lamps screwed loosely into the vinyl-sided wall.

Whether Pratt did it for insurance purposes or to avoid Frannie Bean's complaints, the bulb was there. And it worked.

"Yes!" she said, when she made out Wescott's worried expression, and yelped again when he stooped down and lifted a rock.

The video ran for an eternity, long enough for her to envision how it played out. Television off, Jefferson might've been asleep, maybe even on the sofa where those blankets had lain harum-scarum. She could picture him opening the door after peering through the peephole wondering who would come by so late. Wescott entered. Maybe he rushed in, and Jefferson backpedaled to the kitchen area, attempting to put the bar between them. Or Wescott entered like a buddy, and Jefferson went to get something to drink, maybe even offering Wescott one, too. She hadn't had time to analyze the killing site for long.

Made her wonder if Wescott had done this type of thing before. Probably not, with his lifting the rock. Or maybe so, with his not wanting to leave a weapon behind or awaken the neighbors. Maybe he didn't know what he was doing until he got to the porch, at the last minute taking the rock as insurance.

Quinn's pulse grew faster. Everyone had underestimated Ty. This was an amazing opportunity to say someone else had the potential to kill Natalie.

The unexpected was learning Wescott and Jefferson likely knew each other, as indicated from Jefferson's letting him in.

She couldn't help thinking that if Wescott was willing to kill Jefferson, he could've killed Natalie as well.

She pictured him rushing to leave, deviating long enough to lower the thermostat, a move the average person would not have made.

Finally, Wescott rushed out on video, stopping long enough to hurl something into the woods. The rock. Had to be.

She played the video out, her heart trying to beat through her ribs. "I'd already thought of that rock as a murder weapon, Ty," she said, her voice pitchy at this potential. "Ty . . . a resident spotted it missing, while I stood right there with her as detectives went through the apartment. Y'all . . . the murder weapon might be in the damn woods." She reached over and cupped a hand behind Ty's neck. "You crazy son of a gun, you may have caught him!" she said, raising up the phone to show him, as if he hadn't seen it before. In a spit of emotion, she almost drew him in for a huge smack on the mouth. His eyes went wide. She gave him a light shake instead.

This was wonderful, this could turn things in a different direction, but they weren't necessarily out of the woods. The case, she meant. The trio's relationship. . . was not the critical issue right now.

She'd worry about that tomorrow.

Chapter 26

QUINN CALLED TASSEY, putting it on speaker. "Hey, we're in Charleston, meaning Ty, Jonah, and me, and we have something you need to see."

"The three musketeers, huh?"

They'd been called that by many others many times before, and the world wasn't wrong. She just hoped the three of them would continue to be the same close unit when this case was done. "We work well together, yes. Can we come? Like, now?"

"Can't it wait until the morning? I have a business dinner date," the attorney said.

"No, it can't wait," Quinn said, with the two guys watching. "Don't put on your little black dress for later either, because I suspect we'll be taking up your whole evening. Let me put it this way, Tassey, we have video of Jefferson's killer and the murder weapon. We're on our way, and you'll forget all about dinner." Quinn disconnected. "Your Jeep or my truck?" she asked her guys.

"We're already in mine," Ty said. "Buckle up."

Rush hour had kicked in, in spite of its being a holiday week, because Charleston hosted its fair share of tourists this time of year. The drive took a full half-hour longer than it should.

Tassey texted, *You've got an hour. This best be incredible or you're fired.*

Quinn scoffed at the message, more concerned about traffic, but they made it, parked on the street in one of the spots opening up, and fast-walked to meet Tassey.

None of them had been to the law office's auspicious locale on Church Street, the address wedged alongside several other high-brow firms, but they weren't awed and impressed at the moment.

The scent of clean, circulated air hit them at the doorway, almost frigid compared to the humid heat left outside. A young woman, hair flipped up and neat, remained freshly coifed, even at this hour. She sat behind a long, wide, walnut bar stationed on a riser to place the seated receptionist closer to eye level of a visitor. "Ms. Sterling, I presume?"

"Yes," Quinn replied. This woman probably had waited around solely for them since the Charleston legal community had closed for the evening.

"The elevator over to your right. Third floor. She's waiting for you."

Meaning Tassey's meter was running.

The counselor stood in her doorway, waiting.

Quinn had already transferred Ty's photos and videos to her own phone, and as backup, to Jonah's. She handed her phone to Tassey. Quinn hadn't messaged them to Tassey, not knowing if the attorney would want evidence on her own phone. Quinn lead with the six-and-a-half-minute video. "That's early this morning, before I went to Walterboro and found Jefferson dead. That's building F. That's—"

"Wescott," Tassey said, speaking level to settle everyone down. "Let me study this a second."

The tension in the air was palpable. Finally, the video ended, and Tassey looked up. "Walk me through this, Ty. A firm timeline."

Quinn waited, eager to watch Tassey's face as Ty presented the evidence. Jonah reached over and took her hand, and she gratefully squeezed back.

Once Ty finished, Tassey remained stiff-backed, formal, thinking.

"Well, so much for dinner." She lifted her own phone. The three took furtive glances at each other.

"Sheriff Remington, please," Tassey said, staring up and past the three of them. "Yes, I know it's the end of the day. This is Tassey Talmadge, and this is about the two apartment homicides. Urgent? Honey, I should say so. The detective? No, ma'am. You heard me right the first time. Remington, please."

Didn't take long for Tassey to explain to the sheriff that she was in possession of fresh evidence, and if it was worth her after-hour trip to Walterboro, then the sheriff could stick around.

She got her way and hung up as if that were no surprise. "While this evidence is good," she said, holding up the phone, "that doesn't mean Wescott rolls over. He could always say—"

"That Ty tried to set up him," Quinn said, expressing what had almost spoiled her initial excitement at the video. "But Ty didn't pick up that rock, and the time frame is not on Wescott's side, and he has no evidence that Ty set this up. There's no evidence of Ty going in, while there is of Wescott. And if you put deputies in those woods, you might lay hands on the murder weapon." She was ready to fight this. Every bit of evidence on these cases was circumstantial whether talking about Ty killing Natalie or Wescott killing Jefferson, but reasonable doubt wasn't a foolproof strategy for a defendant.

"There's still no proof he went in that apartment and killed the man," Tassey finished and stood. "Let's drive. Dinner will come and go this evening, people, or so we can hope if this case catches fire."

They picked up Quinn's truck en route, making a three-car caravan to Walterboro—which could've been four counting Jonah's truck, but he was riding with Ty. Someone had to in order to ensure a witness was constantly with Ty. No more going rogue.

Quinn's thoughts raced, hunting for answers, impressions that fell in Ty's favor and against Wescott's. She thought of ways Wescott could get out of this, especially with a good attorney. This double murder of people who lived yards apart could turn into one suspected murderer against the other. Each could point a finger at the other for either murder. If one went to trial before the other, the first had the upper hand, whether acquitted or found guilty, because they'd air all the dirty laundry from their angle, and once the trial was over, that's how the public would remember events, as if they'd been proven as fact in court.

God, if all this went to trial. . . . She counted her blessings she had Tassey Talmadge on retainer.

They were ushered into Remington's office where the sheriff and the two detectives from earlier in the day waited, not particularly happy at their day.

Tassey had copied the evidence on a flash drive, validating the chain of evidence, and made copies of Ty's surveillance log, the likes of which LEOs were familiar, and she handed them out before taking her seat. "Gentlemen, you each have a copy before you of this morning's events. I wanted to be here when you first studied them."

The two detectives sneaked glances at each other, not fond of Tassey's take-charge entrance. Remington, however, let her have her moment, then asked if anyone needed coffee. Politics and experience created callouses and a high threshold for song and dance.

The Tassey crew took their seats. Ty remained eerily silent, as if afraid to sabotage hope. Jonah copycatted his friend.

Those assembled began with the surveillance log. From his expressions, Detective Parker's interest piqued reading it, but his eyebrows almost disappeared into his thinning hairline at the video.

Afterwards, the questions flew fast and furious interrogating Ty, then Quinn, even Jonah who'd had to define the beginning of the timeline when Ty struck out, and the end when he'd caught up with Ty staking out Wescott's apartment. Tassey interjected here and there, keeping the focus on the new evidence and off what they thought of Ty and Natalie.

"Did you speak to Frannie Bean Salvador?" Quinn asked Parker after the first flurry of questions.

"Yes," Parker said, a small degree of comic relief in his expression at the experience.

"She describe the missing rock? Her smoking rock? It has been there for ages, and she used every morning and every evening to put out her cigarette. The rock that had been there the evening before but was noticed gone when you guys showed up."

"She tried to explain something like that, yeah."

Quinn narrowed her eyes. "But did you take her seriously?"

The hesitation said no. Attention fell on him hard in that moment of silence, and it went unsaid he would take it seriously now.

"It's summer. There's still daylight left," Quinn said. "Any chance y'all could get started on hunt for that rock ASAP? Blood, DNA—"

"Cool your jets, Ms. Sterling," said Parker, then after a long, disgruntled stare at Quinn, he left the room to put deputies onto the search.

"I believe this is worth bringing in Wescott," Tassey said to Remington as if they were royalty and the only ones allowed to address each other.

"We will," he said.

"When?" she asked.

"I'm not picking him up, if that's what you mean, Counselor. We'll *invite* him and give him a chance to play nice. This is where you let us do our job."

"We'll wait until we know when he's coming," she said. "I'd consider it a great favor if you'd let me sit behind the glass for the questioning."

"Not happening, Ms. Talmadge."

"When will you try to get him in?" she asked again as if she hadn't already.

"As soon as we can," he said, and when she stared him down, added, "We'll request his presence immediately, but we aren't hauling him in."

Quinn held her tongue in this power standoff.

Parker returned. "Got uniforms headed to the woods. I called Wescott and told him we had new evidence, letting him believe it was on the Natalie Jackson case. Told him we needed his interpretation of it since he was the closest person to Natalie in recent days. He's coming in."

Tassey tried not to smile at Parker's giving things away. Quinn excused herself and stepped out to the restroom, a fast dial to Larry Sterling's cell.

"Listen to me without interruption, please," she said, relaying events in fast speak, hoping he kept up. Time was of the essence if Wescott hurried to Walterboro. He'd been awful quick before to show cooperation in his efforts to remove suspicion.

"Wescott is on his way in," Quinn said. "None of us is being allowed to sit in or listen to the interview, but they might let you." Craven County's trespassing case had been solved, the culprit promptly murdered, yet found by his Sterling Banks people who also presented the evidence on who killed him. Craven was rocking the investigation. How could they not let its sheriff sit in?

"You'd get the interview sooner or later from the SO, Niece."

"Don't brush me off, Uncle. We need you. We need you badly. I've asked little of you over the years, but whatever you think of me and our past, Ty needs you right now. Do it for him, if you have to justify yourself. I don't care."

She lowered a toilet lid and plopped down, phone to her ear, head drooped in her hand.

"Sure, I'll eventually get the interview, but in the meantime, Wescott disappears, or gets lawyered up, or concocts a tale that serves to hurt Ty, or any of a hundred things." *Breathe.*

"Quinn, stop," he said, sounding almost parental . . . almost as if he cared. "The fact it's Ty is clouding your judgment. Listen, they don't want Wescott to lawyer up yet, so they'll court him, maybe bullshit him about Natalie's case, hoping it segues into the other and he says something they can use." He gave her a second. "You understand that."

He was right. Her mind was in disarray for fear of what might happen to Ty if they couldn't make a case against Wescott. But Larry'd underscored the reason they needed him at tonight's interview. "That's the point, Uncle. He might say something they . . . or we . . . can investigate further, or better yet, take to the bank and nail his sorry ass. Can we afford to take the gamble that they'll tell us everything later, or worse, tell us too late to prove him wrong?"

His gravelly sigh came through, but she couldn't read it.

"Let me call and see what I can do," he said.

"Bless you, Uncle."

"For now you do," he said, and hung up.

She sat there in the stall, grateful for the vacuum of silence . . . and feeling guilty as hell. The Sterling feud between them was as much her fault as his. One didn't argue alone. Groveling was not in her nature, but she'd done it. With this being Ty, she'd done it without a second thought. Fear for a loved one had laid her raw, naked enough to show her feelings . . . and also made her feel her own culpability for years of Sterling battle.

Nobody was perfect. Uncle Larry was far from it. He'd networked with Renault in years past, until Graham Sterling was murdered. He'd fought with Archie until he packed his bags and left, not seeing the family for years. He'd stopped short on investigations, taken the shortest route to close one, whether other options existed or not. He'd lost a thousand acres of Sterling land in his affair with a cheap woman who'd disappeared when she realized she wasn't getting a bit of it.

Before Quinn knew it, she was gnawing on old grudges and hating the man while still hating herself for it. A familiar vicious cycle.

God dammit, she didn't have time to mend the Sterling family right now. She leaped up to rejoin the group, hoping to hear that Uncle Larry was coming. If he wasn't, well, she'd deal with those feelings tomorrow.

Quinn walked in on Tassey and Remington talking low, the attorney having moved a chair to the side of the sheriff's desk. The detectives were gone. Ty and Jonah had moved their chairs further back a few feet in an effort not to pry. Quinn joined them, crinkling her forehead in an ask if anything had happened in her absence.

"He got a phone call," Ty whispered. "Pretty sure it was our sheriff." He tucked his head in closer to hers. "Was that your doing?"

"A Hail Mary," she said. "Somebody needs to hear what Wescott says. Since the victim is the suspect of a Craven County case, a taste of professional courtesy might be in order. They play politics, remember."

Jonah looked doubtful. "The trespassing case is nothing compared to murder, Quinn. If it were me—"

"I know, but this isn't your world, Jonah. It works different," Quinn whispered.

"Don't think I don't know that," he replied, hurt and harsh.

"Ms. Sterling," Sheriff Remington said from across the room. "Appears your uncle is dropping in for a visit."

She stiffened, waiting for something negative.

"We're allowing him to watch from behind the glass," he said. "Can't go overwhelming Mr. Wescott when he's volunteering to come in to assist an investigation, can we?"

Tassey gave Quinn a covertly timed wink.

"For now," Remington said, "how about that cup of coffee while we wait." He paused for effect. "Unless you four want to go. You don't really need to be here."

But before Quinn could speak up, Tassey inserted, "Coffee sounds lovely, Otis."

"Appreciate the offer, but I'd rather sit in the car, if you don't mind," Ty said, rising, and in solidarity, the trio thanked the sheriff and left the building.

They sat in the Jeep, tired of the talking, tired of the heaviness of all this. How many times had they said that growing up sucked, each of them missing the time with the JQT club when three children had met in the Windsor tree house to gripe about parents, rant about school, and listen to the slow current of the Edisto water against tree roots and mud. There they imagined how Spiderman would have swung from the Sterling Banks pecan trees to snare Venom and any of assorted adversaries. Or swam in their underwear in the river. Or ate Jule's sandwiches before catching afternoon naps, arms and legs tangled in dreams of what it would be like to live in those tree limbs forever.

They'd had no idea how shaky the shelter of those branches would become under the weight of adulthood.

WITHIN THE HOUR, Ty eased up in his seat, recognizing Wescott's Lexus. Minutes later, Larry Sterling arrived in his personal Chevy Silverado.

Quinn watched her uncle slide out, recalling their old days of back and forth about Chevy versus Ford. He'd dressed in jeans and a button-up shirt, another good ol' boy from the county. *Kudos to you for not announcing your presence, Uncle.*

"What now?" Jonah muttered. "We sit here?"

"Yes, we wait," Quinn said.

Regardless of what Wescott said tonight, Colleton SO would work hard tomorrow corroborating intel. They'd go to the gas station where Wescott had filled up when he'd left his apartment on the way to Walterboro. They'd hunt the rock. They'd study Ty's footage and dissect his surveillance log for irregularities and holes. Fingerprints from Jefferson's apartment would be compared to Wescott's and Ty's. They'd delve into Natalie's financials after learning from Ty about the odd bank account, then they'd contact Natalie's employers about the concerning agreement Natalie had referenced, questioning why she was being paid for providing information on something that made no sense without specifics.

All of these details had the potential of saving Ty. But waiting on law enforcement and attorneys to save your life was paralyzingly scary.

"Pray Wescott lies, y'all," she said, breathlessly. "Pray those detectives know what they are doing."

Ty didn't hide his sarcasm. "Living on prayers are we, Q?"

She grinned sadly at him.

After a while, Tassey's text to Ty and Quinn woke them up from comatose slumps in their seats. *Don't come in. I'll update you later. Your being here won't work right now. Go home and get some rest.*

"I'll be damned if I'm going home," Jonah said. "I'd be up all night anyway, so might as well be here with you guys."

Quinn reached up and rested a hand on his cheek in appreciation, easing it around to the back of his neck for a brief rub, so grateful Jonah had chosen not to mention the kiss.

They exchanged texts with Lenore, Jule, and Archie, assuring them they were fine. Replying in code that new evidence had come to light, they said they were waiting to hear more about it. They were afraid to say more.

The night set dark with only a sliver of a moon in the sky. Windows down in the Jeep, Quinn lay an elbow on the door edge, listening to the trilling of insects in the thin woods in the distance. The center, however, was relatively lit up, almost obscenely so this time of night. They were one of a dozen vehicles in a parking lot that held six or seven times that.

If the worst happened, if their world shifted off its axis over the next couple of days, she wondered if she'd remember back to this moment and wish for the innocence of the not knowing.

"Quinn, he's coming out," Jonah whispered.

Larry went to his car instead of them. Didn't seem long enough for Quinn to feel good about anything. Interviews took a while. Good ones took forever. It wasn't quite eleven.

Meet me at the Waffle House, said his text to all three. Ty turned to Quinn, as if she'd forgotten she had to drive her own truck back, and she wished she didn't have to drive alone. But then Ty looked at Jonah. "Go on, man. You guys will still have eyes on me. It'll be fine."

Quinn and Jonah tried not to scurry, never knowing who watched from inside. She started up the engine and let Ty follow Larry after texting Tassey they were leaving. The attorney didn't reply.

Quinn and Jonah rode in silence the few short miles, and she wondered if his brain was as busy as hers. They quickly pulled up in the diner's parking lot.

"I'm trying to keep Ty at the forefront of everything right now," she said. "His life is in the balance."

Jonah watched the diners inside instead of her. "I understand that. He's important. His wellbeing and mental strength are crucial."

"Right," she agreed, happy to hear him say that.

"There are bigger things than us," he added, and exited the truck.

Chapter 27

THE SCENTS OF bacon and coffee hit Quinn as she followed Jonah inside, who followed Larry. Ty came in right behind them.

The Waffle House staff was accustomed to people rendezvousing in their diner at odd hours. It was a go-to for fresh lovers or clandestine couples, crooks, and cops alike. Business dealings and family gatherings after Sunday service. The four squeezed into the largest booth in the far corner of the eatery, which silently told the waitress to take their orders and let them be. Quinn sat next to her uncle after Ty slid in next to Jonah.

"Wescott's blaming Ty for both murders," Larry said. "Once he saw the video, he claimed he went into the apartment and found Jefferson that way, so Ty must have killed Jefferson beforehand, then took the opportunity to video Wescott and set him up."

"That's bullshit," Ty said, his fisted hand stopping short of smashing down on the Formica table.

Why hadn't Ty taken somebody with him?

"I was afraid of this," Quinn said. She hadn't been sure how shrewd Wescott would be when confronted. Truth was, and Wescott knew it, Ty hadn't proven Wescott went inside Jefferson's apartment, much less killed him. They just both happened to be at the apartments at the same time at an early hour. Each could point fingers at the other. Quinn could only hope Wescott's prints were inside. Easy enough to prove Ty's weren't. Unless they claimed he used gloves. A deputy would think like that, wouldn't he?

"We know Ty was following Wescott," Jonah said. "That put him there, but why did Wescott go in the first place? He have an answer for that?"

Larry looked at Quinn as if saying, *You're gonna love this.*

"Jefferson was working for him, he said."

Plates of eggs and hash browns arrived. Everyone hushed, eager for the waitress to get done and leave. She silently refilled cups and disappeared.

But all anyone wanted to do was nurse their coffee. The weight of Wescott's accusation had ruined appetites.

"But the rock," Jonah said.

"Depends on if they find it, and what they find on it," Larry said. "Wescott said Jefferson asked to meet early, but the man was squirrelly and Wescott was unarmed. So at the last minute he grabbed the rock, and when he hadn't had to use it, he tossed it in the woods."

"Son of a bitch," Ty muttered under his breath. "Can't win for losing."

"From what I saw of Jefferson's head, there will be blood on that rock," Quinn said, searching for hope. "Why did Wescott hire Jefferson in the first place? Did he say?"

"Wescott said he was paying Natalie to be an informant for him, and paying Jefferson to keep an eye on her because she was green at it. He used the name Gabriel as a cover with Cole. Natalie was aware of the pretense."

Cole sure wasn't fond of the man, and, honestly, Quinn wasn't happy with the child being kept in the dark and misguided.

"I'm not believing this," Ty uttered.

But Becca had said Natalie bowed out of the relationship, feeling uncomfortable about Wescott / Gabriel. Cole could have been one of the reasons, if not *the* reason. Natalie's mom instincts had tried to win in the end.

Ty wasn't taking any of this well. "Why would she be an informant? What the hell for?"

"Wait a minute," Quinn said, thinking hard to click some of these pieces together. "Who was Wescott working for might be the bigger question. Wescott wasn't anyone special, and what put him onto Natalie?"

"What would Natalie know to begin with?" Jonah asked. "Nothing against her, Ty, but what the hell would she know that was worth working her like this?"

Ty gave a wilted shrug.

Natalie told her employer that she was not mixing her day job with this freelance business with Wescott, but she could've lied. She could've been digging up intel on clients. That made the most sense to Quinn.

She had one unsolved hunch, though, and she pulled out her phone, checking a couple of sites. It was too late to call SLED, the South Carolina Law Enforcement Division to check a PI license, so she checked two professional PI organizations instead, but Wescott's name wasn't listed. Still, her gut told her she was on track. He was a private investigator, like herself, and also like herself, she wasn't prone to broadcast her profession. If the work was good without a website, why get one? If you had a handful of steady clients, why flaunt your business on a PI society's membership page? Quinn had no office. She met people in the corner of the Jackson Hole diner, with Lenore her unofficial administrative assistant and lookout. She belonged to these professional organizations, but she didn't allow her name on any public, online list, much less her picture.

"He didn't say who he worked for," Larry said. "Nor that he even worked for anyone, but he said he wasn't Natalie's boyfriend. He was Gabriel, and they were working together, pretending to be dating as cover so nobody was the wiser."

"Why the trips to Savannah then?" Quinn asked, really wanting to talk to Becca Blevins now.

"Working together . . . to what end?" Ty scowled hard and deep, and Quinn knew why. He prided himself on keeping up with his family, ex-wife or not. He also prided himself on being a decent investigator, and he'd seen none of this coming. Nothing made sense to him. All he'd ever done had been in the name of doing good and being protective, and it had backfired on him. The good guy was going down for being a good guy. Even following Wescott this morning had worked against him.

They all felt the downward slide Ty was on.

Quinn received a text. Her key people sat with her. Something from the farm? Hopefully, Archie was okay.

The message from Tassey read, *Leaving the SO. Wescott left angry. He's lawyering up. Not sending this to Ty. Talk tomorrow. We need more than what we have.*

Quinn looked up to the congregation waiting for feedback. "Oh, that was Tassey," she said. "Letting me know she's headed home and would call us tomorrow."

Ty wilted. Jonah patted his friend on the back. Larry nursed his coffee, clearly there for his deputy but uncertain how to show it.

The day had started with promise and ended with little more than a wish that a jury would believe Ty over Wescott.

This Wescott situation with Natalie was odd. The situation with Jefferson odder still. What wasn't Quinn seeing?

Or who else might've seen what she missed? A name came to mind.

"Gotta go," she said, downing the last of her coffee, and sliding her eggs toward Jonah to eat.

Ty tried to rise, nudging Jonah to let him out. "I'm coming with you."

Of course he wanted to. He always offered to accompany her on a case, and sitting on his hands was driving him nuts.

Jonah started to slide out to release his friend.

Larry hadn't protested nor offered. Normal Larry behavior—riding that middle lane, straddling that fence.

"No," she said. "I don't need anyone on this. I'm going to see one woman, and this needs to be woman to woman. I'll be at the apartment complex in case you need me, but don't come after me unless I call."

The three men stared from her to each other. Jonah and Larry wouldn't understand, and Ty didn't need to be there.

"I have a firearm. I have a phone," she said. "I'll check in."

"Wescott is out there," Jonah said. "You are not his favorite person."

"I know," she said. "I'll be careful."

Then without waiting for feedback, advice, or question, she made a beeline for the door, cranked up the truck, and headed to building F.

Her clock read almost ten. A little on the late side though not ridiculously so, but if this woman was in bed this early, Quinn would be surprised. And if she was, well, she could wake up and talk.

Almost there. She did make one call, though, in case.

But it went to voice mail.

"Raysor, left your boss's office where they interviewed Wescott. Long story, but he's blaming Ty for Jefferson's death. He left mad, and before his attorney gets involved and this thing blows up tomorrow, I'm going to the apartment complex. Not sure if you're on duty or not but would appreciate you meeting me there. Otherwise, I'll touch base tomorrow."

A long shot. His burly dough-boy self was probably snoring his way through dreams.

The apartment complex looked different this late at night. The streetlights were on but not enough to give a crisp image of anything. Whoever owned the place had spent no more than they'd had to for an occupancy certificate to rent the units, and they'd hired the minimal in Pratt. She was surprised there wasn't more crime at the place before now. After this week, two murders might make them think twice about their security.

She bypassed Pratt's place and drove straight through the parking lot, pulling in front of building F. A Colleton car wasn't there as before, but the deputy could still be making passes through, doing double duty while checking the roads and businesses in the area. Frankly, she was glad she wouldn't be noticed.

She opened her door and heard a television from someone's cracked window, wondering who in their right mind left a window open in July, even at night. And, for God's sake, who left one open after a killing spree? She'd never liked dormitory dwelling in college nor at the academy, and this place only confirmed her dislike for compartment living. Her father would call her spoiled.

From her vantage getting out, she saw lights on at Randleman's and Becca's. Quinn climbed the stairs, noting crime-scene tape re-positioned over Natalie's door, and fresh tape in front of Jefferson's. On this level, that left Tee and Tory on one side and Frannie Bean on the other. Both had lights on. A bunch of night owls.

But she returned down the stairs, deciding another tenant more critical for what may be her only interview for the evening. In their first visit, Becca had been too tight-fisted with her facts, in Quinn's opinion, if Natalie was the friend Becca professed she was. And she'd spoken with Randleman this morning regarding Jefferson but not stuck around long.

Becca also came across as smarter than the average building-F soul.

Quinn stepped off the stairs, approaching Becca's door to her left on the bottom floor. Now that she understood the dynamics and layout, Quinn envisioned Frannie Bean overhead, ever listening, and Baxter Randleman directly across from Becca, unable to hear a thing. She still had doubt that Frannie Bean hadn't heard or seen more than she divulged, but it was too late to face her and Becca both.

Voices came from . . . somewhere. Unable to make out the words, Quinn put an ear up to Becca's window first, grateful for the landing light being dim and no backlighting. While she couldn't make out all of the conversation, she could make out two distinct voices, a man and a woman. They weren't chummy, and Quinn most assuredly caught the word *Jefferson*.

She ran back to her pickup. In the back seat, she kept her fair share of tools, some for the farm and some for her PI work. She was old school in terms of investigations, not having enough complex cases to warrant a slew of technology, but she did have a few gizmos. Surveillance items, mainly. A few bugging pieces, some mobile tracking devices, two insanely decent flashlights, binoculars, a small Canon camcorder, a Canon Rebel camera, and a handful of notepads and pens.

But there was one item she'd never had a chance to use before. Still in the box it came in, she extracted a parabolic listening device, small enough to fit in one hand. She hoped she remembered how to use it, having played with it with Jonah the day it arrived about six months ago. As they'd done as kids, they'd hidden amongst the pecan trees, her testing how far away she could hear him. He tested what kind of language he could get away with and her not hear.

It had been a good day, a really good day. This was before they'd talked marriage, but not before they'd flirted with the thought. Nothing like his painful expression in the doorway of Archie's bedroom when he'd learned of Ty's kiss.

Regret sifted in. He might not be stonewalling her, but he wasn't acting normal toward her tonight. She could feel the other shoe waiting to fall, with Jonah holding off only until Ty's problem was over. She couldn't tell how the chips would fall and didn't want to bother thinking about it anymore.

Item in her hands, she turned and scanned the parking lot for movement, her gaze landing on a white Lexus. *Son of a bitch.* Nobody in this neighborhood drove a Lexus.

Stooping to below car-hood level, she eased back to the building and duck-walked beneath Becca's window, praying she remembered how to use this thing in her hands.

In the meantime, she listened in with ears. They'd turned up the television, damn it. She fiddled in the dimness with the headset, the plug, the recorder, sticking prongs where they didn't fit, hitting buttons that didn't work.

To hell with this. She reached over and slid the device behind the bushes and came back. Taking out her pocket knife, she toyed with the window screen. It lifted easily. Setting it also in the bushes, she returned and went to work on the glass. It felt loose already.

The window went up a quarter inch, then a half. Then she opened a phone app and set it on record, resting the phone on the window ledge facing in.

"I do not work for you," Becca said. No fear in her voice. Nothing like Jefferson leaning on Frannie Bean. "You clean up your own mess."

"He hired us both, so get off that shit," Wescott said. "We work together."

"Not last I heard," she countered.

"What are you going to do then, report to him that I killed Jefferson?"

Quinn could only pray for an admission.

"No, because I never saw you kill him," Becca said. "This was your case, and damned if you didn't fuck it up from here to eternity. Never should've subcontracted outside help, you idiot. Bet that man's background was a clusterfuck." She laughed. "And you call yourself a PI."

Jesus, this was a whole other Becca Blevins. The language, the contrarian, the confident adversary to a man Quinn was positive had killed another man . . . and maybe a woman.

"I liked that girl." Becca's steam continued to build. "She didn't deserve to die. You screwed this all to hell. Her with a kid . . . a good kid. And you're taking away his remaining parent by blaming him."

"Listen to you. You got too close to her," Wescott said. "It's done. The kid's got a grandmother. He'll live. Besides . . ." He talked as if he found himself shrewd. "If his daddy goes to jail, and the kid plays his cards right, the Sterlings will probably give him more than his daddy ever could. You see how close those people are."

If something happened to Ty, Sterling Banks would indeed look after Cole, but who were these people to know that? That would not have been a conversation between Nat and Becca, either. If something happened to Nat, she'd expect Ty to take over, but Nat didn't see herself dying.

Quinn shifted, angling her head better. Becca didn't speak after that, making Quinn wonder if she'd been heard.

"Regardless, he won't be happy," she finally said. "And I'm not vouching for you."

"You'll vouch for me with him, in court, to anybody who brings it up. If I can kill Jefferson, I can deal with you."

Awesome. An admission.

Becca didn't sound stunned, scared, or even skeptical about this man and his sloppy, stupid, lackadaisical admission. She reacted in a manner that took Quinn even further aback.

She laughed. Laughed hard and deep. "He was insane. If he hadn't been, you wouldn't have overreacted. Damn, you beat his face to a bloody pulp." She chuckled again. "He'll have your head."

Quinn adjusted from knees to a squat. *He, he, he. Who the hell was he?*

And all this centered around Natalie? For God's sake, what could she have known or had access to which would warrant all of this? Had to be a client at the attorney firm. Had to be. These attorneys handled family court and real estate, but Quinn could see a child-custody battle, maybe, or some nasty divorce, but the connection wasn't making itself known.

Who the hell was *he?*

The voices went lower, or else the television got louder. What she was sure of was the thump. Then another.

Blinds over the window crunched in, and the back of a head hit the glass. The shock sent Quinn off balance onto the concrete.

Becca screeched long and grating, in an exasperating rage.

Quinn went for a weapon she had left in the glove box, not thinking that conversations with the docile likes of Becca and Frannie Bean would merit a firearm. Quinn leaped up and went to Becca's door, trying the handle. It wasn't locked.

Someone's body went to the floor.

Quinn threw open the door. It bounced off its door stopper, threatening to hit her in return. She kicked it again, foot braced on the threshold, shouting, "Police!" though she wasn't. She didn't rush in, flattening her back against the vinyl siding to the side. More scrambling ensued . . . a surprising amount of scrambling considering this was a man in his forties subduing a woman almost old enough to be his mother.

"Don't come in here," Wescott shouted. "I'll kill her."

Quinn dared to peer in. Furniture had been knocked out of order, a macrame plant hanger on the floor with dirt scattered from a spider plant. A burned lavender smell hung in the air, a candle lying on the rug, wax trailing out and starting to gel.

Wescott's arm encircled Becca's neck. Her cheeks were flushed; her hands gripped the forearm. The gaze, however, didn't fit. It flashed anger, not fear. She saw Quinn but didn't see Quinn, her eyes studying the room. Quinn recognized someone looking for a way to retaliate, and suddenly she wondered if she should be concerned as much about facing Becca as she was Wescott.

After all, they worked for the same boss.

"Let her go," Quinn said, ordering hard from her gut. "Cops are en route."

Wescott looked from Becca and Quinn, to the door, then back to Quinn—analyzing his options. He couldn't say the cops weren't coming because he'd just been there, their interest still vivid in his mind.

He shoved Becca toward the sofa, where she landed belly down, feet knocking the end table. She rolled over on one elbow . . . not in fright but in assessment.

Quinn was missing the point here . . . maybe several points. She had come to interview Becca, only to be confronted with a murderer.

Wescott had erred not going straight home, erred talking too much to Becca, and unknowingly erred speaking of Jefferson's murder loud enough to be heard by Quinn. He'd have to kill both her and Becca to not go down now.

Chapter 28

BECCA EASED UPRIGHT from the sofa, but Wescott's attention clung on Quinn. He wasn't armed or he'd have drawn by now. Not the most astute criminal.

Then Quinn warned herself that underestimating an adversary invited mistakes. She'd learned that at Quantico. Both agents and bad guys did it, resulting in grave results.

"I'll finish both of you before I'm done," he said, standing on the balls of his feet, arms out as if he contemplated a wrestling move.

"With what, another rock? You keep a collection of those, do you?" Quinn slammed the door. She didn't need him to evade her, and she didn't need onlookers in the way.

He made for the door, nonetheless. His threats were empty, and he'd tossed Becca aside only to get in a position to escape.

He tried to elbow Quinn out of the way, but she sidestepped and kicked him behind a knee, buckling him to the floor. She bounced back, purposely not toward Becca. That woman was still a wild card.

Wescott rose, hand on a nearby overturned chair. Standing, he limped once, regaining his balance. Then he charged Quinn, correctly judging which way she'd go, tackling her to the rug.

Laying atop her, front to front, he worked to get upright while seated to hold her down. But as he tried to rise, she cuffed her hands and clapped over both his ears.

"Ahhh!" he shouted, reaching up toward the pain.

Palm up, she lurched and caught him under the chin, snapping his teeth. His head went back, enough for her to sling him off. Scrambling, she rose to her feet, but in a sudden sweep, Wescott took her off them, sending her front down, half in the living room, half on the kitchen tile, similar to where she'd found Jefferson in his own duplicate floorplan.

While Quinn almost equaled Wescott's height, he still had forty pounds on her, and her size didn't grant her the ability to lift a two-hundred-pound man off her back. Her ponytail having long come loose from its cap and rubber band, the long loose tresses only served to give him a handhold to lift her head back then smack her face into the carpet.

Pain shot through her nose, to behind her eyes. *Son of a bitch.*

Oh, no, this isn't happening. Still seeing stars, she pulled her arms and legs in as best she could and pushed to roll over under him and face this idiot. From there she had leverage. She could own him on top. . . .

Suddenly, her effort got easy, and she overcompensated in the roll. She opened her eyes to see the man protecting both sides of his head, one side of which had been nailed with the spider-plant pot.

Wescott climbed to his feet as quickly as Quinn did to hers, neither as fast as they preferred. Both were dazed. Quinn blinked and sniffled, clearing her vision while taking a step back to see Becca five feet to her left, Wescott about the same to her right.

Becca braced herself like someone half her age . . . trained from somewhere in her past. She might be older, she might be rusty, but muscle memory was forever. Wescott advanced, broadcasting his swing, choosing to go at Becca first. She blocked him with one arm and punched him in the throat with the opposite fist. He collapsed back, floundering, groping at his throat as if his hands could free up the air he couldn't take in, but he didn't go all the way down.

So Quinn took advantage of his half balance and took out his leg. He spun halfway around, down on that knee, giving Becca his back. She landed two hits to his kidneys.

The only grunts and groans were Wescott's. The women waited, panting, poised, each watching for the next opportunity. Quinn still kept one eye on Becca, not sure how ally or adversary she was.

Sirens sounded in the background, but Quinn barely heard them.

The closest to the small kitchen, Wescott crawled upright. Then with an unexpected surge, he lunged toward a counter, snaring a knife out of the woodblock collection of six. He hadn't grabbed the largest, but it armed him, nonetheless. "I'll kill you bitches if it's the last thing I do."

"Don't you hear the police?" Quinn said, chest rising and falling, half breathless, half adrenaline.

But instead of talk, Wescott engaged, leaping at the elder, least fit adversary. Backing up, Becca—wide-eyed—followed the wild sweeps of the weapon in his hand.

Pounding sounded on the door. "Police! Open up!"

That split second of distraction was all she needed. All either woman needed. Becca snatched his arm down and back, his wrist downward and against its limit. Quinn heard the bone crack before Wescott's scream consumed the room, and while he focused on the arm, she kicked his feet out from under him again.

The doorframe exploded as Raysor barged in, weapon drawn. Larry followed, at Raysor's shoulder, armed as well. Wescott continued to scream on the floor, his body drawn in on itself. Someone outside screamed.

Up to his knees, Wescott continued to favor his arm, cuddling it against his chest. "You broke my fuckin' arm!" he yelled.

"Good," Becca yelled back, huffing. "Then I did it right."

Larry moved to Quinn who, stooped with hands on her knees, let the adrenaline ebb. "Are you okay?" he asked, holstering his weapon once Raysor reached Wescott.

She laughed once, swallowed, and took in more air, her throat dry from all the breathing. "Happy to see you. Yes, I'm fine."

She tasted blood, and when she touched her face she learned not to. Her nose was broken, and she could only breathe through her mouth. With another deep inhale, she moved to Becca. "Lady, we got a lot to talk about."

"Stand in line," Raysor said, gently cuffing the wrists of a moaning Wescott.

"Is that necessary?" Wescott shouted. "She snapped a damn bone."

"We do this all the time. The cuffs will help," Raysor assured the man, catching a wink from Larry.

This wasn't some Peeping Tom or a two-bit burglar. Quinn didn't care if they'd broken both arms and both legs, because two people had died, the great unknown being whether he'd done both. Besides, he'd just tried to kill two more.

More sirens sounded, and another couple of units arrived outside. Quinn wouldn't have much time before this opportunity was stolen from her.

"Wait a minute," she said to Becca. "Who is your boss? The *he* you kept mentioning?" There was a puppet master in all of this, and somebody needed to cough up his name. Quinn wasn't close to Natalie but familiar enough with her to still be surprised she'd steal intel, dig up dirt, whatever it was she was doing for money under the table, although money was a powerful temptation when it far exceeded what you normally took home each week.

Having seen this grandmotherly yoga lady go toe to toe with a killer and not think twice about it told Quinn she had a history, but Quinn had precious minutes before they hauled her off, too. Best start from the top down with her questions and see how far she could get.

"What the hell were y'all doing and why?" she asked in frustration. The degree that these players had ripped open the lives of people demanded answers, and the cloak of pretense they all performed under, frankly, pissed her off.

"I'm not your enemy," was all Becca said.

Quinn's eyes narrowed. "Convince me."

She nodded toward Wescott. "Thought I just did with him."

"Not even close, lady."

Temper up, potential in her grasp, Quinn saw she'd have to be more direct . . . and make it fast. "Becca . . . Jefferson killed Natalie, didn't he? Not Wescott. And Wescott killed Jefferson to get rid of him and ensure the murder rap stuck to Ty."

Becca only listened, as though measuring like a teacher listening to a student's oral presentation. "Go on," she said.

Larry waited as if on the edge to see when and where to cut this off. Quinn's glances told him he better not try.

Raysor hadn't hauled off Wescott yet, eager to hear himself, while his prisoner stood, half off one leg in pain, his hands tucked against his belly to protect the wrist.

"I want this explained in front of two cops I trust," she said, taking her glare off her uncle and putting it back on Becca. "Yes or no, did Jefferson kill Natalie?"

"Yes."

"Wescott went nuts because Jefferson went nuts, so he killed Jefferson to rid a loose end."

"Yes."

"No proof," Wescott uttered from behind tight teeth.

No proof other than a confession to Quinn and Becca. "So Ty killed nobody," she continued.

"Correct. He showed up that day, collected Cole, and left. Guilty of nothing more than being in the right place at the wrong time."

Emotion pricked behind Quinn's eyes, the relief insanely deep. If only Ty were here. But there was more to this.

Raysor started to move Wescott, telling Becca to come with him peaceably.

Quinn moved in. "No. She's not done!"

Boots sounded outside.

"I'll watch this one," Larry said to Raysor, placing himself next to Becca. "Hold off those guys a minute, if you don't mind. Go take care of your guy and tell your men to give us a second or two."

Quinn didn't waste time waiting for the okay, the sorting out, or the other uniforms to come inside and demand otherwise. "Becca, did you work for Wescott, with Wescott, or independent of Wescott? What exactly was your role?" She had to rush this, and Becca seemed to want to tell her. That would change with an attorney in the room.

"We worked separately," Becca said. "Wescott watched Natalie. I watched Natalie and Wescott."

"What about Jefferson?"

Becca rolled her eyes. "Wescott freelanced on that one. Hired him to keep an eye on Natalie. He was building intel, learning her routine, seeking who she knew who had the connections he needed. Jefferson was already living in the apartment building, a secluded guy who didn't talk much, and he was hired to inform Wescott where Natalie went and who she talked to. No more and no less. That day . . . " Becca stopped, Quinn guessing that she recalled the morning of not three days ago. "That morning," she corrected, clearing her throat, "I'm guessing Jefferson said something to Natalie that gave him away. Natalie wasn't stupid. Jefferson probably took it upon himself to question her about Ty, maybe he was trying to impress Wescott with his independent sleuthing skills. She, being no dumb chick, probably confronted him about watching her or threatened to tell Ty. Jefferson panicked."

A fire climbed from Quinn's gullet into her throat, her injured nose throbbing, and her angry that Natalie and Ty, who were nice, decent folk, had gotten caught up in someone's surreptitious effort to gather information about . . . what? "Who the hell did you work for, Becca? What was the job?"

"I'm surprised, Ms. Sterling. All this originated because of you."

This time Quinn did sit down. "Me?"

Besides snuffing out Cole's mother, this crap had impacted Ty, Cole, Glory, and Archie . . . and, out of concern, Lenore and Jule. And Jonah.

"Ronald Renault, honey."

He. Him. The boss. Renault. Again.

Becca continued. "He wants to know anything and everything regarding Sterling Banks. You, your family, your friends. Anything he can find. Anything he can use. That's all we were told. The why wasn't ours to know, Ms. Sterling, but I imagine you do."

Of course Becca wouldn't be close enough to her boss to understand, but she was correct in that Quinn probably did. He was poking blind at all aspects of Quinn Sterling and Sterling Banks, from any angle, zealous at discreet searches for avenues nobody else might think of.

The man had always wanted Sterling Banks. Going back to her years in high school, ravenous real estate agents, developer moguls, and old Charleston legends drooled over the three-hundred-year legacy and three thousand acres that bordered the cherished Edisto River and led to salt-water marsh at its most southern point.

Looking at Larry, she saw he got it, too. The Renaults had attempted to infiltrate the Sterling Banks universe multiple times. From the in-your-face confrontations, to attempted murder. From so many blind-sided approaches, calls, and visits from real estate agents to people feigning interest in the farm's pecan business. None of the attempts had worked. This appeared to be yet another, using a woman who hated Quinn, hoping her hate would aid his cause.

Only this time, Quinn hadn't intercepted his effort to ferret out any vulnerability that might let him slip in the knife. Natalie had, by refusing to assist him further.

Suddenly the voice-mail message on Quinn's phone made more sense. Natalie wanted to tell Quinn what was going on.

There was one more loose end. Jefferson terrorized children. He'd gone too far and felt he had to do something to cover. Thank God he hadn't crossed the line from killing an adult to children. Question was whether he'd come to Sterling Banks at Renault's direction or from personal need to sabotage Ty's chance for acquittal by scaring Cole to death. Was he that stupid or that smart?

"Are you aware of Jefferson trespassing on my farm and threatening children?" she asked Becca.

The woman hesitated, not remembering such a thing. She shook her head. "No."

Wescott had to have known, but with Jefferson gone, all he had to do was say he was unaware of Jefferson's crazy idea. Easy enough to blame the dead guy.

But nothing would stick to Renault. Chances were, things had gone sideways involving Jefferson, about which he could claim ignorance and blame Wescott. Quinn would bet a thousand acres on it. Renault had hired Wescott as a private investigator. There would be a contract someplace, written in generalities of researching data and filing reports, undefined enough to instill plausible deniability. He also had a team of attorneys.

"Quinn?" Larry sat beside her. "They gotta take the woman now."

Two more deputies had shown up, standing beside Detective Parker inside the doorway.

Becca made toward Quinn, and Larry moved closer on the outside chance of a threat.

"I want you to know," she said, "that I only gathered information in my girlfriend chats with Natalie. No harm intended. I actually came to love that girl, and even called myself trying to keep her out of trouble. I have no direct knowledge of either murder nor had any part of them. Mr. Renault is not going to be happy with Wescott," she repeated, not realizing Quinn had heard her telling that to Wescott twice already as she'd eavesdropped outside the window.

Quinn sighed. "Who are you, really?"

"Retired Marine," she said. "I retired at twenty years and served on the Savannah PD for another fifteen."

"Thought Marines flaunted their experience. Where're your ribbons, flag, certificates, photos?"

"Bedroom," she said. "Trust comes easier when you come across as an innocent senior citizen."

"Thought it might be something like that," Quinn said, while at the same time disappointed that this woman, with her background, could still be bought to use Natalie. Whether she'd come to like Natalie or not, she'd aided her demise by participating in this mess.

Still, she liked to think Becca regretted the ways things turned out.

A deputy took Becca by the arm. She turned back to say, "I took the freelance job so Renault wouldn't give it someone like Frannie Bean, you know. Nothing nefarious in doing my mission at all, Ms. Sterling. Natalie may not have liked you, but she quit with Wescott because she respected you." Then she turned and let them lead her away.

No tears. No despondent regret. A cold Marine lady whose sense of right and wrong had gotten skewed somehow. In the end, however, Quinn had sided with Natalie . . . against Wescott. Something had to be said for that.

Larry came up to Quinn. "Don't forget she obstructed an investigation, Niece. She lied to police."

"Oh, she's guilty of enough," she replied. "But you watch. Renault will have her turn state's evidence on Wescott, and his attorneys will get her off. Wescott will go down with Renault distancing himself since it involves murder."

Larry chewed on the inside of his bottom lip as if he had snuff in there, his jaw tight. "The bastard will keep coming at us."

"You can't arrest people on their plans. Plus, when you hire enough people to do your dirty work for you . . ."

Larry harrumphed.

She hushed, then her stomach growled, churning from Waffle House coffee, no dinner, and utter, painful disappointment at humanity. Human lives were not worth sacrificing over dirt. Her ancestors had spent so many of their lives doing just that, preserving Sterling Banks and working themselves to death. She wasn't sure how proud she was supposed to be standing at the helm of all that.

Natalie's death wasn't worth three thousand acres.

But Natalie's dying was not worth letting Renault get his hands on it, either.

Raysor reappeared, something in his hand. "You forgot your phone."

Quinn snared it. Thank God the detective hadn't grabbed it first. She checked the recording app. "It's still running," she said. Quickly, she read in the time, repeated the date, and signed off, mentioning who was in her presence when she did.

"We'll need that," Parker said, coming up behind Raysor. "Mind if we take it?"

She held it up with a wave. "This is backup to Becca's accounting and mine. This is what helps Wescott go down. I'm not handing you my phone, but I'll send the recording to you. Number?"

He gave it to her, and she copied the recording to him.

He wasn't happy at not having her device, but while Quinn had no problem with assisting them put away Wescott, they weren't pilfering through her phone lock, stock, and barrel to do so.

"Don, Don!" came a lady's voice from the doorway. Frannie Bean scurried in, the scarves around her neck and in her hair accenting a jewel-toned tapestry broom skirt. Way too many clothes for this heat. Her makeup looked fresh for this time of night, the lipstick loud. "I was so frightened . . . and you were amazing!"

Quinn figured who the screamer had been a moment ago.

Frannie Bean engulfed his left arm with both of hers, pressing her ample self against it. "I was the one who called 911."

Damn, was she batting her eyes?

Raysor gave a pleading look to Quinn.

"We appreciate you calling them, too," Quinn said. "You probably saved my hide. Don is quite the hero, isn't he . . . the way he busted in the door."

Frannie Bean cinched her hold on Raysor's arm. "Oh, yes, he is.

And you're quite welcome, Ms. Sterling. You need to watch who you do business with, you know. That could've gone so wrong for you."

"Gotta go," Parker said, headed to a night full of interviews. "We'll be looking to hear from you tomorrow."

"We're going, too," Larry said. "Got to get her nose looked at."

Quinn patted Raysor's cheek. "The deputy here can thank you in his own way, Frannie Bean, but I hope to see you again." She winked at Raysor. "Bye, Dough Boy."

The three of them pushed through the door.

Quinn heard Frannie Bean behind her as she left. "What did she call you?"

"Never mind," Raysor said, and Quinn grinned, enjoying a taste of humor she hadn't felt in a long time, daring to smile at the news she was about to deliver to the folks at home.

Once the waiting EMT outside fixed her nose.

Finally behind the wheel, Quinn received a text from Jonah. *You okay?*

I'm great. I believe all this is over, Jonah. A good good thing.

Coming home?

On my way.

Good, because Archie is packing, Glory is crying, and Cole is locked in his room. Ty disappeared into the grove. Jule is trying to keep Lenore from coming over here since Ty won't go to her. Workers broke a truck and left it in the drive. I'm trying to get it out of the way.

Jesus. She cranked up the truck. *On my way.*

His response took mere seconds. *About damn time.*

Chapter 29

ALMOST TWO IN the morning and the night laid out unending before her. Quinn's nose was bandaged by EMTs who rolled up for both her and Wescott, but she refused the meds and the ride to the hospital, promising to get it looked at tomorrow. Or rather, later today. Quinn worried the drone of tires on asphalt and the black road ahead would let the weariness set in, but she was wrong.

She couldn't shut down her mind.

They'd be free to mourn Natalie now. They could hopefully plan the funeral. They could work on Cole, and with someone in custody, convince him his father wasn't one of them. His mother's real killer had been killed himself. There wasn't much better closure than that, the horrible downside being Cole had had to learn how nasty human beings could be long before he should have. Kids lost a parent unexpectedly to car wrecks and cancer, not murder.

Losing her mother to cancer when Quinn was a child, then losing her father to a murderer, she could relate. He'd be smothered with shoulders to cry on and willing people to ask questions of. Quinn prayed Glory would be one of those souls, but things weren't looking good in that department.

Uncle Larry tailed Quinn most of the way back to Craven County with nary a warning in spite of the fact she drove fifteen miles over the speed limit. She was more sore than exhausted. From Jonah's texts, she expected to find the home place in total disarray, and she held no concept of going to bed before things were righted.

They could be up all night.

Ty should be somewhat easier, but she wasn't in his head. She'd tried calling him, but he didn't answer. She texted that they found who killed Natalie and Jefferson, and that he could breathe easy. She started to add on she loved him, as she'd done by second nature countless times over the years, but tonight it didn't feel proper.

In the half hour it took her to arrive and head through that wrought-iron gate, she had managed to awaken Tassey and feed her the good news, though. As expected, she said to hold onto the original recording. The sheriff's office had enough for now.

Time to deal with home. Jonah rarely cussed, but a multi-front catastrophe had fallen onto his head. He was every bit the leader of Sterling Banks. Whether in his job description or not, whether agricultural, economical, or familial, the buck seemed to stop with him when Quinn was busy, and these days that seemed to be all the time.

She'd had three cases in as many months, each time making Jonah step up to the plate. At least during this time, he'd graduated from hating Quinn's PI work to accepting it, but after tonight she wasn't sure where he stood. Clearing Ty ought to count for something.

But that still didn't make up for . . . everything.

Coming up on the manor, she noted the farm truck pushed to the edge of the trees. At least that was taken care of for the night.

She parked and opened the door to the mudroom. Glory's whimpering and sniffles could be heard from the kitchen table where Jule sat across from her, murmuring while sharing cups of chocolate from the aroma. Bogie sat under the table, head in her lap, her hand moving over him for comfort. It was far too late for a six-year-old, almost seven, to be up, but this night was far from normal. Quinn kissed the child on the head, then asked, "Cole?"

"Finally asleep in his room upstairs," Jule said with a wide-eyed worried expression. To not make Glory lift her head, Jule pointed at her own nose, noticing Quinn's. "You okay?"

Quinn nodded. Jule darted a gaze toward the living room, and Quinn smiled in thanks.

There she found Archie seated in a recliner, eyelids closed, fingers rubbing his temple. Suitcases sat packed at his feet.

As she entered, Archie righted the recliner, stood, and faced Quinn as if he'd been waiting for this moment but hesitated at her bruised, bandaged nose. Bags hung beneath his own filled with fatigue, his complexion pale. He wasn't the gentle, solid uncle she'd visited with yesterday, nor the ill one early this morning, but instead he carried an exasperated, defeated air until he saw her nose.

"Good heavens, Q!"

"Bad guy got in a lucky move," she said, not wanting this about her. "What is this?" She stood fast, waiting for what had pushed Archie over the edge so she could hopefully confront it and turn it around.

"A killer walked through the Fourth of July celebration and cased the place, Quinn. Then he returned that night and made threats to my child."

That was the problem with being left alone too long in your own head. You obsessed on the bad, though, admittedly, the bad had been pretty bad of late. "Uncle Archie, please. We— "

"Don't," he said firmly.

She hushed.

"I told you the other night that the man's picture on your cams looked familiar. His face kept haunting me until it registered this afternoon. I saw him on the Fourth." He pointed toward the front of the house. "Right out there on the grounds."

What? "Are you certain?"

"As certain as I can be about anything," he said. "I noticed him right after Ty arrived . . . right before they took him away."

"Are you saying he followed Ty here?" She thought they were done with surprises, but this . . . she had to think about this.

How had Archie noticed Jefferson that day and she hadn't?

But then he had been watching for people he did and didn't know after being gone so long, while she managed a herd of people, putting out brush fires.

"I saw him three or four times," he said. "He kept crossing our paths. I'm certain that's how he heard the kids' names. He was stalking Sterlings."

Anyone would tell her she had her hands full with the day, with Ty, with Archie's fresh arrival and managing Cole, but she'd not noticed the stranger too conveniently listening in.

A fire stoked inside Quinn, a deep burning wish that Jefferson hadn't died, so he could be tried and sentenced to life. Wescott let him off too easily.

On the other hand, he no longer breathed their air, and the kids would no longer worry. That counted for a lot.

Quinn couldn't assuage Archie by saying trouble had never shown up like this before, because she'd be lying. The problem with a big plantation was one could not fence it all. Add to that the Sterlings being in law enforcement, well known, and affluent, and they came up against more trouble than most.

She could only say the obvious. "I'm sorry, Uncle Archie. Can we sit and talk this out?"

He too quickly indicated otherwise. "Sorry, but my Uber is expected in about thirty minutes."

His announcement stabbed her heart. This wasn't fair. This was

Renault blowback, and she wanted to scream to Archie that this was Ronald Renault's doing, not hers. But his concern was his health and his daughter's safety, regardless of the reason, and he was well grounded in those concerns.

Tears threatened, but she blinked them away. She had wanted to provide both of those things for Archie and Glory. Sterling Banks was their legacy, too. Even in such a short stay, they'd grown on her. She didn't want it going back to just her and Larry.

Glory brought such a light to this place.

"They found the killers, Uncle Archie. All's good now. Ty's cleared. We can go back to normal."

"While I'm thankful for that, for all y'all's sake . . ."

She loved the *y'all* that had creeped back into his vocabulary.

"But I want to head home and think on this a while," he said, and returned to his wait in the recliner, leaving the foot rest down, his focus off of her and onto his bags. Conversation over.

She hated hearing him call San Francisco home again after he'd stated it wasn't. He hadn't blamed her, so why did she feel he had?

"I've got to find Ty," she said.

Archie gave her a small, loving smile, almost like an assurance that he was still her uncle, he loved her, but things weren't working out. With blood family, it seemed as if they never did for her. Well, things weren't going so well in the chosen-family side of the equation either.

She headed out the sliding doors leading to the deep, black thickness of hundreds of acres of pecan trees. She moved away from where Archie could see or hear her, and out of desperation she scrolled her phone, finding the three-day-old call in its history, and dialed. Walking, she struck out for Windsor.

She had to call five times before Patrick answered.

"You awake? I need you to be awake. This is Quinn Sterling." She fought not to sound nasally. Breathing wasn't easy.

Irregular sniffs, a muffled groan, then finally, he made sense. "Quinn?" Then he came to his senses. "Is Archie okay? Is Glory all right?"

"They are sad, but they're physically okay," she said.

The unusual answer drew silence from the other end. "What does that mean?"

"They are leaving Sterling Banks," she said. "Thanks to your boss."

"Why, what happened?"

She gave him the abridged version of Natalie and Ty, Wescott and

Jefferson. The scare with Jefferson and the kids. How proud Quinn was of Glory taking care of Cole. How scared Quinn was when Archie had his episode. "He's called an Uber to go to the airport and grab the next flight. Says it's safer in San Francisco."

"It's the middle of the night, for God's sake," he said.

"I know."

"He's not getting away with that," he said. "How late will you guys be up? I can come right now."

"Um." She hadn't expected that. Without a full grasp of Archie and Patrick's relationship, she wasn't sure she needed that drama spilling into the wealth of drama already on Sterling Banks.

"Now's not a good time. I called to see if you had ideas on changing his mind."

"You said he's leaving in a matter of minutes?"

"Yes, but—"

"To hell with this. I'll be in touch." He hung up.

Jesus Christ, had she just made matters worse?

She got a text. Her pulse tripped seeing Jonah's name. *You here?*

Yes. Where are you and Ty?

Windsor.

Ty had retreated to where they felt most safe, the childhood retreat where their closest secrets and worst fears were shared. Where their JQT meetings had originated, and where time stood still when they fought to solve their ills.

She took a quick sob. Thank God. Ty choosing to go there said a lot. And Jonah was with him. That said even more.

In a trot, she followed the path, unseen in the dark, but crystal clear in her child's eye. Someone could blindfold her, spin her a dozen times, and set her loose and she'd find Windsor. She knew every tree by how their roots crawled underfoot and patterns on the bark. Every tree on Sterling Banks had a soul.

Larry and Archie appreciated the farm. Jule and Lenore understood it. But nobody harbored it in their very being as she, Jonah, and Ty.

She broke into a run halfway there. Once inside the copse of live oaks, the five acres of native trees kept sacred for Windsor, she slowed, panting, knowing most likely they sat upstairs, inside in the dark.

She let them know she'd arrived with her footfalls on the steps but soft enough not to destroy the mood. The screen door creaked as she entered, and while she couldn't make them out in the pitch, she knew by heart where they were.

Ty sat in his rocker. Jonah in the bean bag. Out of habit, she felt for and assumed her place in the straight backed seat. The lone bulb light in the ceiling remained dark.

For a moment, they only listened to the Edisto River making its way south. No bird or insect noises at two in the morning when most forms of life were asleep. A small splash sounded only feet from the tree-house stairs, some nocturnal creature whisking another away for dinner.

Sadly, Archie would be gone when she returned. They'd connected. They could connect again. It was what it was.

Who mattered most sat right here in their usual circle, each tangled in their own warped sense of what was right, what was wrong, and what the hell they'd done to make it worse.

Because fixing the trio mattered more than fixing the world.

Feeling around in the dark, she found Ty's knee and groped for his hand. She drew the hand up and kissed it. "You're no longer a suspect, Old Man. And Cole has his father back." She squeezed hard. "I'm so sorry about Natalie."

"Why did it have to be Natalie?"

She could tell he'd been teary-eyed for a while.

"Why did she get involved with those people?" he said.

Why indeed. Truth was, what didn't merit open discussion was Natalie's jealousy of Quinn. The money had pushed her over the line from thinking about getting even to doing something about it. Somehow, via Wescott, in Renault's digging up dirt, he'd discovered that and snared her as one of his tools.

Natalie and Quinn had never addressed the unspoken rivalry. Ty had tried to assure Natalie that Quinn was nothing more than a dear friend. Quinn thought she was, too, until he kissed her in the living room.

"You did nothing to cause any of this," Quinn said to him.

"She thought—"

"We know what she thought," she finished. "We didn't cause that, and we couldn't change that."

Jonah had remained quiet until now. "This is hard, man," he said. "And I'm not talking Natalie." He sounded sad, and he sounded remorseful, though he was the last person here who needed to feel so.

Quinn was grateful for the darkness.

She wanted to ask how they would move forward, but she was the last one who should ask. She wasn't sure who was the right one, though. They were painted into a corner.

Sight adjusting to the dark, she set Ty's hand on his knee then reached out for Jonah's. He took it. "I love you, Jonah."

She turned to Ty. "Old Man," she started, then stopped, lost how to proceed.

The options were simple. She remained Jonah's fiancé, if he would have her, or she chose to remain single, forever dancing this line. But even that would fracture their friendship. For her to remain single, they would remain single . . . until one found someone outside the circle, and it didn't take a genius to predict that would end their relationship. The sad part was they might all three grow old together, remaining apart for fear of hurting each other . . . while hurting each other.

If either chose to leave Craven County, she'd die.

Both were too damn nice. While either would fight to the death for her, neither would fight over her. But to choose Jonah might make Ty leave. He wasn't in his right mind yet to do anything but mourn Natalie and rebuild his trust with Cole.

"Ty," she started again.

"I'm sorry I came onto you," he said in a tone so sad it hurt. She couldn't tell if he meant the words as an apology for poor behavior, or a reluctant admission to Jonah he had won.

"You're . . . hurt," she said. She almost said *just hurt*, but there was nothing *just* about any of this.

None of this was *just*. Ty's loss of Natalie, his love for Quinn, Quinn's love for her brothers that now had to be reinterpreted as something else. God gave her such wonderful friends only to say later she had to choose one. Like something out of the Book of Solomon, only with no wisdom redeemed from it.

"Let's just . . ." The word stopped her. "Let's sit here tonight and be us. Can we do that?"

They sat in silence, ultimately moving to the floor so they could back up to the beanbag, and they talked in whispers until they napped off and on till dawn.

Chapter 30

YOU DIDN'T SEE dawn creep above the horizon on Sterling Banks. You experienced it. Canopies of several thousand trees made the light fight its way through. The trio felt what time it was and rose from the tree-house floor.

"Holy Jesus," Jonah said, seeing Quinn's broken nose, now black eyes. Ty scowled, imagining what had to have caused it, having missed it last night in the dark.

Quinn would wait on telling them the details. She didn't need guys wanting to deal with the man who had rammed her face into the floor. "Looks worse than it is," she said, though her head felt twice its size, the throbbing demanding aspirin.

They parted, heading into their obligations. Humidity rose with the sun in July, and moisture beaded temples before they'd silently walked a half mile from the river. They fanned out, still with issues unresolved but united in the truth they weren't about to hurt each other in the pursuit. And they weren't doing much about them today.

Jonah went home to shower and start the farm and its workers to buzzing. Ty slipped into Cole's bedroom at the manor, settling into an armchair to watch his child sleep, maybe catch a nap, pondering how they'd start their new life together and how he'd convince his son that nothing on earth would ever bother him again.

Quinn had let Ty go up the stairs first before looking around for any sign of Archie. Finding none, she sighed at the loss. She wasn't letting him get away for so long this time. This fall maybe she'd fly to California. By then, she might bring him around.

Still drained, she intended to take the day easier, not unlike the day after a funeral. God, Ty still had a funeral to plan, but not today. Bless him, he needed to do nothing but love his son and his mother today.

She set foot on the bottom step to head to her bedroom, then glancing across the living room, changed her mind. She crossed the big, high-ceilinged room to the small hall leading to her parents' bedroom. She'd preserved that room for times when she needed to step in, go back in time, and remember. Sometimes to steal a scarf from her mother's collection. Other times to touch things, try to smell them on the clothing in the closet . . . sometimes to sit and heal. On days when the house was empty and echoed too much, she settled into her mother's rocker brought over from Ireland, imagining what it had been like to cradle Quinn and her twin brother at once.

She was tired and aching to stretch on their bed. She eased open the bedroom door . . . and was taken aback at the vision.

Archie and Glory lay across the king comforter, his arm over his daughter and Glory covered in a blanket that Quinn hadn't thought about in ages. Must've been in the closet. Bogie raised his head from the foot of the bed, not wanting to leave, having chosen his person. She might be her dog's master in name only from this point forward.

They were still fully clothed, but there were no suitcases. Quinn eased the door shut, stunned, but more than that, thankful. She had another chance to keep them here.

To feel better, she glanced around the living room and kitchen for the luggage, thinking maybe they hadn't found a flight, but she discovered nothing. Upstairs, she found them in Archie's room.

The house had heartbeats. Tears fell down her cheeks, and, God, she wanted to cry and cry, but the very thing she loved, the heartbeats of the others, didn't need to be disturbed.

She returned down the hall, peering in on Cole. He slept hard, probably exhausted to his bones. In the corner, arms crossed over his chest, on guard for his son, Ty slept hard, too.

Quinn swallowed three aspirin, grabbed a hand towel from the bath, and returned downstairs, retreated out the sliding doors, and escaped into the grove. The deeper she got, the faster she ran. Past the Elliotts, the Sumners, the Cape Fears, and the Stuarts. All the cultivars that the generations before her had struggled to select and cross and design to grow the best pecans with the hardiest means of surviving bugs and drought.

But they weren't a crop right now. They were a haven. They were her lifetime of protection and comfort, and palliative relief from the horrors of being.

There, ahead. Quinn teared at the sight of one of their record-producing trees. In a sprint, she rushed to the arms of Mama Queen. One foot on the trunk, hands grasping the lower branch, in a muscle-memory move from childhood, she swung her lower body up, her knees draping over the next branch in perfect synchronicity. Didn't take but seconds for her to sit back against the massive trunk, legs straddled, the dip cra-dling her backside perfectly.

Then she leaned over the massive limb sprawling out, gingerly sank her bruised face into the hand towel, and cried from a place she hadn't cried from in a long, long time. And there she lay for a long, long time, until she could cry no more, until fatigue let her drape forward, close her eyes, and sleep.

She woke to someone calling her name. Not from the ground, but from the next branch over.

"Princess." A hand stroked her left shoulder blade. Jonah had climbed into the tree, as familiar as she was with which tree served what purpose on the plantation, whether producing pecans or giving solace.

"What time is it?" she said, taking in a deep breath and easing upright, admittedly stiffer than she used to get in these hideaway moments.

"Almost ten," he said, readjusting his posture when she shifted and leaned back against the tree. "Your poor face. You been here since Windsor?"

She reached over for a stem of leaflets and stripped the stem of leaves, releasing the mixed scents of orange, black pepper, burnt sugar, and turpentine. "Pretty much." Then she remembered!

"Archie is still here," she said. "With Glory. Not sure what happened, but they aren't gone. They stayed in Daddy and Momma's bedroom."

"They sent me hunting you," he said. "When you weren't in your room, and your truck was still here, I figured Windsor or Mama Queen."

She leaned over enough for her shoulder to touch his. "Tell them I'm fine."

"No, they said come in and get ready. Apparently, you have a meeting in Charleston."

That woke her to attention. "I don't have an appointment. Who said?"

"Larry called me. Then Archie ran me down. You have them spooked."

This didn't make sense. "But I don't have any such appointment, Jonah." Tassey maybe, but that would be with Ty. The uncles weren't really a factor there.

"Someone made you one, then. Come on down. Get you a bite to eat and take a shower so you don't have to rush." He pushed stray tresses from her face. "Show them how kickass gorgeous you are so they don't see your intelligence coming until you're all over them."

Puzzled, she turned to him. "What's this about?"

"Not my tale to tell," he said, using one of her lines. He slid around to drop to the ground. He reached up, as if she needed help, and she hopped down into his arms to let him feel good about it.

He didn't let go, wrapping his arms further. "I love you, Quinn Sterling. Please hold onto that."

"I'd be a fool if I didn't," she said, leaning into the embrace. Then she did what should've been done already. "I'm so sorry if I hurt you, Jonah. There was so much tension and so much stress—"

"Hush," he said. "I love him, too." He released her. "Go get ready. I hear Larry will be here in an hour."

"An hour?" She pushed hair out of her face. "You coming?"

He shook his head. "Gotta take care of this place. Go on."

She leaned in for a kiss, the first they'd had since . . . well, since. Nothing special, a peck, but his smile from the effort told her how much he appreciated it.

Then she ran to the house.

Archie must have heard her come in because she was halfway up the stairs when he called, "Dress sharp, Niece."

She almost tripped at the comment, spun, and noticed he was decked out pretty damn nice in a suit that made him crisp as hell. "Where am I supposed to be going? Seems everyone knows but me."

He took a second to take in her face. "We're taking you to the big city. Go on now. I'll have coffee waiting for you. Expect a five-star lunch afterwards, unless we run into supper."

She grinned at his use of *supper* instead of *dinner*, like his *y'all* from the day before.

A fast shower, and she tackled what to do with her hair in such short time. Blowing it almost dry, because a full dry took a half hour, she clipped up the sides to leave her face clear of it, and draped the remainder down her back. But nothing could detract from that swollen reflection in the mirror.

She put some makeup over the worse of it then said to hell with it.

Heels for sure, and she went with a pants suit in lieu of a dress, not knowing the situation. Part business and part pleasure, maybe. Suddenly, standing in her bedroom with a sapphire suit in one hand and beige with gold braid along the lapel in the other, her arms dropped.

Both uncles. Jonah said Larry was on his way. Archie was dressed and waiting. What the hell was happening?

How was she supposed to dress?

How was she to mentally prepare?

How was she to not ruin the surprise if it was something special for her?

Moving both outfits to one hand, she stomped to the door in her panties and bra and proceeded back to the staircase landing. "Uncle Archie?" she hollered.

He appeared from the kitchen. "Yes?" He wasn't bothered in the least at her undress.

Damn, he looked sharp in navy. So fetching against his blond/gray waves. Maybe she ought to go with a dress. "Do either of these work?" she asked, holding up the hangers.

"Oh, honey, the blue, for sure. Get a move on." He disappeared to the kitchen.

By the time she'd retouched her face, matching her makeup to the suit, and deemed herself presentable, the hour she'd been given was up. She went to scurry down the hallway to the stairs, but in reaching Cole's bedroom, she had to stop and check in. When she eased open the door, both he and Cole were gone.

She guessed that was a good thing.

"Quinn?" came a yell from downstairs.

"Coming." Larry had arrived. How was this going to work, both uncles in the same room at the same time, much less the same car?

At the bottom of the stairs, she pivoted toward the kitchen for that cup of coffee. Archie and Larry stood side by side, Larry in dress uniform, throwing Quinn's heart into her throat.

Larry winced once seeing her face, but he'd help arrest the cause last night and said nothing about it. Archie simply marveled at how striking she was.

She'd spent her childhood watching them fight, and since high school, hearing about how horribly contrary they were in each other's presence, yet here they were dressed to perform.

Archie handed her a to-go thermos of coffee. "Let's go. I rented us a car. Delivered and waiting."

No piling into her F-150 Super Crew then. No squeezing into one of the sheriff's cruisers. In spite of the Sterling coffers, nobody owned a luxury vehicle. They were too practical. Too busy keeping Sterling Banks functioning. Not interested in pretenses, but they were doing it today.

Larry drove, Quinn in the front, Archie in the back of the white BMW 7 Series. The car rode the highway in a vacuumed silence.

Quinn put on sunglasses. She'd taken off the bandage, praying nothing bumped her nose before all this was over. "Where are we going?"

"Jumping the gun, aren't we?" Archie said. "What about, *why didn't you leave*, Uncle?"

"No," she said. "First, where are Ty and Cole?"

Archie nodded in agreement with her priorities. "Ty took Cole to Lenore's. He said give them a few days."

Probably wise, though she'd miss him, but they'd all been saturated with Ty's issues this week, and he needed distance. She imagined the next they'd hear from him would be for the funeral.

That was going to be tough.

"Okay," she continued, pivoting enough in the front seat to see Archie in the back. "Now, why didn't you leave?"

"Patrick called."

Well, she *had* spoken to him last night in desperation.

"Spoke for an hour, maybe more. He reminded me of our agreement."

He brought it up, so she asked, "What agreement?"

"The condition for me to keep custody of Glory was for me to relocate to Sterling Banks. At least nearby." He said it matter of fact, as if they'd agreed to something mundane such as who got the living room furniture.

"Yet you were leaving last night," she exclaimed.

Larry kept driving like a chauffeur, deaf to the conversation.

"I was," he said. "Didn't seem the right time to be making relocation plans. You have so much on you running Sterling Banks, living your life." He breathed out a short laugh. "Running your PI business."

"Don't discount my PI business."

"I'm not. Just tossing it on your pile. I see you love it. You basically saved Ty, Miss Priss."

Yes, she did, though she wasn't feeling necessarily proud. Natalie was still dead. Ty was still hurt. Cole, poor baby, had to be lost.

"What else?" she asked. An hour with Patrick seemed a lengthy conversation in the middle of the night.

"He felt partially responsible about Renault leaning so hard on you. After all, he's sort of on the Renault team to research Sterling Banks."

Quinn laughed, and looking over at Uncle Larry, laughed some more. "Patrick is a drop in the Renault ocean. Tell him not to feel a thing."

Archie leaned a bit forward, a hard look in his eyes. "Quinn, he feels he's part of a team who killed two people over the real estate Patrick is charged with researching. He's fully aware of Renault's push to own

Sterling land, and his part, though small, fueled the fire. Or so that's how he put it. Ultimately, it threatened his daughter."

Wow, come to think of it, it had.

She wanted to launch into whether Archie was home for good, but they were close to Charleston. "Where are we going, and what are we doing?" she asked. "I don't like surprises."

"You love surprises," Larry said.

She craned her neck at this personal side of the bad uncle. "Depends on what kind."

Larry approached the Ashley River, about to cross from West Ashley to downtown Charleston. The Medical University sprawled ahead to their right, the conical Riverfront Holiday Inn immediately to their left, and she could make out the Arthur Ravenel Jr. Bridge on the opposite side of the peninsula.

They were headed to one of two places.

"Are we meeting with Tassey Talmadge or Ronald Renault?" she asked, needing to reinforce herself either way. She could guess the answer, though. They wouldn't have all dressed to the nines if they weren't infiltrating Renault territory.

Chapter 31

THEY ENTERED Ronald Renault's brokerage office on Charleston's infamous Broad Street as if they were regulars. Quinn still marveled he owned a damn building in downtown Charleston. Archie had told Larry to cave in to valet parking and be done with it instead of worrying over a few dollars. Today was about bigger things.

The brothers strode in, chests out and heads high. Quinn wasn't yet grasping how they'd ridden in the same car, but they appeared very much together. This was no doubt their plan. She'd only been dragged along for show. She'd seen Renault twice in almost as many months, with tension so thick you could swim through it, and hadn't planned on repeating that experience anytime soon . . . if ever.

On second thought, she wasn't there for show. She didn't believe that for one damn minute.

"Lead the way," Archie said, proving her point and holding the door for Quinn. They entered the Renault sanctuary, with the brothers on her left and right flank. She tried not to look up, the high-ceiling marble lobby never failing to impress.

"What are we doing exactly?" she whispered on the elevator, the three of them reflecting in the polished trim around the dark panels on all four sides.

This felt like a formal presentation, only she hadn't one to make.

The previous meetings had to be arranged a day or two beforehand, and both had been in the aftermath of death, the only way the Sterlings had become urgent enough in Renault's universe to warrant attention.

Like now, only this was an even faster turnaround. Had he called for the meeting this time? She understood the place. Renault always met on his turf, which suited Quinn fine since she wasn't letting that son of a bitch set foot on Sterling Banks.

A clerk dressed as if she earned a low six figures welcomed them off the elevator, escorting them to an anteroom. She opened the door to where Tassey Talmadge and Patrick French already waited. A silver coffee service sat before them, and from the looks of the eaten cookies and half-empty cups, they'd waited a while.

Quinn took note there weren't enough cups for the three new arrivals. This was weird. Renault was all about formalities and the most formal of the formal social graces. This felt very ad hoc.

Doors closed behind them, and the doors before them remained shut. Quinn would bet a quarter's pecan earnings that the room was bugged.

Archie and Patrick hugged as if they hadn't seen each other in a while, then Patrick backed up and embraced Quinn. "You look amazing. Knock 'em dead."

But before Quinn could ask what for, Tassey took her aside. "You and I need to talk in a few days. I have a meeting with the Colleton sheriff to conclude things. Expect to be a prime witness for the prosecution. Ty, too. Might be wise to keep me on that retainer to keep things civil." The unsaid being that Renault was on the other side of this court case.

"What are you doing here now?" Quinn asked.

"Renault called me," she said.

"Because we called him," Archie tossed in.

Tassey threw him an agreeable look. Larry stood at the door, waiting for it to open, listening with not much to say.

So odd. So thrown together. The anteroom held the sensation of the moments before entering court on the first day of trial. Last-minute reminders. Straightening ties.

"What the hell is this?" Quinn whispered to Tassey, well aware that any Renault bug would pick up a flea's cough.

"Setting the record straight," she said. "Showing you have the upper hand. Own it." The attorney's hand gripped Quinn's forearm. "Own. It. Hear me? We have to confront him early on. This man needs to see you, hear you, and realize he's been exposed. He called me in to offer to pay my fee, by the way, which I refused. Don't want the first sign of his money staining my bank account."

The doors opened toward the inner sanctum, clipping Tassey short. An assistant poised like something out of Trump Tower, almost wax-figure-like in her structured movements, waved them in. Quinn gave her own outfit a smooth over before entering, Larry and Archie on her heels. When the doors started to close, Quinn noticed Tassey and Patrick remained behind.

"Excuse me, but aren't they invited?" she said to the young woman, who stopped in place, digesting a possible turn of play.

Tassey spoke up. "Patrick and I have each had our meeting, Quinn. This one is yours."

The doors closed, the assistant motioning them to one side of the thousand-square-foot office. The three took their places on a navy leather sofa, with the assumption that the King would be the one in the matching tufted chair. They hadn't sat long enough to be settled before Renault entered through a private door.

"Anything else, Mr. Renault?" the assistant asked, and after a shake of Renault's white-haired head, she disappeared through the same private entrance. The four sat silently until the click sounded on the door. In the last two sessions, they'd agreed on no recordings and no other ears. Quinn wouldn't dare assume one way or the other this time, and would instead ere on the side of caution.

Renault's charcoal, narrow pin-striped suit clearly custom made with the sharp crispness of hems and lapels, spoke mid-four figures, the Oxfords on his feet a couple more. He wasn't a tall man, but the last way you measured Ronald Renault was his height. Quinn couldn't say whether he dressed like this daily, but was well aware he could afford to. Whether he prepped for intimidation, conceit, or habit, however, she didn't care.

She and her uncles had dressed likewise, so that the stage would be evenly set. Stupid to think price tags of clothing had anything to do with the intelligence of the participants, but to people like Renault, it mattered more than a row of PhDs on the wall.

She sat erect as they made eye contact, ankles crossed, hands in her lap, neck straight as a poker. Cue the intro. Open the curtain.

"First, my apologies on the loss of Ms. Jackson," Renault began.

Quinn nodded.

"And these fine gentlemen are your uncles," he said, tone rising as if to lighten things. He leaned toward Archie, hand outstretched. "Don't believe we've met, sir."

Archie rose and returned the grip. "Prodigal son back to the fold," he said. "Last time I came to the Lowcountry was when we buried my brother."

Excellent, Uncle. First shot over the bow.

Renault's smile a hint painful, he sat back and took in the three Sterlings. "I understand there's a fourth as well. A daughter?"

Archie darkened at the mention of Glory. Quinn rested a hand on his leg. "Yes," she said. "There are four of us now. Twice the power of what you originally reckoned with. We're no longer only the simple sheriff and the single girl without an heir."

Renault looked down his nose at her as if she were his, needing a dressing down. "Oh, Miss Sterling."

"Mr. Renault, we've danced this dance before. You always led. This time it's my turn, or shall I say *our* turn."

His posture remained formal, his sleeves resting on the arms of his chair. He waved to proceed, a supercilious effort to maintain the throne. "You requested the meeting. The floor is yours."

You were too curious to say no, you bastard.

"You hired people, three of them, I believe," she began. "One killed my friend's wife, then trespassed on our property and threatened our children, all on camera, by the way. Two of them turned on each other, one killing the other. Then in my presence, mind you, the remaining two fought, professing what had taken place." She leaned forward this time. "Almost what you call premeditation when you stop and think about it."

Renault's tight seams weren't as tightly woven as before, but he cinched himself in and fought valiantly to appear so. A twitch in his arm, his legs recrossing, he waited a tad too long not to show he recognized he was vulnerable. "I did hear how you got caught up in Wescott's misdeeds."

"Misdeeds," she repeated, so Renault could hear how ridiculous a word choice that was.

"Wescott voided our contract when he subcontracted his private investigations work," he said. "Renault Enterprises will not be representing him."

"Distancing yourself, are you?"

"Business, Ms. Sterling."

"But your attorneys will be representing Ms. Becca Blevins, I take it?"

He looked straight at her yet didn't respond.

Of course he'd have her represented, and script her properly such that they cooperated against Wescott to clear their own names.

Quinn had been seated on the edge of her cushion, giving her a more forward appearance as leader, but then in a second thought, she stood. It made him look smaller.

Renault remained in place, regardless, acting entertained, but she could read the questioning in the tenseness of those padded shoulders.

"You and I understand each other." She pointed to him then back to herself. "You want my land. I don't want to let go of it. You protect your wealth. I protect a legacy. You killed my father. I killed your daughter."

He cringed before he could catch himself.

She gave him a second on that one.

"Then you sicced people on me, to see what weaknesses you could learn, what flaws could be found in me, in the people I loved, scouting for weak links you could use to weaken us some way, somehow, or some time down the road. You're creating a Sterling library of data, it seems. You hired Patrick French, thinking a divorce from a Sterling would leave him embittered enough to help you in your efforts to undermine the family, or at least learn of inside issues that might induce a sale. At the same time you had him design the dreams you had for our land, his designs lulling him into a sense of pride, letting him imagine his name on whatever was planned for the future Sterling Banks."

Archie had shifted slightly at the mention of his ex. Quinn had to hope that he and Patrick were of one mind on all of this.

"We've a library of our own, Mr. Renault. Of the attempts you've made. The close calls. The too many coincidences that somehow put you against the Sterlings, without us making the first move. It's clear. You want Sterling Banks. The whole Lowcountry knows it as do several police forces and multiple law firms. You're becoming too anxious, sir. You're overplaying your hand." She hesitated. "And too many people are dying for someone to not to eventually take a look at you."

Her voice hadn't risen, but it had hardened.

"You might not ask what I'm getting to, because how dare you think anyone could ripple the smooth pool of water you think you are, but there is a point."

As dramatic as it seemed, she gave another pause.

"Sterling Banks is not for sale. Not by me."

"Nor by me," Larry echoed.

"Nor by me nor my kin," Archie said.

She pounced back in. "We'll put it in writing if need be. Maybe we'll entrust the entire place in a conservation easement." Her eyes narrowed. "We'll donate it to the state of South Carolina for a state park, if we have to, if we have any inkling of an idea you could get your hands on it." She fought to remain civil.

Larry spoke up as though reading a cue. "We have no need to pursue you, Renault," he said, intentionally leaving off the title. "But my niece isn't exactly flapping in the wind as you may have once thought. When my brother was killed, she stepped into some mighty big shoes, but she did so with guts and intelligence even we in the family had no idea she held. We will not sit by and let you harass her."

Quinn's heart squeezed like a fist hearing his support of her.

Archie rose. "Our name may not be Renault, but to many it's better. It's Sterling, sir. We are the oldest family in the oldest county in the grand state of South Carolina. Three hundred years of blood, sweat, and history, that we intend to continue for three hundred more."

With her chest about to burst with pride, Quinn continued facing forward, all three holding a stare on their host. "One side or the other will subpoena me about Wescott," she said. "Tell your attorney to be careful what he asks for. There will be press in the room that I will court with passion."

In reality, she held little doubt there would be a plea instead of a trial.

She turned to Archie, the closest to the door, to show they were done. He led them toward it.

Hand on the doorknob, she turned around and spoke into the air. "This is Quinn Sterling. Leaving the room are myself, Larry Sterling, and Archie Sterling. Left behind is Ronald Renault. The time is twelve fifty-two on July 8. Recording ended."

They let themselves out, the assistant having rushed in behind them too late to do so.

TASSEY AND PATRICK were waiting for them at 82 Queen for lunch. They'd already ordered appetizers, which arrived as the rest of them took their seats.

Quinn almost groaned seeing the fried chicken livers, and wouldn't turn down one of the fried green tomatoes. The only treat better might've been fried okra, but she'd rather not have to compare anyone else's to Lenore's. Tired of the formality, in spite of being at one of the finer restaurants downtown, she dug in to the livers, spooning a little extra of the country ham red gravy over them.

"Hope you don't mind, I ordered white," Tassey said, nodding to the waiter to fill everyone's glasses. "Since most of the lunch menu is seafood."

"Except for these," Quinn said from behind her first bite. "Hmmmm."

"After that meeting, I'd drink whatever you put in front of me," Larry said, a light groan settling after his words. "But I'm driving, so I'll stick to tea."

"I'm Ubering," Patrick said, "so I don't care." He tried to attract Archie with a wink, who returned a light smile. "Got all the time in the world."

"Yes, he does," Tassey laughed.

Archie peered across the table at him. "What happened before we arrived?"

"I quit," Patrick announced. "Once Tassey had her say, I went in and had mine. I was not going to be used."

Archie had a quick response. "You were all right with it for six months."

Blowing out through pursed lips, Patrick dropped his gaze into his lap. "Well, let's say people dying sobered me. And realizing the man's goal more fanatical than a simple financial interest scared the shit out of me when I saw my family in his crosshairs."

With the hilarity dampened, awkwardness set in.

Tassey held up her wine glass. "I'll have an assistant come get my car if that's where we're headed." She tossed back the drink, though Quinn doubted that woman let too many business lunches compromise her wits.

"Shut up about Renault. I never want to have to do that again. Three times the charm." Quinn pointed to the livers. "Bet you don't get these in San Francisco," she said to Archie.

"Chicken liver pâté is at all the finer dining establishments," he replied, a touch of humor back.

"To hell with the mush," she said, swallowing. "You gotta fry these babies, get some crunch in there."

The release of tension reappeared in the comedic one-liners, the jabs at California, and the order of a third bottle of wine to wash down the crab cakes, flounder, and Lowcountry gumbo.

Ninety minutes or so later, Quinn noticed the time . . . and thought of Jonah back at the farm keeping things afloat and Jule babysitting Glory, while Quinn pretended to be something she was not, in the name of besting Renault.

She'd received no texts from any of them, to include Ty, which she'd sort of hoped for. With a bit of chagrin from behind her wine glass, she scolded herself for expecting them to contact her, a rather Renault-ish sort of behavior, she realized. Time to return to Sterling Banks and shed this costume. She felt dirtier than any of the days she was covered head to toe with Sterling Banks dust from a legitimate hard day of work in the groves.

Time to return and see how they could get back to running the farm, loving the land the good Lord gave her family, and appreciating all those who loved it with her.

Losing Natalie had hit too close to home.

Chapter 32

JULY THE TWELFTH. The party would begin at two, right after the Jackson Hole lunch crowd.

Natalie's funeral took place the day before. The back and forth between planning something so sad and something so upbeat resulted in a messy mixture of opinions on the details, but overall, most agreed that Glory's birthday was not to be overlooked, diminished, postponed, nor overshadowed by the funeral of someone she'd never known.

But was Cole old enough to juggle the incredibly high and low difference between losing his mother and celebrating his new best friend? Should he skip Glory's birthday, but what would he be doing otherwise but wishing he were there?

Postponing Natalie's funeral was a major suggestion for a while, but was it fair to Cole to attend a child's birthday party knowing he was about to put his mother in the ground?

There was no right answer.

So Ty and Archie sat down with Cole and Glory and asked them. They answered easily: the funeral one day . . . the birthday the next. Cole said his mother would want everyone to end on a happy note, not a sad one. Glory said they could cut her a piece of cake and put it on display with a candle and her picture.

Quinn had listened from the next room. She'd had to turn away and grab a tissue. Jule remained dry-eyed and unsurprised. "They think with more sense than most adults if you give 'em half a chance," she said. "They aren't affected by what people may think."

They held the service in Walterboro but buried Nat in a Jackson family cemetery near Jacksonboro. Not having family of her own, Ty felt it proper she rest alongside the family she'd married into. With Cole living with his dad, especially living in Craven County now, he'd want to visit her.

The day of the party, Cole and Ty rose early to assist Lenore with the decorations, the lunch crowd, and the cleaning up. The grandson of a restauranteur had to learn the ropes.

Lenore had decorated corners and ceiling, windows and bar with balloons galore and banners on each wall. She told her regulars as they straggled in for lunch that a little girl had a special day to celebrate, and this day was not one to dawdle. . . unless they had a gift and were prepared to eat a lot of sugar.

After quickly cleaning up the noon-day meal, Lenore posted a sign on the door – *Private Party – Reopen at 6.*

Glory Bea Sterling turned seven today, and Lenore Jackson baked a Funfetti sheet cake full of sprinkles, big enough for half of Craven County. At the birthday girl's request, a huge picture of her and Bogie covered the center, with seven four-inch candles across the top with rows and rows of assorted sizes and colors of flowers filling in the rest. The eater would bite into as much icing as cake. Totally sinful for the adults. Totally awesome for the kids and a few of the older crowd with severe sweet tooths.

Two dozen people sang "Happy Birthday," with Glory standing on a table in the middle of the room, Archie's grip on the back of her dress. Her curls bobbed, and she wound up joining in song with them before the tune was through. Then Lenore put the jukebox on for background music, each song with enough bebop to it to keep people toe-tapping and rocking between the cake on the table and the ice cream and punch at the bar.

After the official candle-blowing, Ty returned to the kitchen, doing the back and forth in keeping the punchbowl poured and the ice-cream orders fresh.

Quinn worked the room, enjoying the laughter after the previous day . . . after the previous week, her nose not as dark bruised and purple. As Glory wanted, a framed eight-by-eleven of a smiling Natalie sat on the corner of the bar next to a piece of cake. Cole had lit the candle, made a wish, and blown it out. Glory made Archie anchor a pink helium balloon behind it with a piece of tape. As the afternoon went on, more things appeared. A bow, a crepe-paper flower, a napkin some creative soul had shaped into an origami bird.

As Glory opened gifts, Ty reappeared from the kitchen and sat in Quinn's working booth in the back corner, where she held clandestine meetings with potential clients. He wasn't exactly melancholy, but his reveling fell short of the quantum effort the rest of the room gave the birthday girl. Quinn slipped toward him, bringing two plates of cake. She'd already had one, but, hey, Ty didn't need to eat alone.

She held out his fork for him to take, then dug into her own slice as if she hadn't had any. "How's Cole doing?" she asked.

"Not bad," Ty said, wincing a little after the first bite. "Damn, this is sweet."

"Yeah," she said. "Makes me want a mug of coffee with it."

He put down his fork. "Here, let me get you——"

"Stop," she said. "I'm good. Sit here with me, okay?"

He dipped the tines of his fork into a flower and swirled it, then ate the nothing-but-icing bite. "I owe you an apology, Q."

She put down her fork and laid a hand over his. "You are a good, good man, Ty, and I love you so much."

"I know," he said, smiling that big man, Old Man smile of his.

She didn't want to say she loved Jonah more or loved him differently. That was nothing but a big BUT. Ty had been through too much to tell him he'd won the consolation prize.

But in these last couple of days, not being around either Jonah or Ty very much with all that had gone on at the sheriff's office, Renault's office, and backed-up business on the farm, the dust had settled as good as it was going to settle.

She loved Jonah. The farm bound them. They had a connection that often spoke without words. His love for her was strong, and respectful. They laughed easily together. Their bedroom affection came naturally, their union in those moments perfection. All they didn't do together was solve cases.

That's where Ty excelled as her partner.

She loved Ty as deeply as she would have her lost twin. Not that she hadn't wondered about Ty being her significant other, how a night with him would feel. He was too fine a specimen of a man not to.

Jonah, Ty, and Quinn. These thirty years of feelings had wrapped the three into an entity that couldn't be separated without hard pain. To cast one out would be as bad or worse than Archie's divorce or Natalie's death.

"I'll always be there for you, Ty."

He played with his cake like his son would do. "I know."

"So will Jonah. And you'll be equally as loyal to us." She started to add a thought, changed her mind, then changed it back again. "Please don't distance yourself. That would kill me . . . kill us. I want you to find someone. Another Natalie. Or someone to bring into the fold . . . make us a quartet, maybe." She tried to laugh a little, to get him to laugh. "She'd have to like sleeping in tree houses."

"And climbing trees," he added.

"Crime fighting?"

His mouth screwed into a crimped shape. "Maybe we need a non-crime-fighter gal to keep Jonah company for when we're leaping tall buildings in a single bound and bouncing bullets off our chests."

"True. True."

This light banter was absolutely glorious after all the last week's crap. Life was coming around.

Deputies had found the rock, with remnants of blood. DNA testing was in process, but everyone held no doubt what would be found. While Ty and Quinn and anyone else would be happy to testify, she'd wager that there would be no trial. Renault would come at Wescott so hard that Wescott would plea to almost anything rather than take a chance with a jury.

Quinn believed they could breathe easier now.

"Q?" Ty said, back to thinking hard again. Quinn expected him to take a couple weeks to dispense of the feeling that a train was coming at him.

"Hmmm?" she said, licking her fork.

"Natalie updated her will two weeks before she died."

That stopped her cold. "Oh wow." She almost said Nat must have forecasted her demise, but no point in Ty hearing that. "Any problems?" she asked instead.

"I'm still executor."

"Good."

"While it doesn't matter anymore, thought you ought to know she put you as guardian for Cole if I wasn't around."

She almost dropped the fork.

"Yeah," he said, the one word saying it all.

She still hadn't told Ty about Nat's voice mail of the Fourth. No point. Quinn could guess what she wanted by now. She wanted to apologize about being the informant, and now Quinn suspected she'd come around and realized that the Sterlings cared for that boy, and in the instance both she and Ty were gone, Sterling Banks was the best place for Cole.

Welcoming in theory . . . but oh so sad in fact. She and Natalie had stupidly lost time being estranged.

Jonah appeared, juggling three slices of cake, and motioned for Quinn to take one about to tip before he sat next to her. "What are we doing here?"

"Not kissing your girl," Ty said, and Jonah's smile slid off like hot butter.

Ty pointed at his chest, then when Jonah looked down, he popped him in the nose and laughed. "That never gets old with you, man. Come on, where's your sense of humor?"

Jonah pushed him over another piece of cake. "I can't get enough of this junk food, y'all. What's that say about me? I'm not sweet enough, or I'm super sweet."

"Geez," Quinn said, rolling her eyes, her insides so tickled with this conversation she could scream. "We were fantasizing about who Ty ought to bring home one day. And what she had to be in order to fit in. Not a super-hero crime fighter like Ty and I are, because you need someone to keep you company, don't you think?"

Now Jonah was making the mouth configurations, part icing, part thinking. "She better be easy on the eyes. If I gotta fill in babysitting her while you hunt bad guys . . . just saying . . ."

"Y'all gotta come dance," squealed Glory, running up to the table. "We're all dancing now." She shouted over at the jukebox where Lenore awaited the order. "Put it on, Ms. Lenore."

Leslie Gore came over the speaker. "It's My Party" dropped in, and Glory hopped over to the collection of admirers, finding Cole to dance.

Quinn pushed her guys out and began her own sashay. Ty moved in on his mother, and Jonah slid arms around Quinn's waist.

"This isn't a slow dance, fella," she said, grinning at him.

He moved in closer. "It's whatever we want it to be."

Glory belted out the chorus again. That girl sure could dance if she wanted.

Quinn moved her arms to around Jonah's neck. "It's whatever the birthday girl wants it to be, my man. We can do what *we* want later."

THE PARTY THAT was supposed to break up at six, continued after eight. Lenore let people come in and out with the partygoers still hanging around, until Glory was being congratulated by dozens more, most of them fascinated there was another couple of Sterlings in town.

The poor dear crashed on the way back to the manor. Archie put Glory to bed upstairs, returning downstairs to have a decompression hour before he crashed as well. Ty and Cole had retreated to their home, and Jonah accompanied Jule back to theirs.

"I've got to have coffee," Quinn said. "You want some?"

"Sure," Archie said. "Then let's sit out back."

Soon they sat in rockers, gazing into the almost night of Sterling Banks pecan trees. The branches hung onto the July humidity, but when you grew up in coastal South Carolina, you enjoyed the back porch in spite of the sticky shade. You took your shoes off and wore clothes you didn't mind sweating in.

As was the custom, they rocked and sipped for a good five or ten minutes, sinking into the evening, letting the business of the day slip loose from their bones before disturbing it with words.

"Been meaning to ask you something," she said.

"Been waiting for you to ask," he replied.

She gave him a cocky side glance. "How do you know what I'd ask?"

"Larry and me?" he said.

She tipped her head he was right and waited for the explanation. That feud was older than the Sterlings versus Renaults, and almost as toxic per stories. As a teenager she'd witnessed the cold shoulders and mean looks, but never an exchange of words. She remembered the passive aggression being intense. Today, them in the car was . . . strange. Was age mellowing the animosity, or had they come to a truce? First, however, what had started the grudge in the first place.

"The night y'all were in the tree house, he and I spoke," Archie said. "We orchestrated Renault, and frankly, I was impressed at Larry's willingness to unite for the Sterling common good. We were no longer teenage boys. Our anger wasn't what we thought it was once we spoke."

Half a century. Damn.

She rocked, waiting. "I want to hear it, Uncle. All the way back. No secrets in the Sterling house, remember?"

Thank God this time he didn't ask about Ty. Hopefully, he'd seen enough between the funeral and the party to see the trio had ironed things out.

"Some people say *It started over a girl*, but ours didn't," he began.

Quinn sucked in a breath. "It started over a . . . boy?"

Archie laughed. "Not quite like you envision, Niece. Let me tell it."

Gladly, because the idea of Uncle Larry carrying on the lifestyle of Uncle Archie didn't fit in her head. To her, Larry had barely graduated from homophobe to homo-tolerate.

"Larry caught me with his best friend under the stairs at the high school," he said. "They both played football."

"Oh, good Lord," Quinn uttered, barely imagining the explosion that had to have caused.

Archie chuckled. "Yep. It was that bad and worse." He turned serious. "Larry gave up his best friend over that. Said he felt duped. He wasn't having that *queer* stigma sticking to him."

"That's it?" That didn't seem to merit decades of hate.

"Then Larry beat the crap out of the boy," Archie said. "Told the poor kid to drop off the team or Larry would out him to the entire school."

Now that sounded like Larry.

"I was livid," Archie said. "But when the kid asked me to stand up for him, I . . . couldn't."

"Oh, Uncle." How sad.

"You have to understand the times, Niece. There was no coming out without the threat of being tossed out of school, your job, whatever you touched, not to mention getting beaten up if not killed. Even with so much improvement still needed, the difference between then and now is incredibly vast." He paused. "Though current times seem to be backsliding a bit."

"So you lost him, too," she said, understanding now.

He nodded. "I tried to stop Larry from all the damage he did, but he felt deceived by the both of us, and he was horribly fretful over being painted with the same brush."

"Did you two fight?" she asked, thinking brothers did so over much lesser issues.

"We did. He beat the shit out of me. I pulled sneakier moves, like sugar in his truck gas tank and a snake in his bed. Pretty sure I remember destroying a term paper that almost failed him in American History." He raised his head. "Almost got him kicked off the team."

A feud indeed.

"So he lost a best friend and a brother," she said. "And didn't know how to cope."

"As did I. And when he couldn't accept I was gay, I refused to accept him at all. I disappeared into my college education, then moved to Charleston afterwards, but even that was too close. Holidays were tense. I started skipping them until I decided to leave. I moved to San Francisco, as far from him as I could get, financing my new future with the money your father paid me for my share of Sterling Banks."

Quinn hadn't realized how still she'd gotten until Archie reached over and pushed the arm of her chair to make it rock.

"So when Uncle Larry lost his acreage in his divorce," she continued, "and Daddy bought it back, that stung even more, because it put the whole plantation in the name of Graham Sterling."

"Yes," he said. "Our foolishness made you the heir of three thousand acres."

"Holy damn," she whispered.

He lightly snorted a chuckle. "That about sums it up."

"Did he apologize? I mean, before we went to see Renault?" She couldn't imagine, but something had to have occurred.

Archie shook his head wearing a soft smile. "He didn't have to. His willingness to join with me, with us, said enough, I believe."

Quinn wasn't quite satisfied with that, though. Larry was a tough nut who expected everyone else to behave to his liking, but this was one example of where he should've bitten the bullet and said the words. "Well, he should. That was horrible what he did."

"Another time, another world. I'm good. At least the story is told now. I told him I'd tell you, by the way."

She leaned in. "What'd he say?"

"Nothing. Nothing either way, which was the essence of him being okay with it. Let him be, Quinn. Let it all be."

She rested back in the chair. The night had arrived. The dozen rows of trees they could see before became two with the porch light off. Quinn liked it off. It made for better talk.

"What else?" Archie asked. She could hardly see his face anymore in the shadows. "We haven't had a chance in a week to talk like we should. Care to know about my Parkinson's? Glory?"

"Patrick," she concluded for him. "Looks like y'all get along okay. He behaved at the party. He resigned from Renault. He was fun at the lunch after."

"And that's Patrick," Archie said. "Fun but not quite the responsible fellow one would like to think."

"Oh, I'm sorry."

"Like Larry, it is what it is. He cares about Glory and me, though."

"Clearly. But explain to me this deal y'all made." If she understood correctly, Sterling Banks was part of the agreement.

"It's simple but smart. He actually took the Renault job for me. Glory and I would come to Sterling Banks, partly to learn about her history and partly for me to have family support. He would live in Charleston as backup. Bottom line, he didn't think he could take care of one of us, much less both of us. Sweet man, but totally unreliable. With me at Sterling Banks and him with Renault, it all worked out."

She had to hand it to Patrick, it did seem to be a great solution if it hadn't been with Renault. "But he quit. What now?"

"He doesn't really have to work, Q."

"So what will he do?"

Archie shrugged. "He'll headquarter in Charleston, but if he gets a hankering to travel, he will, and freelance as he wishes."

Quinn laughed loud. "Hankering?"

Joining her in laughing, Archie gave another shrug. "Guess this place is seeping back into my blood."

Their laughter settled, and they rocked and pretended to watch the trees they could no longer really see.

"This is awkward, but may I ask a favor?" he said, breaking the silence after a long moment. "I mean, we've tiptoed all around it, but nothing's been resolved."

Heart beating harder, Quinn waited, expecting.

"Niece, lovely niece . . . first, are we seriously welcome to Sterling Banks? Glory and I are a handful. There's nothing introverted about that child, and I, well, I'll be a handful one day."

Quinn scooted out of her chair to her knees before him. "I'd be so happy to have you both here. You can't imagine how happy."

The expression on his face almost choked her up. "It's not a proposal. Get off your knees, silly," he said.

She did but sat on the tippy edge of her chair. To have her favorite relative under her roof again, another Sterling. . . there were no words.

"And may I move into Graham's room?" This request spilled quicker than the other, and he almost immediately seemed to regret having thrown it at her.

She'd envisioned him in the room he was in, down the hall from her. But as the senior in the house, and for goodness sakes, with the limitations he would eventually experience, residing in the master bedroom on the ground floor only made sense.

But what would she do with Graham and Maggie's things? "We can move everything out to make room for your stuff," she said.

"Oh no," he said. "To be that close to Graham . . . I would want to keep a lot intact, if you don't mind. I miss him, Q. I miss my big brother more than you know."

"Of course," she said. "Whatever you want. Anything for my favorite uncle."

"For God's sake, don't tell Larry that," Archie said.

Her parents would've loved this moment. The favorite uncle coming home to their daughter who'd been alone in that manor for far too long. The two of them taking care of each other. Sterling Banks taking care of

Glory.

Sterling Banks having an heir. Like they told Renault, it was as if the Sterlings were giving this legacy thing a jumpstart again. Maybe for yet another three hundred years.

The End

Appreciation

A writer can spend a lot of time alone writing a book, and oftentimes it feels like they are the only one making it happen . . . until they see they can't do this alone. This past year was a horrible and a good year, the highs and lows taxing yet gratifying, with each day bringing someone unexpected, it seemed, who I'd like to thank for helping me keep it together.

First and foremost, love to my husband Gary for always asking, "Have you got your thousand words done for the day?" or "Do you need to read a chapter to me?" and most of all, "Do you need more tea in that glass?" He's the guy quietly in the background at events, watching the clock when I speak, and talking to readers as they wait to get their book signed. Someone inevitably asks him, "Are you Wayne?"

Thanks to my blessed threesome, Nanu, Stephen, and Tara, two sons and a daughter-in-law, for supporting my work and bragging to their friends and acquaintances about Mom's latest release. They make me feel way more famous than I am. They've also gotten me into the fabulous Kingfisher gym and into lifting weights, which has made me come alive in different, other ways. Now I believe I can stick around this life even longer to write more stories.

On the other hand, love to my young grandsons, Jack and Duke, for keeping me in my place. "Are you famous yet, Grandma?" Or this, "On a scale of one to five, how famous are you now?"

Thanks to several new librarians in my life, in the South Carolina areas of Edisto Island, South Congaree Pine Ridge, and Chapin. They have welcomed me so warmly into their venues.

Of course much appreciation goes to Debra Dixon who really believes in me and my stories, whose edits only make my fictional worlds that much more believable, not to mention her staff who make a book look way simpler than it is to produce.

And finally, a big thanks to Jerry Caldwell, the outgoing owner of The Coffee Shelf, who believes in me and has represented the South Carolina Midlands headquarters for C. Hope Clark mysteries for years. He just retired from this quaint store and will be sorely missed, but he left behind a stable of phenomenal young baristas who holler, "Hey, Hope," when I walk in the door, and have my large plain frozen latte with two scoops of protein powder ready and waiting about the time I reach the register. They are lovely, beautiful people.

The list goes on and on, from readers to store owners, from chambers of commerce to teachers at the local schools. Everyone who buys a book has no idea how much joy that gives me.

About the Author

C. HOPE CLARK holds a fascination with the mystery genre and is author of the *Carolina Slade Mystery Series*, and the *Craven County Mystery Series* as well as the *Edisto Island Series*, all three set in her home state of South Carolina. In her previous federal life, she performed administrative investigations and married the agent she met on a bribery investigation. She enjoys nothing more than editing her books on the back porch with him, overlooking the lake with bourbons in hand. She can be found either on the banks of Lake Murray or Edisto Beach with one or two dachshunds in her lap. Hope is also editor of the award-winning FundsforWriters.com.

C. Hope Clark

Website: chopeclark.com

twitter.com/hopeclark

facebook.com/chopeclark

goodreads.com/hopeclark

bookbub.com/authors/c-hope-clark

Editor, FundsforWriters: fundsforwriters.com

Made in the USA
Monee, IL
29 December 2023

50618767R00163